MICHAEL PAUL

Blood Money Betrayal

A New York Mafia Tale

To you, dear readers, for making this journey worthwhile
To the city that never sleeps for inspiring this tale
For my parents who would be so proud
To my son Richard – who first heard the completed audiobook version
and to Georgee and my beautiful granddaughters
Rosalee, Isabella and Florence – who are too young to read this now
To my sister Julie and brother Phil
And to my wonderful wife Sheila, my best friend, my greatest supporter, my confidante,
my muse, my love – always ❤
And to my friends

Love triumphs over hate every single time.
Love will always find a way to throw hate into
a trunk, drive it to a remote location, and beat
it to death with a sock full of nickels

- "Love Hurts," by G.K. Chesterton

Contents

Chapter 1: Where the Crows Gather

'Now what do we do, Boss?'

'Well, to start with Frankie, you can shut the fuck up and let me think... that might help.'

The whispered words from the stout, heavy-set man sitting at the head of the table were deep and guttural, his voice resonating low like gravel churning in a cement mixer. The five men who occupied the corner table in the furthest discrete bay window of Alberto's Italian restaurant in Brooklyn, New York, eyed each other hesitantly. Although each was smartly dressed, as a group they looked out of place—bulldogs preened for Crufts; their hard, granite faces and expensive Italian suits doing little to mask the overwhelming probability that they might just be connected with the criminal underworld.

It was a few minutes after noon, and the hushed atmosphere of the restaurant was interrupted only by conversational murmurs emanating from a handful of occupied tables.

The men were all in their early to late thirties, except for the big man, the head of the family, Salvatore Vitalli, who was borderline fifty but looked older as a result of his thin receding hairline.

One of the men, who was sitting with his back to the room, facing the window, was busy chewing his knuckles. His knitted brow and bald head were glistening with nervous sweat and his sharp, narrow eyes were alive with suspicion. Another had his fingers interlocked and was clenching his fists, anxiously. A cigarette somehow defied gravity and hung from the bottom lip of the third man as if held there by an invisible length of thread, and as the ash dropped and splashed onto the starched, white cotton tablecloth, there was no attempt to sweep it away. Only one member of the group appeared calm—the man in charge, the leader, the man who had called the meeting only one hour before.

'Hey Johnny,' he growled, through a fog of cigarette smoke that hung suspended across the corner of the room like morning mist over a links fairway. 'Your ash... it's all over the table.'

'What?'

'Your ash! It's all over the fuckin' table.'

Johnny, sitting two seats to the left of the big man, with his back to the window, looked down. He grunted, then swept the ash away with the back of his hand, which did little but leave an ugly grey smear across the pristine cloth. He glanced at the others, who eyed him with disdain.

'Useless fuck!' muttered the bald man sitting opposite.

'Hey!' interjected the leader. He pointed to the knuckle nibbler. 'It's Happy Hour. Now put a smile on that ugly mug, shut the fuck up, and look at your menu.' The big man switched his attention to the smoker. 'And Johnny?'

'Yeah?'

'What does that say?'

'What does what say?'

'That!'

Johnny looked over at the placard on the wall which said, 'No Smoking'.

He grimaced. 'Jesus Christ! What the hell is the world coming to nowadays? You come to a restaurant, and you can't even have a fuckin' smoke!'

He reluctantly plucked the cigarette from his dried lip. A piece of skin came away with the filter and he dabbed the lip with his finger. He looked at the speck of blood on his fingertip, rubbed it away with his thumb and then, as there was no ashtray, stubbed the cigarette out on a side-plate.

'Now there's a surprise,' grumbled his sour-faced compatriot, sitting across the table. 'I didn't know he could fuckin' read.'

"Two Fingers" Tony, the hefty, bald man who had uttered what was for him an uncharacteristic frivolity, was clearly impressed by the sharpness of his own wit and allowed a hint of a smile to surface across the tepid veneer that barely sufficed as a human expression. The plastic grin looked alien on his hard, leathery face, almost as if it had been drawn on by some prankster at a Halloween party whilst he had been asleep. But then slowly, the stupid, stucco smile slid down from the forced façade, and the box-like mouth returned to the comfort of its furrowed creases and its natural, glum, inverted half-moon shape.

Johnny, who had been the butt of the quip, glanced across the table at his bald colleague and slowly raised a clenched hand with his middle finger extended. His acetic look was met with a scornful frown of indifference from his associate, whose glare was now more akin to that of a judge about to pass a death sentence.

Tony returned his usual double digit 'fuck you' gesture—a gesture he used frequently, and one which had led to him inheriting the pseudonym "Two Fingers", which was often shortened to just "Fingers", or "Two-ee".

'Hey, Boss,' he interjected, leaning over. 'Do we have to sit here and eat with his fuckin' stogie on the table?'

The leader paused for a moment, breathed a heavy sigh and, like a parent having to cope with a demanding toddler at a kindergarten, beckoned a waiter over as he would a childminder. The plate with the offending cigarette butt was removed and replaced with a clean one.

'Hey Johnny,' called the leader. 'Let me give you a tip. Don't antagonise Fingers. He used to be a boxer.'

'Yeah, I know. He had twelve fights... won all of 'em but eleven.'

'Johnny, you're a schmuck!' said the big man, shaking his head. 'You never learn, do ya?'

There was not an inkling of response from Fingers until the dime dropped and he again realised he'd been insulted. His two fingers made a brief reappearance and then disappeared.

For a long twenty seconds, there was quiet until someone felt the need to break the silence. It was Frankie—the leader's son—a slim, fit looking man with immaculately groomed, black hair, which was greased back in a 50s style D.A. — an acronym for "Duck's Arse", owing to the V-shape caused by combing the hair parallel around the sides of the head and parting it centrally at the back. 'Jesus Christ!' he mulled, quietly. 'What the hell are we doin' here, Boss?'

As a sign of respect, and so as not to differentiate himself too much from his cousins and close associates, Frankie always referred to his father as 'Boss'.

The leader glanced to his left. 'You'll find out soon enough. Now button it and look at your menu!'

Frankie, who was sitting nearest the window, snatched the menu from the table and opened it.

Frankie Vitalli was a style guru, or thought he was. He wore elaborate gold rings on the fingers of his right hand and a Rolex Daytona chronometer, with the steel and gold Oysterlock bracelet, on his left wrist. His fingernails were immaculately manicured and appeared pearlescent white against the sunburned skin of his hands. A glint of sunlight reflected from a heavy gold bracelet on his right wrist and caught the eyes of the man opposite. Out of the five men, Frankie was the only one wearing a light suit, and the only one wearing an open shirt through which a solid gold chain glinted in the refracted sunlight coming in through the window. For all intents and purposes, he looked like a white version of a Harlem pimp from the 70s—all that was missing was a wide brim Panama fedora.

The leader of the group, who appeared to have added a few extra pounds to his middle-aged paunch whilst merely looking at the menu, leaned into the table, his belly swallowing the table's edge. His menu was still raised and to anyone looking on, he appeared to be discussing its content. His accent was broad New York/Italian, and he spoke confidently, again with a throaty growl caused by years of smoking Cuban cigars. 'Right,' he said. The tone of his voice was soft and lethargic. 'Would one of you clowns like to tell me what the fuck happened this morning?'

The men looked at one another.

Frankie turned away and looked out of the window as if he'd washed his hands of the whole affair.

Johnny was still dabbing his lip, but was now using a napkin, the corner of which had become peppered with dots of dried blood. He took a deep breath and then said nervously, 'Boss, I hate to say this, but we screwed up this morning!' A comma of hair fell across his right eyebrow as he spoke.

'Well, I can see that, you asshole,' said the ringleader. 'Why the fuck do ya think we're here?'

Then Johnny added, quickly with outstretched jazz hands, 'But it ain't nothin' we can't fix, Boss.'

The leader's hooded eyes narrowed into inquisitive slits as he waited for what he knew would be a bullshit explanation.

Johnny, realising it had fallen to him to explain, shuffled uncomfortably on his chair. He brushed aside the misplaced lock of hair from his wrinkled forehead and glanced around at the others. He wiped his face with the napkin as the comma of hair fell back-across his brow—he left it hanging.

'Well, we did exactly as you said, Boss,' he began, folding the napkin. 'Me, Joey, Fingers and Sash found the guy's house and waited across the road like you told us. It was a long wait. I guess about three... maybe four hours. It was getting hot and the A/C in the car was busted, so we had the windows down. We were thirsty and hungry and was thinking about getting something to eat, but...'

The leader eyed him as though he had every intention of throttling him if he didn't get to the point quickly.

Johnny sensed the danger signs and again brushed the offending curl of hair from his weathered face. 'Anyway... I'll get to the point.'

'Please do,' said the leader, 'and preferably today.'

'Well,' continued Johnny, who again nervously glanced around at the others. 'We waited, and eventually a white Lincoln pulled into the drive. Sash thought we should wait until the guy went into the house. He was unsure about the car, though... said the guy always drove a Cadillac. Anyway, it was Joey who surprised us. Without saying a word, he jumped out the back of the car, raced across the road, took out his piece and shot the guy in the back. Sash and me ran out after him. It all happened so quick. But then when we got there and rolled the guy over, we saw…' Johnny took a deep breath and lowered his head as the images came back to him. He let out an edgy sigh and gulped, as if the words he needed to use had become too bitter to pass between his lips.

'Saw what?' asked the ringleader, whose patience was wearing thin.

Johnny raised his head—the lock of hair was still across his brow, hanging like an inverted question mark.

'Saw what!' reiterated the leader.

'Sorry, Boss. If Joey hadn't been so quick out of the car…'

'SAW WHAT!' grimaced the big man.

Startled by the sudden, angry retort, Johnny blurted out the damning words. 'That useless fuckin' godamncocksuckin asshole, Joey; he went and shot the wrong guy, Boss!'

Johnny's use of profanity was so intense, a spitting cobra suffering from Tourette's would have been impressed. 'The guy's dead,' he said solemnly. 'We brought the body with us. It's in the trunk of the car.'

The leader's face remained stolid. Undisturbed. Frozen.

The others studied him, waiting to see which way he would go. The options were few. Anger or humour. Which would it be? Either would do, as long as it was not you on the receiving end of whatever emotion surfaced.

The leader nodded—slowly at first. An eyebrow rose involuntarily, and he clacked his teeth as he continued to nod, looking at each of them in turn. Then he said conversationally with the same dry throat: 'I've heard the Cannelloni's good here. Anyone tried it?' He looked around the group. 'Frankie?'

Frankie frowned and shook his head.

'What about you, Fingers?'

'No, never had it, Boss.'

'Sash?'

Sash, sitting on the opposite side of the table facing the leader, was a handsome, tall, wiry black African American with short, cropped black hair. He shook his head too and kept his eyes low. He'd been there. He was the most experienced of the four tasked with undertaking the 'hit'. Even though it was Joey who pulled the trigger, he knew the blame could so easily be placed on him.

'What about you, Johnny?' The leader's lifeless gaze came back to Johnny. 'You ever had the Cannelloni here?'

Johnny was confused. He found himself shaking his head. What the hell was going on? They had made a big mistake that morning. They had killed the wrong man, and he had just delivered the bad news. But from his boss's demeanour, it was as if the last 60 seconds had been erased, as if his declaration of their error had never been mentioned. For him, as a kid, punishment had always been swift. A slapped ear with the back of a hand was expected, but this reaction, or lack thereof, was completely unexpected. It felt wrong, out of place. But it was worse than that; there was an inconclusive emptiness which you could grasp, which you could feel, and it felt detached and icy cold.

'So, no-one's tried the Cannelloni, huh!' continued the leader. 'What about the meatballs? Sash?'

'No, Boss.'

The leader looked towards Frankie. Frankie knew the score; he'd seen this type of behaviour before and knew what to expect. 'Yeah, the meatballs here are good, Boss,' he said.

'Oh, fuck me. So, someone *has* eaten here. Good. OK, in that case, I think I'll have the meatballs. What about you, Johnny?'

Still dumbfounded, Johnny said, 'Yeah, sure, Boss. I agree, the meatballs here *are* good.'

'Oh, another fuckin' connoisseur. Sash, what are you having?'

'Yeah, the meatballs are OK by me, Boss.'

Fingers, who rarely said much on a good day, glanced over the top of his raised menu and grunted his approval.

'And what about Joey?' I guess with him being a fuckin' meatball, he'll go for the meatballs too, huh?' The leader hacked a sardonic laugh. The others joined in hesitantly, uncomfortably. 'Anyway, where is the stupid prick?'

There was a pause as they all looked at the empty seat to the right of the big man. Fingers said, 'He's in the John, cleaning up.'

'What? He's cleaning the fuckin' restroom?'

'No, himself. He got a bit messed up this morning.'

'I bet he fuckin' did.' The leader turned and beckoned the waiter across. 'Hey, bring us a couple of bottles of your best red, would ya? But nothing too heavy. You got a good Chianti here?'

'Si, we have a fine Chianti.'

'Well, I don't want one that's just fine. I want one that's a cut above the rest! And don't sting me on price either! In fact, fuck the Chianti, bring me a Valpolicella. You got any of that?'

'Of course, sir,' said the waiter, who noted the order and sped off towards the kitchen as if his legs were on tram rails.

The big man turned to face his crew and lowered his voice. 'You gotta watch these bastards,' he muttered. 'They bulk buy cheap five-dollar bottles of Marsala, replace the labels, and charge fifty. Assholes!' The leader took a deep breath and then centred his attention back on the group. 'So, tell me,' he continued. 'If not, the asshole we intended to rub out this morning, who's the unfortunate fuck lying dead in the trunk of my car out there?'

Johnny took a sideways glance at Sash. But Sash was non-committal and Frankie's attention had reverted outside—back to where the car containing the dead body was parked.

Johnny, who now believed his boss had taken the bad news rather well—much better than he had ever expected—was now feeling more assured and added some detail. 'Oh, I don't know. Just some jerk-off who happened to be in the wrong place at the wrong time, I guess,' he said. 'We didn't pay much attention once we realised it wasn't "Cadillac" Tony. But I did get his wallet. Let me check his ID.'

Johnny plucked the wallet from his inside jacket pocket and slid out a driving license. He looked at it and gave a momentary double-take. Then, the brow of his face slowly concertinaed into a row of hard ridges and his jaw began to twitch like a ventriloquist as he silently mouthed the name on the card. His frown intensified.

Something was wrong.

All eyes bored down on him quizzically, and the faces of his compatriots all leaned in.

When you're the only one harbouring knowledge of bad news that needs to be shared, the weight of that knowledge can crush you, and Johnny suddenly felt as though gravity had increased its force by ten to the power of nine. Had a black hole opened beneath where he was sitting at that moment, he would have gladly jumped in, rather than divulge what he now knew to the man hunched over towards him at the head of the table.

'Who is it?' asked the leader.

'Jesus Christ!' trembled Johnny.

'What, his name's Jesus Christ?' grinned Fingers. 'If this was the second coming, He didn't fuckin' last long, did he?'

'That ain't funny,' said Johnny. 'Neither's this. Boss, it says here that the guy's name is… Dino Marmarella.'

Suddenly, in a stop action moment, the entire world exploded in the corner of the restaurant as the leader leapt to his feet, taking the edge of the table with him, upsetting the drinks which spilled across the tablecloth

'Dino Marmarella!' he raged in a suppressed yell that lay somewhere between blind fury and a choked laugh. 'Dino fucking Marmarella! Are you kiddin' me!'

Frankie snatched the ID card from Johnny and inspected it. 'Well, fuck me sideways,' he said. 'He's right. Look!' He passed the card to the big man.

Attracted by the outburst, a waiter appeared and was at their table in three strides.

Frankie got to his feet. 'Hey, you!' he snapped quickly. 'We've spilled some drinks here. Quick, fetch a cloth!' He turned to his father. 'You OK, Boss?' The waiter was standing as if frozen to the spot. Frankie turned to him. 'You still here? There's a three-thousand-dollar suit there goin' to ruin! Now fetch a fuckin' cloth!'

The waiter left them with a napkin that was across his arm, span on his heels and quickly weaved his way miraculously between the tables like a gridiron running back dodging a defensive blitz.

Frankie paused for a moment, and then calmly took his seat. The head of the family was still standing, his face red as if he'd been holding his breath since the Big Bang. The restaurant was gradually filling with groups of people, but Frankie remained cool and had the presence of mind to realise that it only takes one individual to be inquisitive enough to make such a flare-up a memorable event. 'Boss,' he whispered urgently. 'We're causing a fuckin' scene here.'

The leader gulped a huge lungful of air. 'Don't you fuckin' tell me what to do!' he said pointedly, as he slowly lowered himself onto his seat and tried to regain his composure. 'I don't believe it,' he continued, trying to suppress the all-consuming rage that burned within. 'I don't fuckin' believe what I'm hearing. You've killed Louie Marmarella's only son?' He shook his head. 'You dumb fucks! And if that ain't bad enough, you've got the useless mother outside, lying dead in the trunk of my car! HAVE YOU LOST YOUR FUCKIN' MINDS?' He glowered at each of them in turn—each glaring look a single hard lash from a bull-whip.

Frankie, the explosive situation now all but defused, looked as surprised as his boss. He turned towards the window. This was news to him. He didn't know about the blunder. Intrigue enveloped him, bringing his attention back from the sidewalk and into the room. Bubbling below the surface, he sensed scandalous excitement—mixed with a sense of relief that on this occasion he hadn't been directly involved. And as if to reaffirm the fact, he said, 'Boss, I don't know what happened today. I wasn't involved in this one. But don't worry, we'll sort it out.'

His Boss was still dazed. 'Dino Marmarella,' he muttered quietly, 'For fuck's sake!' The leader buried his face in his hands and then surfaced for air. He looked as if he was teetering on the brink of inflicting catastrophic violence and was only just managing to keep his simmering emotions from hitting boiling point.

The others had never seen him this angry, and it came as a surprise to each of them. The leader was powerful; a feared and well-respected businessman, highly ranked amongst the criminal elite. Nothing ever fazed him—until this.

The waiter arrived and swiftly stripped and replaced the drink-soaked tablecloth and then distributed fresh napkins. Frankie quickly shooed him away, as if brushing aside a persistent fly from his face. All eyes were still on the leader, who slowly raised his head like a condemned man waiting to receive the blade of a sword from an executioner bent on prolonging the agony of his victim.

Everyone waited. Like a courtroom gallery seconds away from learning the verdict of a jury, their anticipation was soon to be quenched.

'We're in deep shit!' said the big man resignedly, his teeth gritted. 'Unless we find a plausible solution, we're fuckin' dead meat!'

'No, we're not,' countered Frankie. 'We can fix this.'

'Fix this? Are you fucking kiddin' me?' How the hell do we fix this, Frankie? We've killed Louie Marmarella's only son. Do you understand what that means? Have any of you any idea the repercussions facing us when this gets out? Jesus Christ! Louie Marmarella is a Made Man! And so is his fuckin' son, and this ain't gonna end well.'

The men all knew that a Made Man is deemed untouchable, and as such can only be dispatched if there exists good enough reason, and only then, if the mafia family's hierarchy grants permission. To become a Made Man and a fully-fledged member of the American and Sicilian Mafia; a man must be of Italian descent through their father's lineage and must be sponsored by another Made Man. The inductee is required to take a code of silence which prohibits any discussion with authorities relating to a family's criminal investigations. Such is the level of loyalty within Mafia culture, it is considered deeply shameful, even for opposing families, to betray one of their own to the legal establishment. Any grievance, physical or otherwise, is usually avenged within their own ranks, which is why many mob murders go unsolved. To attack, let alone kill, a Made Man is seen as punishable by death, and it was to this strict ruling to which Salvatore Vitalli was referring.

Just then, the sixth member of the group, the triggerman, Joey, emerged from the restroom. At twenty-one years old, Joey was the youngest of the group and, as such, was always trying to prove his worth to the others. His tendency to be over exuberant often led to him making clumsy mistakes. But he was a favourite of the leader, who usually cut him some slack, however today, the length of slack had run out, leaving the spool spinning empty.

Oblivious to the mood of the moment, Joey sauntered nonchalantly across the restaurant and joined the others. He pulled out the empty chair to the right of his Boss. His suit and demeanour matched that of the other men, although his hair was less immaculate, and he had the appearance of someone who had missed his train and had run all the way to an important meeting. He sat and immediately picked up a menu. But as he flipped through the scant pages, he sensed unrest, and his eyes were everywhere other than on the printed words.

Gradually, he became aware of the heavy silence that seemed to resonate uncomfortably around the private bay window enclosure occupied by the six men. It was the kind of silence you can feel, silence you can almost grasp and taste, silence that drains your mouth of moisture, leaving you feeling isolated and exposed in a vacuum of fearful uncertainty.

Joey now knew something was wrong, and he surreptitiously searched the forlorn faces of his companions. Eventually, his eyes met the bent gaze of his boss sitting alongside to his left. 'What's up?' he asked nervously.

The empty hush abated, replaced instead by the low, severe, gravelly voice of the big man who held all of his respect. 'Did you shoot and kill the wrong man this morning, Joey?' The question was asked quietly and ineffectually, almost as if the man was addressing a child or asking a stranger for a light for his cigarette.

Like a lizard's flicked tongue probing the air for scent, Joey's fevered eyes again raced around the table searching for a clue. But the dour poker faces that staring back at him provided little to help his read of the situation. Joey's breathing became laboured as panic grasped him by the throat.

The leader stood, and with an ugly snarl, raised a napkin and swiped Joey once around the face with it, and then immediately sat down.

Joey raised his hand to his face—shocked by the violent action. He looked at his boss with almost teary eyes, but nothing was said, and silence again filled the pregnant void. The charged atmosphere gained intensity until someone spoke.

'For fuck's sake, Joey,' said Frankie. 'You missed some.'

'What d'ya mean?' asked Joey, his voice shaky.

'You still got some blood on your face… there.' Frankie threw Joey a napkin and indicated an area on the line of his chin beneath his ear. Joey wiped the speck of blood away, looked at it, and then surreptitiously glanced around to see if anyone had noticed.

They all had.

'Eh, that's not from the body,' he said anxiously. 'It's mine. I just nicked myself shaving.'

Joey had fast growing facial hair, a genetic condition that required him to shave twice a day if he was to keep his five o'clock shadow from appearing around lunchtime. And if he was out during the evening, a third appointment with his razor blade in a single day was not unusual.

The leader glared at him.

Joey's worried eyes met those of the big man alongside. 'Boss, I'm really sorry,' he said. 'It was a genuine mistake. But the dead guy… he was just some ordinary guy, wasn't he… some nobody?' He looked around for affirmation, but nothing was forthcoming from the forlorn faces observing him.

'No, he wasn't some nobody,' replied the big man bitterly. 'The man you killed was Louie Marmarella's only son, Dino.'

Joey's mouth fell open. 'OH NO!' he garbled as his hand flew to his mouth. 'I'm so sorry.' He looked around at the others, whose scornful faces regarded him as if he'd been pronounced dead at the scene of an accident. Joey fidgeted on his chair and tried to find the right words. 'Look… I said, I'm sorry.'

The leader eyed him as a father would a disobedient son. 'Don't apologise,' he said gravely. 'This goes well beyond apologies. You fucked up again, Joey, and you know it. We know it… and it's becoming a habit. You seem to fuck everything up just lately. But on this occasion, you really fucked up big time. So, let me explain. You were sent to do a number on some guy known as "Cadillac" Tony, right?'

'Yeah,'

'Cadillac Tony,' repeated the big man, empathising the two words.

'Yes, sir.'

'Repeat after me, Joey... Cadillac Tony.'

'Cadillac Tony, Boss.'

'AGAIN!'

'Cadillac Tony.'

'So, when someone showed up this morning at Antonio DeVille's house driving a fuckin' Lincoln, didn't you first think to check before pulling the trigger just in case it was the wrong guy?'

Joey looked confused.

'The clue is in his name, dumbass! He's called "Cadillac" Tony because he only ever drives a fuckin' Cadillac!'

Joey gasped and tried to get a word out.

'Don't you fuckin' speak to me!' urged the big man, sitting back in his chair. 'I've heard enough from you today. You should have listened to Sash. Now I gotta sort *your* shit out again.'

At the mention of his name, Sash shifted uneasily in his seat. For him, he felt an overwhelming sense of relief. Those few glorious words had totally exonerated him from any blame, and he quietly wiped the sheen of perspiration from his shiny black face.

The leader paused, gathered himself with a heavy intake of breath, and then said, 'Have you left it clean in there?' referring to the restroom

Joey nodded.

'Are you sure?'

'It's spotless, Boss.'

'Yeah, like your chin. Joey, I'm not sayin' you're a liar, but if you told me it was raining outside, I'd have to open the fuckin' window to check.' Salvatore Vitalli turned his attention to the tall black man sitting opposite. 'Sash, go check the washroom.'

As the lithe, athletic man began to rise from his chair, the waiter's face appeared again alongside. Sash glanced at his boss, who motioned for him to remain seated.

'Gentleman,' said the waiter breezily. 'Are you ready to order?'

Frankie threw him a look that should have killed him stone dead where he stood. But now the leader of the group was composed, and his face broke into a peculiar Santa Claus smile as he said, 'Yeah, I think so. Meatballs for six,' he announced.

'I don't like meatballs, Boss,' said Joey.

The leader turned his head and glared at him. Again, there were no words—and none were needed.

The waiter paused. There was an anxious question mark look on his face.

'Like I said, meatballs for six,' repeated the leader, as his hooded eyes again met those of the younger man sitting next to him who bit his lip and glanced up at the waiter and nodded.

The waiter immediately span on his heels and quickly embarked on his now familiar flight path back to the kitchen.

The leader, whose eyes had only briefly left those of Joey's, waited for the inquisitive faces on the other tables to lose interest. Then, his smile slipped as if his facial skin had suddenly lost its grip on his skull. He raised a finger, pointed at Joey, and spoke with deadly sobriety, his mouth hardly moving. 'Fuck up again, an' I'll kill ya. Do you understand me, Joey?'

Joey's face remained comatose; his eyes averted.

'Look at me! Do you fuckin' understand what I just said?' The voice remained calm and together. 'Son, I'll kill you with my own hands if you screw up one more time.' The heavy-set man paused and then added with deadly menace, 'And you know I fuckin' will!'

Joey's ashen face, shocked by the intensity of the threat, showed no emotion. Then he nodded, as if bowing to the great man's wisdom. 'Sorry, Boss,' he said again, quietly.

'Don't apologise to me,' said the big man. 'Just do things right. I love you like my own. You know that, Joey. But you got a clumsy attitude, and one of these days you're gonna end up dead! And you'll probably end up taking us with you... if you haven't already! Now all of you, shut up, and let me think!'

Joey raised his hooded eyes and looked at Frankie on the opposite side of the table. Frankie winked as if to say, 'He don't mean that. It's just his way. He's angry. You'll be OK.'

The six men had arrived at the restaurant twenty minutes earlier. Alberto's restaurant was reputed to be one of the best in Brooklyn, but on this particular afternoon, food was the last thing on their minds. The job should have been simple, yet vital—a contract kill that had become so regular amongst the warring families they rarely made headline news. "Cadillac" Tony DeVille was a professional hit man associated with their arch-rivals, the Marmarella family. It should have been a simple task for four mobsters and would have removed a recent threat aimed at one of the Vitalli family's close associates. But now, with the son of such a high-ranking mobster lying dead, the stakes had risen exponentially.

'Now listen to me,' said the leader, lifting his round, heavy head, his authoritative poise now fully returned. He leaned into the table, his voice quiet. 'Did anybody see what happened?'

'Yeah, we all did,' said Johnny.

'No, you fuckin' idiot. I mean, did anybody in the neighbourhood see what happened? Were there any people around… witnesses?'

The men looked at one another and collectively shook their heads.

'Are you sure?'

'The street was empty, Boss,' said Johnny. 'The house was situated at the end, tucked away in the corner… ya know?'

'No, I don't fuckin' know. That's why I'm askin' you!'

Again, the men eyed each other.

This time it was Sash who interjected, 'Boss,' the black man's voice was deep, melodic and credible, with all the hallmarks and qualities of a jazz singer from Harlem. 'There was nobody about,' he continued easily. 'We'd been casing the joint for hours. The place was deserted.'

The leader's eyes bored into him from the opposite side of the table. 'Deserted? Good. So, there were definitely no witnesses.'

'No.'

Salvatore Vitalli's face was fierce. 'So, am I *really* to believe that nobody saw this fuckin' idiot shoot and kill Louie Marmarella's son?'

The men shook their heads.

'Right,' continued the leader. 'And what about the gun?'

'It was a .45,' said Joey. 'I had a silencer attached.'

'Oh, really?'

'Yeah.'

'And you've got rid of it, obviously.'

'What... the silencer?'

'No, the whole fuckin' thing! Combined, it's a murder weapon... idiot! But You got rid of it, right?'

'Got rid of it?'

'Yeah, you know, disposed of it. Incriminating evidence, and all that.'

Joey eyed the others, hoping for support. When none was forthcoming, he turned to face his boss, whose eyes were already waiting for his to return. 'Well, no... not yet, Boss.'

'You haven't got rid of it yet?'

'No.'

'Where is it?'

'It's in the car.'

'It's in the car.' A single sardonic smile mixed with a double dose of incredulity came to the leader's face. 'The same car that's got the fuckin' stiff in the trunk?' The smile slid from his face again.

Joey bit his lip like a guilty schoolboy and gave a single nod of his head. There was a sudden hubbub of chatter from elsewhere around the restaurant as a group of people arrived and were seated.

The leader had slowly buried his face in his large hands again, momentarily shutting out the world and wiping away the cacophony of incompetence that had enveloped him. Eventually, after what seemed like a lifetime of exasperation crammed into a few seconds, he surfaced for air, his red face straining to quell the angst which was again building within. 'So, let me get this straight,' he said gloomily, the expression on his face looking like a deflated souffle as he addressed them all. 'You've got a dead body in the trunk of my car, and the murder weapon with Joey's prints all over it, in the fuckin' glove compartment.'

The five men around the table, realising what was about to come, waited— their eyes trained on a spot six inches in from the edge of the table where each of them sat.

'You know something?' said the leader. 'I'm not even gonna pass comment about that. I'm not gonna mention anything about how dumb you are. And I'm not just talking about Joey now. Everyone knows he's a dumb prick. I'm talking about *you* five as a collective. I'm not even gonna compare your intelligence to that of my three-year-old nephew who's at home right now playing with his fuckin' building bricks, and who's probably got a higher I.Q. than the sum total of you fuckers put together. No. I'm just gonna move on, because with all due respect to the stiff lying in the trunk of my car out there, from the neck up, you fuckers are just as dead. Christ, I've listened to some dumb shit in my time, but this charade today takes the fuckin' biscuit!'

The big man paused for a moment, which ran to a full minute of deep reflection. Then he reached into his pocket, took out a small silver pill case and carefully placed a white tablet from it into his mouth. He swallowed it back with a slug of water from his glass and then began.

'Now, listen up,' he said with deadly intent in his voice. 'Here's the deal. This is what you're gonna do. And I'm gonna spell it out, so that you know exactly what I expect.'

The leader's penetrating gaze fell upon each of the men individually, like the twin muzzles of a loaded shotgun. Then the instructions began— the leader's mouth hardly moving, his eyes and face totally devoid of any emotion as he fired a cartridge of verbal buckshot at each of them in turn.

'Johnny, you take the car, clean it and lose it. I don't care where, but make it good. You know what to do. And get rid of the fuckin' gun... but make sure it's clean of any serial numbers first. Frankie, tonight, you dispose of the body... in pieces. You know the routine; you've done it before. Bag the bits and dump 'em outta town... separate locations. And this time I don't want you to Fed-Ex 'em all over the state, understand? Using the mail service to dispose of stiffs brought the heat down on us last time.'

Johnny interjected. 'Yeah, and it's a criminal offence to abuse the mail service... right, Boss?'

The leader, whose mouth was open and ready to continue, checked himself as Johnny's comment percolated down to his subconscious, struck something hard, and stopped him dead in his tracks. He turned to Johnny. 'Hey fuckwit, do you think this is funny?'

'I didn't mean it to sound funny, Boss. But the Fed-Ex scam worked.'

The ringleader had another thought, he thought momentarily about shooting Johnny there and then. But after dismissing the notion, he moved on. 'No,' he continued, 'it was sloppy. And we ain't doing that this time. This time I want a proper job. Bury the bags in woodland...deep. No shallow holes! They need to be at least five feet in the ground, otherwise the stink permeates up through the dirt and attracts squirrels and shit. They'll scrape and dig to get at the meat. Then the next thing you know, some fuckin' numpty out walking his dog finds his mutt wandering around with a foot in its mouth.'

The men looked at one another. The vision of a dog proudly parading around with a severed limb between its teeth conjured up the merest hint of a smirk on Johnny's face. It didn't go unnoticed.

'You still think this shit's amusing, don't you, Johnny?' said the leader in a whisper, which was barely audible.

Johnny, realising he was in deep trouble again, tried to deflect the wrath from his boss before it fully surfaced and went nuclear. 'No, sir. I do not,' he said nervously. 'We know the score, Boss, and we'll fix this thing.'

'Damn right you will. Cuz if we don't, we might just as well all climb in the fuckin' trunk alongside that dead mothafucker out there, and head for the woods with him. Understand?'

Johnny nodded as silence again fell around the table. The waiter appeared again but a smouldering no nonsense rebuttal from the leader sent him scurrying back to the kitchen.

The leader continued, his voice subdued, his eyes moving from one face to the next and back again. 'Frankie, I want you to speak to Gianni. He'll be back later. Tell him to get you some equipment...rented! Don't use anything we own that could be traced back. And I don't want no calling cards. Tell him to use fake ID's and cash. No fuckin' plastic! But don't tell him why. He's a nosy bastard, and even though he'll probably guess, I don't want you to admit a fuckin' thing to that sonofabitch. Do you understand me?'

Frankie nodded. 'What shall I say if he asks?'

'Asks what?'

'Asks what I want the tools for.'

'How the fuck should I know? Tell him you took up gardening or something. Use your fuckin' loaf. And avoid chainsaws! I don't like 'em... they're too noisy and too fuckin' messy. A handheld saw with a serrated blade and lopping shears should do the job. It won't be as quick, but it's quiet.'

'Lopping shears?' enquired Johnny.

'Yeah, haven't you heard of those? You use them to cut the limbs off trees, and useless dumb fucks like you. And Frankie, make sure you dispose of the hands properly. We don't want that fuckin' dog walker turning up next week with a handful of fingers in his mutt's mouth for the cops to trace.'

The leader glanced around the table.

'You'll need a car too,' he continued. 'Again, don't use anything we own. We got a ringer back at the warehouse... a station wagon. It's got fake plates and a new paint job. Use that. Sash, you help Frankie cut the body up... bathtub! Rent a motel room. Somewhere quiet outta town. Same applies... cash. No plastic. Fake IDs. And you gotta be naked when you cut this asshole up. We don't want any of that DNA shit coming back and biting us in the ass. And use plastic bags, garbage bags... double 'em up. This fucker's gonna stink. Drain as much of the blood as you can before you dismember it. And clean and disinfect the room after you're done. And then, when you're finished... set fire to the fuckin' joint. Got it?'

'Boss?'

'Joey, do yourself a favour and shut the fuck up! Sash, you drive. And don't speed. I don't want any drama. You get stopped... you're on your own. And you'll take the rap. Right?'

The black man nodded and glanced at Frankie, who returned the barbed look with interest. It was an unwritten law that if there was ever any police involvement in any of their activities, the members at the core of the family would disavow any involvement. It was also unwritten that Frankie and Sash didn't get on. There was history between them—something to do with Sash and Frankie's wife. Everyone around the table knew that Frankie's wife—Debbie—a beautiful, voluptuous blonde from Vegas with large breasts and a sex drive that could power the national grid, was reputed to have a weakness for black men. That is, everyone but Frankie, who was the last to find out—and only did so when someone tipped him the word that some of the blacks in the neighbourhood had been calling round to service her in the afternoons, and usually in gangs of three or more—or so it was rumoured. Sash had always denied any direct involvement with her, but Frankie had his suspicions.

The leader looked at each of the faces around the table. The instructions from the big man continued. 'After you're done, dump the car and equipment... and no prints! Use gloves... those thin transparent ones that surgeons use. I shouldn't have to tell ya this stuff. You should know already.'

'We do, Boss,' said Frankie, who then added. 'But it doesn't hurt for others to be reminded.' He glanced at the others, and then fixed a momentary stare on Sash. Sash sensed it but ignored him and refrained from eye contact.

The leader paused and looked at each of them again in turn. 'Gentleman, listen up,' he said grimly. 'This has to be clean and clinical. Every angle covered. Attention to detail is paramount. This guy needs to disappear... as if he just boarded a plane and fucked off, never to return. Think before you do anything. Any more fuck ups like this morning and we'll all be sleeping with fuckin' fishes.' Again, he eyeballed each one of the faces individually. Each of the men nodded in turn as his hooded eyes fell upon them.

The table went quiet for a while and then the big man's voice broke the silence again. 'I just remembered. Johnny?'

'Yeah.'

'I want you to pick up someone from the Hill next week.'

'The Hill' is the name some use when referring to New York's Elmira Correctional Facility; an adult all male maximum security prison. Salvatore Vitalli's crew eyed each other with curiosity and shook their heads in bewilderment as they tried to work out to whom their leader was referring. There were a number of associates incarcerated throughout the state, but none of them knew of anyone within their immediate circle who was due for imminent release, and their look of enquiry eventually returned to the big man at the head of the table.

It was Johnny who asked the question. 'So, who's being sprung, Boss? Is it anyone we know?'

'Yeah, it's someone you all know. An old friend's being paroled over the next few days.'

There was a pause as each of the men looked at one other, and then Fingers said, 'Who the fuck's caged up in Elmira? I know Layzee's there, but he ain't due out yet.'

There was a triumphant look on Salvatore Vitalli's face. 'Yeah,' said the big man. 'Layzee Dawson's coming home.'

'Oh, fuckin' hell!' muttered Frankie. 'I thought that mother had another two years to serve.'

'Well, he's been a good boy,' said the leader. 'And good boys get parole.'

'Parole? Who the fuck signed that off?' protested Frankie, as he stopped rocking on the rear two legs of his chair and leaned in. 'Jesus Christ!'

The big man turned to face him. 'We've been working on a few things behind the scenes,' he said. 'He'll be fine.'

'Boss, he's a liability and a fuckin' head case. Did you see what he did to that hooker?'

'Yeah, I saw the pictures.'

'He broke her jaw, her cheekbone, and stabbed her in the neck with a plastic fork... at a fuckin' KFC diner! What the fuck was he thinking? The place was rammed, thirty-one eyewitnesses.'

'Thirty-two if you count the Colonel,' mumbled Johnny.

'I know, I know, and I'm not making any excuses on his behalf,' explained the leader. 'How could anyone? But if you're in a tight spot, say a fire fight, would you want anyone else standing alongside you?' The big man again eyed each of them individually. 'He's good, but he's bad, too. I know that.'

'Bad, he's a fuckin' psycho!' continued Frankie. 'And what about his wife?'

The big man raised his finger. 'Well, as we know, she's disappeared, and someday I'll tell you a story about that fuckin' bitch! Listen, Layzee Dawson is loyal, capable, and he's one of us, and he's coming home. Although now there's a delicate problem associated with his release. One that you fuckers should have sorted out today.'

Just then, the waiter arrived with their food in a large white dish. He placed the dish of chopped, processed meatballs, smothered in tomato sauce, in the middle of the table and then liberally applied freshly ground black pepper over the whole dish from a mill longer than his arm.

'Food looks good,' said the leader.

'Buon appetito, signori!' said the waiter with a flourish as he stepped back and left the men to their meal.

'See, I told you this was a class joint,' announced Johnny proudly.

'What the hell do you know about class?' grumbled the leader. 'The only class you know is the one you used to fuckin' dodge when you should have been at school.'

Fingers, who was a big eater and had already helped himself to a plate full of food, grunted a laugh at the big man's comment—a laugh which transformed into a heavy, guttural belch, which reverberated hideously around the room, attracting the attention of a couple of elderly women diners, who frowned their disgust. Fingers nodded as if pleased with himself.

The leader also fired a look of repugnance. 'Hey! What's the matter with you?'

'He can't help it,' said Johnny. 'Look at him! He wanted to lose 10lbs this year. He's only got thirteen to go.'

Fingers continued filling his face as if suddenly struck dumb and deaf.

Just then Frankie, who was again rocking on the back legs of his chair whilst still monitoring the going's on outside, said quietly. 'Well fuck me, look who's just turned up.'

All heads swung towards the window and strained necks stretched to see.

'I don't believe it,' groaned Frankie.

'Who is it?'

'I'm not lying, Boss. But Louie Marmarella just got out of a car with a couple of goons. Looks like the fat fuck's heading this way. He's coming into the restaurant.'

'And those two bookends with him,' added Johnny, '...are those dumb shmucks the Capelli brothers.'

'Jesus Christ,' said the leader. 'As if today couldn't get any worse.'

Chapter 2: Rough Justice

T he crack of a of a prison officer's nightstick across the head of a felon is a sickening sound, and more often than not results in the recipient having to visit the prison infirmary. But recently, on one particular occasion at New York's Elmira Correctional Facility, the penitentiary sometimes referred to as 'Hellmira', it was not an inmate who was hospitalised after sustaining a head injury with a nightstick, but three prison officers.

The incident occurred when an inmate refused to enter his cell after attending a disciplinary hearing that resulted in an extension to his sentence. The inmate, who was being accompanied by a prison officer back to his cell, grabbed the officer's baton and struck the guard twice on the head with it, before four other officers scrambled up the stairs across the landing of the cell block to restrain him.

The brute had the strength of six men. One of the officers was picked up and thrown down the stairs. Another was punched in the face and struck with the butt of the baton, injuring his eye socket before the inmate was eventually overpowered.

Still fighting and kicking on the floor whilst being cuffed, the man cursed and fought like a Trojan but was then administered pepper spray and was dragged away across the landing yelling obscenities as he passed Layzee Dawson's cell who was watching the scene unfold from the relative sanctuary of his bunk. Layzee turned his head away and continued to read his book. He had seen it all too often.

That was just one of three incidents that occurred during that week at the prison.

The first was when officers had to deploy a chemical agent to stop half a dozen inmates fighting in the recreation yard. The second being when an inmate, high on an unknown intoxicant, stabbed his cellmate with a shiv for snoring, the blade of which was found to be hidden within the wooden structure of a crucifix adorning the cell wall, which was cleverly being used as a sheath.

The weapon was one of several seized during that week, some of which were positively genius in their design. A crude shotgun made from bedposts, with lead from curtain tape used as the charge combined with batteries and match heads to be ignited using the filament from broken lightbulbs. Another was fashioned with stolen items from a prison workshop. A simple knuckle duster made from a rasp attached to a handle. A particularly nasty find was a whip, comprising razor blades attached to a strip of leather. More flamboyant was a fake machine gun made from a grease injector. And more commonly, knives made from the lids of sardine tins. Even an everyday padlock dropped into a sock to be wielded and swung like a mace can cause massive head trauma.

The man who had witnessed all of this was Layzee Dawson, who was not averse to physical violence himself. After all, he was a multiple killer. Although in his defence, he would say that he never dispatched anyone who didn't have it coming. A bald-headed heavily tattooed muscular heavy, Layzee had been sent down for four years, not for any felony related to murder, but as a result of being found guilty on two counts of assault in the first degree.

The first charge was for stabbing a prostitute in the neck with a plastic fork in a fast-food diner. The second was after his wife called the police, who arrested and took him away when they arrived at her home to find it trashed and his wife battered and bruised.

Whilst the first crime was indefensible and was supported by a barrage of eyewitnesses from the diner—when it came to the second charge, Layzee Dawson was innocent—he never laid a finger on his wife. Her injuries were self-inflicted, a ruse she manufactured to finally rid herself of the man whom she had come to hate during their fifteen years of marriage.

The case involving his wife became the primary focus of media attention during the trial. Layzee pleaded "guilty" to his assault in the diner, but rightfully entered a plea of "not guilty" to the charges brought against him by his thirty-eight-year-old wife. Throughout the proceedings, he maintained his innocence on the second charge, but to no avail, Layzee was found guilty on both counts, largely as a result of meticulous planning on behalf of his scheming wife—that, and an Oscar-winning performance staged by her on the witness stand. Her testimony had everything: drama, intrigue, and treachery. And from the very first day, Mrs Dawson played her part to perfection. After all, she he had had years to prepare, and Layzee never stood a chance.

When she arrived at court on the first day, she was unrecognisable. Gone was the healthy and attractive, middle-aged, motherly figure. Instead, it was a frail and distraught-looking woman who turned up for her court appearance, her once shining blond hair looking like grubby rat's tails. She looked tired, gaunt, and malnourished, not as a result of the strain and worry associated with a destroyed marriage, nor at having to face the shame of a stressful court case, but as a result of deliberately starving herself in the weeks and months leading up to the trial in order to attain a certain guise that, if she played it right, might just sway a court's decision in her favour.

During that time, she had become the apotheosis of a method movie actor. A haggard, frail, pale-looking victim of domestic abuse, supposedly tortured by an evil monster during years of persecution and suffering. She had purposely dressed down for her court appearance and when she stepped out of the car, her semblance was more akin to that of trailer trash than a middle-class socialite. And that's how she intended to play it, as she took the stand.

'Could you please explain to the jury how you sustained these injuries, Mrs Dawson,' announced the prosecuting attorney as he rose from his chair and theatrically uncovered a sizeable A-board displaying several enlarged photographs of cuts and heavy bruises across Mrs Dawson's face, arms, and shoulders.

Stifled intakes of breath from both the public gallery and jury members reverberated through the courtroom as they recoiled against the vile images of Mrs Dawson's unbeknownst self-inflicted injuries.

The attorney paused for effect as the jury settled, and then he repeated the question. 'Mrs. Dawson… and I know this is difficult. Are these the injuries you sustained at the hands of your husband on the night in question?'

Layzee Dawson jumped up from his seat and pointed at the pictures. 'I never touched her!' he remonstrated. 'That's how she fuckin' looked when I got home that night!' Again, he was told to sit and be quiet. He lowered himself onto his chair.

The question was repeated.

'Yes,' whimpered Mrs Dawson quietly, her head lowered as though she was struggling through the hurt and pain of recollection as she convincingly acted the part of an abused and victimised woman. 'He came home late,' she continued. 'Drunk as usual and stinking of alcohol and perfume. He could barely stand.'

'You won't be able to stand by the time I've finished with you,' muttered Layzee beneath his breath.

'He told me he had found another woman and wanted me to pack my bags and leave that night. I tried to reason with him. But how can you reason with an animal like that?' She pointed from the dock to her husband, whose jaw had dropped and who looked completely baffled by his wife's claims. His perplexed expression switched to anger, which he was having trouble suppressing but endeavoured so to do, as he had already received many warnings from the female judge for verbal outbursts and whose patience was wearing thin.

Mrs Dawson lowered her head in shame as if the words were too horrific to repeat. She took a sip of water, and then glanced up at the judge, who asked if she was able to continue, or if she needed time to compose herself.

Maria Dawson shook her head and then resumed her testimony. 'And then it began, as it had so many times before,' she said pitifully. 'He grabbed me and hurled me across the room. I struck my head on the table. And then he reached for a baseball bat, which he kept behind the door in case of intruders. I begged him not to use it on me, but he began hitting me with it. Eventually, I think I passed out.'

The courtroom was deathly quiet, the jurors hanging on her every word.

'Is this the baseball bat that he used on you, Mrs Dawson?' queried the attorney, holding up the exhibit like a trophy of victory, which in its plastic bag looked battered and stained with dried blood.

Mrs Dawson looked across and winced. She nodded, 'Yes.'

Layzee was writhing in his chair with raw fury and then exploded out of it again like a captured bear from a trap. 'You're a fuckin' lying, BITCH!' he yelled.

The judge cried out for order and banged her gavel, but the prosecutor continued through Layzee's ranting. 'The very bat shown to have had your wife's smeared blood all over it,' continued the attorney, desperate to get his point across.

Again, Mrs Dawson nodded, as Layzee once again stood up. 'HEY! The only thing I've ever hit with that baseball bat was fuckin' baseballs!' claimed Layzee vehemently. 'And yeah... I'd had a drink, so what? But she's talkin' shit! I never fuckin' touched her!' Which was the only truth spoken during that week-long trial. Layzee was forced into his seat by his legal representative, as the judge again asked for the defence attorney to control his client.

The courtroom refocused on the witness stand as Mrs Dawson rose to her feet. 'You punched my face,' continued his sobbing wife, quietly, as if in a trance-like state. 'Over and over. Look at what you did.' She pointed to the damning pictures and then looked towards the jury members. Her eyes were filled with tears, a river of black mascara running down her face—as she knew it would. 'He then dragged me by my hair to the bedroom. And then he beat me again. I pretended to be unconscious. That's when he left the bedroom and began trashing the house. Eventually, everything went quiet. I think he must have passed out with the booze. That's when I called the police.'

Which was an untruth. The police were called the moment Mrs Dawson heard her husband's car pull into the drive.

By now, Layzee had had enough. He slowly stood up and began applauding. 'That's fuckin' brilliant,' he announced, turning towards the gallery behind. 'What a performance, huh? You should be on the fuckin' stage,' he yelled, his arms outstretched. 'Meryl Streep couldn't have played it fuckin' better.'

The judge again silenced the room and warned Layzee for a final time. 'Another outburst, Mr Dawson, and you will be held in contempt of this court, and you *will* be removed.'

Layzee was having none of it. 'When I got home... she looked like those fuckin' pictures. I said to her, what's goin' on? Who the fuck did this to you?'

'You did,' cried Mrs Dawson from the dock, still standing.

'There she goes again. Fuckin' lying bitch!'

The judge had had enough. Again she banged her gavel. 'I am adding a further 30 days to your sentence, Mr Dawson.'

'What for?'

'Contempt of court. You were warned, Mr Dawson.'

'That's bullshit!'

'60 days!'

'Fuck you!'

'90 days!'

'Up your ass!'

'Bailiffs, will you please remove Mr. Dawson?'

'Hey, come near me and it ain't gonna end well for you!'

Four bailiffs descended on Layzee Dawson, with all the speed of a quarterback blitz, and brought proceedings to an end.

The following week, whilst being sentenced and despite being implored by his attorney beforehand to remain calm, Layzee Dawson was about to fully demonstrate his violent motivational intent towards his now estranged wife, who was present in the gallery and was watching stoically as his sentence was handed down.

On the day of the sentencing, Maria Dawson appeared at the courthouse smartly dressed and although still very thin, she looked groomed and attractive—a completely different persona to that of the dishevelled abuse victim she had so convincingly portrayed throughout the trial.

Gone were the bedraggled ropes of sullied, yellow hair. Gone also was her pallid, white complexion. The tatty grey threadbare house coat dress she wore day after day was also absent, replaced by a sharp, tailored black business suit. Her blond hair was now styled, and her face exhibited meticulously applied makeup, which appeared to be the work of a professional beautician. She looked twenty years younger and the complete antithesis of her former self, or rather, the self she portrayed leading up to and throughout the trial.

There was a buzz of scandalous intrigue both outside and inside the courtroom as she entered proudly, like a film star on a catwalk. She wore Christian Louboutin shoes and carried a Louie Vuitton monogrammed clutch bag. She knew where Layzee would sit alongside his attorney and took her seat directly behind and a few rows back, knowing she would be well within his eyeline if he turned his head.

Her remarkable change in appearance was no accident. It was predetermined to infuriate her husband, as if twisting the blade of the knife, now firmly embedded deep in his back for however long the court was about to adjudicate. Now that the guilty verdict had been pronounced and set in stone, Mrs Dawson no longer had to act the part, and felt comfortable that she could now enjoy the remains of the legal process and bathe in the afterglow of her successful brush with the scales of justice.

Her metamorphosis did not go unnoticed by her husband, as he was brought up from the cells into the courtroom to hear his fate.

He arrived wearing a loose-fitting orange prison jumpsuit, his wrists cuffed and chained to a belly restraint. Attached to his right leg was an electronic stun cuff capable of delivering an extended 50,000-volt charge, which the judge could activate if required.

Upon seeing his wife, Layzee yelled, 'Hey! Look at her today. Don't she look peachy? Whatever happened to that fuckin' old, ugly, lying cow from last week, huh? Nice threads, though, girl. Who d'ya fuck to get them?'

Again, having walked only four steps into the courtroom, Layzee already had to be warned about his behaviour.

'Mr. Dawson!' said the judge. 'You have been informed that if you disrupt proceedings today, you will be removed, and your sentence pronounced in your absence. You *are* a security risk, Mr. Dawson, and if you show any further form of unruly behaviour or violence, I *will* activate the device attached to your leg. And it *will* incapacitate you and be painful. Do you understand?'

'Yes, your Lordship. But no one's listening. I admitted to stabbing that fuckin' hooker. But I never laid a hand on that bitch!' Layzee span round and pointed to his wife, whose face showed not a single ounce of reaction. 'She's stitched me up!'

'Mr. Dawson!' continued the judge. 'You have the court's verdict.'

'Yeah, but it's fuckin' wrong, Your Grace,' said Dawson.

'Mr. Dawson, you will refer to me as "Judge" or "Your Honour". Now, continue to stand and listen to the sentence of the court.'

A defiant Layzee Dawson sat down.

'Stand up, Mr Dawson!' ordered the judge, 'Or I will activate your stun cuff.'

Dawson remained seated. Then suddenly, he screamed and was shaken rigid by the electric shock current from the stun cuff attached to his ankle, which shook him from his chair and sent him crashing to the floor. The courtroom gasped and then fell quiet.

Slowly, Dawson moved and then got to his feet. 'Fuck me, that tickled. Can we do that again?' he said. He remained standing.

The judge spent the next ten minutes summarising the court's jurisdiction before announcing a four-year prison term that Dawson was to serve at the Elmira Correctional Facility, an all-male maximum-security prison in Chemung County, New York.

Unsurprisingly, Layzee didn't take it well. And although shackled, suddenly tried to vault the wooden partition to get at his wife sitting behind him. 'You fuckin' wait!' he yelled. 'I ain't done with you by a damn sight!'

Almost immediately, the judge reactivated the stun cuff and Dawson screamed again for a full five seconds. Then, once deactivated, four uniformed court security officers leapt on him, dragging him back from the partition and forcing him to the floor, batons clattering and boots scuffing the floor as the men wrestled with him.

'I'll get you, you fuckin' lying bitch!' came the muffled voice from beneath the tangled heap of wrestling bodies as the chains of restraint jangled amidst the melee. Such was his strength, the four bailiffs struggled to take the raging man away, but eventually they got him to his feet.

'She's a fuckin' liar!' he yelled as he was dragged out of the courtroom and forced down the tight corridor leading to the cells, fighting, and ranting every inch of the way as echoes of, 'I'll fuckin kill her!' receded into the distance.

Exasperated, Dawson's defence attorney, who was employed, and on the Vitalli crime family's books, cast his eyes to the ceiling and wondered if his fee was worth the grief. He then momentarily wilted and buried his face in his hands, almost in relief that the sentence was relatively light, but also relieved for himself that his dealings with this latest family misdemeanour were, for now, over.

Layzee Dawson's violent display proved that he had both the intent and the physical resource to endanger the life of his spouse. However, Mrs Dawson was ahead of the game and had that behavioural trait of her husband covered. Before the onset of the trial, she had already requested law enforcement assistance. She had struck a deal with the authorities and agreed that if she testified against her husband—for her safety—she could enter the Witness Protection Program, which would provide her with anonymity and a new identity.

On the day of sentencing, yet unbeknown to both Mr and Mrs Dawson, sitting in the shadows in the corner at the back of the packed public gallery, was Salvatore Vitalli, who eyed Mrs Dawson with quiet intrigue mixed with loathing. He was sitting with a close associate of the family, Doctor Lucas Roberts—the family's physician. They watched as, with head held high, she proudly left the courtroom accompanied by an entourage of police officers, to be whisked away to begin a new chapter of her life somewhere.

Vitalli knew she had lied and had lied convincingly. It had certainly been an impressive show, but he knew she had fabricated every single facet of her carefully conceived story, and then delivered the performance of a lifetime. He turned to his associate. 'What a bitch!' he whispered.

The doctor nodded his agreement. 'Yes... quite a performance,' he said.

Salvatore Vitalli was impressed at the lengths Mrs Dawson had endured to convince the jury. Her injuries *were* substantial, however conceived. But nothing could detract from his dislike of her. For a wife of a family associate to demonstrate such flagrant disrespect for her husband so callously, and so publicly, was, to put it mildly, unforgivable. In *his* world, there was an unbreakable code. Families stick together. And wives know their place. Now, with Layzee Dawson's incarceration, Vitalli had temporarily lost a valuable family asset, and he hoped at some point in the future an opportunity would present itself to remedy the court's injustice, and that Mrs. Dawson would get her comeuppance.

Despite the treachery of his wife, for a man who lived his life by inflicting brutal violence almost every day, four years was an incredibly lean sentence for Layzee Dawson, when really, he should have been sent to death-row for the multiple murders he had committed spanning many years of mob activity. But such were the organisational skills and the meticulous planning that had become a hallmark of the Vitalli crime syndicate; the police could never compile sufficient evidence to build a murder case against him, or any of the Vitalli family, for the matter of that. And well-paid lawyers and money grabbing corrupt police officers ensured that any jail-time that a family associate had to endure was kept to a minimum. Such was the length of influence they possessed; it even stretched as far as New York's Elmira Correctional Facility, that had been Dawson's home for the past two years.

Whilst incarcerated, and to increase his chances for early release via the parole system, Dawson had been advised by his firm's legal representative to become a model prisoner—an unlikely scenario given his quick temper, but one he fulfilled, even on the day when his wife paid him a visit twenty-three months into his prison term and a week before his scheduled parole hearing.

'Hello, Layzee,' she said, via a telephone handset from the safety of the reinforced glass window that separated her from her husband in the dismal visitation room. 'I bet you didn't expect to see me again, did you?'

'I have every intention of seeing you again,' he snarled.

Layzee, wearing his scruffy spruce green prison scrubs, glared at the woman who, since seeing her last, had put on a little weight, and looked curvaceous, affluent, and frankly stunning, wearing a royal blue polka dot designer dress by Gucci. Her blond hair was fashioned into a neat bob cut and she looked tanned, radiant and, yes, attractive.

Layzee could have refused the visitation, but when he heard of his wife's request to see him, he felt intrigued to see what she wanted. With his parole hearing due within days and the prospect of imminent release soon after, he fully expected her to be afraid, remorseful, and beg for forgiveness for what she had done. But then he realised there might be an alternative motive for her visit—a sly plan, perhaps, to keep him banged up in jail. Despite that, he felt compelled to see her and added her name to the short list of those allowed to visit him.

'I know what you're doing,' he said calmly from the other side of the Plexiglas screen in the cramped visitation stall, when he realised that forgiveness was not, and perhaps never was, on his wife's agenda.

Mrs Dawson smiled. 'And what's that?' she asked.

'You've come to taunt me, you bitch!' he whispered, fully aware that a prison guard standing close by was watching, and not wishing to be placed on report. 'Huh, I should have fuckin' realised that,' he growled. 'You know I have a short fuse. So, you've come to make me angry, create a scene and jeopardise my chances for early release, haven't you?' He looked smug at the notion that he had solved the riddle of her late visitation. 'Well, you can fuck right off!' he whispered. 'Because nothing you say or do is gonna ruin my chance of getting outta here next month. And then paying you a fuckin' visit.'

Mrs Dawson's smile remained, and there was an air of confidence about her. 'You'll never find me,' she said. She leaned back from the cubicle and looked around the bland grey walls of the sterile room, which reminded her of a school canteen. A few other visits were also taking place. At least the visitation room appeared clean, she thought. Lord knows what the cells looked like.

When she arrived, she had to undertake the usual protocol of identification checks. Then the metal detector procedure ensued, whereby she had to remove outer clothing, shoes, and jewellery. That was followed by a frisking and a handbag search, all of which she found utterly absurd, since hers was a non-contact visit. Even if she wanted to, how could she possibly pass anything to her husband if he was effectively in another room separated by a glass screen? After her hand was stamped with ultraviolet ink, which would be checked on her departure, she was then sent to a holding room whilst inmate number 42439 was brought from his cell. And now here she was. She turned back to face him.

Layzee's eyes bored into her, fuelled by seven hundred days' worth of incarcerated hatred. She refocused her attention. It was one of the few times during their marriage where she really felt she had the upper hand, and she was going to enjoy this moment. 'So, how is it going with those anger management classes of yours?' she asked, feigning interest but determined still to twist the knife before she got round to the real reason for her visit.

'Fuck you!' snarled Layzee down the telephone, his hand tightly gripping the handset as if throttling her throat.

'Oh, I see. They're not really working, are they?'

Layzee's glare of unbridled anger should have permeated the glass window separating them but seemed impotent. Almost as if his wife was wearing an emotional bullet-proof vest. He noticed something about her, a side he had never seen before—an unusual air of supremacy. She spoke differently, too. And that air of pre-eminence was again apparent in her next few words. 'You see, I'm no longer afraid of you,' she said. 'Those days are long gone.'

'Is that so?' replied Layzee, his chin resting in the palm of his hand. 'Feeling safe with your new identity and life now, are you? Where are you shacked up nowadays?'

'Wouldn't *you* like to know?'

'You can't fool me. I can smell your fear even now, from this side of the fuckin' screen.'

'No, it's not fear you can smell, Layzee. The only smell you have under your nose is probably Vaseline. Have you been enjoying the showers, Layzee? I hear a lot of that goes on.'

Layzee Dawson sat bolt upright, his eyes narrowing into angry slits. This certainly was a side of her he had never seen before. His free hand formed into a clenched fist, his knuckles tight like a row of white onions. But then he checked himself and released the tension. 'Nice try, bitch,' he snarled.

Mrs Dawson mirrored his smile. She lowered her voice as she spoke into the mouthpiece. 'Word on the street is that it's *you* that's turned into a bitch.'

'You nasty fuck!' he said, raising his voice. 'Yeah, you talk the talk from that side of the glass, don't you? How about you fuckin' come round here?'

'HEY!' yelled the prison guard, pointing towards Layzee's stall with his baton. 'Are we good there?'

Layzee leaned back. 'Yeah, no problem, Boss,' he said.

Mrs Dawson scoffed at her husband. 'Boss? Look at you, bowing down to them. The big man reduced to a pussy. You've lost all sense of self-respect, haven't you, Layzee?'

The look of unfettered hatred in her husband's eyes would have been sufficient years ago to have reduced her to a quivering wreck.

'No,' she continued, as she met his thousand-yard stare with that of her own. 'Like I said, I'm no longer afraid of you.'

'Well, you should be,' he whispered, leaning forward into the stall, his fierce, red face only inches from the glass window. His lips formed into a thin scowl. 'But just know this. Once I'm out of this shithole next month. I will not rest until I find you. And after what you've done to me. You know what's fuckin' coming.'

Mrs Dawson grinned as if impervious to the threat. She leaned back and calmly opened her handbag. She sifted through some items and took out a photograph.

Layzee strained his neck to see. 'What's that?'

His wife turned the photo around and pressed it against the window. Upon seeing the picture, Layzee's eyes narrowed, and his jaw dropped into a puzzled look of enquiry which deepened as he focused on the image. The photograph was that of a man he recognised from news reports he had seen through the years. A man he had never met. It was Louie Marmarella's associate and chief enforcer, "Cadillac" Tony DeVille.

Layzee assumed this to be the new man in his wife's life, and that she was about to gloat about how much better a lover and companion he was. But he was mistaken.

'See this man,' said his wife icily, her smile now gone, the telephone handset still firmly pressed against her face as she spoke. 'This is the man that I have hired to kill you.' Her tone was calm and matter-of-fact, as if discussing her preference for a movie she fancied watching that evening. 'I thought you should know that,' she added. 'Because he's very good at his job and never fails. He has a one hundred percent success record, and you would probably never know, even when you draw your last breath, who it was that finished you. I thought it was only right you see his face.'

Layzee felt the blood rise again to the point of lift-off, but bit his lip and quelled the rising tide. Over the years. He had heard of this man's work. It appeared to be nothing remarkable, just a different approach to achieve the same objective. Whilst his own method of problem elimination was raw, brutal and always up-close and personal, this man's style of assassination was reputed to be more clinical. But then, the two had never met and Dawson's self-belief in his own ability, by way of his sheer arrogance, was such that should that day ever occur, he would always back himself to prevail. He looked across at the woman who had issued his death warrant. 'Anything else?' he asked.

'No. That's all,' said his wife simply, putting the photograph back in her handbag. 'I'll leave you now to dwell on that thought. And with regard to your parole board review... you might now want to reconsider your tack. You might be better off failing that interview and serving out your full four-year sentence. But I'm afraid that will only prolong your inevitable demise. So, perhaps best get it over with quickly, don't you think?'

Layzee couldn't help himself and spat at the window.

'HEY!' called the guard, who took a step forward.

'It's OK,' said Layzee, his hand raised. 'Just blowing my wife a goodbye kiss.'

Mrs Dawson glowered frostily at him through the slime of sputum sliding down the pane of glass. 'Goodbye Layzee,' she said, as if closing the lid on a coffin in a funeral parlour. She rose from her seat, turned and, without looking back, walked majestically out of the room.

# # #

A week later, it was time for Layzee Dawson's parole hearing. The comprehensive report submitted by the warden to the parole board highlighted the lack of any infractions in his two-year prison conduct record, and his physical, mental, and psychiatric examinations were deemed satisfactory. It was said that his behaviour and his attitude towards his fellow inmates and prison society in general left no cause for concern and as such he was awarded "good time" or "meritorious credit", which had helped bring forward his parole hearing. It seemed the only issue that could hamper Dawson's early release was a failure to show plans for employment. However, the board was satisfied that a job as a driver for a pharmaceutical company—unknowingly for them affiliated to the Vitalli family—had been secured, and as such his parole was granted on the understanding that he adhere to the usual constraints regarding regular visits, reporting to his parole officer as and when required.

'So, you're getting out today, Dawson,' said Officer Dale Birch, one of two correctional officers who were processing Dawson for release. 'Frankly, I'm surprised. It beats me how anyone on that fuckin' parole board could possibly believe that you could ever become a useful member of society.

How the fuck did you swing that one, Dawson?'

Layzee remained silent.

'What's the matter, tough guy?' continued Officer Birch. 'Cat got your tongue? Ah... you'll be back. And pretty soon, I reckon. I guarantee it. In fact, I'll keep a cell warm for ya.'

'Don't bother yourself,' said Layzee. 'I got other plans.'

'Well, we'll see. I have to say though, your ex-missus looks a dish. Nice rack. I bet she's really been putting it about whilst you've been banged up here.'

Layzee, who would have normally flown at the officer, allowed the comment to wash over him, but it was noted and filed away, perhaps to be released and dissected at some appropriate time in the not-too-distant future.

The second officer, a younger, less experienced man, asked. 'By the way, Dawson, you never told us what those tattoos on your neck signify?'

Layzee was covered in tattoos. 'What these?' he said, pointing to an acronym of four elaborate letters tattooed just below his neck. The letters were A C A B. 'They stand for "Always Carry A Bible",' he said.

'Really?' queried the less experienced man.

'No, they don't,' said Officer Birch. 'I've seen plenty of those tats. The letters stand for "All Cops are Bastards". Ain't that right, Layzee?'

'Huh... you should fuckin' know.'

'No, I didn't mean *that* tattoo,' said the younger security guard. 'I meant those tiny daggers. 'What do *they* mean?'

Layzee had a grid of about two dozen tiny knife emblems grouped closely together on the side of his neck. Most of the criminal underworld in the know knew they represented murdered victims—and it was thought he might have got the idea from 2nd World War fighter pilots who marked their kills on the side of their planes.

'Yeah, what do they mean, Dawson?' snarled Officer Birch.

Layzee stepped forward. He decided to enlighten the officer who had made a habit of baiting him during his time in prison. 'What these?' he said, pointing to his neck. 'OK, I'll tell ya. Each one represents the wife of a cop

I've fucked. Look... there's yours.'

'You bastard!' sneered the officer.

Layzee leaned forward and smiled threateningly in the senior officer's face. He lunged as if going for him, which made the accompanying officer grab the hosel of his baton. But before the conversation escalated, Dawson scooped his stuff from the table. 'Fuck you very much,' he growled, as he made his way towards the gate to freedom. But before walking through it, Layzee couldn't help himself. He paused, looked back, and said to the senior officer, 'Hey, Birch! I might be seeing you sooner than you think... but not this side of the fence. When we meet again, it'll be on my turf. And I'll ask my tattooist to get his needles ready.'

The correctional officer, who knew he had just been threatened, watched as the brute of a man exited the prison facility to a waiting yellow taxicab. He thought about reporting the incident to the warden, but with Dawson now a free man, he thought better of it and decided to say nothing, a decision he might live to regret.

Chapter 3: A Dish Best Served Cold

The six men sitting at their dining table in the restaurant's secluded bay window watched as the new group, headed by Louie Marmarella, entered the Italian restaurant. The waiter that had attended to the Vitalli group greeted the newcomers and there was a brief exchange before Marmarella and his two bodyguards were led to their table on the other side of the room.

The six members of the Vitalli family remained silent as the Marmarella contingent was seated. Although separated by several tables, the six men could just make out what Louie Marmarella was saying to the waiter. 'I'm expecting my son Dino to join us,' he said. 'Let him know we're here when he arrives, would ya?'

'Si, senior,' said the waiter, who passed each of them a menu and asked if they would like drinks.

'Err, no thanks, we'll wait until my son gets here,' said Marmarella.

Fingers, sitting at the Vitalli table, looked up and glanced outside at the car containing the dead body of Dino Marmarella. He sneered and then whispered beneath his breath. 'It'll be a fuckin' long wait.'

Everyone at the Vitalli table stifled a laugh, except Joey and the big man. 'Shut up!' said the man at the head of the table. 'Keep your voices down and keep your cool. We're here just to have lunch. Now let's eat.' Joey's emotions were still in disarray over what he had done.

The men helped themselves to the meatballs and spaghetti, which they first dusted with grated Parmesan cheese. Nothing was said as the large dish was passed around from man to man with a basket containing garlic bread—the red wine followed.

The mood at the secluded bay window table had switched and had become as solemn as a holy communion service where priests offer, in the form of holy bread and wine, the body and blood of Christ for each of his kneeling congregation to consume. The Vitalli crew kept their heads down and continued to eat quietly, except for Frankie, who had one eye outside on the car containing the body of Dino Marmarella.

Unlike Salvatore Vitalli, who was an overweight, tall man, Louie Marmarella was a man built wide rather than tall. Despite his modest stature, Marmarella cut an imposing figure for a man of fifty something years old. His body was short and squat, with a protruding midriff that appeared fat, though his upper torso looked well-muscled and powerful. His arms were strong but compact, and the backs of his blunt, leathery hands were covered in a fine black mat of hair. He walked with a wide, awkward gait—a slow, lumbering motion borne from his low, heavy centre of gravity, reminiscent to that of a sloth moving through the limbs of trees.

Marmarella's tanned face was round and unassuming, appearing heavy atop his broad shoulders. There was no discernible neck to talk of, just a roll of fleshy fat separating his head from the starched white collar of his shirt. A thick, unkempt mop of black hair topped his head, with a grey streak running down the centre, making it appear a skunk had crawled up there and was taking a nap. His eyebrows seemed permanently knitted into a scowl, and his voice was a gruff bark—more suited to issuing orders than polite conversation. He wore a pencil-thin black moustache while the rest of his face remained cleanly shaven. His jowls were beginning to sag beneath his square jawline and aggression seemed to ooze from every pore—like sweat. One didn't maintain a position of power in Marmarella's criminal empire by being soft—*he* ruled through fear, intimidation, and a blatant disregard for law or human life. Those foolish enough to defy him had a tendency to disappear without a trace.

Today, he wore a pinstriped tailored navy-blue suit which appeared one size too small for his stocky, powerful build. The ensemble was completed by a loud polka-dot tie and a pair of black patent leather shoes, cementing the probability that he, too, had an association with organised crime.

As the minutes passed, Marmarella appeared to get more and more agitated as he waited for a son that would never arrive. Eventually, he pulled his cell phone from his pocket and angrily punched a few keys.

Louie Marmarella's voice had a unique pitch that even when he spoke quietly would travel inexplicably, and the six men in the bay window had no problem hearing his words. 'Where the hell is that idiot son of mine?' he remonstrated, shaking his head. The two men sitting with him glanced at one other and shrugged simultaneously.

At that exact moment, at the Vitalli crew's table, a muffled melodic ringtone sounded, and Joey pulled a cell phone from his inside jacket pocket and answered it. Then, his eyes widened, and a startled look appeared across his face—a face which had turned ashen white.

Frankie, sitting opposite, raised his eyes.

The men listened as Marmarella spoke. 'Dino,' he said bluntly. 'Where the hell are ya?'

Joey, sitting with his back towards Marmarella's table, pressed the cell phone against his ear. Then, he said quietly, 'Eh, sorry. You got the wrong number,' and promptly hung up.

He reached into his jacket and pulled another phone, this time his own phone, which was a similar make. He compared them. Realising his mistake, he pocketed both phones and glanced over his shoulder towards Louie Marmarella, who was looking at his own cell phone with a look of puzzlement.

'Oh, no,' muttered Frankie, as realisation dawned that something monumental had just occurred. 'You fuckin' idiot,' he whispered across the table to Joey. 'You dumb, fuckin' idiot.'

'Hey, what's going on?' asked the leader.

Frankie leaned across towards his boss, his eyes fixed on Joey, his voice but a whisper, 'Boss, we may have a problem. I think numb-nuts here must have taken Dino's cell phone this morning. And I think he just answered

Louie Marmarella's call.'

The leader's face sank as if his facial skin had again suddenly lost its grip. In doing so, it added another fold of skin to his double chin. He turned and shot a look of angry intent at Joey as the cell phone in Joey's pocket rang again. Beneath the table, he grabbed Joey's leg and squeezed it hard. 'Leave it!' he said sharply, like a ventriloquist speaking through taught stationary lips.

The phone rang—and rang.

Joey grimaced under the pain of his boss' tight grip as the infuriating, muffled ringtone continued. Marmarella turned and looked across the room and over towards the six men who had hunkered down and who appeared to be busy stuffing their faces with food. He had a puzzled look on his face.

Joey prayed for the ringing to stop. It did, but the inquisitive frown on Marmarella's face remained.

'Give it to me!' snarled the leader, who grabbed the phone, switched it off and passed it to Frankie, who slid it into his jacket pocket.

Frankie, who was directly in Marmarella's line of sight, had no option other than to deflect his rival's enquiring look of bewilderment by acknowledging the man. Although he couldn't stand the sight of him, Frankie raised his glass. 'Hi there, Mr. Marmarella,' he called. 'How ya doin'?'

Louie Marmarella paused for a moment, spotted Frankie, and then got up from his seat. He slowly ambled across the room to the partially concealed bay window table where the six men were eating and placed his hands on the back of the chairs where Fingers and Joey were seated. Then he leaned over and said, 'Well, if it ain't Francesco Vitalli. I'm fine, thank you for asking. How ya doin' Frankie?'

The ploy seemed to have worked, decided Frankie. 'Not as well as you,' he said to his family's archrival.

'And how's that lovely wife of yours?'

Frankie shrugged. 'She's doing good.'

'You mean someone else is doin' her good,' laughed Marmarella. 'And probably right now.'

Frankie, who was sitting on the other side of the table, exploded out of his chair, his face livid with anger as he stood bolt rigid, his fists clenched.

'Whoa... I think I hit a nerve there, didn't I, Sash?' smiled Marmarella, taking a step back and bringing Sash's rumoured relationship with Frankie's wife very much into play.

The black man also got to his feet. 'Hey, mister,' he said. 'You're bang outta line with that.'

'Hey, talkin' of 'banging', have you seen her lately, Sash? Or are you at the back of the bangin' queue right now? Perhaps she's found a brother with a bigger dick!'

'You fuckin' asshole!' intoned Frankie through grated teeth.

The leader of the Vitalli group also stood and quickly intervened. 'Now look here, Louie,' he said authoritatively. 'Me and my boys are just out having a pleasant lunch... much the same as you. So, there's no need for this antagonism, is there? Now, what do you want?'

'Well, well... if it ain't Salvatore Vitalli. I didn't see you there, Sal. How the fuck could I have missed you?' The comment was delivered, and received, as a slant on the big man's considerable size. 'It's a real family get-together you got going here. How's the world treating you nowadays, Sal? You're not having much luck with that fuckin' treadmill, by the looks of it. Have you tried Yoga?'

Salvatore Vitalli's lips narrowed. 'You got a vicious tongue, Louie,' said the big man. 'You always have had. You've no right to come over here, spoil our fuckin' lunch and insult Frankie and the boys that way.'

Marmarella smiled. 'Just being sociable. Christ, you have put some weight on, though, Sal. What about Pilates? I hear that's good for the waistline.'

Johnny, who still had the food menu close by, scanned the listing and frowned when he couldn't find a dish named "Pilates".

'I don't need your fuckin' advice,' growled the leader. 'Now what d'ya want?'

'Ah, you know me, I don't mean nothin' by it,' said Marmarella. 'Or do I, Frankie? Ha!'

Frankie, who had slowly lowered himself onto his chair continued to glower at the leader of the Marmarella family, his hooded eyes betraying the unbridled hatred that burned beneath his sun-tanned face which was beginning to glow a dark shade of red as anger fuelled his rising blood pressure.

Marmarella, who always seemed to know which buttons to press, was clearly enjoying the moment. 'Hey, take it easy, Frankie,' he said, suppressing a smirk of satisfaction. He leaned towards Frankie's boss. 'I'm just fuckin' with him, Sal. He's a bit touchy today though, don't ya think? I'm surprised you let him off his leash.' Marmarella winked and blew a kiss at Frankie, whose stare remained fixed and threatening. Marmarella continued, 'Hey, Frankie,' he said, 'When I'm dead and gone, you'll realise what a real friend I was.'

Frankie leaned forward. 'Yeah? Well, why don't you drop dead now so we can test your theory?'

Marmarella began to applaud as he laughed. 'Huh, very funny. Frankie, you should show some respect. Acting like a dick won't make yours any bigger. Ain't that right, Sash?'

'Hey!' intervened the leader, his patience all but expired. 'What exactly do you want, Louie?'

Marmarella gestured with his outstretched arms. 'Nothin'. Like I said, just being sociable while I wait for my boy to arrive. It's a beautiful day. Just thought I'd say hello, that's all.'

'Well, you've said it,' said the big man. 'So, now, if you don't mind...'

'It's called FUCK OFF!' finished Frankie. 'And it's located over there!' He gestured to the other side of the room.

'Oh, I see. It's like that, is it?' said Marmarella, backing off, his palms raised, feigning an apologetic attitude. 'I know when I'm not welcome. By the way, I sent the chef here my secret recipe for those bad boys.' He pointed towards the bowl of meatballs they had all been eating. 'They got a special ingredient,' he said, his eyes widening conspiratorially. 'I bet ya didn't know that. Speaking of bad boys, did you ever find out what happened to that guy of yours who went missin' a few months back? What was his name? Big fucker. Oh yeah, I remember. "Spaghetti" Sam, wasn't it? Wasn't he closely related to you, Sal?'

'He was my brother,' said Salvatore Vitalli as their eyes met. 'And you know that.' In that single glance, a silent, wordless conversation passed between the two men, their eyes speaking volumes.

Marmarella's conceited gaze held steady, for just a fraction too long, as if savouring his own smugness. 'Huh… enjoy your fuckin' meatballs,' he said, as he winked, turned, and sauntered back to his table and sat down, a proud smile of victory beaming across his face.

Salvatore Vitalli looked around at the puzzled faces of his crew. An air of distaste had spread like a radiation cloud as appetites around the table faded, snuffed out by the implied suggestion that their food might contain a grotesque beef substitute. The men looked at the balls of meat on their plates, and then at one another. They all knew that one of Marmarella's business interests included a slaughterhouse on the dockyard, which supplied meat to the local markets, butchers, and restaurants. They also suspected it was used for other purposes.

Fingers, who still had a mouth full of food, stopped chewing. His sour face, which looked sour even when he slept, froze for a moment at the thought of what, or who, he might be eating. With his mouth still full of food, he said, 'I knew this meat tasted funny.'

'Didn't stop you fuckin' eatin' it, though… did it?' said Johnny.

Fingers began to cough and choke, as if on the verge of vomiting. Then he angrily spat out the remnants of the grey meat, reached into his jacket, pulled out his nickel-plated revolver and rose from his seat. Sash was quick to respond and grabbed his arm and sat him back down before anyone could see what was in his hand.

'Put it away!' barked the leader.

A sudden ripple of chuckled hilarity rose to a crescendo of jeering from the Marmarella table, who had been watching the fallout of activity from the other side of the restaurant.

Frankie was seething, and shoved his plate away. His eyes were fierce and overflowing with raw loathing as he glared across the restaurant at Louie Marmarella, just as a Dean Martin ballad began playing through the restaurant's PA speaker system. 'I fuckin' hate that bastard,' he said.

'Who? Dean Martin?' said Johnny. 'I kinda like his stuff.'

'No, stupid... that fucker over there! One of these days, I'm gonna put that sack o' shit through his own fuckin' meat grinder.'

Fingers added his two twopenn'orth to the conversation. 'Yeah, while he's still breathing!'

'Jeez! You're a real charmer, ain't ya, Fingers,' said Johnny.

The leader leaned into the table. 'HEY! Why do I have to repeat myself? Keep your voices down. Can't you see he's just tryin' to bait us? What have I told ya? Never show your emotions. Never let a guy like him know what you're thinking.'

Louie Marmarella again glanced over and said something indistinguishable which made the Capelli brothers, Marmarella's security contingent, look across and grin.

The Capelli brothers were not just brothers, they were twin brothers—identical in every way. That is until they smiled. For when they smiled, that's when the symmetry ended. For whilst Ricco Capelli had perfectly aligned bright Da Vinci veneered white teeth, Rocco Capelli's teeth were crooked, like a ragged, blackened line of cracked and broken tombstones, embedded in the soft purulent flesh of his yellow diseased gums. His was an ugly mouth—the ugliest—borne from years of poor hygiene and a phobia of dental surgeries.

Estimates suggest seventy percent of Americans suffer some form of dental phobia, ranging from mild anxiety to absolute psychological trauma, often resulting in a complete refusal to undertake any treatment whatsoever, irrespective of the consequences. Rocco Capelli was one such individual. Whilst his brother Ricco had spent a fortune in dental fees over the years to acquire that "Hollywood smile", Rocco had always embarked on a circle of avoidance whenever a need for dental treatment arose. The only positive outcome of this behavioural trait was that it provided a means for people to tell them apart, but only when they smiled—which was not very often.

Both Capelli brothers were tall, of medium build, and wore closely cropped dark brown hair. They both had the same blue-grey narrow eyes and oversized Roman noses, which accentuated the angular shape of their square jaw lines, which were furnished with neatly trimmed goatee beards. They both wore matching fashionable rectangular-framed metal glasses.

But there was a cruelness about their faces with their dead, lifeless eyes which never appeared to blink, almost as if living in a state of perpetual trance beyond the tinted blue lenses of their spectacles. The twin brothers were also devoid of any smile lines and, as demonstrated by a lifetime of violence, both were completely bankrupt of any moral standing. To say they looked unusual would be an understatement, but it was their facial complexion, which was visually their most alarming feature. Both had pale skin with a washed-out watercolour pallor, almost as if a light dusting of Oshiro powder, used so effectively by Japanese Geisha girls, had been applied to their faces. They looked ghostly—unnatural. But apart from their striking appearance, it was how they sometimes communicated with one another that left most within earshot of their vocal exchanges bewildered.

Generally, twins have an innate understanding of one other, and often, as in the case of the Capelli brothers, speak using their own code. As they spend so much time together, from an early age, a twin can pick up words said wrongly by the other twin, which they fully comprehend, but which can be perceived almost as a foreign language by other people. The Capelli brothers expanded on this trait and carried it into adulthood, using it to their advantage all their criminal lives, and sometimes seconds before dispatching unfortunates to the hereafter.

The two men were always immaculately dressed. Their suits and casual attire always matched—almost as an intentional trademark, not dissimilar to that of their lifelong heroes, the infamous London gangsters, the Kray twins.

Today, as they sat and waited with their mentor Louie Marmarella, for the arrival of his son Dino, the brothers wore matching black pinstriped suits and black shirts with thin silk black neckties which, ironically, wouldn't have looked out of place at a graveside burial gathering. Perhaps owing to their unique look, women were drawn to them and found them handsome. However, it was Ricco, with his perfect smile, who attracted the most female interest. Rocco, with his dental horror show, had had to get used to paying for his pleasures.

The Vitalli table had fallen quiet until Frankie, who was still watching the comings and goings outside, said suspiciously, 'Hey, what the fuck's going on out there?'

Again, the men strained to look outside.

'What is it?' enquired the leader.

'Eh… there's a waiter and some other guy looking under our car. This don't look good. The guy's pointing something out.'

'What d'ya mean, pointing something out?'

Frankie looked pensive. 'I don't know. He's kneeling and pointing beneath the trunk. I don't like the look of this. Hold on. They're coming back in.'

The door of the restaurant swung open and then the waiter who had been outside spoke with the bartender. The bartender pointed towards the men in the bay window. Then the waiter walked across. 'Scusi, gentlemen,' he said. 'Apologies for disturbing your lunch, but is that your black Chrysler in the parking lot?'

'Yeah,' said the leader. 'What about it?'

'Well, it seems it's leaking fluid, sir.'

'Really.'

'Si, but the leak's not coming from the engine compartment… how do you say in Inglese? It appears to be coming from the trunk at the rear. It is causing a mess of our car park.'

The leader glared at the waiter. 'Jesus Christ! What are *you* now… a fuckin' grease monkey?'

'I do not understand, sir.'

Frankie put his hand on his father's arm. 'Boss, he's just trying to be helpful,' he said.

'Well, it don't fuckin' sound like it to me. Alright,' groaned the leader, turning to the waiter. 'It sounds like a problem with the rear axle. We'll sort it out.'

'Grazia signore,' said the waiter, who added, 'Happy to oblige.' And then left.

'What's up with the axle, Boss?' asked Joey.

'Nothin', you idiot,' whispered the leader, his mouth hardly moving. 'There are bullet holes in the floor of the trunk... it must be blood coming from Dino's body.' Salvatore Vitalli looked exasperated. 'Didn't I leave instructions for our mechanic to weld those holes shut? We need to sort this shit out, and quick.'

'I'll go check,' said Frankie, who rose and left the table. Fingers followed him out. A few minutes later, both men returned and walked purposely across to the group's bay window table. Frankie leaned over towards the big man. 'Boss, we've got a problem.'

'Jesus Christ! What now?'

'The stiff in car ain't stiff.'

'What d'ya mean?'

'He ain't dead.'

The big man's forlorn face took on the relative dimensions of the Grand Canyon as the lines of his furrowed brow deepened. Slowly, he raised his head. 'What?'

All the men leaned in closer.

'The stiff in the trunk ain't dead,' repeated Frankie. 'He's alive.'

'Well, if he ain't dead, course he's alive,' said Johnny. 'There ain't no grey area with that, is there? He's either dead or alive...'

'Shut the fuck up, you!' interrupted the big man. 'Hang on a minute. After all this shit... are you sure, Frankie?'

'Yeah, he's breathing. We've tied and gagged him for now and left him in the trunk. He's unconscious, but we need to get him outta here in case he comes round and starts kickin' off.'

Bewildered, the leader paused for a moment and looked at Fingers for confirmation.

'Yeah, Boss. It's legit, he's alright. When I say he's alright, he's fucked up, and he's been shot... but yeah, he's alive.'

'I don't believe this,' said the big man.

Fingers continued. 'It looks like Joey's bullet hit him in the arm or somewhere round there. I... I don't know. But he's lost a lot of blood and needs to get to a hospital.'

'Hmph… fuck that!' growled the big man. 'No hospital!'

'No?'

'No!'

Joey grabbed Fingers' arm. 'I don't think I shot him in the arm. I think I shot him in the back, didn't I?'

All five of the men turned to Joey.

'Son, you couldn't hit a bull's ass with a barn shovel,' said the leader, his deep baritone voice again triggering a grumbling chorus of muted 'useless fuck' comments around the table.

Frankie allowed for the murmuring to subside and then whispered to the main man, 'Boss, why don't we just finish him?'

'Who… Joey? Good idea.'

'No, the stiff. After all, ten minutes ago, we all thought Dino was dead, and we had everything planned. So, let's just finish him! He's always been a piece of shit… he's a rapist and a woman killer.'

'No, no, hold on,' said the big man, raising his hand. 'Yes, I agree. He deserves to die. But this could work to our advantage if we play it right. Let me think.'

Frankie waited, watching the cogs and gears of criminal intent engage as his father explored his options. The others remained silent as the waiter cleared the table of the dirty plates and uneaten meatballs. A dessert menu was then distributed to each of the men, after which the waiter left.

The big man eventually raised his head. 'I think we now know what happened to my brother, Sam,' he growled, his eyes almost covered by his lowered eyelids as if offering condolences to a distraught widow whose world had just caved in. Only this was *his* world, and it had become all too personal. How dare Marmarella come over and publicly taunt him and his family in the manner in which he had?

Salvatore Vitalli looked up at the audience of faces hanging on his next few words. Words that they knew would trigger some kind of terrible reprisal. 'Perhaps it's time for some payback,' he said grimly. 'Anyone got any ideas?'

He looked around at the faces.

Joey was the only one not paying attention. He had a glazed, catatonic look about him, like that of a student who had fallen asleep with his eyes wide open during a three-hour lecture on knitting.

'Hey!' said the big man. He waited, but Joey didn't respond. He looked at him quizzically. 'Is he asleep?' he asked. 'HEY! Douchebag!'

Fingers nudged Joey's leg beneath the table.

Joey shuddered himself back from his daydream. He looked around and realised he was being spoken to.

'Hmm... nice of you to join us,' remarked the big man. 'Where ya bin?'

'Eh, sorry, Boss,' said Joey, looking confused. 'Half my mind was elsewhere.'

'And I suppose the other half went looking for it. Did you hear what we were discussing?'

Joey looked startled, like a rabbit transfixed by car headlamps. He noticed the dinner plates had disappeared and grabbed a dessert menu. 'Yeah,' he said, worriedly. 'Was it something to do with dessert, Boss? I'll have the Key Lime Pie.'

The leader glared at him. 'You'll be buried in lime if you're not fuckin' careful,' he said. He turned his attention to the others. 'Well, we all figured those bastards had something to do with Sam's disappearance, didn't we?' And now I think we know. So...' He gestured to the car containing Marmarella's son. 'Now, it's *us* holding the winning hand. How do you think Sam would have played it?'

Salvatore Vitalli had two brothers, Lorenzo and Samuel Vitalli. Lorenzo, his older brother, and Joey's father had been dead some ten years—a car accident. Sam, affectionately known as "Spaghetti" Sam, was Salvatore Vitalli's younger brother. Before his disappearance, he handled the family's finances and was particularly inventive when it came to laundering money. He acquired his nickname not as a result of his passion for spaghetti, but as a result of his dislike of pasta dishes generally. Sam had now been missing for almost six months and was presumed dead, although his body had never been recovered. Suspicion pointed to Louie Marmarella. Whilst Salvatore Vitalli would have nothing to do with narcotics, other crime families were heavily involved in drug trafficking. Anything DEA related attracted heavy prison sentences, and Vitalli knew, to avoid decades in prison, those arrested for drug related crime would often turn snitch to get a lighter sentence. And he did not want any of that threatening *his* empire.

His brother Samuel had been publicly critical about New York mafia involvement in drug trafficking. And in order to alleviate the stigma from his own family, he had given an anonymous interview to a journalist which was published in the New York Post damning the Marmarella syndicate's involvement with cocaine smuggling, sighting Louie Marmarella's brother in Southwest Florida as the main kingpin. Had word got out regarding the source of the article? Was that the reason for Sam's disappearance?

Maybe.

If it was, and if it could be proved that Louie Marmarella was responsible for Sam's disappearance, then a line had certainly been crossed. But this was not the only issue with Marmarella's organisation. They had violated other unwritten rules. Louie Marmarella had been accused many times of exceeding his area of responsibility, sending his soldiers to threaten businesses where the Vitalli family had long had a vested interest. The whole thing was becoming increasingly ugly, but so typical of how warring crime families have operated through the decades. Greed breeds power, which often leads to expansion—which inevitably leads to conflict.

'OK, we'll discuss our options later,' said the leader. 'Fingers, go sit in the car until we leave. We don't want Marmarella's son sounding off, do we?'

'Yeah, OK. You got it, Boss.' Fingers got up and headed back to the car park.

Salvatore Vitalli continued. 'Frankie, later I want you and the boys to take the car and get Dino to the "Warehouse." Make sure you cover your faces. Put him to the medical bay in the bunker. Are you sure he didn't see who shot him?'

'Positive,' said Johnny. 'He was walking up the drive. Joey was behind him.'

Joey fidgeted in his seat. 'I shot him in the back twice. I'm sure I did.'

'No, you didn't,' said Frankie. 'One bullet hit the top of his shoulder blade. That's all I could see.'

Joey was upset and clearly confused. 'But I shot him twice.'

'Yeah, the second bullet's probably somewhere in Pittsburg,' growled the leader. 'Anyway, it doesn't really matter now, does it? What matters is how we handle this. So, get him to the Warehouse. When he eventually comes around—if he comes round—I don't want him knowing it was us responsible for the gunshot. I'll make a call and have our doctor look in, and check his condition.'

'What about you, Boss?' queried Frankie.

'Don't worry about me. Just do as I say. And make sure nobody else knows we have him... OK?'

'Sure. But what about you? You stayin' here?'

'Yeah, just for a while,' said the leader, who was smart enough to realise that if the car was pulled over by the police and a body was discovered in the trunk, then he, too, would be implicated.

'OK,' said Frankie. 'But I need to clean up first.' He straightened up, brushed himself down and sauntered over to the restroom, which was close to where Marmarella was sitting.

'Hey, Frankie!' called Marmarella. 'Whilst you're in there, you better get some rubbers. After shaggin' the neighbourhood, I suggest you use one next time you fuck your wife. Who knows what she's caught? Those STDs can be a real bitch to cure. Especially the ones that itch!' Marmarella laughed heartily.

Frankie's head turned in a flash.

'That does it!' The words formed silently on Frankie's taut lips as the red mist descended. Suddenly, in a handful of strides, he bounded over to Marmarella's table and lunged at the man.

The two men met.

Marmarella's chair and table gave way beneath the weight of the two locked bodies, as they crashed to the floor amidst a crescendo of splintered wood and glass. Frankie's raised fist came down hard on Marmarella's exposed jaw with a sickening thud, just as the two Capelli brothers reached into the melee and grappled with the flailing arms and legs. In the same instant, Johnny and Sash were up out of their chairs and halfway towards joining the fracas when a loud blast from a handgun halted them in their tracks.

Everything stopped, and all eyes turned to the bay window.

Salvatore Vitalli was standing at his table, his hand raised theatrically—a gun pointing towards the ceiling. His shoulders were covered in a thin layer of powdered plaster dust, which continued to fall like sifted icing sugar on a Yuletide log. 'OK,' he yelled, as silence fell across the room. 'That's enough!'

Frankie seized an opportunity to land one last blow and took it—his fist thudding into the raised mouth of Rocco Capelli, whose rotten front tooth, one of two, shattered as blood spurted from the obscene gash that sufficed as a mouth for the ugly twin.

'Boys, we're leaving!' announced the leader. 'Frankie, get up. Sash, pay the waiter.'

As Frankie rose from the floor, something fell from his jacket pocket and slid beneath an upturned table; it went unnoticed.

Salvatore Vitalli had reconsidered, and owing to the fracas, decided to leave with his crew.

'HEY, Frankie,' said Louie Marmarella as he got up off the floor. 'You got a good left hook there for a trumped-up tart. I'm impressed. I'll be seeing you around.'

'Fuck you, asshole!' said Frankie as they quickly backed out of the room and then made their way to the black Chrysler.

Louie Marmarella watched from the restaurant doorway as the Vitalli family crammed themselves into the car, which dropped several inches as the suspension struggled to cope with the sheer weight of six men, plus the half-dead body in the trunk. Other diners, some of which had only just ordered food, quickly gathered their belongings and also vacated the restaurant.

Two minutes later, the place was empty apart from the staff, Marmarella, and his two minders, one of whom had rushed to the restroom to fix his bloodied face. 'Well, that was a fun day out,' said Marmarella to Ricco. 'Shame my boy hasn't turned up yet. He'd have enjoyed this. He likes a bit of banter.' Marmarella glanced down and noticed something lying on the floor. It was a phone—a cell phone—but not just any cell phone. 'Hello,' he said. 'What do we have here?' He picked it up, looked at it quizzically, and turned it over. On the back were two initials—D. M.

'Hey,' said Ricco Capelli. 'Ain't that Dino's phone?'

A frown of intrigue formed across Louie Marmarella's face, which began to redden as his blood pressure rose, the blood vessels on each temple pulsing noticeably. He took out his glasses and inspected the cell phone carefully. 'Yes, it is,' he said as the bitter taste of treachery and dread filled his senses.

The two men turned to the window and watched as the black Chrysler containing the Vitalli crew limped from the car park like an overladen dump truck, its exhaust scraping on the sidewalk as it turned and disappeared into traffic.

'What the fuck's going on here?' snarled Marmarella. 'And where the hell is my boy?'

Ricco Capelli sat at a table and checked the call data on Dino's cell phone. The restaurant was now deserted except for the staff, who were clearing up the mess. Ricco explained his findings to his boss. 'When you called Dino earlier, Mr. Marmarella,' he said. 'The call was definitely answered on your son's cell phone.'

Louie Marmarella, who wasn't exactly au fait with the nuances of modern technology, asked, 'How the hell do know you that?'

Ricco pointed to the call log on Dino's phone. 'Look, it shows here. You certainly didn't ring the wrong number. Even though the guy who answered it said you had. The time stamp on Dino's phone and your phone match exactly.'

'So, what does that mean?'

'Well, with Dino's phone being found here, it can only mean one of Vitalli's crew had it and answered it when you called. Don't know why they would do that, but it's the only explanation.'

Marmarella raged. 'MOTHAFUCKERS! So, how come they had it? And where the fuck is Dino? If ever they've hurt my boy… God help me, I'll fuckin' tear 'em apart!'

It was then when Rocco Capelli burst through the doors of the restroom, clutching a blood-stained hand towel to his face. 'HEY!' he yelled. 'Look what they did to me!'

He removed the bloodied towel, leaned forward to his two associates, and opened his mouth. Both his brother and Marmarella grimaced and took a step back. One of his two eye teeth was missing, and the other one was broken; a black jagged piece of discoloured tooth, all that was left at the front of his mouth.

Louie Marmarella looked up at him and inspected the damage. 'Ah… it's a fuckin' improvement if you ask me,' he said, dismissively. 'Now, let's get outta here. I need to find my boy.'

Chapter 4: The Doctor and the Donor

Salvatore Vitalli's impressive house sat deep within sprawling, lush grounds, positioned far from its protective boundary of high walls and tall trees. During the property's extensive renovations years earlier, the garden's bushes and foliage had been strategically planted to ensure no windows or doors could be viewed from outside the grounds of the estate. A point Vitalli had specifically emphasised when discussing security matters with his contractors.

'Hey, listen up. You installation bozos are bustin' my balls, you know that? I don't mind you squeezing me on price—I know that's your racket. But them cameras better be placed perfect, understand? I need security here to be as tight as a nun's crutch. We clear on that, or do I gotta spell it out for ya?

And so it was. Very little real estate escaped the gaze of the security cameras around the perimeter of the property. But security precautions did not end there; there was also a manned gatehouse, and meandering around the various neat paths that circumnavigated the house were a couple of bored-looking personal protection men. They each wore dark suits, beneath which were hidden automatic weapons, no doubt capable of inflicting mass destruction. While nearby, a couple of gardeners sporting their own weapons of moss destruction tended to the lawns and lavish borders, which were neat and bursting with colours of red, yellow and blue from the roses and azalea bushes.

A spacious terrace at the back of the house led to a flawlessly manicured lawn, rivalling even the fairways of the Augusta National golf course. About a hundred yards beyond, but still within the property boundaries, stood a substantial outbuilding. Within the family, it was known as "The Warehouse". To outsiders overhearing this term in conversation, it would seem unremarkable. But for the family, the name "Warehouse" held a special meaning, and had nothing to do with a typical storage facility in some business park. It was the name given to something altogether different. For "The Warehouse" was a large garage, or part of one.

From outside, it appeared to be just a single-story brick building with three double-sized overhead wooden doors. It contained a workshop, a small canteen—used by mechanics and staff—and space for six cars. It was kept as pristine as a new car showroom, but what made Salvatore Vitalli's garage exceptional, and the reason for the name, wasn't the building itself or its contents, but what lay twenty feet below—a network of corridors and rooms. A secret cellar. A disaster bunker which immediate family members could use as an underground "safe house" if ever there was a serious threat up above.

On a smaller scale, safe rooms or panic rooms in private homes provide shelter during break-ins, home invasions, or severe weather. These spaces contain emergency supplies and communication systems to contact authorities. Basic versions are box-shaped with reinforced walls and a sturdy deadbolt door, while expensive options feature steel plates, Kevlar, or even bullet-proof fibreglass.

Salvatore Vitalli conceived his disaster bunker idea over a decade earlier while visiting Jersey in the Channel Islands just off the Northwest coast of France. There, he toured the German Underground Hospital—a subterranean structure carved into a hillside during World War II. Originally built to store armaments and withstand allied attacks, it later became a museum, and it was this facility that inspired Vitalli's secret underground "safe house" and would lead to its construction ten years ago. While the excavation might have drawn attention, it blended seamlessly into the busy construction work on the main house. After completing the underground shell in just months, Vitalli built the garage above it, and both the house and the entire hidden complex were finished within a year.

The underground structure was self-contained, with three bedrooms containing bunk beds, a large living area with a kitchen, and several storage rooms housing refrigeration and appliances. Specialised food, capable of being stored for two decades, filled the storage pantries with enough evergreen and freeze-dried meat, fruits, and vegetable products to sustain several people for many weeks of co confinement. The bunker contained water reserves, first aid supplies, hygiene kits, and a small armoury of weapons and ammunition. Power came from generators and solar panels, feeding underground to storage batteries, with emergency lighting and propane cylinders for cooking and heating. The facility also featured a well-equipped medical theatre and external communication systems that could monitor conditions above ground during a crisis.

Upon its completion ten years ago, family members were gathered and informed by the construction engineers that such was the integrity of the bunker's solid foundation, even if a nuclear incident ever occurred, the structure would survive, as well as the occupants within.

It was Johnny Vitalli who questioned that assurance, reportedly saying to the builders, 'Hey, listen, you! We've paid a fortune for this sewage tank. If a nuke drops and this thing fails, we expect some kind of compensation from you guys, understand?'

To which Fingers replied, 'Hey, fuckwit. How the hell are you gonna get compensated after you've been vaporised? Fuckin' idiot!'

Access to bunker's living quarters was via a long underground passage, barely wide enough to accommodate the movement of appliances and supplies. It was situated in the basement, the door of which was in the hall just off the main kitchen.

The entrance was next to a large safe in the cellar, which also contained a hefty workbench and household tools. The bunker's heavy access door was rectangular, ten inches thick, and was made of military grade composites, similar in heft to that of a Fort Knox vault door. Once the deadbolt door was closed, without the access code, it was impossible to get in; a point delicately raised by Johnny during the briefing.

'What if we forget the code? You'd need a fuckin' nuke to get in there.'

'I got your access code, dumbass,' commented Fingers. 'We've all got our own. I've got yours. It's simple to remember, and it needs to be for you. I'll spell it for ya—I M A T W A, double T.'

'Eh, what's that? Are you trying to be funny? Have you developed a sense of humour overnight, Fingers? So, my password reads what—I'm a twat? Hilarious. Is that the best you can manage? You can't even spell "twat" right. It's got one T at the end, not two!'

Within the largest of the bunker bedrooms, a vertical shaft led up to a concealed exit hidden beneath the vehicle inspection pit in the garage directly above. The mechanics and utility staff were unaware of its existence, and it could only be opened from within the bunker by triggering an electronic charge designed to blow out the inspection pit. This would then allow occupants to climb the twenty-foot ladder to get out. But this was last-resort usage only. Access was strictly limited to the underground passage from the basement in the main house, the length of which was over a hundred metres.

During the ten years since its construction, the bunker had never been used, and as employees and associates had come and gone, the secret dwelling had almost been forgotten. After equipping it with survival supplies, the close family members agreed the bunker remain a secret, never to be discussed outside the family circle. And so it came to be. A folly of sorts, but one that was well maintained should it ever be needed. And today, it would be needed.

The large metal gates at the entrance to the grand house swung open as the black Chrysler filled with the six Vitalli family members returned from the Italian restaurant, with Dino Marmarella still lying in the trunk. The heavily laden vehicle swept through and along the winding gravel drive and pulled up at the entrance to the house where the family doctor was waiting on the steps.

The big man, Salvatore Vitalli, stepped out, and the car's suspension breathed a sigh of relief. He walked lethargically up the steps and greeted the doctor with a handshake, whilst the car and the remaining family occupants continued to the rear of the house, where Dino Marmarella's unconscious body was lifted from the trunk into the kitchen. He was quickly carried along the underground warehouse passageway and placed in the bunker's emergency medical room, where the Vitalli family doctor examined him and rigged him to a drip and life support equipment.

Over the course of the next hour, the doctor performed a delicate surgical procedure and successfully removed the bullets fired by Joey. But then he appeared to hit upon a major problem and asked to speak privately with the head of the family.

Salvatore Vitalli was in the middle of a telephone call when the doctor arrived at his door but beckoned the doctor into his ground floor study and invited him to sit. 'I'll just be a minute,' he said.

It was a warm day outside, and the air was filled with the delightful fragrance of freshly mown lawns, the scent of which mingled with the sweet aroma of lavender and honeysuckle, which drifted in through the open French doors of the study.

Whilst waiting, the doctor looked around.

The study's focal point was a vast stone fireplace, its mantle carved from a single slab of Italian marble. A large mahogany bookcase spanned the full length of one wall, antique leather-bound books in Italian and English filling its shelves, a faint whiff of cigar smoke forever trapped within their pages. Another wall was covered floor-to-ceiling in framed family portraits—a procession of dour-faced patriarchs staring sternly across the generations, the most prominent being Salvatore Vitalli himself, immortalised in oil paint as a younger, fitter man wearing an impeccably tailored suit.

Overall, the room exuded an aura of studious intimidation. A testament to power, wealth, and an uncompromising vision of legacy.

The family leader finished his call.

'So, what are you telling me, Doc?' he asked, as he sat hunched behind his large mahogany desk, the surface of which was clear save for a vintage green glass banker's lamp.

Doctor Lucas Roberts was sitting opposite in one of two high-backed red leather chairs, their cushions well-worn from years of conspiratorial conversations and backroom deals.

The doctor suddenly realised that the chair on which he was sitting was about six inches lower than that of Salvatore Vitalli's, so he was always subordinately looking up at the man, and he wondered if that was coincidental or by design?

The doctor was a tall, grey man with a lean profile. He was in his mid-forties, had lengthy, grey monochrome hair and his creased grey suit hung loosely from him as if he hadn't had a decent meal in weeks. He had been the crime family's physician for many years and was a trusted confidant, a professional, well-spoken, unimpassioned man. But when about to deliver unwelcome news to the head of the Vitalli family, he found much of his self-assurance seemed to ebb away, receding to a private place somewhere perhaps where fear, dread and nightmares linger.

'Well, it isn't exactly good news,' said the doctor awkwardly.

'OK. So, what exactly is it then?' queried Vitalli, his eyelids heavy with the strain of overbearing responsibility.

Slumped in the chair, the big man cradled a whisky glass and looked relaxed to the point where he might almost have been asleep. The doctor shifted uncomfortably and carefully repositioned a lengthy grey fringe of hair that covered half his forehead.

'Eh... his condition is unstable, bordering on critical,' he replied, in a matter-of-fact manner, his sense of professionalism partly restored as he took solace in the secure comfort of his medical knowledge and expertise.

Salvatore Vitalli's eyes closed, and for a moment the doctor thought he was asleep, and he hesitated.

'Go on. I'm listening,' said Vitalli, opening one eye.

'Eh... of course,' said the doctor. 'Well, the first bullet hit high on the back of his upper arm and was deflected inwards from the humerus bone, across his scapula... the inner section of his shoulder blade, if you will. Then, it struck and shattered his clavicle and finally lodged in his chest cavity behind the first rib. It was a heavy calibre weapon, hence the bullet's momentum and subsequent damage.'

'I see,' said the big man. 'You said first bullet?'

'Yes, the second bullet was embedded in his gluteus maximus, his right buttock.'

'You mean his arse.'

'Yes.'

'So, what you're sayin' is... he's now got two arseholes.'

The doctor, whose studious, analytical brain, devoid of any genuine sense of humour, looked puzzled. 'Eh... yes, I suppose you could say that, yes.'

'Personally, I'm fuckin' surrounded by 'em,' complained the big man. He inhaled a deep lungful of grass scented air provided by the light breeze coming in through the open doors. 'Well, considering the bullet was fired by Joey, who just happens to be a complete fuckin' arsehole, I suppose I'm not that surprised.'

Salvatore Vitalli's attention was momentarily distracted by something he had spotted on one of the dozen or so security monitors that were such a prominent feature in the bookcase opposite his desk. He leaned across and pressed a button on a stemmed microphone. 'Hey, you!' he rasped. Several heads outside swivelled as his voice boomed around the grounds of the property. 'Those roses. Don't prune 'em now. You only prune 'em when the bush is dormant. We're a full month away from that. So, holster those fuckin' shears.'

The gardener raised a hand, and Vitalli's attention again returned to the doctor. 'See what I mean? New gardener. Been with us for a week. Before I employed him, I asked him what qualifications he had. He said he was outstanding in his field. Now he's out, standing in mine. Ha! Anyway...'

The doctor looked confused and slightly bemused.

'So, where are we with this Dino guy, Doc?'

'Well, I have to say, unfortunately, indications for Dino's recovery are not favourable, perhaps 50-50 at best. And that depends.'

'Depends on what?'

'He needs a blood transfusion urgently, or he'll die. And he needs it within the next 24 hours.'

Salvatore Vitalli frowned. 'OK, well, give him one then.'

'I can't do that,' said the doctor.

'Why not?'

'He has an exceedingly rare blood group.'

'Well, we have blood banks, don't we? That shouldn't be too much of a problem, should it?'

'Ordinarily, it wouldn't be, but it is. You see, there are eight main blood groups and many more with varying subtypes. Dino's blood is AB Positive but with a very rare Ro subtype. People of any ethnicity can have this combination. Although, it's a strange fact that people of black heritage are ten times more likely to have it than white people. Either way, donors are extremely difficult to find. In fact, only two percent of donors have this combination and the moment the local blood bank is dry. They have nothing at all of Dino's particular blood variant.'

Vitalli looked thoughtful. 'Hmm, can't we look elsewhere?'

'I've tried. Believe it not, the closest blood bank supply is in the UK, and I do have connections there. But, even if they agreed to release it, by the time it arrives here, Dino would be dead.'

'So, what do we do? Surely the blood bank has a list of local donors.'

'Yes, they do, and I've checked. But their records show only two donors with Dino's specific blood type combination. One of them died two years ago, and they don't know where the other one is.'

The big man shrugged. 'Well, can't they find him?'

'Well, to start with, "he's" actually a "she", but there's more.' The doctor pulled a face of resignation, and then lowered his voice and said, 'The second donor on their records, the woman with Dino's exact blood type match, is actually someone we know.'

The leader's face stiffened. 'Who?'

'Layzee Dawson's wife.'

'You gotta be fuckin' kidding me!' snarled the big man, who appeared to have just sucked the juice from half a dozen under ripe lemons.

'No, it's true. If you were to check her medical records, you would see for yourself that she does have AB Positive blood with the rare Ro subtype. It also shows on her prison record.'

'What, she's an ex-con?'

'Yes.'

'Well, fuck me sideways till Sunday. I never knew that.'

'I doubt her husband knows, either. She did time in Idaho. Pocatello Women's Correctional Facility to be exact.'

'Really? When was that?'

'Oh, a long time ago. Well before she met and married Layzee Dawson. She was sentenced to fifteen months for trafficking.'

'Drugs?'

'Actually no. But I'll come back to that.' The doctor uncrossed his legs, repositioned himself in his chair, and then continued. 'You see, Mr. Vitalli, Maria Dawson, is an ingenious individual. We saw that in the courtroom two years ago. She knows the rarity and value of her blood and has been selling it for years.'

'What? She's been selling her own blood?'

'Yes. Like I said, she's a smart woman.'

The big man hacked a laugh. 'Huh, I don't know why I should be surprised. She's always been a conniving bitch. But we're fucked! With her sitting pretty in the Witness Protection Program, we haven't got a cat in hell's chance of finding her.'

The doctor smiled a curious smile of intrigue. 'So, I understand,' he said. 'But I know where she is.'

The big man frowned. 'You do? If she's in the Witness Protection Program, how the fuck is that possible?'

The doctor leaned in. 'Well, actually... she found me. Like I said, she's been selling her blood for years... TO ME!'

'Selling it to you? Get the fuck outta here!'

'No, it's true. On the Black Market, her blood type commands top dollar. Over the years, there have been instances where I've had cause to use her blood type on certain individuals. You know, those associated with... shall we say, our method of commerce.'

'Wise guys?'

'Yes. Individuals that need urgent medical care but also need to remain...'

'Backstairs?'

'Covert… yes.'

'Huh, and I don't suppose Layzee ever saw a fuckin' red cent of that blood money?'

'I suppose not,' agreed the doctor. 'Or any of the money associated with her other bodily donations.'

'What d'ya mean, other bodily donations? There's been other stuff?'

'Yes. She also auctioned one of her kidneys and a liver lobe on the internet.'

The big man looked astounded. 'Jesus Christ,' he said, 'If she ever has a sale or offers a discount on Black Friday, give me a call. I need a new heart, but then again, not one as fuckin' cold as hers.'

The doctor smiled. 'Ah, now you've happened upon the reason she went to prison, Mr. Vitalli.'

'What do ya mean? Explain!'

'Well, let's go back eighteen years. Our young Maria would have been in her early twenties and was working as a receptionist at a local funeral home. A small family business run by two brothers, but one that was operating a racket involving the sale of human organs and cadavers.'

'What d'ya mean?' said the big man. 'Dead bodies?'

'Yes. Instead of cremating all the dearly departed deceased entrusted to them. The owners of the funeral home had a little side hustle going on.'

Vitalli frowned. 'A side hustle?'

'Yes, they were harvesting, limbs, spines, brains, organs anything really from the human remains. In fact, sometimes complete corpses, selling them to body-part brokers.'

'Body part brokers? What the fuck! You gotta be kiddin' me.'

'No, no. But there was a problem, you see.'

'A problem?'

'Yes. The problem was, they were doing this without the consent of the grieving families.'

The big man feigned a look of surprise. 'No shit! How inconsiderate of them.'

'Quite. Mind you, at the time, it was a very profitable scam for the two brothers. They would forge the donor documentation, and would think nothing of selling kidneys, hearts and the like, even from bodies with hepatitis and HIV. Falsifying the documents, they would pass them off as organs derived from healthy donors.'

'Nasty fuckers,' said the big man. 'Fancy being on the receiving end of that shit?'

'Yes, but they got clumsy.'

'Clumsy?'

'Yes, especially with bodies destined for cremation. You see, following the cremation of a loved one as you know it's common practice for the ashes of the deceased to be returned to the family in a cremation urn, but when there is no body to cremate as a result of its illegal sale, there are no ashes to return.'

The big man mulled over the problem. 'Yeah, I can see how that could be a real bitch?'

'Exactly. Of course, the funeral home had to make good, and families would receive their precious urns. But a replacement for the missing ashes had to be found. So, they used a derived powder concoction. A sediment substitute, if you will.'

'A sediment substitute... for the ashes.'

'Yes. They filled the urns with pulverised cement. It looks very convincing.'

'Yeah, it's a good medium. I've been in the funeral business myself. I've buried many people in cement over the years, and their families never complained. And those that did... got buried too.'

'Eh... yes. But my point is, Mr Vitalli, people would never question something as sacred as the contents of a cremation urn, would they?'

Vitalli raised his head thoughtfully. 'No, I guess not.'

'So, the funeral home scam could have gone on for many more years?'

'So, why didn't it?'

'A former disgruntled employee from the funeral home blew the lid off the whole sordid business when she reported the goings on to the police.'

'What a bitch! I'd have soon found a fuckin' urn for her.'

'Yes, of course. Being in the medical profession, I remember this case very well. And it didn't end there. The funeral home caused quite a stir. They even went as far as extracting and selling the gold teeth of the deceased.'

Salvatore Vitalli's mouth dropped open, and he grimaced as if looking down at the contents of an unflushed toilet bowl. 'Jesus Christ! he said, gravely. 'Have people no scruples? That's like something out of the fuckin' holocaust.'

'Yes. Anyway, the owners and Maria Dawson were arrested for, amongst other things, defrauding relatives of cremation services. They were all found guilty, of course. I think Maria Dawson was just a courier, or something like that. She got a lighter sentence and was released after serving only nine months. But the funeral director brothers were not so lucky. They were each sentenced to eight years.' The doctor paused and then said conspiratorially, 'But for Mrs. Dawson, this for her, was a learning curve and an introduction into a very niche market. She knew she had a very rare blood type. And once she discovered the value of it on the Black Market, she decided to cash in. And has been doing so ever since.'

'Unbe fuckin' lievable,' said Vitalli. 'And Layzee knows nothing about this?'

'No. If what she told me is the truth, apparently not.'

Vitalli shook his head. 'No, he doesn't know. He would have said something. He wears his heart on his sleeve. Or, perhaps after what you've told me, it's probably some other fucker's heart? See, you think you know people. But you never really do... do ya, Doc?'

'No,' replied the doctor. He leaned in towards the big man across the table. 'But, Mr. Vitalli, there is one little detail I have omitted to relate concerning this little story.'

'And what's that?'

'The two brothers who ran the funeral home were twin brothers... identical twin brothers.'

The big man's eyes widened. 'The Capelli brothers?'

'Yes.'

Salvatore Vitalli sank back into his wide leather chair, which creaked under his weight. 'Well, well,' he said resignedly. 'Why ain't I surprised? Ain't it a small world, huh?'

'It certainly is,' said the doctor, who also sat back in his chair, content that the man opposite seemed pleased with his findings.

The big man pondered for a moment and then looked puzzled. 'How long have you known about this?' he asked.

'I've known for quite a while.'

'And you never thought to tell me sooner?'

The doctor stiffened in his chair and writhed uncomfortably. 'Eh... well, at the time, I... err, until now, I didn't think... I didn't think it relevant.'

'Well, you should do less of it. Thinking I mean. Why don't you let your brain take some fuckin' time off, Doc? Let it go on vacation for a while.' Vitalli decided not to press the issue on this occasion and curbed his annoyance. He needed the doctor now more than ever. 'So,' he continued with a wry smile. 'Time's running out. And I've got another meeting. Let's get back on track. When did you last see Mrs. Dawson?'

'About three months ago.'

'Do you know where she lives?'

'No, but I have a contact number for a friend of hers. She relays my messages. Mrs Maria Dawson now goes by the name of Matilda Jacobs.'

'Hmm... does she now? So, tell me, how does this blood deal work with... Tilly?'

'It's straightforward enough, really,' said the doctor, who was feeling a little more confident and at ease. 'I call her, and we arrange to meet at my surgery here in town. You see, she provides me with a unit of blood, which is about one pint in "old money", every sixteen weeks. The human body contains approximately ten units of blood, so taking any more than one unit at a single sitting would be unwise. That is, unless an urgent situation arises. And that's when the big money kicks in. You see, Mr. Vitalli, the sale of human organs across the world is a very lucrative business and is worth millions.'

The big man leaned towards the doctor across his desk and smiled. 'Listen,

Doc,' he said pointedly, as if about to share the name of a horse from a rigged race. 'If you ever need a donor who's brain dead with a heartbeat, I've just the guy.' Salvatore Vitalli was still smarting from the botched assassination earlier. 'His name's Joey. His brain's worth fuck all, but his others bits might be useful.'

The doctor was not quite sure how to take the big man's offer. Was he joking? 'I'll bear that in mind,' he said quietly.

Vitalli looked satisfied and contemplative as he sat back in his chair. He cupped the glass of whisky in his broad hands. And then realised the doctor was without. He poured a second glass and slid it across his desk to the doctor, who he had forgotten was teetotal. 'Remember two years ago, Doc, when we both sat in that courtroom and watched her walk out?'

The doctor nodded. 'Yes.'

'Well, well… Mrs. fuckin' Dawson, huh?' Who'd have thought that? What a piece of fuckin' work she is… the bitch!'

'Eh, quite,' agreed the doctor as he puzzled over the glass of whisky in his hand. 'She certainly is an interesting character. And over the years, Mrs Dawson has profited handsomely from her various medical donations, and continues, so to do.'

The doctor looked thoughtful and then a rare, dubious expression of cunning manifested itself across his gaunt, serious face. 'Which begs the question,' he said quietly, almost as a whisper. 'I wonder how much Louie Marmarella would pay to keep his boy alive?'

Salvatore Vitalli smiled wickedly, and his eyes narrowed as he realised what was being implied. 'Doc,' he said. 'You're a conniving bastard, and I love ya. Now tell me, exactly how much of this rare blood do you need to keep Dino alive?'

The doctor nodded his head thoughtfully. 'Probably about ten units.'

'And how much blood can be drained from one woman's body?'

'Funny you should ask,' said the doctor, raising an eyebrow. 'I would say about ten units.'

'Hmm, I see. And if that were to happen,' said Vitalli, reflectively, 'I'm a fair man, Doc, and I wouldn't want you to be outta pocket. So… how much is a pint of that fuckin' antifreeze that flows through her vein's worth to you, Doc?'

The doctor stated the value, which was substantial.

'CHRIST!' said Vitalli. 'I don't know about lucrative. That's daylight fuckin' robbery.'

The doctor twisted uncomfortably in his chair. 'Like I said, Mr Vitalli,' he continued, trying to justify the amount. 'The black-market price for human bodily components is almost self-regulating and is naturally governed by supply and demand. As a highly educated man, you will know that, as with all commodities, the rarer the product, the higher its perceived value.' The doctor paused and looked a little confused. 'But do you not like the idea of blackmailing Dino's father to keep his son alive? I thought that was a valid suggestion.'

Vitalli's facial expression remained glum. 'No,' he said. 'Yeah, we could shake down that scumbag and it is a valid suggestion, but it's me who wants to keep his son alive.'

The doctor frowned.

Vitalli leaned in. 'You see, Doc. If Dino dies, and Louie Marmarella was to find out it was us that shot him, which he would, he would wage an all-out war. He's got his brother working the drug runs down in Florida with an army of fuckin' Columbians to call upon. They'd be on our ass faster than shit through a goose. We'd get wiped out. And that's why it's imperative Dino pulls through. So, I'll be funding this transaction. Understand?'

'Oh... I see,' said the doctor attentively, who looked pensive.

Salvatore Vitalli could see the doctor had an issue. 'What's the matter?'

The doctor inhaled a lungful of air. 'This will sound selfish, Mr Vitalli. But the problem for me would be that by draining Mrs. Dawson's entire body of blood, she would obviously die. Which means personally, purely from a financial standpoint, the source of future supply and therefore future revenue for me would also die with her.'

The big man regarded the astute doctor with hooded eyes. He had been in enough business negotiations to recognise when an individual was about to pitch him a deal. 'I see what you're getting at,' he said with a grin. 'You took your fuckin' time. You're a slippery fucker, ain't you, Doc?'

The doctor regarded the big man's smile with a double shot of angst. Was it a smile of suppressed annoyance or a smile of mutual respect for a like-minded businessman? He couldn't tell, but hoped it was the latter. He painfully gathered his thoughts and tried diplomatically to find the right words of justification. 'Like yourself, Mr. Vitalli, I pride myself that I too am a businessman, albeit on a far less lofty level than that of yours.'

'Hey, don't get defensive, Doc,' said the big man. 'You were doin' alright there for a minute. I get the deal. You normally drain one pint of blood every four months from this bitch, don't you?'

'Yes.'

'So, pumping the whole fuckin' lot out of her now would equate to just over three years' worth... right?'

The doctor nodded. 'And... four months.'

'... and four months. So, in just over three years... and four months, by virtue of the fact that she no longer exists, your income source would also no longer exist. I understand that. Whereas, if she were to remain alive, you would continue to benefit financially for as long as she's willing to donate. Which could be a decade or more.'

The doctor looked astonished at how quickly the big man had worked the numbers, and the timeline. 'Yes, that's absolutely correct,' he said.

'So... you're asking me to compensate you for what you'll lose beyond those three years, is that right?'

The doctor looked a little flummoxed, but was impressed by Vitalli's incisive methodology and direct approach. 'Eh... yes, sir. Well, I suppose I am. But it only seems fair that...'

'OK! Now we understand each other,' interrupted the big man. 'So, let's just cut the crap and get to the bottom line, shall we?' Salvatore Vitalli leaned in on his desk and eyed the doctor as if he was about to put a gun to his head and pull the trigger. 'So how much d'ya want, Doc?' he asked. 'And don't go all around the fuckin' houses. I know you got a number worked out already.'

The doctor knew he was now at the point of no return. Should he play safe and request a modest sum or be bold? But the doctor harboured a secret. Unbeknown to Salvatore Vitalli, he was a habitual gambler and owed money all over town. He regularly played poker at underground private games for high stakes where the Buy-In could be thousands of dollars. Over the years, he had performed well and had won tens of thousands. Although, what he won on Poker he tended to lose on his preferred game of choice, Blackjack. That is until he learned the art of card counting—a method used by many players around the world yet reviled by casino Pit Bosses and Floor Managers. Some tolerate its use, as most card counters are bad at it. But that was not the case with the doctor. His analytical mind and propensity for quick thinking and mental dexterity had, over recent years, held him in good stead, and he had become quite accomplished at winning using his card counting technique.

The basic premise in Blackjack is that high cards benefit the player, whilst low cards benefit the dealer. If a player can calculate the likelihood of the next drawn card, one can gain an advantage and swing the odds of winning very much in their favour. There are various card counting techniques, but the doctor preferred the running count method. Whereby he would assign a positive, negative, or zero number for each card dealt, depending on its value. His running count would then determine whether the dealer or he would have the advantage on the next hand, and he would bet accordingly—more if the count was in his favour, less if the count, and therefore the advantage, was with the dealer. Good card counters will either go unnoticed, or if discovered, will be asked to leave the property, or even be banned—or worse. Violence against card counters or anyone thought to be cheating was not uncommon in the gambling world.

Yet, the doctor had managed to stay south of the Pit Bosses radar, and the all-seeing eyes in the sky—those all-black spherical globes that look down from the ceiling in every casino, searching for those trying to cheat.

He had been lucky. He had never been caught or even raised suspicion. But he was a careful man. When the count swung in his favour, he would refrain from repeatedly winning too much. "Too much" attracted attention. He found "just enough" was the best strategy. Every so often, he would purposely lose, so as not to draw suspicion. Then he would thank the dealer, leave a tip, and move on. But recently the doctor had hit a bad losing streak, a streak that had lasted now for many weeks. As a result, his concentration had suffered, to the point where his counting had become less accurate. His losses had mounted and now he was heavily in debt. In debt to a man, you should never owe money to. But the situation that had presented itself today with Salvatore Vitalli might, for him, be fortuitous and could change everything.

The doctor felt his current bargaining situation with the head of the Vitalli family was not that dissimilar to that of a card player at a Blackjack table. Someone who had perhaps just drawn sixteen whilst the dealer was sitting on a picture card—the worst possible starting hand any Blackjack player could have.

But now, the decision was his to make. Should he play safe and request a sensible amount from the head of the crime family? Or should he go all in? It was a decision filled with jeopardy, especially when sitting opposite a man as intimidating as Salvatore Vitalli.

So, what should he do? Stick or twist—stand or draw?

He looked into the cold, piercing eyes of the dealer, who once again was leaning forward across his desk, waiting for his response.

'Well?' enquired the big man. 'Name your price.'

Without another thought, the doctor swallowed hard and went for broke. 'My price, Mr Vitalli, is one million dollars?'

The doctor's tone was less of a request, more a polite plea, and he hoped he hadn't busted his hand.

The big man eased his considerable bulk back into his chair and took a sip of whisky from his glass. He thought for a moment, whilst quietly enjoying the hooked wriggling fish sitting opposite that was tethered to his line. 'Huh... that's a big number,' he said, his gaze rising to the ceiling in thoughtful contemplation. 'But I guess I can live with it.' His eyes panned around and fixed on the man opposite. 'You've got a deal, Doc,' he said.

The doctor leaned forward. 'Thank you. But, there is just one problem, Mr. Vitalli.'

The big man looked at him severely. 'Don't you give me shit now, Doc. What is it?'

'I need to forward Mrs Dawson part payment first. She always insists on that. I usually send her a bank transfer, but currently, and this is a little embarrassing, my finances are tied up elsewhere. I wasn't expecting to have to do this today.'

'I see,' said Vitalli. 'How much are we talking?'

'She normally asks for fifty percent of her full fee upfront—in this case one hundred and twenty-five thousand dollars.'

'Does she?' The big man nodded, contemplating, whilst the doctor waited.

It was crunch time, thought the Doctor. Right here and right now, everything hung on the big man's next few words.

After careful consideration, the mob boss pointed across the desk at him. 'Right. I ain't paying her that,' he said. The doctor's heart, which was beating twice its normal rate, sank. Then the leader continued. 'But here's what I'm gonna do. Two hundred and fifty thousand dollars will be in your account within the next two hours. That's twenty-five percent of your fee. You can use whatever of that you need for any upfront payment to this bitch. Personally, I ain't sending her a fuckin' red cent. I intend to remain in the background with this. So, any upfront payment that's required, you pay that out of what I send you. And that will be between you and her, not me. You'll handle that transaction. Do you understand what I'm saying?'

'Eh... yes, sir. I understand,' said the doctor.

'And do you understand why I need for it to be that way?'

Yes, you crafty bastard, thought the doctor. Anonymity was crucial for Vitalli, as it would allow him to maintain a position of deniability. He wanted to ensure there was nothing that could implicate him in any way should things go south. 'Eh, yes, I do understand,' said the doctor. 'And had you not mentioned it, I was going to suggest we do it that way. For a man in your position, it's a wise move.'

'Good. The rest of your fee you'll get at the conclusion of our agreement. The deal being... you get the blood you need from Mrs. Dawson, and Dino Marmarella remains alive and recovers from his injuries. Is that acceptable?'

There was an audible hiss of relief from the opposite side of the desk as the doctor relaxed his taut, stifled frame, his suit now looking noticeably a size too large.

'Yes, thank you,' he said. His heart was momentarily filled with exaltation at the realisation that Salvatore Vitalli had agreed to pay him a quarter of his fee in advance. But now he was locked into the arrangement and, as such, was indebted to the man. How clever of Vitalli to do that, he realised. And how stupid of himself if ever he had second thoughts and wished to renege on the deal.

Salvatore Vitalli extended his hand.

The doctor quickly wiped his sweaty palm on his creased trouser leg and shook the big man's hand, and the 'blood deal' was sealed. But when the doctor tried to retract his hand, Salvatore Vitalli held onto it.

'Now that we have a deal,' said the big man menacingly, as he tightened his grip on the doctor's bony appendage. 'Don't let me down. That would not bode well for you. Set up a meeting with this bitch within the next twenty-four hours, get the blood you need, and let me know when she's dead.'

The doctor stared into the eyes of the man opposite, who had just signed another death certificate, as he had so many other times in this room. His hand was released, and he nodded and smiled a nervous smile. He couldn't believe it. He couldn't believe the big man had swallowed everything he had told him; for the Doctor had LIED.

Everything he had said during the past half hour had been fabricated—all of it. Mrs. Vitalli's blood was not of a rare type, neither was Dino Marmarella's. It was all a carefully conceived ruse the Doctor had manufactured. Even the part involving the Capelli brothers, and the trafficking of human organs was pure fiction. Using nothing but cunning and his intellect, the doctor had used Salvatore Vitalli's hatred for Mrs. Dawson against him and was about to extort money from the very man who was an expert at extorting money. It is sometimes said that the easiest man to sell to is a salesman. And now all he needed to do to secure the remaining seven hundred and fifty thousand dollars of the one-million-dollar blood money deal was show up tomorrow with ten 450 ml blood bags containing what Vitalli would perceive to be Mrs. Dawson's rare blood type and finalise the deal.

In time, Dino Marmarella was always going to recover, irrespective of a blood transfusion. He didn't need one. The doctor knew that. His plan was to keep him sedated. Then, in a few days, he would declare that Dino was out of trouble and on his way to a full recovery. Salvatore Vitalli would then honour their deal and he, Doctor Lucas Roberts. would be richer to the tune of one million dollars.

Huh, my God... for him, this was life changing, decided the doctor. No, correct that—it was lifesaving! It meant he could now get away, go abroad somewhere. Buy some time and set up a new life under a new name. But wait, he was getting away from himself. He hadn't got the money yet.

Exaltation quickly drained away as if someone had turned off his life support as he realised what he had done and the consequences if he failed to pull off the deception. But there was no backing out now. He was committed—committed the second he veered from the truth. He forced a smile as a nagging thought broke free and raced to the forefront of his subconscious. It was a frightening thought of catastrophic doubt. A thought that prompted a question that up until that handshake had never entered his mind. Now that he had duped the man—could he really get away with it? He suddenly felt small, as if sitting in a child's chair, and felt as though he was being throttled. He ran an anxious finger around the collar of his shirt. He needed to get out—get out of the damned room and get some fresh air.

In stark contrast, Salvatore Vitalli bore no sense of anxiety. His cool persona remained. He was happy with the blood money deal. If Dino lived, one million dollars was a small price to pay to prevent a war between the two rival families. And in addition to that, as a sweet bonus, both he and Layzee Dawson would get their revenge on the woman they loathed, the woman that they perceived as having betrayed them both.

The crime family leader raised his glass to offer a toast. Through a sharp fog of uncertainty, the doctor remotely fumbled for his.

'Cin Cin, Doc,' said Vitalli, smiling broadly as the two glasses clinked together. 'Here's to Mrs. Maria fuckin' Dawson. But Doc, there's just one thing I need to add.'

The doctor looked anxiously across the desk.

'I wanna see her dead body when this shit-show is done.'

Chapter 5: Beauty and the Beasts

Where to, mister?' asked the cab driver earlier that same day, as Layzee Dawson jumped into the back of a dusty yellow taxicab for the first time in two years.

'Do you know a good steakhouse in Manhattan?' he asked.

The cab driver, whose craggy face bore the wizened lines of an old rocker from the sixties and who wouldn't have looked out of place as a band member with the Rolling Stones, eyed Dawson through his rear-view mirror. 'Sure, I know one or two. What you after, something fancy or cheap?'

'Do I really look as though I give a fuck?' replied Layzee. 'After the shit I've been eatin', I just need a decent steak. So, let's go. And don't hold back the fuckin' horses.'

The rear tyres of the cab took purchase, bit into the black bitumen, and screeched away from the penitentiary that had been Layzee Dawson's home for the past two years. As the yellow taxicab raced along leafy tree-lined Davis Street towards the Southern Tier Expressway heading for Manhattan, Layzee looked back up the hill at the prison's uncompromising brick walls and watched for a moment as its distinctive pale green roof disappeared into the distance. 'Fuckin' shithole!' he muttered beneath his breath.

'Why did you insist on a yellow cab anyway, mister?' asked the cab driver. 'It would have been a whole lot cheaper if you'd hired a cab locally.'

'Yellow's my favourite colour,' grumbled Layzee. 'And the local cabs look too much like fuckin' cop cars.'

Again, the driver glanced curiously into his rear-view mirror. 'What were you in for anyway?' he asked.

Layzee's aggravated eyes looked back at the driver through the same mirror. 'Well, if you really must know, First Degree Murder. I shot a nosey cab driver in the back of the head cuz he wouldn't stop yackin'. Layzee leaned forward. 'In other words, it's none of your fuckin' business what I was in for. And I ain't in the mood for discussing football scores, your favourite baseball team, or how often you have to wipe jizz stains off your rear seats, either. So, just drive the fuckin' cab!'

Layzee Dawson's release from New York's Elmira Correctional Facility occurred two weeks earlier than expected, and on the same day, the Vitalli family attempted to assassinate "Cadillac" Tony DeVille. But Layzee kept his early release low-key and knew nothing of the failed attempt on DeVille's life or even that there had been such an attempt. He decided not to inform Salvatore Vitalli of his early release as he had a few errands to run, and he knew that once back in the family fold, it would be difficult for him to free up some time. Besides, he also felt he had bought himself two weeks grace, as Tony DeVille would still believe him to be in prison and would therefore not yet try to find him.

It was a four-hour drive from Elmira to Manhattan, the whole four hours spent in silence, which suited Layzee. He had had two years to work out how and what he was going to do after his release. But now he was out, all of that seemed to pale to insignificance, almost as if the planning process had been just a psychological mechanism for getting him through his jail time. Whilst in prison, in between heavy gym sessions banging weights, much of his time was spent reading criminal justice books relating to procedures and legislation, paying particular attention to the sections covering NYPD policy and law enforcement procedures for arrest, search and seizure. Perhaps, owing to his tough-guy image, Layzee seemed to be a magnet for NYPD cops, particularly regarding their highly controversial random stop, question and frisk practice, despite the ruling that such encroachment on an individual's privacy should only be undertaken by officers if there existed sufficient belief that an individual was engaged in criminal activity. But then Layzee always looked as though he was involved in criminal activity. For now, though, he was content just to sit, let the world go by, and distance himself from the fortress prison he had come to loath. Even the overwhelming sense of revenge that coursed through his veins on the day he was sentenced had tempered with each day of his incarceration. That is until his wife's unexpected visit rekindled the dying embers of hatred he felt for her. Now, with a contract out on his life, he knew he needed to be vigilant. *He* needed to be the one to strike first—but all in good time. First, food was on his mind.

It was late afternoon when he arrived in Manhattan, his yellow cab swallowed up by the yellow river of dozens of identical cabs shuffling along the grid-locked streets. After two years of prison food, Layzee was desperate for a proper meal in proper surroundings, amongst proper people. Manhattan was a place he rarely visited, but he knew that once lost amongst the manic bustle of busy side-walks buzzing with city slickers and tourists, there was less of a chance of him being spotted. And that's why he insisted on a yellow cab; he felt he needed to blend in and become that grey man. He was taking no chances and had also avoided his usual local haunts as word of his early release might filter back to DeVille and compromise his advantage.

After stopping off at an Outback steakhouse on West 23rd Street where he had wolfed down two thick-cut rare sirloins and a few Budweiser's, it was early evening when he hailed another cab which took him via the Robert F. Kennedy Bridge over the East River into Queen's. He was returning to Fresh Meadows and the house he once shared with his estranged wife. Under cover of darkness, he was dropped off a few streets away and made the rest of his journey on foot.

# # #

Meanwhile, on the other side of town, the night had finished chasing away the last remnants of sunset, leaving a warm evening, although the sky was as black as coal, with hardly a dusting of starlight to illuminate the streets.

Debbie Vitalli—Frankie's wife—drew the drapes in her living room window and poured herself a tequila. Her husband had called earlier to inform her he wouldn't be home for a few days; some urgent family business had cropped up that needed his attention, he had said.

Well, whatever, she thought. She wasn't about to let the evening go to waste, that's for sure. She glanced at herself in the wall mirror and smiled at her reflection, satisfied that she had fixed her blonde hair and makeup just right. She liked what she saw and gave a nod of approval. Her daily speed walking and cardio exercise routine had certainly helped her maintain her voluptuous shape; for although in her mid-thirties, she looked ten years younger and as fit as she was when she was an exotic dancer at the Paladin Club in Las Vegas.

She was wearing a black silk dressing gown beneath which was very little, just a lace-up, transparent chemise negligée, which left nothing to the imagination. Although impractical, stockings and patent black stilettos completed her look. She smiled. Her new boyfriend liked her looking that way. Everything was ready, and everything was just right.

A log fire crackled and cast its red glow into the room, and the lights were dimmed. She made herself comfortable on the couch and nestled herself between a couple of oversized cushions. Earlier, and after she had finished speaking with her husband, she had called her new man to let him know she would be alone and available that evening, and had purposely left the French doors to the rear garden unlocked.

The carefully conceived setting was all part of a fantasy role-playing game that she liked to enact. She would sit demurely on the couch sipping a drink whilst flicking through a magazine, and then her new lover would quietly enter the house as if he had just broken in, creeping through the rooms dressed as a burglar wearing a black hoody and ski mask to hide his face.

She found the scenario incredibly erotic, and her black lover was only too willing to go along with the pretence.

Upon seeing him, Mrs. Vitalli would shriek and there would be some fanciful interplay between them, during which she would be harassed and violated. She would scream, feign fear and outrage. Then his black hands would be all over her body, confusing her senses deliciously. He would gag and restrain her whilst at the same time groping and sexually teasing her. Then he would ravish her in front of the fireplace for hours. And she would let him, although she would struggle and feign attempts at resistance as if genuinely being forced. But she loved it. And so did he.

All of that she was looking forward to, but later that evening her new lover had telephoned and apologised, saying that an unexpected urgent business issue had surfaced which needed his input and that he was unsure if he could get away to see her that evening, but he would try. If not, he said he would call and see her the following day. Mrs. Vitalli was disappointed. But she hoped he *would* turn up, even if it was later that night.

She fussed with her long blonde hair and positioned a few strands around her shoulders and across the deep cleavage of her bosom. She would remain dressed as she was, just in case he arrived. And if not tonight, then there was always tomorrow. After all, her husband had told her he would be away for a few days, so there was plenty of opportunity. She had a couple more drinks whilst flicking through a magazine, and then in the cosy warmth of her living room, she fell asleep on the sofa.

Sometime later, she was awakened by the creak of a door being opened. She sat up. She suddenly felt elated. So, he had managed to get away— wonderful!

She longed for his probing rough hands about her, and expectation fuelled her excitement, causing a breathless flutter as her heart skipped a beat. Again, she heard the creak of a door. But the sound was not coming from the door she had left unlocked for him; the sound was coming from the side entrance kitchen door.

Was this some new ploy he had thought up to further enhance their fantasy sex game? she wondered. She felt her pulse race. How exciting!

She leaned across and turned off the table lamp. Now only the glow from the log fire illuminated the room. She could hear the shuffle of his footsteps in the kitchen and the sound of drawers being opened and closed.

What was he doing?

Whispers. Low whispers. My God, she thought. How authentic. He was certainly making an effort at realism tonight.

Suddenly, his dark shape appeared through the shadows as he stepped into the room. She gasped and rose from the sofa, her dressing gown gapping open, revealing her sexy lingerie, and that she was not wearing any panties.

'Oh, my God! What are you doing here?' she demanded, playing her part as she always did. 'Who the hell are you? What do you want? Get out of my house!'

Then, something strange happened.

To her absolute horror, another figure emerged through the shadows and into the dim light.

What the hell!

Two men wearing matching suits and identical black balaclavas looked at one another and then back at the half-naked woman. Both men then lifted their masks as if to get a better look, but by doing so revealed they were two white men, and strangely, they had almost identical facial features, even down to their two matching goatee beards.

Mrs Vitalli gasped. 'Who the fuck are you?'

This time there was no need to act the part. She was genuinely frightened. She grabbed her gown and covered her body.

'Hey,' said Rocco Capelli, his voice soft and low, a gun hanging loosely in his hand. 'There's no need to cover up on my account, lady.'

'Nor mine,' said his brother, Ricco Capelli. 'Why don't you just loosen that gown, lady, and let it drop? We won't hurt you.'

'That's right,' said Rocco. 'We were admiring the view. That's some body you got there, girl. Shame to cover it up.'

Mrs Vitalli gulped and inhaled a lungful of air as if to cry out.

'Hey, hey... shh!' said one of the men. 'Don't you make a fuckin' sound, lady, or else?' He emphasised the gun in his hand.

It was then when Mrs. Vitalli realised she was in big trouble. Who were these men? What did they want?

They stood looking at her; leering like two predators stalking their prey.

'Drop the gown, lady,' said Rocco Capelli. 'And if you scream, I will fuckin' shoot you.'

'You better do as he says,' said the other man. 'He ain't fooling around.'

Fearing for her life, almost hypnotically, Mrs. Vitalli found herself slowly complying with their instruction and she released her flimsy dressing gown and allowed it to fall to the floor. Her mind drifted back to The Paladin Club in Las Vegas when she would do this daily in a room filled with strange men. But standing almost naked before these two brutes and knowing where this might lead. She found herself shaking with fear. 'I'm expecting my husband home soon,' she said pitifully.

'Ah, good. We're looking forward to seeing him,' said Ricco Capelli. 'But we can have some fun first, can't we, lady?'

'What do you mean, fun? Look... take what you want and get out!'

The two leering brothers smiled at one another and took a step towards her. 'Now, that's not very friendly, is it?' said the man holding the gun. 'What do you take us for, thieves? We're ain't robbers, are we?'

'No. We're lovers,' said the other man.

'Yeah, that's right,' said his brother, moving nearer. 'Lady, have you ever been fucked by two men at once?'

Mrs. Vitalli's eyes widened as Ricco took a step forward. 'NO! Don't you dare come any closer!'

'Yeah, how do you fancy giving that a try? You might like it.' Ricco slowly walked around and positioned himself behind the voluptuous married woman. 'And talking of fucking,' he whispered in her ear. 'Ain't that what you're dressed for, lady?' He placed his hands on her waist and drew her towards him.

Mrs. Vitalli shivered with shock at his touch and gasped. 'NO! Get your hands off me... please.'

'Shut the fuck up!' said Rocco Capelli as he holstered his weapon and pulled out another.

Mrs. Vitalli's mouth gaped open as she looked down at what he had removed from his pants.

'Why don't you put that lovely mouth of yours to use, lady?'

'Oh, my God,' she mouthed silently.

'You're gonna love this,' said Rocco Capelli. 'Go on, touch it. Ever seen one that size before? And my brother's got one just like it.'

'Don't you dare!' jabbered the petrified woman. 'Leave me alone!'

'Shh... just enjoy it. You know you want to.'

'FUCK YOU!!'

'Now, now. That's our job, ain't it? Just relax lady, and let it happen.'

The two brothers now had her surrounded, and they both slid their hands beneath the silky chemise negligée and on to her warm soft skin.

Mrs. Vitalli whimpered as she tried to fend them off, pushing their arms away, but they were too strong.

'Stop fighting,' said Rocco Capelli as he cupped her breasts whilst his brother slid his hands down from her waist and began kneading the swell of her naked buttocks, between which Mrs. Vitalli felt something hard as Ricco pressed himself against her.

'Get your filthy hands off me!' she said tearfully, as the two large pairs of hands began to intimately explore her body in earnest.

'No! NO!! Don't... please!'

The two men scooped her up, and as she cried out, a hand covered her mouth. Then, she was carried upstairs, wrestling and kicking, her muffled cries for help useless as they took her into her bedroom.

# # #

It was just after midnight, on the other side of town, when Layzee Dawson picked up a rock from his garden, smashed a window at the rear of his house and climbed in. His wife, who had abandoned the house on the day he was sentenced, had changed the locks during the weeks leading up to his trial.

Inside, the house was dark and had that boiled cabbage smell of damp neglect. The power had been disconnected, and there was very little in the way of furniture left, just a threadbare upturned armchair and a three-legged coffee table with its broken appendage lying alongside. The windowsills around the house were a graveyard of dead flies, and spider webs hung heavy in every nook and recess, thick with the dust and grime of abandonment.

'What a fuckin' shame,' grumbled Layzee, as he surveyed the wreckage of his marriage and recalled the happier times when this empty husk of a house was a home. 'That lyin' two-faced bitch!' he mouthed, as the image of his wife materialised in his mind's eye.

In the cold darkness, and like a blind man knowing every square inch of his environment, Layzee felt his way to the kitchen and found an old flashlight in his utility drawer. It still worked, and he found the door to the basement where there was a generator. After tinkering with it for half an hour, he got it working and then the lights illuminated the unwanted sorry state of the house. In the cold light, he grimaced as he looked around. He felt like a grieving relative at a funeral gathering.

He shrugged off the memories and hurled the sentimental bullshit out of the broken window. There were more important things on his mind, like staying alive. But how would he do that? Without a gun, he felt as naked as a newborn child. And with Marmarella's hitman, "Cadillac" Tony DeVille on his case, he knew he needed to at least try to level the odds.

A thought came to mind. He remembered that many years ago; he had secreted a handgun in part of the wall of the attic where one of the roof joists met the brickwork. He quickly marched upstairs, pulled the drop-down loft ladder, and climbed up.

With only the torch for guidance, he picked his way along the roof joists. He was looking for a house brick he had marked years before with telltale scratch marks along its face. He found it and, using a bread knife, he began scraping away at the weak cement surrounding it. The brick came away from the wall. He reached into the narrow recess between the outer and inner walls and felt around. He remembered having wrapped the gun in an oily rag, which he had placed in a plastic bag. With his arm elbow deep in the wall, he cursed as his hands blindly explored the sharp shards of concrete and the tangled mess of cobwebs.

Then, his fingers touched something hard and square. What the hell was that? He had forgotten he had also hidden a box of ammunition there and felt buoyed by the finding. Seconds later, he had located and withdrew both the box and the plastic bag. He unwrapped and took out the 38-calibre snub-nosed revolver and inspected it.

It looked perfect. But would it fire?

On his way down the stairs, the doorbell at the front door sounded, and he went into full defence mode. He quickly loaded a couple of rounds into the gun as he swiftly strode over and peeked through the door's spyhole. He then cursed himself for the schoolboy error and slammed his body against the adjacent wall.

'IDIOT!' he remonstrated. How many dumbass people had been shot through the eye doing just that? However, before he pulled back, it had registered with him that standing outside was a withered old man; the nosey neighbour from next door, who looked startled when Layzee snatched open the door.

On seeing Layzee holding a gun, the old man took a giant step back—almost fell—and then steadied himself as he fought to regain his balance. 'Eh… I thought I heard something,' croaked the old man, his open mouth devoid of any teeth.

'Well, that's good to hear,' snarled Layzee. 'At least you ain't fuckin' deaf yet!' And with that, Layzee slammed the door shut and continued loading his handgun.

The doorbell rang again.

Layzee grimaced and opened it. 'You still here?' he snapped.

'Yeah… there's been some trouble around here lately,' snivelled the old man.

'There'll be some trouble if you don't fuck off!' growled Layzee.

'No, no, you don't understand,' continued the man. 'I'm trying to help. I've had to call the police a couple of times over the past week. There's been someone snooping around the neighbourhood and around your property.'

Suddenly, the old man had Layzee's attention. 'Who? What did he look like?' Layzee found himself peering over the shoulder of the scrawny man, scanning the dark, empty street for movement.

'I don't know,' said the old man. He pointed a shaky, withered finger towards the street. 'Over the past week, I've been seeing the same car, driving slow up and down the road out there.'

'What? Like it was casing the joint?'

'Yeah... I suppose you could say that. I figured whoever was driving it was up to no good.'

'What sort of car was it?' asked Layzee.

'A white one.'

'A white one? Well, that narrows it down to several fuckin' million. What sort of white one? Was it a Cadillac?'

As the old man's thought process struggled through the gears of recollection, his head shook as if his jaw was vibrating on a spring. 'I... I don't know,' he said eventually.

'Think!' urged Layzee impatiently. 'Could it have been a Cadillac?'

The man thought for a while longer, and then, when he had finished thinking, said, 'It might have been. What do they look like?'

Layzee leaned in. 'What? A Cadillac? Don't you know what a fuckin' Cadillac looks like?'

'Does it look like a Chevy? I had a Chevy once. A green one.'

'Congratulations,' said Layzee as he eyed the old man severely. 'OK, did the car have fins on the back?'

'What? My Chevy?'

'No! The fuckin' car you saw!'

'What d'ya mean, fins... d'ya mean like shark fins?'

'Yeah, like shark fins.'

The old man frowned and then said. 'Err... it might have done. It was a white saloon. It said 'Eldorado' on the trunk; I remember seeing that the one time when it drove off.

'Jesus! Why didn't you say so?' Dawson bit his lip and shook his head. 'So, it was a Cadillac,' he muttered to himself. 'Yeah, that figures. An old white Eldorado Seville. That would definitely be Tony.'

'That's him,' said the old man. 'Tony. He said his name was Tony.'

Layzee looked exasperated at the old man. 'What? You fuckin' spoke to him?'

'Err... no.'

'Well, how do you know his name's Tony? What did he do, leave a fuckin' calling card?'

'No. Well... I don't think he did. He spoke to my wife.'

'He spoke to your wife?'

'Yeah.'

'What did he say?'

'He said his name was Tony.'

'OK... I got that bit! What else did he say?'

'Err... he said the weather was cold for the time of year.'

'Did he?'

'Yeah. That's what she said. But I thought it was a peculiar thing for him to say.'

Layzee frowned. 'Why?

'Because my wife thinks it's warm for the time of year. Don't you think so? Anyway, she said he liked the biscuits.'

'Biscuits?'

'Yeah. He liked my wife's biscuits; the ones he had with his coffee.'

'He had coffee?'

'Yeah.'

'Where?'

'In a cup. How do you drink yours?'

By now, Layzee had had enough. 'Right, you're a real piece of fuckin' work, ain't ya?' he said. 'I'll tell you what to do. YOU... go home! And when you get there, go into your kitchen. Turn on your gas stove and put your fuckin' head in it.'

The old man looked at him quizzically. 'Should I light it first?'

'No.'

'Why not?'

'Because you've lived too long. Now go and do us all a fuckin' favour.'

The old man nodded and then said, 'Tony did ask if we'd seen you recently.'

'Did he?'

'Yeah. he said he was an old friend of yours. But I think he was lying.'

'No shit.'

'Yeah.'

Just then, there was movement behind where the old man was standing. Slowly, through the murk of the night, the lengthy twin barrels of a shotgun emerged and came to rest over the left shoulder of the old man, aiming directly towards Layzee Dawson's head.

'Are you alright, Harvey?' croaked a feeble voice. It was the old man's old lady.

'Jesus CHRIST!' grunted Layzee as he stared down the shotgun's double barrels.

'Hilda! What are you doin'?' groaned the old man. 'Is that thing loaded?'

'I heard voices,' said the old woman.

'Hilda, take your finger off the trigger,' urged the old man. 'Is that thing loaded?'

Hilda, who appeared unstable as she struggled with the heavy weapon, said, 'Don't you move, mister!'

'Hilda, put the gun down!' urged Layzee.

'HEY!' yelled the old woman. 'Shut your fuckin pie hole. You may be bigger than me, but guess what, it's me holding the fuckin' gun. And if you budge an inch, I'll blow ya fuckin' head off!'

'HILDA!' called the old man, whose shoulder was still supporting the weight of the weapon. 'If you pull that trigger, you'll also blow my fuckin' eardrums apart. Now put the gun down!'

The old man's wife paused and then asked, 'Who is this pencil dick, anyway?'

'He's our neighbour, Mr Dawson,' replied her husband. 'Don't you remember him? He's been away for a couple of years.'

The old woman frowned. 'Oh, yeah. I remember you. Layzee, ain't it? Harvey said you'd been on a round-the-world rowing trip. How are ya?'

'I'd be feeling an awful lot better if you were to put that gun down, lady,' said Layzee.

'Oh, of course. It's not loaded, anyway.' The frail old woman struggled with the weight but withdrew the heavy shotgun from her husband's shoulder and dropped the butt to the ground. It landed heavily, at an odd angle, and there was an almighty... *BANG!!* And a red flash as the weapon went off and buckshot blasted from the barrel.

Her husband hit the ground like a slab of damp clay.

'Jesus Christ, lady! What have you done?' yelled Layzee. 'You've fuckin' killed him!'

Her husband lay flat, face down and as still as death, as time slowed, and the world stopped turning. Layzee Dawson and the old woman stood rooted to the spot where they were standing, paralysed by the gravity of the moment.

Slowly, the woman stepped forward, knelt and touched the lifeless body of her husband. 'OH NO!' she cried. 'Harvey! Harvey, wake up!' She raised her hand, which was covered with blood. 'Oh, my God!' she whimpered. 'This is terrible. And it's his birthday tomorrow. He'd have been ninety-two. I already baked him a cake. What am I gonna do?'

'I don't know, lady,' said Layzee.

The old woman's frown intensified. 'I don't even eat cake,' she said, worriedly. 'Do you eat cake?'

'Listen, lady,' said Layzee. 'FUCK THE CAKE! Don't you realise what you've just done?'

'Oh, I know,' groaned the woman. 'He was a good man. Grumpy at times, I know, and he snored and passed wind a lot, but he was a good man. Apart from his drinkin' and swearin'. But I didn't mind that so much. It was his incontinence that I couldn't stand. That stink of old man's piss and having to empty that damn colostomy bag six times a day. I hated that. An' I ain't even gonna mention the performance I used to have changing his diaper. After all, his memory deserves some level of dignity, don't ya think? Although, some days, I swear he'd sit in his own shit for hours.'

The old woman looked loving down at the crumpled body of her husband.

'In years gone by, he used to be a lot better though,' she continued. 'You know… he was regular like. Every day, he'd wake up at six in the morning and have a piss. And then and six-thirty he'd have a shit. But there was a problem with that.'

'Really?' said Layzee. 'What was the problem with that?'

'He never got outta bed 'til seven.'

'Oh, Jesus Christ, lady!'

'But do you know what was worse?'

Dumbfounded, Layzee regarded her with puzzled awe. 'I'm all ears,' he said.

'He used to masturbate a lot.'

'He what?'

'Yeah, it's true. He was an obsessive wanker. I often found him jerking off in the outhouse. Can you believe that? A ninety-one-year-old whacking his wiener at two in the morning.' The old woman looked down at the flaccid body of her husband. 'That's where he used to hide his smutty magazines… the dirty bastard!'

Layzee felt as though he'd been transported to another dimension. 'Is that so?' he said, dazed.

'Yeah… he was a big tit man. He liked norks. Nowadays, mine hang too low. He had an annual subscription to that girlie mag. What's it called, eh, Double D Dames? Have you seen the size of the top bollocks on the women in those books?'

Bewildered, Layzee shook his head. 'Top bollocks?'

'Yeah, you know, their Brad Pitt's… tits. They're huge! They're like fuckin' barrage balloons. Fun bags he used to call mine.'

'Yeah… I know what you're referring to, lady.'

'Last year, he wanted me to get them fake things. Ya know… those silly cyclone implants? He said they'd help give him wood. But I had to remind him we got rid of the log burner. We got an electric fire now… so there's no need. Well, he won't be needing them big tit books no more. You can have them if you want. There's dozens in the outhouse.'

'Thanks for the offer,' said Layzee. 'But I think I'll take a raincheck on that, if you don't mind.'

'So, what shall I do?' queried the poor woman. 'Some of the pages are stuck together, but I suppose I could donate them to the thrift store.'

Layzee looked to the stars. 'Kirk to Enterprise,' he grumbled. 'If you're listening Scottie; beam me the fuck up, would ya?'

The old woman looked forlornly at the body of her husband. 'There's not much else I can do, is there?' she said sadly, a note of resignation in her voice.

Just then, remarkably, her husband stirred, and he looked up at her from where he lay. 'Argh... what about calling me an ambulance, you stupid bitch?'

'OH! Harvey!' yelped the old woman, her wrinkled face acquiring a few more. 'You still with us? Are you alright?'

'What do you think? No... I'm not! I'm pissed off. Don't you dare touch my collection of Double D Dames!'

'OK! That does it for me,' said Layzee, who reached for his phone and punched 9 1 1 onto the keypad.'

'9 1 1—what's your emergency?'

'I need an ambulance,' said Layzee.

'What's the problem, sir?'

'I need you to send paramedics for an injured guy who's been shot, and a straitjacket for his wife, who's batshit crazy and needs to see a shrink.'

'Sir, let's deal with the injured man first. Is he still breathing?'

'Hold on. Harvey, are you still breathing?'

The dispatcher went through her scripted procedure, during which Layzee described the events leading up to the accident. When asked for his name, Layzee, not wishing to divulge his identity, gave *his* own name as Mr. Geoffrey Mitchell. A few minutes later, an ambulance arrived, followed by a police patrol car.

The paramedics attending the incident concurred that the old man had only a slight flesh wound to his right hip; most of the shotgun pellets had missed, although his colostomy bag had burst where he had fallen, and there was a strong sewage smell about his person.

'Oh, he always smells like that,' complained his wife, who again took the opportunity to relay every detail of her husband's bodily waste dysfunctionality, as well as his masturbatory habits. 'Is it natural for him to be whacking off at his age?' enquired his wife.

'Will you just shut up, Hilda!' groaned Harvey, as he was loaded into the ambulance, which then took them both away to the New York Hospital Medical Centre, leaving Layzee with the two police officers.

'OK, Mr. Mitchell. I think we have everything,' said the taller of the two officers, a burly man who stood well over six feet tall. 'We're happy there was no malicious intent here. She's an old lady. It's a shame, and she is a little confused.'

'Confused?' queried Layzee, eager to get rid of the two cops. 'Personally, I'd say she's a fuckin' ravin' headcase. But you write up what you want.'

After the officers left, Layzee returned to his house, and the street emptied of emergency vehicles, or so he thought. A few minutes later, there was a knock on the door. One of the paramedics had returned.

'Christ, now what?' called Layzee through the closed door

'My apologies, sir. With everything that was going on, I forgot to check you for trauma,' called the paramedic. 'I just need to perform a few quick tests. It won't take long. Otherwise, I'll be in deep shit. You know how things are.'

'*Deep shit...* is that a technical term?' Layzee reluctantly opened the door, turned and the medical man followed him into the house.

'Thank you, sir. This won't take long. After experiencing a distressing event, Mr. Dawson,' explained the paramedic. 'Psychological trauma can be extremely damaging.'

'OK, I know you got your job to do,' said Layzee, who then, realising he had not disclosed his true identity to the police or any of the ambulance crew, wondered how the man knew his real name.

He turned and faced the man.

Standing against the black silhouette of the open front door to the house was "Cadillac" Tony DeVille, garbed in the uniform of a paramedic. He had a Smith and Wesson .357 Magnum revolver raised, the barrel of which was pointing directly at Layzee's head. He also had a smug look of triumph about him. Layzee's own handgun was tucked in his belt behind his back, but knew if he went for it, he would be shot dead in an instant.

'Huh... I've seen your face before,' remarked Layzee. 'My wife showed me a picture once. I remember thinking, fuck me... ain't that an ugly mug? Fancy going through life having to wear that shit!'

DeVille refused to take the bait. 'I like moments like these,' he said calmly, his voice low and tinged with a throaty purr. 'Those final few seconds before a man dies. I find it so cathartic. It makes me wonder when my time comes, what my last few words will be.'

Layzee smiled. 'Well, why not pass me the gun, and you can have your moment,' sneered Layzee.

'You're a funny man, Dawson,' smiled DeVille as he cocked the hammer of his revolver. 'And what will your last words be?'

Layzee frowned. 'A question.'

'A question? OK, I'll grant you that. But make it quick. I need to collect my fee tonight.'

'Well, you saying that has now spawned a second question?' remarked Layzee.

'OK... what's the first?'

'How much is that bitch wife of mine payin' you?'

'Plenty. And your final question?'

'How did you find out I'd been released early?'

DeVille's smile broadened. 'Huh, that's a trade secret, and I ain't about to tell you that, am I?'

'Well, what's it matter if I'm gonna be dead soon, anyway?'

DeVille thought for a moment and then said, 'That's a fair point. OK... I'll tell ya. Someone tipped me the wink.'

'Who?'

'I received a call earlier today from someone we both know.'

Layzee tried to puzzle whom it might have been. As he had informed no one outside of prison of his release—the list was short. 'Let me think. It wouldn't happen to be that motherless rat bastard Officer Dale Birch, would it?'

'Bingo!' mused DeVille. 'Birch, don't like you much, does he?'

'I know… the feeling's mutual,' grinned Layzee. 'And it's the only thing we have in common. But I know this year he's gonna be really disappointed.'

'Why?'

'Because he thought I'd be back soon to keep him company. You see, he's got it worse than me. He's in prison every fuckin' day until he retires. But that ain't the main reason he'll be disappointed.'

'Huh… well, now I need to know, don't I? So, what is?'

'Because, owing to the fact he's been a complete shit stain, I've removed him from my Christmas card list. That's gonna really piss him off.'

DeVille frowned. 'That's a joke, right? How can you be joking with only seconds of your miserable life left to live?'

'I'm an optimistic type of guy,' grinned Layzee. 'You never know what might be waiting just around the corner.'

'Huh, Birch was right about you,' remarked DeVille with a frown of incredulity. 'You're either quite clever in your own way, or a brainless dullard. I'm leaning towards the latter. Perhaps we'll find out for sure when your brains are splattered all over your floor. But before I complete my contract, Dawson… Officer Birch did request something.'

'I bet he did, and you can't wait to tell me, can you?'

DeVille smiled as if humouring the condemned man. 'He suggested I make you suffer before I put a bullet through your sorry head.'

'Did he?'

'Yeah. And he was quite specific and suggested a number methods for me to consider.'

'Such as?'

'He suggested I blow torch your eyes out, or maybe I try flaying your skin using a dermatome. You know… those nasty electric shear implements they use for skin grafts. I've used one before. The pain's excruciating when anaesthetic's not applied. But there was one suggestion he put forward that was particularly creative, and one I haven't tried yet.'

'I'm all ears,' mused Layzee.

'He suggested I hang you by your rectum using a meat hook 'til your heart gives out.'

'Nice!'

'Yeah, but that would take too long, and I ain't that cruel. Anyway, I do rather like the effect a bullet between the eyes has on a man's head and the adherence that process has on Sir Isaac Newton's third law of motion.'

'Ah… an educated man. And what's that, professor?'

'You know every action has an equal and opposite reaction… right? No? Huh… I can see you have no idea what I'm talking about, do ya? An' I ain't about to waste my time tellin' ya. Besides, my arm's starting to ache holding this piece. I'll just say this. It's that split-second look of surprise when the bullet hits. I never tire of seeing it. In fact, before I enjoy that moment with you, Dawson… I have to say though, I am surprised by you.'

'Really?'

'Yes.'

'And why's that?'

'Well, for a supposed professional, I'm surprised that when you let me in, you failed to spot the absence of a medical vehicle parked outside. Especially with me dressed as a paramedic. That was sloppy of you, wasn't it?'

'Yeah,' said Layzee. 'I'll give you that one. I *was* slow to spot that.'

'An observation you now regret, I expect,' said DeVille.

'Yeah, but I did spot something else,' said Layzee. 'I noticed a cop car returning a couple of minutes ago. Did you spot that?'

'Police FREEZE!' called a voice from behind where Tony DeVille was standing. 'NYPD! You with the gun! Kneel and lay the weapon on the floor. Do it now!'

Tony's eyes widened, and he froze rigid.

'I guess not,' said Layzee. 'How sloppy of *you*. An observation you now regret, I expect. And hopefully for a fuckin' long time.'

Standing in the doorway with his gun trained on DeVille's back was the tall police officer with whom Layzee had been speaking a few minutes earlier.

'Sir, do it NOW!' repeated the cop. 'Or I will shoot you!'

DeVille stood as still as an ice sculpture, weighing his options and then realising he had none, lowered himself to the floor and released his revolver.

'Hands behind you head!' screamed the cop's partner, his gun also trained on Marmarella's hitman.

DeVille slowly complied and looked up at Layzee. 'I ain't done with you yet, Dawson,' he said menacingly. 'The cops have nothing on me. I didn't pull no trigger. I ain't shot anyone... lately. I'll be out in a day or two. And I'll be seeing you around, Dawson. So don't get too comfortable.'

'SHUT UP!' said the taller of the two police officers, who was busy cuffing the man. The officer turned to Layzee as he escorted his captive out of the house. 'And you! Stay where you are... I'll be right back to speak with you!'

'Why? What have I done?' queried Layzee. 'Nothin', that's what.'

The tall cop and his colleague walked Tony DeVille to the squad car and bundled him in. The tall officer then sauntered back up the drive to Layzee's house, as if bored with the whole mundane affair.

Layzee watched him. 'Oh, for fuck's sake, now what?'

The lanky officer, who was closer to seven feet than six, had to duck his head through the aperture of the door as he re-entered the house. 'Sir, you gave us a false name earlier,' he said. 'I ran a check on your address just after we left. Turns out your name's Dawson; released from prison only a few hours ago.'

'Oh, yeah... that, OK. It must be a real slow night for you guys. Ain't you got any fuckin' murders to attend to. Because I can guarantee you right now that some fucker's getting killed somewhere, and you're breakin' my balls my over a fuckin' name?'

'Sir, I came back to warn you that under New York Penal Law section 190.23; providing a police officer with a false name is a Class B misdemeanour, punishable by up to 90 days in jail.'

'Yeah, yeah, yeah... I get that,' said Layzee. 'But only if you warn me of the consequences first. See... I know something of the law too. I've had two years to read up on it.'

The officer frowned and considered Layzee's reply for a moment. Then he said. 'Technically, that *is* correct.'

'Yeah, I know.'

'So... consider yourself warned.' The officer went to leave and then turned back. 'You're a lucky man giving us that fake name, Dawson,' he added.

'Why's that?'

'Otherwise, we wouldn't have come back. And you too might have been heading for the hospital. And probably straight to the morgue.'

'Yeah, see how lying can save your life,' remarked Layzee, as he looked up at the towering police officer. 'By the way... do you get headaches?'

'What d'ya mean?'

'There can't be much oxygen up there at that fuckin' altitude.'

'Hey! I don't like you!' said the officer.

'Oh, what a disappointment. And there's me thinkin', we're gonna be drinkin' buddies.'

The officer looked down his nose at Layzee's petulant face, smiling back at him. 'Dawson, you've been out of prison less than a day and already you're involved in an incident.'

'But I ain't done nothing.'

'So, it seems. And I suppose by calling 9 1 1, you probably saved that old man's life tonight. So, I'll let your petulance slide this time. But do yourself a favour, Dawson... quit whilst you're ahead.'

With that, the police officer left and Layzee walked down the drive and continued his rash behaviour by enthusiastically waving them off.

'Now then,' he said, as he turned and looked up and down the empty, dark street. 'I wonder where Tony parked his Cadillac?'

Chapter 6: Phobia

J oey Vitalli sat mournfully in the small underground medical ward and looked at the man whom he had shot earlier that day. Apart from the injured man, Joey was alone in the underground bunker complex.

It was Louie Marmarella's son, Dino, who lay on the bed before him. He was unconscious and fighting for his life. He was on life support, breathing via a ventilator and had nasogastric and various IV tubes inserted into his body. ECG electrodes were connected to a screen above his bed, which bleeped continually, monitoring heart rate, blood pressure and other vitals. His condition was said to be critical but stable, but he had lost a lot of blood, about twenty per cent, or so the doctor had said. His right shoulder and upper torso were heavily bandaged after undergoing surgery to remove the bullet—the bullet *he* had fired.

Joey was distraught.

What the hell had he done? Today, he had committed the unthinkable act of deliberately taking another man's life. And for what? To impress his family members? To show them he was worthy to be amongst them. And if that wasn't bad enough, not only had he shot the wrong man, he had also incurred the wrath of his uncle, the family leader, who had been, and probably still was, apoplectic. He had always wondered how it would feel to shoot someone. Well, now he had, and it felt cheap, and in the manner in which he had done it, shooting the man from behind, it felt cowardly, too. He had not yet thought about being labelled a murderer. That thought had not yet entered Joey's mind. He just hoped the man would survive. But Joey had learned one thing today: he wasn't cut out for this lifestyle.

Or was he?

He felt confused and his emotions were in disarray. What was this feeling he hated so much—this unexpected feeling of guilty sorrow that had impacted his conscience like a freight train doing ninety? Such things never seemed to bother the other family members. They talked of killing and death and seemed completely oblivious to remorse. And he was cut from the same cloth—so why did *he* feel this way?

He was surprised by his reaction, and he hated himself.

He hated the damn Warehouse too. He had an unnerving dislike of enclosed places. His was not full-blown acute claustrophobia, but it was a recognised psychological condition, an unusual anxiety complex known to behavioural therapists as cleithrophobia—the fear of being trapped or locked in a confined space without a means of escape. And that was the reason he had spent so much time in the restroom in the Italian restaurant, that, and his overpowering feeling of culpability for what he had done.

After Joey had shot Dino outside "Cadillac" Tony DeVille's house, Johnny and Sash, thinking Dino was dead, had quickly scooped up the body, dumped it in the trunk of their car and drove away. And it was then as they accelerated away from the scene of the shooting, that the thought of Dino's confinement in the trunk triggered Joey's phobia. He could imagine himself in that situation, locked away, unable to get out, and it was this that filled him with overwhelming dread. Dread, coupled with guilt and blind panic, which had resulted in a severe case of nausea on his arrival at the restaurant, causing him to rush to the restroom, and into a stall to throw up.

It all began years before. As a young kid he had developed a fear of coffins—borne from a visit to the Chamber of Horrors exhibition within Madame Tussauds waxwork museum on 42nd Street. He should not have been in there. He was only nine years old but defied warnings that that particular section of the museum was for "Adults Only", and he had sneaked in, regardless.

Inside were frighteningly realistic scenes of murder—captured frozen moments in time that would strike terror into the heart of any child.

In the final section, there was a theme of historical British murderers—Jack the Ripper dissecting the bodies of his victims; John Haigh, the acid bath murderer; Dr. Crippen, dismembering his "patients" before hiding them within the walls and floors of his house. But it was a scene depicting the exhumation of a woman's corpse by two infamous Irish body snatchers, Burke and Hare, that was to linger in Joey's memory and fuel his nightmares into adulthood.

Like the other gruesome scenes, the exhibit was set in semi darkness and was horrifically staged. Amongst the shadows, yellow impact lighting illuminated the evil faces of the two men who were holding shovels in a cemetery alongside an exposed grave. A coffin had been dug up and opened to reveal the body of an old woman recently buried. Horrific enough, but it was the coffin lid that, as a young child, had terrified Joey so, leaving him indelibly scarred for life; for inside the coffin lid were scratch marks—scratch marks streaked with blood that alluded to a terrible and tragic accident. The woman, thought to be dead, had been unwittingly buried alive, and had regained consciousness sometime later, whilst laying beneath six feet of soil, entombed in her sealed coffin. The scratches on the inside of the coffin lid were from her fingernails, broken in a frenzied effort to escape as she scrapped and clawed to get out, only eventually to suffocate to death in the cramped darkness.

Ironically, had it not been for the two criminals, no one would ever have known. Which led Joey to wonder just how many others out there in the cemetery had also been accidentally buried alive.

The nightmare image of the woman's horribly contorted face, so effectively lit and replicated in Madame Tussauds' vile diorama, had remained with Joey ever since, and he often found himself imagining the frenzied fear the poor woman must have suffered as she hopelessly fought to escape the cramped coffin. And how gruesome her eventual death must have been with no room to move, and no air to breathe.

Joey shivered at the thought.

And now, here he was in the Warehouse, an underground bunker tantamount itself to a crypt. Here he was, sitting alongside a near corpse, waiting and hoping for it too to come back to life.

As a form of penance for shooting the wrong man, Joey's uncle, Salvatore Vitalli, had sent him down into the bunker to babysit the patient, whilst he met with the doctor in the main house.

The Warehouse was dark, cold, and apart from the beeping heart monitor, was eerily quiet and harboured a strong earthy smell of rising damp which was inescapable. It was probably a similar smell experienced by the buried woman when she regained consciousness, surmised Joey, and he again wondered how long she would have lasted before the blessed release of death ended her agony.

Suddenly, in the darkness outside the room, a voice broke the silence.

'Hey, any dead bodies down here?'

Joey leapt from his seat and for a moment he was back in Madame Tussauds' Chamber Of Horrors. 'Jesus Christ!' he shrieked, as a face appeared through the fog of gloom.

'You two getting to know each other?' said the voice.

'Damn it! Frankie,' gasped Joey. 'You nearly gave me a heart attack.'

'Well, you're in the right place for that, kid,' smiled Frankie as he stepped into the room. 'Jesus Christ, look at all this hospital shit. I ain't been down here for years. Guess the old man's getting a bit paranoid, huh?'

Joey held his chest and tried to catch his breath. 'I dunno, maybe. Frankie, you scared the living shit outta me.''

'For fuck's sake, kid,' urged Frankie. 'What's the matter with you?'

'Nothing. It's just that you startled me, that's all.'

Frankie passed Joey a coffee mug. 'Here, take this, and cheer the fuck up.'

'Thanks.' Joey went to take a sip but stopped himself. 'What is this?' he queried.

'It's a cup of who gives a fuck,' said Frankie. 'Now, get it down ya neck.'

Joey sniffed the cup. 'What is it... whiskey?'

Frankie glared at him. 'Paraffin.'

'What?'

'I'm kidding, it's Jack Daniels. It's from Fingers' secret stash, Joey. Just drink it. You'll feel better.'

'Feel better? I feel awful.'

'Well, I feel better having found Fingers' secret whiskey stash. Anyway, what d'ya mean, you feel awful... why?'

'Why?' Joey gestured to the injured man. 'Look what I did.'

Frankie shrugged his shoulders. 'I know. It's a terrible shame.'

'Yeah.'

'I mean, shame, it looks like he might pull through.'

'You think he will?'

'I don't know, maybe.' Frankie took a closer look at the unconscious man lying on the bed. He frowned and then added, 'Mmm... I dunno. Doesn't look too good. Maybe not. Anyway, who cares?'

'I care,' trembled Joey.

'You care? You fuckin' shot him!'

Joey's demeanour slumped. 'I know. I'm just glad the second bullet missed.'

'It didn't miss.'

'What d'ya mean?'

'Your second bullet hit his ass.'

'It hit his ass? Oh, my God!'

'Exactly. Kid, let's face it, you're a lousy shot. Your aim's all over the fuckin' place. You really need to spend some time down the shooting range and learn to group your shots.'

'What?'

'Yeah, kid. Practice is the key. Had you done that, this useless fuck would be dead, and it would be happy days.'

'Happy days?'

'Yeah. I'd be looking forward to a night out with a young lovely. And you'd be doin'... whatever it is you do. Now you been and got the boss man all riled up. But that's your problem, kid. You're too fuckin' jumpy. You gotta be like me, Frankie V.' Frankie adopted a pose with his arms extended.

Joey regarded him with a spiralling feeling of despair and envy. For although he found it difficult to share Frankie's views on certain family practices, he looked up to him. He was different to the others. As Salvatore Vitalli's son, he seemed to be granted a higher degree of latitude when he strayed from the usual and expected protocols of the Vitalli way of life. Protocols that if broken by his cousins, Johnny or Fingers, would certainly attract some form of reprimand from the big man.

'Well, we can't all be like you,' said Joey.

'Why not? Look… I know you've had a bad day, kid. But when nothing's going right, go left! Try something different. I mean, nothing really bad happens to me now because I got my shit together. And that's something you must try and do. And then you'll have… you'll have good times too, I promise you.' Frankie paused, then put his arm around the younger man and said, 'But remember, always be true to you, and always strive to be your best version. That's what I say, and that's what I do. And stay cool, for the love of God!'

Joey tried to lift himself from his slump but couldn't. 'I try to, but I get nervous. Not everyone can be cool.'

'I know. And believe me, kid, "awesome" takes practice. Anyway, listen up. The boss man wants to see us all again.'

'What… me too?'

'Especially you.'

'What?' Joey again felt that all familiar sinking feeling as if an elevator had a broke free and was plummeting twenty floors.

'Ah, I'm fuckin' with you, kid. Relax, I don't know what he wants, but something's going down. Anyway, there's a close friend of mine on her way down here. Greta, you'll like her. I met her at a nightclub a few days ago. She got dressed up like a nurse when we got back to her place for drinks. Then I found out she was one… huh! Turns out she ain't got much of an idea about medicine, she's still training, but… well, she's a bit cock-eyed, if you know what I mean. But she certainly knows how to give mouth-to-mouth and resuscitate a guy's…'

'Frankie! I'd rather not know if it's all the same to you. Anyway, aren't you supposed to be married?'

'Yeah, I know I am. But us wise guys, we're allowed a few indiscretions, aren't we? Bangin' babes is all well and good, and there's fuck all wrong that. But love, marriage? That's different, kid... it's a completely different animal. You're talking about lifelong commitment, something authentic and genuine. It's about accepting each other's flaws. It's about support, respect and understanding. You'll learn all this as you go through life. Especially if you find the right girl.' Almost as an afterthought, Frankie added, 'Of course, I love my wife.'

'Yeah, I really like Aunt Debbie too,' said Joey. 'She's always been kind to me. She gives good advice, and she makes the best milkshakes.'

'Now, that *is* a fact,' said Frankie.

Joey frowned. 'But what about what Johnny and Fingers are saying? You know about those neighbourhood guys calling to see her when you're not around? Doesn't that bother you? That ain't right.'

'Hey, kid! They're just neighbours... friends. Don't believe everything you hear from those clowns upstairs. They know nothin'. She's a loving wife, and as loyal as they come.'

'Sure... sorry, Frankie.'

'Ah...that's OK, kid. You're still young. You gotta lot to learn.'

Frankie leaned over the bed and looked with distaste at the unconscious, heavily bandaged man fighting for his life. 'Anyway,' he continued. 'Greta will be here soon. She'll keep an eye on this fuckin' skid mark while we go and see what the boss wants.'

Joey gestured to the man on the bed. 'Why is he so hated?'

A scowl formed across Frankie's face. 'Huh! I don't think you've heard *all* of what he's done, have you, kid? He's a fuckin' psycho. He once shot and killed a guy who accidentally put a ding in the door of his Lincoln in a car park at some grocery store. But that's nothin'. A few months back, one of his associates snitched to the police to save his own ass. This piece of shit got word of it and called at the guy's house one evening and shot and killed him, but not before he put a bullet in his wife and two kids first. He forced the guy to watch *them* die before *he* got his. Word is, he tortured the guy for a few hours until he got bored and then finished him. And that don't even scratch the surface for this piece of dog dirt. Which is why I'd put that pillow over his face and shoot him right now, if I could. But... I get it. The boss needs him alive to avoid an all-out war. Huh... fuckin' politics pisses me off.'

Joey regarded the man lying on the bed and found it difficult to picture that the sleeping man could perform such atrocities.

Frankie picked up on his hangdog demeanour. 'Don't waste your time feeling sorry for *him*, kid. He's a complete fuckin' stain on his family's name, which, let's face it... ain't the rosiest, is it? But he's protected, see. If I had my way, he'd already be dead. When we have a few spare hours, I'll fill you in on the rest of his résumé.' Frankie looked down at the heavily sedated man and grimaced. 'See, he's no different to his fuckin' father. The apple didn't fall too far from the tree when this asshole entered the world... that's for sure. Besides, now you're older, kid... there's something I think you should know. But now ain't the time. We'll talk later.'

Just then a petite, pretty young woman arrived at the wardroom looking smart and regimental, wearing a starched white nurse's uniform. She was carrying a small holdall. 'Ah... here she is,' said Frankie. 'Greta, meet Joey. Joey... Greta. Ain't she a dish? Look at her. She'd brighten anyone's day, right?'

'Yes,' said Joey. The two shook hands.

'Hi, Joey,' said the nurse. 'I've heard a lot about you.'

Joey frowned with embarrassment as he regarded the pretty girl admiringly. They appeared to be about the same age. 'Really?' he said.

'Ehmm... right!' interrupted Frankie. 'Joey, could you just hold the fort here for a few minutes? I need to explain to Greta about that medication that arrived today. It's in the storeroom.' Frankie took the nurse by her hand. 'Greta, come with me.' He winked at Joey as they left the wardroom.

Whilst gone, Joey regarded the man lying on the bed with a growing sense of awe, and wondered what Frankie wanted to tell him, and why it had to wait until he was a suitable age.

Ten minutes later, Frankie returned alone, looking somewhat flushed. 'Right,' he said, checking his watch. 'It's almost seven. Come on, kid... we better get going.'

They both made their way back along the underground passageway to the house where Johnny, Fingers and Sash had already gathered. The five men congregated around a solid oval oak table set in the middle of the kitchen and waited for the leader to arrive.

The kitchen was spacious. It had an exposed beam vaulted ceiling and bare brick walls on which hung rustic dark wood shaker cabinets above a countertop perimeter of brown marbled granite. The room looked intentionally distressed, as if in need of a revamp, although the large stainless steel cooking range appeared unused. One of the strict house rules was that if anyone did use it and failed to leave it looking brand spanking new afterwards, they might just as well climb in the trash dumpster at the rear of the house and wait for the garbage truck to take them away. Consequently, most of the meals eaten at the house by the family members were either cooked by the housemaid, delivered, or they ate out.

'Any idea what this is about?' asked Sash, slumped over the table above which, suspended from the ceiling high above, hung five brass domed pendant lamps.

'I don't know,' shrugged Fingers. 'I just hope he's laying on a few canapés and drinks. I'm fuckin' starving.'

'Jesus H Christ,' muttered Frankie. 'You eat like a god-damn horse!'

'Yeah,' said Johnny. 'What say you get over to that stove and cook something up? You know something, Fingers, I have never ever seen you prepare a meal or anything for anyone.'

'Hey, that's a bit harsh,' grumbled Fingers. 'I happen to be a good cook. I cooked a meal for a lady friend only the other week.'

'Yeah, I heard about that,' said Johnny. 'She's still in fuckin' hospital. Although, she did say it was the best slice of soup she'd ever had.'

'Blow it out your ass,' grumbled Fingers.

'I think she blew it all outta hers.'

'You're fuckin' disgusting. Why you gotta be like that? As it happens, we had a very pleasant evening. I prepared her a nice steak.'

'Yeah... she said she wanted some peace and quiet whilst you cooked it. So, she took the batteries outta the fuckin' smoke alarm.'

'Hey, Johnny!' Two words—*fuck* and *you*.'

Just then the door of Salvatore's study burst open and out walked the leader together with the family doctor, who were concluding their discussion. Immediately, the light-hearted mood in the kitchen dropped several levels and arrived at the one marked *sombre.*

'Yes... OK, Mr. Vitalli. I'll get on and make that call,' said the doctor, who hurriedly headed for the door leading to the garden. He opened it and stepped out onto the large terrace where a number of benches faced the recently mown lawn. He noticed, looking down the steps to the lawn, that from where he was standing, there appeared not one single weed or blemish of any description across the expanse of green turf, which was beginning to look slick as dew formed.

Fifty yards beyond was the garage where the external lights had just come on as daylight began to fade, and chirping crickets made their presence known. It looked like it would be a warm evening, but the doctor was now filled with cold apprehension over what he had agreed to do.

Salvatore Vitalli ambled into the kitchen with all the impregnable attitude of a chairman walking into a board meeting surrounded by "yes men" directors. He slid out a chair which scraped across the cold stone floor like fingernails drawn down a chalkboard.

Joey shuddered.

The leader sat down, wrung out his hands, and placed them on the table. He was still wearing the trousers to his suit, although his jacket had gone and his tie hung loose from his white shirt collar, the top button of which was open. It was the most relaxed he had looked all day. He looked around at the now forlorn and expectant faces staring back at him. His crew were all sitting in the same positions as in the restaurant. Similarly, apart from Frankie, their jackets had also been discarded. The five men were waiting to hear why, for the second time that day, they had been called together.

'Who's with Dino?' asked the big man, as he stripped off his tie and threw it on a nearby chair.

'Greta,' replied Frankie.

'Who?'

'She's a nurse, a friend of mine.'

'Is she a qualified?'

'I'll say.'

The big man's-tired gaze eventually fell on Joey to his right, who sat nervously on tenterhooks, waiting for what he knew would be coming. He did not have to wait long.

'Joey,' growled his uncle, the family Don—the crime family kingpin. 'Your fuck-up cost me a pretty penny today, son. But there might be some good that comes out of this shit, but it's gonna need work and a lot of luck.' He paused and, without embellishing further, asked the group, 'Do you guys know why I gave the order to whack "Cadillac" Tony DeVille this morning?'

Each of the men frowned and looked at one another as if each expected the other to provide the answer. But none of them had been told, which, for them, was standard operating procedure. Once such a directive was issued by any capomandamento, it was expected to be fulfilled without question and generally no explanation was offered. The big man's eyes looked at each of them as they collectively shook their heads.

'Boss,' said Frankie. 'You know we never question why an order's given. We just carry it out.'

'Well, you didn't today, did you?'

'*They* didn't, Boss... I wasn't there.' Frankie glanced at Joey, who was biting his quivering lip. Frankie turned to his father. 'Look, Boss... the kid's just learning. We've all fucked up at some point in our lives. Can't we just lighten up on him? Look... the kid's trembling.'

'I agree,' added Sash. 'Can't we just please move on, Boss? Besides, I for one, would really like to know why we needed to ice that guy.'

The leader scanned the faces and nodded his head slowly. 'OK,' he said. 'Do any of you have any ideas why I ordered that hit?'

There was silence before Frankie offered a suggestion. 'Was it payback for Spaghetti Sam?'

'No, but that's a fair shout.' He looked around. 'Anybody else any ideas?' The others shook their heads. 'OK. Well, I'll tell you. As you know, Layzee Dawson is being released and is due out next week. And guess who paid him a visit last week? His fuckin' wife! It's taken that bitch almost two years to go see him. And do you know why she went? Well, I'll tell you now, it wasn't to apologise and beg forgiveness for framing his ass...'

'I know why she went,' interrupted Johnny, halting the big man in mid-flow. 'Conjugal rights! She wanted a shag.'

'Hey, dickwad!' snarled the big man.' You gotta learn when to appreciate when I ain't in the mood for your fuckin' dumbass humour. And just in case you ain't noticed, that would be right about fuckin' now!'

'Sorry, Boss,' whimpered Johnny. 'Just tryin' to lighten the moment.'

'Well, thank you very much, but don't. Thanks to you useless fucks, this thing might blow up in our faces, when it should have been put to bed earlier today!' The leader twisted his neck to release a knot of compressed tension, which cricked as he straightened his bent posture. He again looked at each of them and continued. 'The reason she went to see him was to tell him that she'd taken a fuckin' contract out on him.'

'What... to kill him?' queried Johnny.

'No,' said the big man. 'It was a contract offering a fuckin' job flipping burgers at Mackie D's. Of course, to kill him, you fuckin' idiot!'

'Johnny,' said Fingers. 'Why don't you just wind your neck in and let the Boss talk?'

'And obviously "Cadillac" Tony was given the contract,' nodded Frankie thoughtfully.

'Yeah, that's right,' said the big man. 'And that's what she told Layzee.'

'What... she actually told him that?' intoned Frankie. 'Face to face?'

'Yeah.'

'Wow... that was bold.'

'Or stupid,' added Sash.

'Well, there was a reinforced Plexiglas window separating them,' explained the big man. 'Otherwise, I'm sure Layzee would have fuckin' throttled her. But yeah... she told him. Can you believe that shit?'

'What a cruel, conniving ho,' said Sash. 'That's just plain mean, Boss.'

'Ahh... I get it,' said Johnny. 'So that's why we went after "Cadillac" Tony. To whack Tony before he whacks Layzee.'

'Fuck me! You catch on quick, don't you Johnny?' muttered Fingers. 'Jesus, you ought to be running the fuckin' country.'

The big man sitting at the head of the table pointed his finger. 'Shut up, both of ya.'

'So, we now got two problems,' said Frankie.

'Yeah. And by now Tony will know for sure something's up.'

Johnny looked puzzled. 'But how would he know that?'

Salvatore Vitalli grimaced. 'Because Dino Marmarella's car is parked outside his house. And by now, they'll know Dino's missing. You fuckers were so eager to leave after you botched the job, you left Dino's car there... for God's sake! Tony DeVille don't need to be a rocket whizz to realise someone tried to whack him outside his house today and screwed up, does he? Christ, why didn't you just leave him a fuckin' calling card too?'

'I... I don't think we had one of those, Boss,' said Johnny.

'It was a rhetorical question, you fuckin' wank splat,' blustered the big man. 'Which brings us to problem number two. Dino Marmarella himself.'

'Oh, why don't we just finish him, and have done with it, Boss?' pleaded Frankie. 'All this medication and surgery crap. Just bury him in the garden. Who would know?'

'Yeah,' said Johnny. 'He'd be good fertiliser for the cabbage patch. Next year, we might get a bumper crop.'

'What?'

'You're disgusting'

'What d'ya mean? I bet Fingers wouldn't think twice about chowing down on Dino flavoured cauliflower cheese... would you, Fingers?'

Fingers shrugged. 'Wouldn't bother me.'

'HEY!' barked the big man. 'Have you quite finished?' The bickering faces around the table turned to face the big man. 'Dino's death would do us no good at all,' said the leader. 'We need to keep him alive.'

'What for?' queried Frankie.

'Well, let's think about this for a minute.' The leader rubbed his chin with his thumb and forefinger. 'We still can't be absolutely sure my brother's dead, can we?'

'Well, didn't Marmarella intimate as much in the restaurant, Boss?'

The leader thought for a moment before answering and then said, 'He did. But I'm not buying it. I think he said that to provoke a reaction. I think Sam was kidnapped and may still be alive.'

'You think so?'

'Yeah. Why would Marmarella burn him? He's more useful to him alive.' The big man shook his head. 'No. Until we find clear evidence of Sam's death, and I have a feeling we won't, keeping Dino alive gives us a huge bargaining chip.'

'What about his phone, Boss?' queried Sash. 'There might be something on that that might give us a clue.'

The big man nodded appreciatively and then said, 'That's what I like about you, Sash. You don't say much, but when you do, it's usually something worth listening to. Good thinking. Frankie, pass me Dino's phone.'

Frankie reached into his jacket, but then looked confused as his hands rummaged through his pockets. His searching became more frantic.

'What the fuck?' All eyes focused on him as he patted and again checked each pocket, but his hands emerged empty. 'Where the hell has that gone?'

The leader turned to him. 'In the restaurant, I did pass it to you, didn't I?'

'Yeah, you did,' replied Frankie as he continued to check his pockets. 'I put it here inside my left jacket pocket.'

'What about that fight?' commented Sash. 'That skirmish you had with Marmarella.'

'Fuck me, yeah,' remarked Johnny. 'That'll be it. I bet you it fell outta your pocket then.'

The leader's face hung heavy. 'For fuck's sake!' he groaned. 'If ever Marmarella's found that in the restaurant.'

Johnny gestured to the others. 'He'll know for sure we got it from his son!'

'Ha! No shit,' mumbled Fingers. 'You worked that out all by yourself? Guys... he worked that out all by himself. Jeez, you must have a fuckin' college degree in the bleedin' obvious, Johnny.'

'Ah, shut up you!'

'HEY! This is no laughing matter,' said the big man. 'This is some serious shit. If Marmarella found Dino's phone in the restaurant, he'll know we're involved. He might look it, but he's not that fuckin' stupid.'

'I disagree. He does look it, and he *is* that fuckin' stupid,' added Frankie. 'Even more reason for us to just finish Dino off and bury the fuckin' body.'

'No! If there's a chance Sam's alive, we ain't doin' that. Nobody's died. So there ain't any real damage done yet... is there?'

'No,' agreed Sash. 'Apart from Dino being banged up.'

'Yeah, that's right!' The leader pointed to each of them individually as he hammered home his directive. 'So, our priority is simple. *We* make sure Dino pulls through.'

With all the talk of food, murder, death and decomposing bodies, Joey could feel pressure building within both mentally and physically and he again felt sick. He couldn't contain himself and was on the verge of vomiting. 'Sorry, but I really need to go to the toilet, Boss,' he whimpered, waiting for permission.

'OK, GO... for Christ's sake!' barked the big man. 'And whilst you're in there, why don't you stick your head down the bowl and flush some fuckin' sense into it?'

An awkward silence fell across the kitchen as Joey got up and left the room, his head hanging like a dog scolded for leaving a deposit on the floor.

'So, what do we do, Boss?' queried Frankie.

'Well,' said the big man, his eyes still fixed on where Joey had been sitting. 'First of all, we need to make sure Dino survives,' he said. 'But there's a problem with that.'

'What sort of problem?' asked Frankie. 'He looked OK to me.'

'What are you on about?' snapped the leader. 'He's fuckin' half dead. And the other half will follow if he we don't get a blood transfusion soon.'

'OK, but can't the Doc sort that out?'

'It ain't that simple. Apparently, Dino's blood's a rare type. But the Doc and I have a plan for that.'

# # #

Outside, sitting alone in the garden on a bench in the sunset, was the family physician, Dr. Lucas Roberts.

He was deep in thought. Although gathering speed beneath the cloudless evening sky, a hurricane force of doubt was beginning to overpower him. He was there under the pretence of ringing Mrs Dawson but had been staring at his phone for over ten minutes, paralysed with trepidation and foreboding; for after he had switched it back on, following his meeting with Salvatore Vitalli, he discovered he had five missed calls from someone. Someone he really didn't want to speak to—although he knew he must. His emotions were an uncomfortable cocktail of apprehension mixed with a feeling of euphoria as two things occupied his mind, fighting for priority.

The first was his blood money deal and the fact two hundred and fifty thousand dollars would soon be in his bank account. The second was that he could now finally pay off a long overdue debt—the seventy thousand dollars he secretly owed Louie Marmarella. Money that, unbeknown to the Vitalli family, had been loaned to him, and that he had used to pay off his gambling debts.

He knew he should have asked Salvatore Vitalli to help him financially, but he was embarrassed, and as his practice sometimes exposed him to the Marmarella family members, when Louie Marmarella offered to help, he did not believe accepting his offer would be an issue—as he had every intention of repaying the loan quickly. But losses from recent poker games had been considerable. Lady Luck had not smiled on him once. In fact, he felt as though he had never met her. How foolish of him to have accepted Marmarella's offer of a loan. At the time, desperation had clouded his judgement, and now he regretted his decision with every ounce of his being. The doctor stared at the phone cradled in his hands and his heart sank. It was Louie Marmarella that had repeatedly tried to call him.

In the idyllic, tranquil quiet of Salvatore Vitalli's immaculately landscaped garden, and as the day entered a glorious twilight, the doctor began listening to the messages. After the third, in which Marmarella's tone had become increasingly agitated—each message hitting a new level of annoyance, underlined by an increasing amount of expletives—the doctor was suddenly startled as the phone vibrated and rang in his hand; 50,000 volts of horror running up his arm and coursing through every fibre of his body.

His eyes widened and his jaw dropped in awe as his head sank back and his eyes rolled to the heavens. Without looking at the number, he knew who it would be. He lifted the phone to his face.

'Hi, Louie,' he said, endeavouring to maintain calm. 'How are you?'

'How am I? intoned Marmarella aggressively. 'I've been trying to get hold of you all fuckin' day. Don't you ever return a call? Five fuckin' messages I left!'

'I'm sorry,' gulped the doctor. 'I forgot to charge my phone last night. It's been off most of the day. I've only just switched it back on. I do apologise. What can I do for you, Louie? Has anybody been hurt?'

There was a pregnant pause, and the tension thickened, before a rather timid response finally broke the silence. 'My boy is missing,' growled Marmarella.

The doctor was taken aback. 'Oh, good grief, Mr Marmarella... missing? What do you mean, missing? Eh, who's missing... err, who... who?'

'What are you... a fuckin' owl?'

'Who is missing... Dino?'

'Of course, Dino. He's the only one I got. I don't suppose you've seen him, or heard from him, have you?'

'Who... Dino?'

'Yeah, Dino!'

'Eh, Dino?'

'Yeah... DINO! What's the hell's the matter with you?'

'Eh... no, Mr. Marmarella, I'm sorry, I haven't heard from him.' The doctor swallowed hard. Technically, he wasn't lying. He had not heard from Dino, because Dino was incommunicado.

'OK, then,' said Marmarella. 'That's all I wanted to know. I think the Vitalli's have something to do with this. In fact, I'm fuckin' sure they have.

If you hear anything from those bastards, you'll let me know, won't you, Doc?'

Louie Marmarella was no fool. He knew all about the doctor's close relationship with the Vitalli family and relished using the doctor's fallibility to drive a wedge through it.

'Of course, I'll let you know, Mr. Marmarella,' said the doctor.

There was a further awkward moment of silence before a question materialised. 'And what are you doin' about that money you owe me?' growled Marmarella.

'Eh, good news. I'll be able to settle what I owe you later tonight.'

'Yeah, that's long overdue,' said Marmarella. 'And with the interest, it ain't so little, is it?'

'The interest?' stammered the doctor. 'How... how much interest?'

Marmarella paused and then said, 'We agreed a thousand a day. So, what's it been, twenty days? That makes an extra thirty thousand, don't it?'

'Err... twenty thousand,' corrected the doctor.

'Are you fuckin' arguing with me?'

'No, sir.'

'Good. Thirty it is then. That makes a nice round one hundred thousand. I look forward to receiving it. Wire it to me later.'

'Eh... right,' said the doctor.

'Good. Glad to hear your luck has changed. And next time I call, Doc... answer your fuckin' phone!'

The call ended abruptly.

'Damn it!' mouthed the doctor. He rarely cursed, but on this occasion, couldn't help himself. He closed his eyes and grimaced. 'You bloody fool!' he raged quietly to himself.

Then, a weak voice from behind said, 'What's the matter, Doc?'

The doctor sprang to his feet and span round. It was Joey Vitalli, who had wandered outside to get some fresh air and was standing directly behind him.

CHRIST! thought the doctor. How long had he been there?

And how much had he heard?

Chapter 7: The Eighth Act of Mercy

The wretched smell of nervous bodily sweat mixed with the eye watering sting of cigarette smoke can be oppressive around a high-stake poker table at two in the morning. Beneath the dim lights, after many had been eliminated, the shifty eyes of those players remaining in the game continued to study every nuance of one another's behaviour, searching for clues, a "Tell", or anything to determine what cards an opponent might be holding, or whether a bluff was being played; that is, if the eyes can be seen at all, for many players try to conceal what their eyes might betray behind sunglasses, or beneath headwear, until either they fold their hand or the winner of that particular round of play is decided.

It is then, after intense hours of play and during the cold-hearted finality of the game when the once friendly banter can often yield to more visceral verbal baiting, accompanied by homicidal looks of loathing as victory in the winner-takes-all game draws near.

For those final few players remaining at the table, they still have a chance, albeit one proportional only to the size of the stack of casino chips before them. Those with short stacks find themselves in a desperate situation, and further hampered by the mandatory cycle of blind bets that drain a player's resource of chips which, after all, are the oxygen of the game. For them, time is the enemy, and they know only too well that pending being dealt a miracle hand, they are doomed. All too quickly, their stacks reduce in size, and eventually they are forced to either bluff or go "all-in" with a weak hand that otherwise would never be played and would end in the "muck"—the aptly named pile where weak cards are discarded.

Inevitably, those clinging on with short stacks get called out, only to crash out, having lost their stake, their prestige, their standing, everything. And their stake can be considerable; many tens of thousands at some games. But having lost, there is only one thing left for a stone-cold loser; the walk of shame as they rise from the poker table, gather their scant belongings and, like a jilted lover, limp forlornly out into the cold morning air, defeated, crushed and broken.

The remaining players watch in silence, all thinking the same thought, '...there but for the grace of the Poker Gods go I.'

Eventually, just two players will remain sitting at the table with their Manhattan skyline of stacked columns of casino chips, hoping this time the Gods will smile favourably upon them as they go head-to-head to determine the winner of the huge cash prize. But this is the lure of poker and of blackjack, and of gambling generally. The hope and belief that next time, you will prevail—that you *can* win. That is, if you can afford the stake to buy a seat at the next big game—and you know you must. Because next time you may unknowingly have walked in with Lady Luck on your arm, destined to leave with a small fortune—that, and the kudos that comes with beating the best players. And it is that very notion that is so irresistibly delicious to habitual gamblers—gamblers like Doctor Lucas Roberts.

Success is the culprit and always will be—the all too infrequent taste of winning; that is the drug! And once savoured, its sweetness is never forgotten. Winning is the heroin of the gambling world. Winning, and the superlative high that comes with it, is as attractive to a gambler as crystal to a crack-head. And like an addict, endeavouring to replicate the sheer ecstasy of that first narcotic fix, the sweet taste of glorious triumph will always guarantee that a high stakes card player will return to the tables, much the same as a heroin addict will always reach for that grubby syringe, a gambler will always find a way to raise money to play again, even when they have no money. And there lies the dichotomy. For then, looming in the dark waters of financial destitution await the loan sharks—those carnivores of misery. They will always be there, ready to emerge from the shadows and gorge on the weak and the financially crippled.

And for the doctor, it was no different. Even though he was a professional man with sound financial acumen, he too had fallen into that particular bear trap. Over recent weeks, a streak of bad beats and poor luck had wiped him out. And unforgivably, he had allowed emotion to creep into his game and cloud his judgement. He had lost tens of thousands and had vowed to give up gambling and tried to stay away. But he couldn't. Like an alcoholic drawn to a liquor store, he would often be seen at the local casinos watching the rolling dice at the craps tables or the ivorine white ball, known as a "pill", revolve and bounce around the spinning wheel of the roulette. Even when he had no chips with which to play, he felt compelled to be there. He *needed* to be there. Like a pilot fish, attached to a shark, he needed at least hoover the essence of success and savour the adrenaline rush of the winners, and, of course, witness the empty heartache of the losers. In a strange way, he took solace from both. But after a week or so of watching, and when watching became intolerable, he too would arrive at the shady door of the Shylocks—the loan sharks.

A few days before Joey shot Dino Marmarella, Doctor Roberts found himself at the business end of a private high-stakes poker tournament. The doctor enjoyed the taste of illicit underground cash games—knocking on heavy doors in seedy backstreet locations where shifty eyes and secret codes pave the way to a chance of winning a fortune was, for him, the fuel that stoked the flames of excitement—it was where he felt most alive.

On that occasion, thirty players had enrolled in the unlicensed winner-takes-all tournament, which began with three tables of ten players, each player receiving an identical stack of casino chips with which to play. The stake that each player had to pay to enter the tournament was forty thousand dollars, and the prize for winning—a cool $1 million. That is, after the organizers had taken a hefty 17% rake—their commission for hosting the game.

The doctor had a slow start and was soon down $3000 worth of chips, but recovered during the first three hours when the three tables were reduced to two after ten players lost all their chips and were eliminated—largely as a result of rash "all-in" bets with weak hands. Three hours later, the second table was closed when a further ten players crashed out of the tournament.

After playing carefully, the doctor entered the eighth hour of play and found himself in a heads-up confrontation on the final table with just one other player remaining—all the others had been eliminated, but some hung around the ever-growing crowd of spectators to see who would prevail.

Over the years, the doctor had clinched victories in several minor tournaments, some legitimate, some not. Those events offered modest prize pools, to be distributed among the top five finishers based on their final rankings, with the winner naturally receiving the lion's share. However, this was the doctor's first brush with a truly monumental, life-altering cash prize in the brutal winner-take-all format. In this high-stakes game, second place held no value—it was all or nothing. But he had played well, and all that stood between him and a fortune was the man sitting in the shadows opposite. A ruthless, well known Irish poker player who had won numerous international tournaments and was known in poker circles as "The Barracuda", his real name being Michael O'Malley.

The youngest of six children, O'Malley grew up in a working-class family in Dublin, Ireland, where gambling was almost part of the school curriculum. He started playing cards almost before he learned to read and write, learning the nuances of the game from his grandfather, a former bookie and greyhound dog racer. During his adolescence, O'Malley had numerous brushes with the law, but by his late teens, he had already made a name for himself in local games in the backstreet pubs of Dublin. He had the uncanny ability to interpret the gaunt faces and body language of his opponents, seemingly knowing when and when not to gamble or bluff—his aggressive style of play, and his incessant talkative demeanour, earning him his infamous nickname.

On his twenty-first birthday, O'Malley made a decision that would change his life. He left Dublin with nothing more than a tatty old suitcase and the skills he had honed as a poker player. He boarded a plane and headed for the bright lights of Las Vegas, the original home of high-stakes poker. His notoriety for aggressive play grew quickly, his barracuda-like petulant snarl earning him a reputation for unnerving his opponents even before the cards were dealt. The doctor had watched him play many times, but this was the first time he had ever played against him, and he had to admit, he *was* intimidated.

'Why ya lookin' at me, ya fucka,' said O'Malley in his broad Irish lilt as they sat to resume their game. 'You'll not get a read from my face. Whereas you... you remind me of someone who'd shit on the table to keep the flies off the sugar, ya gobshite!'

Charming! thought the doctor. Don't let him get to you.

O'Malley's most notorious moment came during the World Series of Poker in 1988, when he won a $700,000 pot with nothing but a pair of twos against his opponents' two Jacks. Once the 5-card flop was revealed, he found a third two on the river card, the final card, which gave him his victory. There was only a five percent chance of hitting *that* card, but that audacious stroke of good fortune cemented his status as a respected player and one of whom one should be wary. However, that was short-lived. O'Malley's career had not been without controversy. He had been accused of cheating multiple times, though nothing was ever proved. There were whispers about his connections to Irish mobsters and his involvement with dealers in rigged underground games—dealers with an ability to set up a deck whilst shuffling the cards when in collusion with a player. Skilled dealers, using sleight of hand, can deal seconds, which means knowing the value of the top card on the deck and dealing out the second card whilst saving the first, usually an ace, for his cheating, playing partner.

Despite the rumours, or perhaps because of them, O'Malley remained one of the most feared players in high-stakes private games. Now in his late 50s, "The Barracuda" showed no sign of slowing down. He travelled the world, moving from one big game to the next, leaving a trail of empty wallets and broken spirits in his wake. To his followers, he was a poker genius. To his opponents, he was a ruthless predator. But to Michael O'Malley, that was all just part of the game.

After a thirty-minute break, and on the hour at 4 am, the heads-up game resumed, and Doctor Roberts sat down opposite O'Malley with a stack of chips roughly equal to that of his opponent. Despite his wealth, O'Malley was wearing a scruffy grey hoodie and his trademark green narrow brimmed trilby hat. Cradled around his neck was a pair of headphones, which sometimes during the tournament he would put on as if bored with the banter and the process of playing the game.

'Are ya ready to get beat then?' said O'Malley. 'Cuz, oi think oi've got the measure of ya.'

The doctor kept his eyes low. He had no intention of entering into dialogue with this man. He needed to remain focused.

The deck of cards was shuffled, and the dealer dealt each of them two cards face down. When the doctor lifted the corners of *his* cards, he saw he had the Q♠ and 4♠ —a possible flush draw if he could hit three more of the same suit, when the flop was revealed—the community cards each player could use to make a poker hand. He bet 20k and was immediately called by O'Malley, who matched his bet, after which the first three cards of the flop were dealt by the dealer and splayed out in the middle of the table: Ace♥ 4♣ 8♠.

The doctor now had a pair of 4s and a third spade *was* there, which meant his flush draw was still a possibility. He felt had to represent the ace and bet a further 20k and without hesitation was raised by O'Malley to 50k.

So, what did O'Malley have, wondered the doctor? Was O'Malley holding an ace?

They exchanged glances.

The doctor had paired his 4, but it was a weak pair. Had O'Malley paired the ace on the flop? The doctor met O'Malley's raise with 30k in chips, hoping for another 4 or a spade to be added to the flop. Both men looked to the dealer. The turn card was revealed, and it was the Ace♠.

Wonderful, thought the doctor—another spade, which meant he now had four spades. He needed five, but the flush draw *was* still on—that is, if the final river card turned out to be another spade—any spade. But now there were *two* aces on the flop. Had O'Malley just completed trip aces, he wondered? Was he holding a third ace? If another four was revealed, that would give the doctor a full-house—three fours and the two aces. But if

O'Malley was holding an ace, his ace filled full-house would be the winner. No, the doctor's best bet was for another spade to appear.

He looked across the expanse of green baize.

O'Malley's eyes were shielded by the brim of his hat. He looked up. 'So, what d'ya think oi've got then?' he said. 'Come on! Oi've an awful pain in me bollux waiting for ya to make ya mind up. But oi have to admit… oi got a good hand here.'

The doctor said nothing and kept his gaze low, refusing to be swayed by O'Malley's chatter. But was he bluffing? Perhaps O'Malley had a handful of nothing. Or was he slow-playing a strong hand? With two aces on the flop, he might have the other two aces, which would give him four aces. "Quads" — "the Nuts", the best possible hand!

No… highly unlikely, but he might have one, though. That would give him three aces! A very strong hand that would beat his pair of 4s. The nature of O'Malley's next bet might provide a clue. But now it was the doctor's move. Should he raise, check, or fold his cards?

'Come on, ya gobshite!' jibbed O'Malley. 'You'd bore a hole off a golf course. What are ya feckin' waitin' for?'

The doctor refused to be pressured by the Irishman's verbal baiting and offered no bet. and checked to O'Malley, and fully expected O'Malley to also check—but he didn't.

O'Malley looked across at him. He smiled as if knowing exactly what cards the doctor was holding and reached for his chips. After a moment of contemplation, during which O'Malley watched carefully for a reaction from the doctor, he made his mind up and pushed half his stack of chips into the middle of the table. He had raised the doctor $100,000.

The doctor tried to curb his astonishment. The slightest twitch on his face might disclose how weak his hand *was*, and O'Malley would pick up on that. Sensing blood on the table's green baize cloth, O'Malley's bold raise evoked a collective intake of breath from the partisan Irish contingent amongst the crowd of onlookers. The doctor's face remained impassive, but beneath his frozen features, a maelstrom of mental activity was taking place.

Damn it! He *must* have an ace! thought the doctor. In poker, you don't play your hand, you play your opponent. Was O'Malley playing *him?* Of course he was. Unless the river card was a 4 or a spade, all the doctor had was a weak pair of fours to align with the two aces on the flop.

Should he fold, or match O'Malley's $100,000 bet?

He tried to fathom the odds. He estimated he had about a 30% chance of hitting his flush draw on the final river card, but to find out would cost him $100,000 from his stack of casino chips, which would leave him vulnerable. Again, he could feel O'Malley's stare boring into him.

'I might as well go home and firkin' come back tomorrow,' said O'Malley. 'Perhaps by then you'd a made ya mind up!'

The doctor showed no reaction but was beginning to believe that O'Malley was holding an ace, and with the odds against him of making his flush, he reluctantly folded his hand and tossed his weak pair of 4s into the muck.

The pot of chips was promptly scooped up by O'Malley, who smiled wickedly and then arrogantly flipped over and showed the doctor *his* two cards. They were the 7♦and the 2♣—statistically, the worst cards you could possibly be dealt by a dealer.

O'Malley leaned across the table. 'Oh... ya feckin' blitherin' eejute, ya must have taut oi had an ace, did ya?'

The doctor was horrified and felt humiliated as the baying crowd jeered.

O'Malley had had nothing—not even a pair! He had beaten the doctor with garbage, a stone-cold bluff, and with the weakest possible hand. The doctor didn't need a flush draw, his pair of 4s would have won. And that was how the remainder of the session would unfold.

Thereafter, the doctor won a few hands with small pots, but he was outplayed by the Irishman, who appeared to know when and when not to bet, and when to bluff. It was cold-blooded murder, almost as if someone was watching over the doctor's shoulder and informing O'Malley of his hole cards each time they were dealt.

The final agony came when O'Malley had ninety percent of the chips, and the doctor went all-in with a pair of nines. Of course, he was called by O'Malley and they each revealed their cards and waited for the flop to determine their fate. O'Malley had A♣10♦versus the doctor's pair of nines.

It was a coin toss. The chances of winning before the flop were roughly even, but fortune favoured O'Malley, who paired his 10♦ on the fourth "turn" card with the 10♥.

Now the doctor could only win with a nine on the final "river" card, which, when revealed, turned out to be a queen—a cruel queen, her face fixed with a Mona Lisa smile staring up at him.

It might just as well have been a joker card, thought the dispirited doctor, as cheers rang out around the room.

O'Malley had won one million dollars, and the doctor had had it snatched from right under his nose. And, to add insult to injury, he had also lost his $40,000 stake—the last of the money he had borrowed from Louie Marmarella.

The doctor walked across to congratulate his opponent, but as O'Malley began to celebrate with his entourage, who were whooping and hollering, the Irishman turned to him.

'Oh, feck me. Don't take it too hard,' he said with a smirk one would associate with a Luddite. 'A fella like you was always gonna get beat. Oi always knew what ya had... see. Oi could feckin' read ya like a book.'

The doctor turned to leave, but O'Malley hadn't quite finished. 'And by the way,' he said, savouring his moment of victory, twisting the knife in the defeated man's back. 'Thanks for ya forty grand. Oi look forward to spending that. Just remember me name... Michael O'Malley.'

Taken aback by the sheer arrogance of the man, the doctor looked into the gloating face, which hung heavy with a smirk of petulance.

'Yes, I will,' he said. And with that, Doctor Lucas Roberts gathered his things and left the room, dragging his black cloud of despair out through the door behind him.

# # #

It was now nighttime a few days later, but the pain of that loss after being so close to winning one million dollars still festered like an open wound. And again, the doctor tried to shrug off the disappointment and focus his attention on his recent telephone conversation with Louie Marmarella, who was expecting the doctor to pay his $100,000 debt that evening.

He looked up at the sky. 'What a bloody mess!'

He was alone sitting on a bench in the garden at the rear of Salvatore Vitalli's house, when a voice from behind broke his train of thought. 'Doc, are you OK?'

'Huh!' The startled doctor sprang to his feet and span round. It was Joey Vitalli, standing in the moonlight behind the garden bench. The doctor had only just finished speaking with the head of the opposing crime family. The man to whom he owed so much money.

Christ! How much had Joey heard?

'Eh, hello Joey,' he stammered quickly, endeavouring to maintain his composure. 'Yes, I'm fine. Thank you for asking, and how are you?'

Joey looked puzzled. 'Was that Louie Marmarella you were talking to, Doc?' queried the young man.

'Eh, yes,' said the doctor in a matter-of-fact manner. 'He rang me to ask after his son Dino?'

'What? He has your number?'

The doctor realised he had to play this down. 'Yes, of course, as a doctor my contact number is readily available, Joey.'

'Oh, but does he know we have Dino?'

'Eh, no, no. Of course not. It was just a general query. Of course, he doesn't know we have Dino.'

'But... but why was he ringing you, Doc?'

'I know that sounds odd, Joey. But it's nothing sinister. Mr. Marmarella called me for a professional opinion, and as a doctor, I am obliged to help anyone who needs medical advice.'

'I heard you mention money, Doc. Are you sure you're OK?'

Joey was privy to the rumours of the doctor's interest in card games but was unaware of how deeply entrenched his gambling addiction was or how the Doctor had compromised his loyalty to the Vitalli family.

'Eh, yes. Of course, I'm alright, Joey,' replied the doctor. 'Why don't you go check on Dino?'

'Err... I don't need to, Doc. He's being watched over by that nurse. Eh... what's her name, Greta?'

Just then, Frankie stuck his head around the French doors leading to the kitchen. 'Hey, you two lovebirds, knock it off. Doc, have you got a minute? Boss wants a word.'

'Of course,' said the doctor, grateful for the interruption. 'Joey, we'll catch up and talk later.'

The doctor, who was still clutching his cell phone, stepped into the kitchen.

'Ah, there he is,' said Salvatore Vitalli, rising from his chair at the table where the rest of his crew were gathered. 'Doc, there's a change of plan about that thing.'

The doctor frowned, as did the others around the table who knew nothing of "that thing".

'Change of plan?'

'Yeah, follow me, I'll explain... and bring your case.'

Doctor Lucas Roberts picked up his bulky Gladstone medical bag and followed the big man through the door leading to the basement below the kitchen.

The men at the kitchen table looked at one another. 'What the fuck's all that about?' queried Johnny.

'Perhaps he's decided to finish Dino off, like I suggested,' said Frankie.

'No, I don't think so,' voiced Sash. 'His mind's already made up on that.'

Once out of earshot of the others, and as they made their way down the steps to the basement, Salvatore Vitalli said to the doctor, 'I was gonna wire you that two hundred and fifty G's we agreed on, but thinking about it, that would leave a paper trail. And I don't need that at the moment. So, it's gonna have to be cash instead.'

'Oh... I see,' said the doctor thoughtfully, who would have preferred a bank transfer of the money but knew it would be pointless to object.

Beneath the dull fluorescent lights of the basement, the leader walked over to where an old large Winchester safe stood next to the passage door leading to the bunker complex. The safe was grey, shoulder height and had an old-fashioned mechanical dial combination wheel beneath which was a lever. Before he dialled the safe's three number combination, the family boss glanced at the doctor who was watching him. 'Hey, do ya mind?' he grunted, gesturing for the doctor to avert his eyes.

'Oh, of course, sorry,' said the doctor, who, whilst still holding his cell phone, turned and respectfully looked away, and appeared to be checking something on his phone.

But he was doing much more than that.

Surreptitiously, the doctor had activated his phone's video recording function, aiming its 'selfie' camera lens behind him and towards where Salvatore Vitalli was preoccupied with opening the safe.

The big man's blunt fingers turned the safe's dial anticlockwise four revolutions until the first combination number aligned with an index marker at 12 o'clock on the dial's outer ring. He repeated the action clockwise for three passes and again anticlockwise for two passes, carefully aligning each rotation to the specific combination number, which no one else knew, and which he had long ago committed to memory.

The fourth spin of the dial involved no number, but completed the process and then he twisted the safe's handle, which retracted the locking bolts with a mechanical 'clunk', and the heavy door swung open.

On hearing the bolts unlock, the doctor turned and saw that inside the safe, amongst a few books, papers, and at what appeared to be jewellery and watch cases, were regimented lines of neatly stacked bundles of banknotes.

Each cellophane bundle was the size of a house brick and contained five wrapped packets of dollar bills secured by mustard coloured currency straps. He knew from his casino experiences that that particular colour of paper strap indicated high denominations and was used to wrap a hundred one-hundred-dollar bills; equating to ten thousand dollars in each separate wad; and it appeared there were five wads in each of the cellophane wrapped bundles.

The doctor's hungry eyes salivated at the sight, as he quietly pocketed his phone for fear of raising suspicion. Forever the opportunist—he wondered if the camera had captured the turning of the safe's combination dial. And if it had, would the video footage show the three combination numbers?

Oblivious to what the doctor had tried to do, Vitalli picked out five bundles and placed them on a bench next to the safe. He turned to the doctor. 'Each one of these contains fifty thousand bucks,' he growled. 'Do you have a problem with hard cash, Doc?'

'No, not at all,' spluttered the doctor. 'Cash is fine.'

'Good.'

The doctor glanced into the safe. There were many more identical bundles of sealed dollar bills, dozens of them. Each of the three shelves in the safe were filled with the same wrapped packets of ill-gotten gains—ill-gotten gains that perhaps only organised crime can produce.

'I'm rather surprised you have no security cameras in here,' said the doctor, looking around.

'There are no cameras anywhere within the house,' growled the leader. 'I don't trust 'em. I heard the cops can patch in and watch everything you say and do. See, they don't need to plant bugs any more, Doc. They just hack into your Wi-Fi... fuckin' bastards! And we're supposed to be the criminals? I tell ya, there are more crooks on the law enforcement side of the fence than on our side. Anyway, I had all the internal cameras taken out. There's plenty outside overseeing the perimeter of the property, but nothing indoors.'

The doctor, who was still looking at the contents of the safe as if struck by love, appeared dazed. Salvatore Vitalli picked up on his demeanour. 'What's up?' he asked.

'Eh, nothing,' stammered the doctor who, having never seen so much money in one place in his lifetime, quickly quelled his astonishment. 'I was just thinking through what I need to do tomorrow,' he added, as he opened his medical bag and reached to pick up the bundles of money from the bench.

The big man grabbed the doctor's arm and looked severely into his anxious eyes. 'Did you speak to her?' he asked pointedly, referring to Maria Dawson, his penetrating gaze unyielding. 'I'm putting a lot of trust in you, Doc.'

'Eh, yes,' said the doctor. 'Everything's arranged,' he lied, knowing anything less would be unacceptable to the crime family boss.

'What did she say?' The big man's eyes were wide with cunning expectation.

'Nothing unusual,' remarked the doctor. 'She knows the drill. We've done this so many times over the years. I explained to her that I had an urgent requirement for a pint of her blood. We agreed on a price which I inflated to make it more appealing, and we've arranged to meet tomorrow morning.'

'OK. So, where and when?'

'Eh, my surgery... at 11am.'

'Good,' smiled Vitalli. 'Make sure things go as planned. And don't you let me down, Doc.' There was the threat of menace in Vitalli's eyes, and the doctor realised that the outcome of such disappointment would be catastrophically severe for him. 'And don't forget, when it's done, I want you to arrange for me to see the body. I need to be somewhere tomorrow, but perhaps the next day.'

'Yes, her body will be in the morgue.'

'But you can arrange a visit... yes?'

The doctor hesitated. 'It will not be easy... but yes.'

Vitalli's large face moved closer. 'Because, as agreed, the remainder of your payment depends on that. Correct?'

'Of course.'

The broad hand of the big man released the doctor's arm, and he closed and locked the safe's door and span the combination dial to neutralise it.

'But I do need to ask a favour of you, Mr. Vitalli, if I may,' said the doctor.

The leader turned and waited; his hooded eyelids heavy with the stress of the day. 'What?'

'I wonder if I might spend the night here tonight. Your house is much closer to my surgery than mine. I need an early start tomorrow, and I would also like to monitor Dino overnight, in case his condition deteriorates.'

'OK,' agreed the leader. 'Good idea. We're not that dissimilar, are we, Doc... you and I? Like you, I'm used to spilling blood too, but I'm not used to bagging it once it's spilled... if you know what I mean.'

The doctor knew exactly what he meant and nodded awkwardly at the not so veiled threat. He turned his head away and grimaced as he finished placing the five bundles of cash into his bag. 'Eh... shall I take one of the rooms in the bunker complex?' he asked.

'No, no... stay in the house,' offered the big man. 'No one's ever slept down there, so there's bound to be damp on those beds. We got plenty spare rooms upstairs. You can take the Caravaggio Room.'

The doctor frowned—he had never stayed overnight at the house before. 'The Caravaggio Room?'

'Yes. When we renovated the house, we named each of the guest rooms after famous Italian artists.'

'Ah, I see. A homage to the old country,' nodded the doctor appreciatively. 'I didn't know that. That's a nice touch, but I could really do with being a little closer to our patient, Mr. Vitalli.' The doctor didn't fancy the idea of staying in the main house. He wanted to distance himself.

The big man looked tired and, not for the first time that day, appeared irritated. 'Look,' he announced unequivocally. 'Frankie's got that nurse looking after Dino. She's being well paid. And it looks like you've got him hooked up to every fuckin' medical alarm in the northern hemisphere. If they all go off at once, the country will probably be put on nuclear alert, and we may all get a warning from the fuckin' President that we've moved to Defcon 1.'

The doctor looked bemused. 'Eh, what do you mean, I don't understand?'

The big man frowned, and then a rare smile materialised on his face. 'It's a joke, Doc. For fuck's sake, lighten up, will ya? Ah... it's too late in the day. Doesn't matter. Anyway, take the 'Caravaggio Room', I insist. It's left at the top of the main staircase and it's the second bedroom on the left, overlooking the rear garden. I need you rested and on point tomorrow.'

'OK, that's very kind of you, sir,' said the doctor. 'Thank you. And if you don't mind, it *is* late, so I think I'll retire now.'

'Good call,' muttered the big man. 'I'm beat too. And hey, Doc! Big day tomorrow. Get a good night's rest.'

'Yes. I'll see you in the morning,' said the doctor. 'I'll be up at around seven?'

'I'll be up around nine.'

'OK, sir. Goodnight.'

Ten minutes later, Doctor Lucas Roberts lay upstairs on the large bed in the opulent Caravaggio guest room, which was tastefully decorated in neutral colours with sweeping drapes and antique art offerings being the only splash of colour on the plain walls.

One feature piece of artwork opposite the bed was one the doctor was familiar with, a full-size replica of Caravaggio's famous masterpiece, "The Seven Acts of Mercy"—the theme of which centres on the material needs of others. The seven compassionate acts depicted in the painting are—visiting the imprisoned; feeding the hungry; burying the dead; sheltering the homeless; clothing the naked; attending the sick and refreshing the thirsty.

The doctor paid little regard to the personal needs so beautifully depicted in the painting but instead lay on the bed contemplating his own personal needs. He couldn't stop thinking about the bundles of money sitting in the safe just two floors below. His own part payment of five fifty-thousand-dollar bundles lay next to him on the bed. And he opened one to confirm what he had hoped; that the wads of one-hundred-dollar bills were not new banknotes which would have sequential numbers, but used banknotes and, as such, where untraceable—they all were.

He lifted two ten-thousand-dollar wads to his face and sniffed them, rifling through them like he would a deck of cards. Although used bills, they still retained that intoxicating chemical fresh ink scent of newly printed bank notes, and he exhaled and then again breathed in the luxurious perfume of wealth.

As he lay there staring at the ceiling, a repetitive quick mental calculation cycled through his thoughts. The safe contained three shelves—five rows of fifty-thousand-dollar bundles, stacked three high and probably four deep. If that assumption was correct, he calculated that each shelf in the safe contained three million dollars—and there were *three* shelves!

'Jesus Christ!'

He sat up and swung his legs off the bed. That would equate to nine million in cold hard cash, and maybe more. Does organised crime pay? he asked himself. Damn right it does!

He looked at the Caravaggio masterpiece on the wall opposite. There should have been an eighth act of mercy depicted in the painting, he surmised; *enriching the needy.*

He pulled out his cell phone and stared at it. Had his video recording captured the movement of the safe's combination dial? And crucially, would it show the exact numbers that needed to align with the dial's index marker for the safe to open? If it did, he would be in possession of the safe's combination.

He fumbled and found the recorded video file on his phone. In an odd way, he hoped it showed nothing, in which case there would be no temptation, and the decision would be made for him. Then, he would have no option other than to proceed with the blood money plan. But... what if the video clip showed the safe's combination? What then?

He raised the phone, and with a shaky finger, pressed "play". The video playback began, and it drew every single ounce of his concentration.

The video imagery was shaky and dark. But he could clearly see Salvatore Vitalli's hand on the safe's dial. And yes, when he magnified the grainy image by spreading his finger and thumb across the phone's screen, he could just make out each of the first two turns of the dial, and the combination numbers that aligned with the index marker on the dials outer ring. The first two numbers were 13 and 25.

'Fuck me!' he said, uncharacteristically—he rarely used profanity.

He continued watching, his eyes wide as if on stalks, but then his brow knitted itself furrowed lines of concern. The third turn of the dial was slightly out of focus and partly shielded by the big man's broad hand.

'Damn it!' he hissed. He could feel his heart pounding. What was the last bloody number?

The third turn looked as though it might have aligned with the number 57 detent on the dial, but he couldn't be sure; the final combination number was hidden behind Vitalli's thumb and forefinger. He played the video again, his eyes straining to decipher the muddy sequence. He paused the video and advanced it frame by frame. Now it was a little clearer. The final number was either 55, 56 or 57. But which one?

The doctor checked his watch. It was just after 1 am. He could hear a kerfuffle of noise outside his room and then recognised the voices of Frankie, Johnny and Fingers. It appeared they were also staying over for the night but couldn't give a damn who they disturbed whilst making their way to their own bedrooms.

'*I'm trying to get some sleep in here... shut the fuck up!*' bellowed a faint voice from a bedroom somewhere along the corridor. It was the voice of Salvatore Vitalli.

The doctor smiled to himself. Amidst the hubbub of thoughts running rampant through his head, it provided a moment of light relief, and he lay back on his bed.

The noise in his head returned as he wondered where Sash and Joey were. And Joey? What was he to do about Joey? The kid was a liability. And if ever he informed Salvatore Vitalli that he had overheard him speaking with Louie Marmarella, perish the thought of the consequences.

But nine million dollars, just sitting there—it was probably money waiting to be laundered, surmised the doctor. But what the hell was he thinking? He had two hundred and fifty thousand dollars right now, and right there next to him. And he had agreed to a deal for one million. But that would involve him faking the murder of Mrs Dawson, and all the unpalatable problems that would entail. And Mr Vitalli had insisted on seeing her dead body—that was certainly a fly in the ointment. And it seemed his seven hundred- and fifty-thousand-dollar final payment might depend on that. But how could he overcome a physical inspection of Mrs Dawson's dead body—when there was no body? How was he to achieve that?

He closed his eyes and exhaled a heavy sigh of breath.

Yes—he could delay such a visit for a few days and try to put Vitalli off the idea. He could forge a death certificate and show him that. But if Vitalli still insisted on seeing her body, then he would have no choice. He would have to utilise an emaciated corpse in the morgue—a cadaver with similar features to Mrs Dawson and pass it off as if it were her.

The doctor's head dropped to his chest in despair and again he emitted a heavy sigh. How could he do that? Resemblance would be the obvious issue. He cycled through his wheel of logic. With his extensive medical knowledge, perhaps he could dazzle Vitalli with science. But how?

Start at the beginning, and work the problem, he urged himself.

He began. Salvatore Vitalli had not seen the woman for over two years—FACT. And when he last saw her at Layzee Dawson's trial, in the courtroom she appeared gaunt and malnourished—FACT. As time goes by, people inevitably transform, and in death, their once familiar facial features sink and contort—FACT again.

So, he would simply describe the technicalities of how the body's altered appearance was as a result of the embalming process—which he would say he had authorised to conceal the so-called 'murder'.

During embalming, the body's blood is replaced with formaldehyde-based chemicals; methanol, sodium nitrate, glycerin and colouring agents.

Yes, that explanation would fit the crime perfectly, thought the doctor. And it would make sense to Vitalli. He could further explain that any lack of resemblance to the woman Vitalli once knew was simply as a result of that process. But how could he affect a facial likeness?

He thought for a moment.

Over the years, he had witnessed many mortuary cosmetologists—he had seen them apply morticians wax, camouflage cover cremes, and blemish concealers to great effect. With a fair wind and following seas, it shouldn't be too challenging for him to replicate that process. And with a perfectly styled wig, accompanied by meticulously applied makeup, that should suffice—and the forged death certificate should seal the deal.

The more he thought about it, the less of a problem it appeared to be. Thank God Vitalli had to leave for a meeting in Chicago. At least that would buy him a day or two. But then another concern etched itself across the doctor's every growing list of immoral turpitude.

'Bugger and damnation!' he grimaced, as he realised that as Vitalli had paid him in cash, he would now need to personally visit Louie Marmarella to pay back his one-hundred-thousand-dollar debt. Earlier, he had informed Marmarella that he would wire him the money that same day, and now he was overdue.

'Damn it!' he mouthed—another complication. He quickly turned off his cell phone. The last thing he needed was a ranting Louie Marmarella, berating him at one in the morning. But nine million dollars, sitting in the house, just two floors below.

For the love of God! If he could just find a way to take it all, he would be set for life. But could he? Should he? He had been waiting for such an opportunity for two years.

Owing to his doubt over the final combination number, he realised three attempts might be required to open the damn safe, but that was no real issue, was it? Time was on his side. He had all night. If luck was with him, it might even open on the first attempt. But could he get away with stealing so much money?

Christ! If he did, he would be hunted for the rest of his days. But with nine million, he could go anywhere, be anyone. But how would he get it all out of the house? Five bundles were manageable in his medical bag, but if his calculations were right, each shelf might contain 60 bundles—180 in total. But if he took it all, what if the leader had recent cause to again open the safe? Once he saw the money had all gone, all hell would break loose.

The doctor realised he would need to buy some time to get away. But how could he do that?

It was then when a lightbulb of an idea materialised amongst the fog of doubt in the doctor's conniving brain. What if he didn't take it all, but left just a line of bundles across the leading edge of each shelf—like a false front with empty space behind? Should anyone open the safe, in the subdued lighting of the basement, a cursory glance would raise no suspicion. The contents would appear untouched.

Such a deception might buy him a few precious hours, maybe even a day or two, or perhaps a week. That could be crucial. Yes, he would lose 45 bundles in creating the deception, but 135 plus the five he already had still amounted to just over seven million dollars.

Suddenly he realised he was planning to do this, and momentarily the doctor felt fear mixed with excitement—so often a deadly cocktail when combined.

But if he *could* do it, not only would he avoid faking a murder, he would also have no need to tangle with Louie Marmarella. He would just simply disappear into the lap of wealth and luxury. And he would particularly look forward to spending Marmarella's one hundred thousand dollars.

He buried his face in this hands and gritted his teeth.

Oh, for the love of God—what should he do?

Chapter 8: Getting Served

I t was mid-morning in New York, and two days after the disappearance of his son, Dino, when Louie Marmarella found himself standing in one of his black marbled bathrooms; his recently acquired luxury penthouse apartment had five.

He had for the past hour been busy entertaining a guest, but found it necessary to freshen his appearance. He was dressed casually in a white sea island cotton shirt, a pair of black Luca Feloni chinos, and was wearing his usual Giuseppe Zanotti patent leather shoes. His eyes rose from the washbasin and met their reflection in the large backlit wall mirror as he continued to wash his guest's blood from his hands—blood which spiralled around the basin, forming a red vortex before disappearing.

His swank New York penthouse apartment was situated in central Manhattan and occupied the entire top two floors of an exclusive fifty-four storey residential building. Marmarella's principal residence was a waterfront mansion on Marco Island south of Naples in Florida and was purchased as a result of his Caribbean-based drug links with Puerto Rico. But for his New York business purposes, Marmarella needed a suitable New York base, and so had agreed a standing arrangement with an American billionaire who owned many similar apartments throughout Manhattan.

Today happened to be the first anniversary of the death of the middle-aged billionaire, who tragically met his demise under peculiar circumstances whilst on a skiing vacation in Aspen, Colorado.

The man was an average skier at best, and it was deemed odd that he would even consider tackling such a difficult black run alone and so early in the morning in the notorious Hanging Valley Headwall area of the Aspen Snowmass. What made it more peculiar was that the ski lifts had not yet opened on the day of the tragedy, so how he got up there to attempt the run was a mystery. If via a Skidoo, then its tracks had long since disappeared beneath falling snow, rendering the solution to the conundrum unresolved.

The ski run was steep and narrow, with hundreds of aspen trees along its length. It is said that the largest living organism by area on planet Earth is a group of aspen trees called a 'stand', each tree a replicate of its neighbours and connected under the soil by their roots. Apparently, it was one such replicate tree that got in the way of the billionaire as he was undertaking his steep descent of the mountain. It was reported he died instantly his head impacted the tree. Although, there were some that suspected that the only piece of wood involved with his fatal head trauma on that tragic day, had nothing to do with a tree but was more likely the result of someone wielding a baseball bat within close proximity of his head.

For him not to be wearing protective headgear on the ski slopes, and the impact injury being on the back of his head, when, in all probability, he would have been moving forward, suggested a significant whiff of foul play. There was further intimation that he could have been murdered, and then his body placed there via a helicopter, which are often used to drop explosive charges to free avalanche threats each morning. A theory which gathered credence when it was later discovered that the billionaire had altered his Last Will and Testament one week before the tragic accident, scandalously betrothing his luxury Manhattan duplex apartment to one, Louie Marmarella.

In the days that followed, the coroner, who initially thought the man's death was suspicious, appeared to have a sudden change of heart during his enquiry, despite the broad circumference of the tree failing to match the narrow circumference of the indentation on the back of the dead man's head. The coroner's evaluation concluded that, in all probability, the man had caught an edge on his skies and pirouetted into the tree backwards. An unlikely scenario, given the injury mismatch, but cause of death, although deemed violent and unnatural by the coroner, was declared accidental.

Had someone got to the coroner during his evaluation? The circumstances and the unexpected alteration to the man's Will, which would remain hidden until a later date, left the hypothesis open to interpretation; however, those in the loop had unwavering certainty that foul play *was* the root cause.

Such was the brazen nature of the man; a week later, Louie Marmarella attended the funeral of the billionaire and was seen to be comforting his widow and two young children. Even by his standards, a heinous act of stagecraft, a vulture praying on the weak during their deepest hour of grief. He hardly knew the woman and despite his attempts at compassion; for he knew what was coming—it would be a relationship that would fracture irreversibly during the following few days, when the contents of the man's Will were disclosed, and the keys to the luxury apartment handed to the crime family Don.

What made the billionaire change his Will was shrouded with mystery. Although it was alleged the billionaire company chairman had used Marmarella's influence to permanently remove an associate from his board of directors who was about to go public with evidence of significant financial fraud.

The director, who was a hobbyist flyer, soon met with a fatal accident when the plane he was flying, his Cessna Skyhawk, appeared to suffer a system component failure shortly after take-off from New York's Jamestown airport. Engulfed in flames, the plane crashed in a lightly wooded area close to a field in western New York, killing the Managing Director. There was very little of the plane left, only parts. And very little of the Managing Director, too. Following the subsequent investigation into the crash, the NTSB, the National Transportation Safety Board, decided that, although inconclusive, the probable cause was a defective part in the fuel system.

The billionaire was then blackmailed by Marmarella when he later revealed the existence of a secret video recording, showing the billionaire discussing the contract kill with himself and some shady individual purporting to be an aircraft mechanic.

There was a shortened version of the video, which was carefully edited, removing sections featuring Marmarella, but revealing the billionaire discussing his murderous intentions with the maintenance man. Soon after, the changes to the billionaire's Will were made and filed with Marmarella's law firm, after which the maintenance man disappeared without trace.

It was unsurprising that other law firms throughout New York all turned down what would have been a lucrative case to overturn the contents of the Will when they discovered who they would be fighting. Especially when a partner of the first firm approached by the man's disgruntled widow also disappeared, only to reappear a few days later dead on the road below the balcony of his thirty-two-story condo with a pair of small antique kitchen scales lying alongside his body; the scales representing a legal symbol of justice, and a clear warning aimed at any other law firms who might consider taking the case. Again, the coroner came to Louie Marmarella's aid—*accidental death* was pronounced.

Following up on the story, a reporter working for the New York Post somewhat cynically wrote that for the man's death not to have been attributed to murder was a flagrant miscarriage of justice. If not murder, then it meant the man must have slipped and fell out of his kitchen window, perhaps whilst weighing flour to bake a cake, taking the scales with him.

Louie Marmarella finished preening his thin moustache and eyed the image, looking back at him in the bathroom mirror of his recently acquired apartment as a scowl of frustration developed across his leathery face.

He had been angry all morning, still was, and was waiting to continue his questioning of his guest, who happened to be Frankie Vitalli's wife, Debbie Vitalli, the former exotic dancer from Vegas whom he had savagely stripped naked upon her arrival at his apartment before beating her, and who had now been locked in the searing heat of his home sauna for over twenty minutes.

The sauna was on the lower of the apartment's two floors, the upper floor of which, with its arc of floor-to-ceiling glass walls dedicated to living space, luxurious reception rooms, a kitchen, which was never used, a study, and four bedrooms, all of which had their own lavish en-suite black marbled bathrooms.

Marmarella grabbed a nearby towel to dry his hands. He wiped his face and then meticulously ran a comb through his thick, black, mop of hair, neatly adjusting the grey streak that ran down its centre, which had become dishevelled during his exertions whilst 'welcoming' his guest.

His henchmen would normally administer such punishment, but Marmarella liked to keep his hand in. To anyone who knew him they would agree that accompanying the grey streak of hair on his round, blunt head was a sadistic streak, deeply entrenched within the psyche of both him, and his son, Dino, who was cut from the same cloth, both of whom appeared to take pleasure from experimenting with new techniques with which to extract information from their rival business associates and, for the matter of that, anyone who got in their way.

In the quietness of his bathroom, Marmarella could just make out the woman's banging on the wooden door of the sauna, but her cries had faded in the dry one-hundred-and-ten-degree heat, and now the beating of the door had also ceased. He wondered how long she would last before her heart gave out.

An hour, maybe?

He didn't know. Perhaps that might be an experiment for another day. He didn't want her to die just yet; he was desperate for information. But he knew that in situations of extreme heat, when warm blood reaches the skin of the human body, pores expand to secrete perspiration by way of eccrine sweat glands. He was fascinated with the physiology of the human body and was well read on the subject. Furthermore, he also knew that to reap the cooling effect of sweat, the salty liquid must evaporate from the skin. Under normal circumstances, the beads of fluid vaporise, blood cools and temperature equilibrium is restored. But if sweat is unable to cool the skin, as would be the case with Mrs. Vitalli sitting in, and unable to escape the fierce heat of the sauna, then the situation would worsen, as her brain would inevitably overheat, and her central nervous system would collapse. If left too long, severe dehydration and confusion would be the result before heat-stroke and internal burning would lead to coma, and eventually her death. After which—Marmarella's eyes lit with excitement at the thought—her corpse would over time, literally cook.

He decided to leave her for another twenty minutes—perhaps then she would be willing to talk, that is, if she had enough moisture left in her mouth to utter a sound.

He hadn't asked her a single question yet. When it came to questioning someone, he liked to think outside the box. Why waste his breath asking questions at the onset of interrogation, only to hear denial after denial and lie after lie?

No, he preferred a different approach—demonstrate the violent rami-fications of non-compliance first, *then* ask the questions. That approach, although brutal, seemed to work for him every time.

He looked at his reflection in the mirror and put a question to himself. What if the intense heat rendered the whore's vocal cords inoperable? For he regarded her as nothing more than that—a whore. They might shrivel up, and she would then be incapable of speaking. That being the case, he decided, so be it. It wouldn't matter; she could write down her responses. Either way, he didn't care. He just needed to know one thing, and one thing only before she expired: the whereabouts of his son.

Marmarella left his bathroom, crossed the corridor, and stepped out from his air-conditioned lap of luxury onto his terrace, which afforded panoramic views of the Hudson River, New York Harbour, and, in the distance, the Statue of Liberty. Today, even fifty-four floors up, it was pleasantly warm outside, but nowhere near as warm as the room on the floor below. He shrugged his indifference and a thin, wry smile momentarily formed across his face at the thought of Frankie Vitalli's wife suffering the worst day of her life.

What was it hookers called the process when their pimps beat them up—getting served? Yes, that was it. She was getting served.

He basked with nefarious pleasure at having that level of control over his rival's woman. He felt powerful, a feeling he relished. When beating her, it was almost like beating her husband.

He smiled.

That lucky punch Frankie Vitalli landed on his jaw in the restaurant had already been returned with interest.

Marmarella's intention the night before had been for his two Capelli brother associates, to snatch Frankie Vitalli from his home. But when it was discovered, he was not there, and after waiting the entire night for him to return, Marmarella ordered for them to bring his wife instead. She would have to do. After all, it was from Frankie's pocket that his son's cell phone had fallen in the restaurant. So, he *had* been involved. That being the case, it was a fair assumption his wife would be privy to such knowledge and could provide him with the answers he needed. But would she?

As he looked out over the impressive Manhattan skyline, he expelled a spent lungful of frustrated breath through his nostrils. His eyes narrowed. God forbid, if ever they had hurt his boy!

The fresh air did little to curb his anger and, if anything, inflamed his resolve further. His hand inadvertently rose to the slight swelling on his face where Frankie Vitalli's fist had impacted his jaw. Well, now it was time for some payback. And as Vitalli wasn't here himself, thought Marmarella, he would vent his revenge on his whore wife!

He glanced down from the lofty perch of his terrace at the hundreds of people six hundred feet below swarming the New York city sidewalks like an army of soldier ants. He snarled his distaste at them, as if he had happened upon a cockroach, and suddenly felt the desire to squash them all with his foot.

He promptly turned, strode off and went back indoors, walking purposefully as he skipped down the spiral flight of stairs to his home spa, the wellness centre of his extensive apartment complex, which today had little regard for the wellness of anybody.

Ricco Capelli was sitting inside the locker room when his boss burst in like a whirlwind. Marmarella nodded and the Capelli twin brother smartly got to his feet and followed him through to the wet room, where the twin brother was motioned to fetch the woman.

Capelli duly unlocked the wooden door of the adjoining sauna, which released a torrid wave of blistering hot air, causing him to recoil back as if he had opened the door to a furnace. Debbie Vitalli had collapsed and was lying unresponsive on the floor of the sauna, the temperature of which had been cranked up to the maximum. She was dangerously dehydrated, panting for breath, and by the look of her glazed eyes, appeared delirious.

Capelli allowed the hot thermal draft to dissipate and then stepped in and dragged out the naked, sweat drenched woman by her feet. He looked down at the wretched body that he and his brother had violated the night before. Gone was the vivacious sex siren. She now had the appearance of a boiled lobster.

He pulled her through to the wet room, which often doubled as an interrogation room, as any bodily fluids spilled there during a session of 'questioning' could easily be washed away. He released her feet, and her legs dropped to the floor with a wet 'slop'.

Marmarella's henchman picked up a wooden bucket filled with iced cold water and threw it over the poached, pink skin of the helpless woman, who shrieked at the sudden shock of its contact and rolled herself into a ball.

'HEY! Watch my fuckin' shoes!' bellowed Marmarella as he danced his feet away from the creeping deluge of water, his voice reverberating between the marbled walls of the wet room.

Capelli nodded his apology like a mute.

Debbie Vitalli groaned, which refocused their attention, and then her contorted body uncoiled, and she slowly moved, like a slug, across the wet slime of the marble floor. She seemed to sense liquid near her mouth and lapped at the wet marble, which amused Marmarella.

'Huh, look at that,' he said. 'Thirsty, are you?'

The hapless woman raised her head; her once immaculate blonde hair now matted and saturated with sweat and clinging to her skull like a biker's crash helmet. 'What do you want?' she croaked; her dry eyes incapable of shedding a single tear as she sobbed, such was the level of her dehydration.

Ricco Capelli glanced over at his boss, who was sitting on a marble bench.

'I have two questions for you, Mrs. Vitalli,' said Marmarella matter-of-factly. 'Question one, would you like to continue living your life? Which, I might add, appears to be a life filled with excess and luxury. And question two, where is my son?' Now, those are two simple questions. I would like an answer to both, but I suggest you pay particular attention when answering the second question.'

Mrs. Vitalli again raised her head from the wet tiled floor. Above her, she could just make out a large meat hook attached to the ceiling, which bothered her. Her eyes widened, and she looked across at the man. 'I don't know what you're talking about,' she sobbed, her eyes again glancing up at the sharp metal hook hanging from the ceiling.

'Ah, no, no, no... that was not the response I was hoping for,' said Marmarella. He noticed she had seen the meat hook. 'How disappointing.'

He glanced at Ricco Capelli, who produced a hard rubber Kosh from within his suit jacket. He quickly stepped across the woman's body and raised it in readiness to strike. The poor woman emitted a hoarse scream and pulled herself into a tight, fetus position to protect her head, face, and mouth, which was still oozing blood from the beating she had endured earlier.

'STOP!' ordered Marmarella, before the twin brother struck the defenceless woman. Marmarella leaned forward. 'Mrs. Vitalli,' he said, wiping a rivulet of sweat from his furrowed brow, his eyes forming narrow slits of intent. 'This could get an awful lot worse for you,' he continued. 'My Wellness therapist here who is kindly organising your spa treatment today is a particularly skilled manicurist. Although, when attending to the nails of his clients, I think he tends to be a little over exuberant, sometimes taking off a little more nail than he should, if you understand what I am saying. Just my view, of course, but I have noticed he sometimes goes beyond the cuticle on occasions... if you get my drift.'

Marmarella paused for effect, allowing the not so veiled threat to register with the poor woman. 'So,' he said, licking the sweat from his lips. 'Before we get to that particular part of your treatment program, which would then be followed by *that*,' he pointed to the meat hook. 'I strongly suggest you try answering those two simple questions again. Would you like for me to repeat them?'

Mrs. Vitalli tried to focus as Marmarella's eyes bored into her, as if invading the very soul of her being. There was something about his eyes;

they could feign friendliness, but then, in the very next second, they were empty, black, and soulless, like the dead eyes of a shark. They offered not a single ounce of empathy even when he smiled that sickly smile, and she knew that trying to appeal to the compassionate side of this brute would be useless, as, for him, compassion had never been borne into existence.

She felt tired. Resigned almost to her fate. Exhaustion had replaced fear, and she closed her eyelids. Of course, she wanted to live, but such was her state of mind, she would now gladly accept the blessed release of death if it came painlessly. She knew nothing of this man's son, and nothing of him, whoever he was.

How had this happened?

She thought back to the horror of the distressing night before when she had been horrifically abused and then raped by the two twin brothers, whom afterwards bound and gagged her.

They had waited a couple of hours and, upon realising her husband was not coming home, trashed her house. Then, after a violent skirmish that occurred when Mrs Vitalli needed to use the bathroom, they injected her with something, wrapped her in her dressing gown, covered her head and face with a hood, and bundled her into the trunk of a car. That was when she passed out, and now here she was. She realised she had no idea where she was, which was terrifying. She thought wrongly that it was some kind of spa centre. At first, she thought she had been kidnapped, perhaps for a ransom. But the past hour confirmed money was not the motive. Without saying a word, this man had beaten her, stripped her naked and had her flung into this hellhole and had said nothing about demanding a ransom. So, blackmail appeared not to be on his agenda. But who was he, and why her? She didn't know him—she had never seen him before in her life, but assumed now that the man must somehow be linked with her husband's activities, whatever *they* were.

What the hell had Frankie been up to? And what was that about this man's missing son? She was never told much, rarely informed of any of the family's business, and preferred it that way.

'HEY!' snapped the man.

Through blurred vision, she looked up at the face speaking to her. His expression had slid to a new level of morose anger, and there was no doubt whatsoever in her mind that this individual was capable of dealing death and thereafter sleep as soundly as a newborn.

'I am usually a patient man,' said Marmarella. 'But I am getting a little... PISSED OFF!'

Mrs Vitalli shuddered at the final two words, which were spat like a snake ejecting venom. Then, he appeared to quench his anger, and spoke softly again in a refrained, pathetic tone, as if speaking to a child.

'Do you know who I am?' he asked, his mouth remaining open, his face nodding slowly as if, like a teacher to a young pupil, encouraging her to reply.

'No,' she whimpered. 'I don't know who you are. And I don't want to know. I don't know who your son is either... or where he is. I just want to go home. If you let me go, I'll say nothing of this... I promise.'

'BULLSHIT!' raged Marmarella through grinding teeth. 'You seriously expect me to believe your husband doesn't discuss such things with you?'

'He doesn't.'

Again, as if a switch had been thrown, the refrained tone continued. 'My name is Louie Marmarella,' he said softly. 'Have you heard of such a man?'

Oh, my God! Of course, thought Mrs. Vitalli, as she tried to suppress the look of surprise from her battered face. This was now beginning to make some sense. Of course, she had heard of him. She knew the name, knew he was associated with a rival family, but up until that moment, she had no idea what he looked like. 'No,' she lied. 'I don't know who that is.'

'Huh... you have not heard of me?'

'No.'

The short, squat, heavy man sat back on the marble bench as if personally offended. 'I find that interesting,' he said. 'As my men found certain items at your house, that would suggest otherwise.'

Mrs. Vitalli frowned. What things? He was lying.

'Well, that doesn't matter for now,' he continued. 'Are you going to answer my questions, Mrs. Vitalli?'

'Yes, of course I want to live,' she sobbed.

'Good. That's the correct answer to the first question. Now the second. Tell me, where is my son?'

Now she knew who this man was—she knew that the son to whom he was referring was Dino Marmarella—his only son. She had heard Frankie sometimes speak of him, always with distaste. He was a young thug, a privileged, despicable man. She had heard stories of robbery, rape and, worse, involving the young mobster, who seemed untouchable, residing within the shadow of his father's reputation. Was Frankie responsible for his disappearance? She didn't know. But of course, now she knew why she was there. As Marmarella couldn't get to Frankie, *she* was the substitute. But she knew nothing of his son's whereabouts, or if her family had him. And if they had, good! She felt steely resolve course through her veins.

Fuck Marmarella and his cohorts! Oh, how she longed to spit those words in this man's face. But for now, she needed somehow to survive this ordeal. But how?

'Where is he?' growled Marmarella.

She looked up into the eyes of the man. 'I'm sorry. I don't know,' she said simply, dreading the repercussions of those words. She would not have to wait long.

Fuming, Marmarella could not contain himself any longer.

He exploded to his feet.

'LYING BITCH!' he raged. He stepped across the wet marble floor, pushed Capelli aside, grabbed the woman by her greasy hair and lashed the back of his hand across her face, which opened the wound to her mouth and spattered a stream of blood across the wet marble walls. But he wasn't finished yet. He reached down and grabbed her hair again, lifting her head, and struck her a second time, raging as he did so.

Her naked body fell back, cracking her head against the floor—and that was all that was required to render the poor, naked woman unconscious, as she slid limply to the floor like an oily, wet, slaughtered seal.

'DAMN IT!' snarled Marmarella. 'Look at my fuckin' shoes!' He snatched a handkerchief from his pocket, stooped and wiped away the droplets of water from his precious patent leather loafers.

Almost as an afterthought, he leaned over the woman and checked for a pulse. It was still there, barely. 'Get her out of here!' he snarled. 'Take her to the dockyard.'

Ricco Capelli hesitated. 'You mean?' he gestured a cutting action with his finger his across his throat.

'No, no... not yet,' said Marmarella. 'Perhaps she doesn't know anything. But let your brother spend some time with her. He has a persuasive way with women. But keep her alive for now. Let him get to work on this bitch. See if he can get anything out of her.'

'And if he can't?'

'Then lock her up, but keep her isolated. When I find Dino, and if it transpires that the Vitalli's *are* involved in his disappearance, which we know they are, then you can take her to the slaughterhouse. You know what to do. But keep their heads. One of our Russian friends likes to keep them as a souvenir. Grimy bastard! But there again...' A wicked smile formed across Marmarella's face. 'Someone needs to be taught a lesson. I might just forward them on later. Two heads for the head of the Vitalli family. Ha, ha...'

Chapter 9: A Matter of Life or Death

Doctor Lucas Roberts was still lying on the bed in the Caravaggio guest room of the large Vitalli family home. He had been gazing at the painting on the wall, but seeing nothing for what seemed like hours, but in reality was only a few minutes.

The replica painting of Caravaggio's masterpiece was of museum quality and a fine reproduction of the original which resides as the altarpiece in a church famous for its artworks, and for which it was commissioned, Pio Monte della Misericordia, situated in the historical centre of Naples in southern Italy. But all the doctor could really envisage, as he stared blindly at the painting, was a large safe filled with a fortune in one-hundred-dollar banknotes.

Somewhere in the sprawling house, the faint sound of an old grandfather clock chimed half past the hour somewhere, but did little to mask the bagpipe drone of someone snoring in one of the other bedrooms along from where he lay. Fingers, decided the doctor—that would be Fingers. His sleep no doubt induced by a belly full of food, half a bottle of whisky and whatever else he had been drinking during the day.

It was one thirty in the morning. The clock's chimes seemed to break the doctor's trance, and he rose from the bed. Resolutely, he grabbed his medical bag containing the five fifty-thousand-dollar bundles, left his room, and crept quietly downstairs and into the kitchen.

There was nobody about, and even if there was, he had done nothing wrong yet; he was just a concerned doctor on his way to check his patient in the bunker complex. But he had made a decision—a life-changing decision. A decision that would not only affect *his* life but the lives of two others.

For one of the people concerned, it would mean they would, for now, be spared, but for the other, it meant their future was less certain.

He silently descended the stairs into the basement and stood before the tall grey safe. He raised a hand to his face and pondered for a moment. The moment extended to two or three minutes as he mentally rehearsed his intentions. But where had he parked his car?

Yes—he remembered. His Ford Expedition SUV was parked at the side of the house, close to the kitchen's French doors. With two rows of seats collapsed and over a hundred cubic feet of space available, there would be ample room to transport the money. He estimated he would need about a third of that space and the car's rear privacy glass would hide the vehicle's contents. And he had reversed the car in, as he always did when parking any vehicle. That would make loading the car easier.

Good. He didn't want to have to move it and risk waking anyone. But how long would it take to carry over a hundred and thirty bundles of cash up from the basement, out through the kitchen and into his car? Fifteen minutes—maybe twenty. And what would he use?

He recalled there being some crates of medical supplies in one of the storerooms in the bunker complex. Perhaps he could empty one and use that. He would need multiple trips, but he could just pile the money into the back of his car, conceal it, and be gone.

'Oh, God!' he mewled. This was all too real. He had in his possession two hundred and fifty thousand dollars in cash. He could leave right now with that, but seven million. Seven million just sitting there waiting for him. This was a once in a lifetime opportunity, and surely it had to be grasped.

The heavy, steel door of the passageway leading to the underground complex was open, and he decided to look in on Dino, mainly to check on the nurse and whoever else might be down there. After all, he still didn't know the whereabouts of Joey or Sash.

With his mind made up, he grabbed his bag purposely, and walked the dimly lit thoroughfare to the underground complex and entered Dino's wardroom. The monitoring machines were still beeping their signs of life for the unconscious man lying still on the bed. But there was no sign of the nurse.

He looked down at his patient, who looked pale but comfortably sedated. If he decided to steal the money and disappear, the physician realised he might still be signing the man's death certificate. Despite the leader's insistence the man should live, one of the other Vitalli's might just be rash enough to execute him—Frankie, in particular. Although there was no solid evidence, he knew Frankie still blamed the Marmarella's for the disappearance of his father's brother, Sam.

A callous thought came to the doctor's mind. 'Ah, well, Dino was just another mobster. They all usually live and die by the bullet, anyway. So why should *he* be concerned?'

The doctor left the room and headed along the cold corridor towards the main living area of the bunker complex. Sitting there was the nurse and Joey. A TV was on in the background, but the sound was turned down.

'Oh... hi, Doc,' said Joey. 'I thought I heard something. What's up? Can't you sleep? I heard you were staying over tonight.'

The nurse shuffled uncomfortably on the sofa, acknowledged the doctor, and got up to leave. The doctor fired her a look of disgust. 'No, Joey. I'm just checking on our patient.' He was annoyed. 'You should be in there,' he said to the nurse. 'Are there any issues?'

'No, he seems OK,' said the nurse.

Yes, as if you would know otherwise, thought the doctor sardonically. 'You're being paid to sit with him,' he snarled as she hurriedly left the room. 'Now please, stay in there until you hear from me.'

Joey grimaced and also rose from the sofa. Fearing the doctor's mood, he said, 'Well, that's me done. I'm off to bed. See you tomorrow, Doc... or should I say later today?' He switched off the TV and headed for the passageway to the main house.

'Are you staying over tonight, Joey?' queried the doctor.

'Yeah. I'll be in the Botticelli room if you need me, Doc. It's left at the top of the main stairs, third room on the right. Eh, what room are you in, Doc?'

'I'm in the Caravaggio room,' said the doctor.

'Oh, right? Although, I don't like that room much. That dark big picture opposite the bed gives me nightmares.'

'Yes, the painting *is* dark, Joey. But intentionally dark. Caravaggio's use of light and colour to symbolically highlight each of the seven acts of mercy depicted in the painting *is* dramatic. Those good deeds almost leap from the canvas against the surrounding mass of dark tones. It's a clever technique, and I tend to see something new each time I see the work.' The doctor quickly realised his words were lost on Joey. 'I suppose it *is* an acquired taste, though,' he added. 'Is there a painting in your room, Joey?'

'There are paintings in all of them. The one in mine's something to do with Venus, but I've looked, and I can't see any planets.'

The doctor frowned. 'You're joking, right?'

'What do you mean?'

'Oh, you're not joking. Ah... right? Well... your painting will be Botticelli's *'The Birth of Venus'*, Joey,' explained the doctor. 'It's nothing to do with planets. It's about the birth of the goddess of love and fertility who emerges from the sea fully grown.'

'Oh, right,' frowned Joey, 'What... and she's just been born? That don't work, does it?'

'Figuratively, it does. She was born of the sea spray, carried by the wind, and arrived on the shores of Cyprus. She embodies the rebirth of civilisation.'

'Yeah, she's got a fit body... I'll give you that. Is that why she's naked?'

'Well, again, it's symbolic, Joey. The painting has several divine and mythological meanings.' Again, the doctor realised that his elucidation had sailed clear over the young man's head and was perhaps already through the stratosphere and well on its way to Venus.

'Johnny thinks she's got nice tits,' added Joey, with all the uneducated aplomb of a juvenile delinquent.

'Huh... yes. I guess he would,' said the doctor.

Joey shrugged. 'Oh well, bedtime. Goodnight, Doc. See you in the morning.'

'OK, Joey... goodnight. Eh, Joey, before you go, any idea where Sash is? I thought everyone was staying over tonight.'

'Eh, yeah. He went to bed early... said he was tired.'

'Oh, I never noticed. I must have been outside. OK... thanks, Joey. Get a good night's rest. See you at breakfast.'

It was all falling into place, contemplated the doctor, as Joey sauntered off, heading for the corridor towards the main house. Everyone was now accounted for, and the window of opportunity that had serenely yawned open, now gaped wide, to the point where you could almost drive a dump truck through it.

The doctor quickly made his way along the dank corridor to Dino's wardroom. He needed to reaffirm an earlier instruction. 'Ah, there you are, Greta. I'm sorry I was a little testy just then. It's been a long day... for all of us, I guess.'

The nurse smiled. 'It's OK, doctor,' she said, as she wrung out her hands nervously and wiped them down her uniform. 'It's just that it gets a little scary down here.'

'Eh, yes, I understand. But I really need you to be professional and brave and sit with our patient for a few more hours. Someone will come and relieve you later. But remember, should any of the alarms on these machines sound, you have my contact number. Just call me, irrespective of the hour.'

'Yes, sir,' said the nurse.

The doctor went to leave and then hesitated. He turned and asked, 'Eh, how did you end up being employed here, Greta?'

The cheeks on the nurse's face reddened with embarrassment. 'A few months ago, I was on duty in A & E at the hospital when Frankie came in. He offered me a job.'

'Ah, Frankie... yes. I see,' said the doctor. And without an interview, background checks or any other form of due diligence, he surmised. 'That explains everything,' he said. 'Good. I'll see you later.'

The doctor left and headed down a short corridor leading to a storage room. He couldn't help but reflect on how fortunate it was that the duty nurse that night in A & E, when Frankie had cause to visit, was an attractive and fit young woman. Had it been an ugly, overweight matron with a stern attitude on duty that night, it would have been unlikely *she* would have received an offer to join Frankie's entourage of family associates, despite no doubt having far more experience and knowledge than the young nurse he had just left.

Inside the storeroom were twenty feet of shelves on either side of the room filled with dry food provisions, water containers, and several storage bins containing medical supplies. He pulled a crate from the shelf which dislodged something.

What the hell?

It was a black pair of women's lacy knickers.

'Oh my God! Frankie,' he said with little hesitation. 'I wonder who he's had down here recently?'

He didn't have to look too far.

Using his finger and thumb like medical forceps, he placed the underwear to one side, and then emptied the contents of the crate, stacking the items back onto the shelf. He took a couple of the money bundles from his medical bag and placed them into the crate. A quick arithmetical calculation suggested that the crate would accommodate about two dozen bundles. He estimated each bundle would weigh about a pound, around half a kilo. So, six trips, he decided. Six trips from the safe, up the stairs, through the kitchen and to his car.

He frowned. But twenty-four bundles? That might be too heavy and cumbersome. He couldn't risk dropping the crate and making a noise. So, perhaps eight trips. Yes, he could manage that.

He left the storage room with the crate half-filled with medication and a blanket. He would use both to conceal the money. He followed the corridor back to the basement and once there, he quietly closed the heavy passage door. He placed the crate on the bench, emptied it, and then eyed the safe's combination dial.

So, could he do this?

He felt apprehensive.

He mentally rehearsed the actions. Left—four revolutions to number 13. Then right—three complete turns of the dial to 25. And then finally, left—two revolutions to either 55, 56 or 57.

He took a deep breath, but instead of embarking on his task, he crept up the basement stairs, listening for noise.

All was silent, apart from the muffled sound of snoring coming from up above.

On the kitchen table were the remnants of the leader's meeting with his crew. Empty glasses, cigarette ashtrays—and in the air, there was the lingering smell of the leader's cigar smoke that had been so overwhelming in his study.

The doctor crept to the kitchen's French doors and quietly opened them. Outside, it was dark, all but for a few external lamps which were trained on the house frontage and a few of the large specimen trees in the landscaped garden. His car was nearby in shadow and, using his remote key, he unlocked it but left the doors closed. If someone appeared now, there would be no issue. He would say had just finished treating his patient and had stepped out for some fresh air. He took a deep breath of that fresh air which still had the damp, earthy scent of freshly mown lawns. A thought came over him. Was he being watched, he wondered?

His eyes narrowed as he looked around for security cameras, but he couldn't see any. As far as he was aware, over the years, there had never been a major security threat at the property, and perhaps the Don's attention had waned in that regard.

He knew that through the trees at the top of the long, winding drive, there would be one of the two security guards on duty in the gatehouse. He knew both of them well—well enough to know that when he left, he would not be challenged. They had become accustomed to seeing him come and go at peculiar hours. Once again, he took a deep breath. OK, now to see if he could open the safe.

He made his way back down to the basement and stood before the steel monolith. He found himself rubbing his thumb and fingers together like a safe-cracker in and film noir movie.

He smiled. It was a nervous smile. And he could feel the jib of his chin chatter. He couldn't believe he was doing this. After all, he was a nice man—but why not?

He thought back to the recent poker tournament and the one million dollars he had come so close to winning, and the sheer arrogance of Michael O'Malley. The disappointment of that painful loss spurred him on. Especially when he envisaged the image of a light aircraft, piloted by O'Malley, towing a banner through the sky with the words '*Nice men always finish last!*' written upon it.

He grimaced. Wasn't it about time he changed that narrative?

Yes, it was!

With acid determination and shaky fingers, he gripped the combination dial, and turned it four revolutions counter-clockwise, stopping when the number 13 aligned with the twelve o'clock index marker on the outer ring. Then he reversed the motion three revolutions, stopping at 25.

OK, now for the acid test. He turned the dial left for two revolutions, stopping at 55. And then gripped and tried to turn the lever.

Nothing.

He quickly span the dial and began again. On the third revolution, he tried 57. He grasped the lever, but again, when he applied pressure, it wouldn't budge.

'Fuck!' He spat the obscenity for a second time. Had he misread the video recording? Again, he delicately undertook the same process and this time on the third pass aligned the number 56 with the index mark. He grasped the lever and applied pressure.

He gasped. The lever moved, and the locked bolts retracted with a distinct...*CLUNK!*

'Jesus Christ!' He hadn't noticed that when the leader opened it! He winced at the colossal sound and snap-turned his head towards the steps leading to the main hall, his ears already probing the stillness for any sign of movement from above. Standing there, he couldn't believe silence could be so loud.

He waited. But all appeared to be quiet.

To be on the safe side—and he cringed at the term—he needed to avoid being trapped. So, he quickly and as silently as a ballerina, leapt up the steps and into the kitchen. He stood by the French doors, ready to jump into his car and drive away should anyone respond to the noise. But he could hear nothing and he gradually tiptoed back towards the basement.

He waited two, or was it three full minutes, before descending the basement steps? And there it was. In the gloomy room, the powerful, immovable safe stood like a veritable financial cenotaph with its welcoming door slightly ajar, beckoning for him to come closer, inviting him in to explore its precious contents. He walked toward it and opened the door wide. Now he could see three-dimensionally, what the video recording had alluded to. There were the three shelves stacked with bundles of money. But were they stacked all the way back? He began removing them, placing each one in the medical crate. My God, he had never felt so alive. And, yes, they *were* piled to the full depth of the safe. He quickened his movements. Within sixty seconds, he had the crate almost full, but it *was* too heavy for him to lift. He took a few bundles out and then carried the loaded crate up the steps and into the kitchen. He paused and listened.

But there was nothing. Not a sound from anywhere, apart from his thumping heart, which he felt might awaken the whole neighbourhood.

Suddenly, fear gripped him, and he felt strangely naked as he realised he had passed the point of no return.

He pressed on.

He remembered back to the conversation with Salvatore Vitalli. How stupid of the man, he thought. Fancy removing all the internal security cameras, *and* with having so much money stashed in the house. He wondered what the true worth of the man was. It was certainly a damn sight more than seven million.

He got the crate outside, and then quietly opened the rear door of his SUV. It took him only another minute to quickly stack the bundles in the back of the car. Then he was back in the basement again, repeating the process.

This was too easy.

He was high on adrenalin, the most powerful natural drug in the world, and he found he could manage more weight. He spent the next fifteen minutes emptying most of the bundles from the safe, carrying them up the basement steps and loading them into his car, together with the boxes of medication and a blanket which he used to crudely conceal the packets of cash. When almost finished, he counted out 45 bundles and began carefully stacking them at the front edge of each of the three shelves, as he had planned. He stepped back and admired his accomplishment.

Yes, that looked perfect. The safe looked untouched, and the shelves looked filled to capacity. He checked to see if there was anything else in the safe of value—*there was.*

At the bottom, there were three watch cases. One of which stood out, as it was a two hundred-thousand-dollar diamond encrusted gold Hublot from their "Big Bang Collection". He remembered seeing it in a GQ magazine. He also remembered seeing it once on Salvatore Vitalli's wrist when he had been invited and accompanied the family to a Christmas Ball. The watch's case, bezel and bracelet were adorned with over five hundred tiny Baguette-cut diamonds—totally ostentatious, thought the doctor, but nevertheless, a true gangster's timepiece.

He considered taking it, but decided not to. Yes, he needed to buy some time, but stealing this? No. He didn't want a missing watch to prematurely alert Vitalli of his theft of the money, especially as he had done such a convincing job of re-stacking the leading edge of the shelves. He closed the heavy safe door, locked it, and reset the combination dial. As an afterthought, he then wiped the dial and lever with his handkerchief. Now he was thinking like a criminal, too.

He paused.

Suddenly, he felt strangely delirious, as if the weight of the moment had caught up with him. He began to feel very warm, and his vision began to blur. He felt breathless and his body appeared to shudder as if going into spasm—as if something, or someone, had cut the ground from beneath him. He sank to his knees and his eyes felt heavy, as if he was about to faint. Then, he became aware of a presence.

Through a fog of dreamy images, he could see Greta, the nurse. She was standing there. She must have been on the other side of the safe door as he closed it. On seeing the doctor, the nurse immediately took off down the passageway leading to the bunker complex.

The doctor was suddenly perplexed.

Oh, no! What should he do? Should he leave, after all, he had what he wanted, and she was running nowhere, heading towards a dead end.

His mind was in turmoil. Panic had him by the throat, and he was floating in a sea of doubt. But then he felt himself running too—running after her. Then he was in the bunker storeroom, reaching out, grabbing the girl, spinning her around, muffling her mouth with his hand. *There* was the underwear he had discovered earlier. He reached for them and stuffed them viciously into the nurse's mouth—they were probably hers, anyway.

As she struggled and kicked, he forced them hard to the back of her throat. Then his hands were about her neck, and he knew just where to place his fingers and thumbs as he throttled her.

He remembered his training. When pressure is applied accurately to the carotid arteries of the neck, it takes only ten pounds of force and approximately ten seconds for a person to lose consciousness when being strangled. Once pressure is increased and the trachea is closed, the sudden decrease of oxygenated blood to the brain causes a state of hypoxia, and brain death usually occurs around four to five minutes later.

The doctor grimaced as he pressed his first and middle finger below the jaw and into the hollow depression alongside the girl's windpipe. Amidst her choking, silent wails for help, he gritted his teeth and increased the pressure until her muffled cries waned to stifled silence and her thrashing limbs lost their struggle for life.

The doctor was on the floor. He kicked himself backwards, distancing himself, and then took stock.

'Huh? What had he done?' But then he realised he wasn't in the storeroom at all. He was still in the basement and there was no dead body lying alongside. 'Damn it!' What the Hell was going on! Was he going mad? My God, his mind really *was* fucking with him!

What was this—some kind of psycho catharsis? Yes, it must be—it must be something like that. Again, his medical training kicked in, as he somehow recalled reading somewhere that psychologists referred to such events as a concept of psychoanalytic theory, a powerful emotional release that could be triggered by intense traumatic events—traumatic events, like trying to rob someone of seven million dollars. Is that what he had experienced? Had his mind dumped the negativity of his predicament through hallucination?

His heavy breathing slowed, and clarity returned, almost as if his mind had survived the initial force of a hurricane, and he was sitting calmly in the eye of the storm.

He scrambled to his feet and felt suddenly buoyed that he hadn't murdered the girl. He shook himself free of the notion. Perhaps the girl had been there, perhaps she had not. But even if she had, it didn't really matter, did it? How would *she* know who was, and who was not allowed access to the safe?

Funny how a guilty mind can cloud a criminal's judgement, he concluded. For that's what he had now become, a criminal—a criminal stealing from a criminal. Does that make it OK?

Maybe.

Almost blindly, he crept up the basement steps and glanced back. The safe was locked, wasn't it? He felt as though he couldn't trust his senses anymore. He likened the feeling to being drunk, whilst endeavouring to undertake a delicate task requiring serious concentration.

He looked again. But everything appeared to be as it should. He quietly tiptoed into the kitchen, and then something caused him to stop. Somewhere above, he could hear the sound of a toilet flushing. Then, came the soft distant echo of a door on the gallery landing being closed, and the shuffle of footsteps. Footsteps coming down the grand staircase.

More mind tricks, he wondered.

No, no—this was real! Damn it! He couldn't leave the house now, could he?

What to do?

He found he couldn't move. Panic had rendered him paralysed, and his mind again was at sixes and sevens. The sound of the shuffling footsteps grew louder. And then, Two Fingers Tony Vitalli, wearing a loud pair of yellow and blue polka dot pajamas, ambled into the kitchen.

Startled upon seeing the doctor, Fingers jumped back. 'Jesus, Mary and Joseph!' blurted the bald man. His last three remaining strands of hair looking dishevelled on top of his head. 'Doc, you fuckin' scared the livin' shit out of me! And I've just had the mother of all shits! I came down to find a shovel to break the fucker up.'

'A shovel?' garbled the doctor.

'Yeah... it's a joke, Doc. Anyway, what you doin' down here?'

'Eh, Dino,' said the doctor. 'He's having a difficult night.'

Fingers opened the fridge door, took out a fried chicken drumstick and began tearing it apart with his teeth. 'What's bin the problem?' he asked, feigning interest.

'Err... his heartbeat's irregular,' said the doctor.

'Is he dying? Do you want one of these, Doc?'

'Eh, no thanks. And no, he's not dying. He's stable now, thankfully. I just came up to get some fresh air.'

After stripping the drumstick of every morsel of meat, Fingers tossed the bare chicken bone into the sink, punched the air, and grabbed himself another. 'You sure you don't want one of these, Doc? They're really Yum Yum. I don't know what spices they use, but they got the balance just right... d'ya know what I mean? And they taste just as good cold too.'

The doctor felt confused—Yum Yum? Was he hallucinating this scene, too? 'I'm sure they do,' he said. 'I understand the mix of spices they use are a closely guarded family secret.'

'Is that so?'

'So, I believe.'

Fingers tore off another chunk of meat. 'Although, I don't much care for their fuckin' nuggets. I've heard they're made from testicles and stuff from the head.'

'Really?'

'Yeah, I thought you knowing everythin' about everythin', you'd know that, Doc.'

The doctor, not wanting to get involved in a protracted discussion concerning the nuances of a fast-food diner's menu, said, 'No. Ah, well… duty calls. I'd better get back to my patient.'

Fingers, whose mouth was still full of meat, nodded as the doctor headed for the basement. 'See ya later, Doc,' he spluttered through a sprayed saliva cloud of chewed chicken.

'Always a pleasure,' said the doctor as he left the kitchen. He descended the basement steps and waited at the bottom. He could hear Fingers in the kitchen as the sound of another bone hit the sink. Would Fingers go outside, he wondered? His eyes widened as a terrible thought materialised. Had he closed the rear door of his SUV?

'Oh, BUGGER!' he hissed. Alarmingly, and before he processed that concern, the doctor caught the sound of another pair of footsteps shuffling along the top of the staircase.

What? Who the Hell would this be? He peered up the basement stairs. It was the worst-case scenario. Salvatore Vitalli was coming down the staircase.

'Jesus!' murmured the doctor. No, no, no… NO!! Now what should he do? Stay calm, stay calm. STAY CALM!!

He thought quickly. Should he meet jeopardy head-on, before Fingers could intervene? Yes! The best form of defence is also to be on the offensive.

He stepped up from the basement and, despite his racing heart, walked nonchalantly back into the kitchen. 'Ah, Mr. Vitalli,' he said. 'I thought I heard your voice.'

The family patriarch turned. 'Doc, what are you doin' up? Is everything OK?'

'No, Dino's fuckin' dyin', garbled Fingers, whilst masticating on his fourth drumstick.

'Dying! What you mean dying?' said the leader.

'No, no, no, he's not,' intervened the doctor. 'There was a moment where he had an irregular heartbeat. But thankfully, I was here.'

'Is he OK?'

'Yes, he's stable now.'

The leader threw a scolded look towards Fingers. 'You fuckin' drama queen!' he raged, pointing his finger. 'See, this is what I'm talking about. This guy...' His pointed finger swung towards the doctor, '...is a conscientious professional. He gets the job done. Not like you fuckers! And why do you have to empty the fridge of everything edible? No wonder I can never find anything to eat in my own fuckin' house.'

Fingers shrugged, muttered a half-backed apology, and grabbed another drumstick before closing the fridge door and stepping aside.

'Hey, Doc!' said the leader, diverting his attention fully to the medical man. 'I've been thinking. I got a little bonus for you. I was gonna wait until breakfast, but you know what I'm like. I wanna do this now. Come with me.'

There was mystery in the leader's voice. Or did the doctor detect menace? The big man left the kitchen and made his way down the steps to the basement.

Horrified, the doctor followed him.

A bonus? What kind of bonus? Had the big man lied about having no security cameras in the house? Perhaps he had been watching him robbing his safe all along. Was the bonus—a bullet? That would be so gangster-like.

Oh my God, thought the doctor. Was he about to die?

Again, the big man gestured for the doctor to avert his eyes, as if he was about to dial the combination on the safe door. The doctor slowly turned his back, his mouth open, his eyes closed tight, as he waited. Would he hear the shot? Or would oblivion drown the sound?

'Hey, Doc,' said the leader. 'Look!'

Astonished that he was still breathing, the doctor slowly turned back round. The safe door was open, and there were the three shelves, the bundles of money along the front edges of each exactly as he had placed them only a few minutes ago, concealing his colossal crime.

'I wanna show my gratitude, Doc,' said the big man. 'For what you've done over the years, and for what you're about to do later today,'

The doctor prayed that the crime family Don was not about to reach for another bundle of banknotes; for if he did, he would see that upon removing it, behind lay nothing.

The big man's large hand hovered around the shelves, but then he crouched and lifted a watch case from the bottom of the safe. 'Here, this is for you,' he said, as he rose to his feet, a rare smile materialising across his wide face. 'We intercepted a shipment of three hundred of these last week. It's an Omega Seamaster GMT. It's the same watch that guy wears in those British secret agent movies. What's his name?'

'Bond' said the doctor. 'James Bond.'

'Yeah, that's him. You like those movies?

'I prefer the books.'

'Really? The Bond books? Never read 'em. But I think you could almost pass for that guy,' said the leader. 'You got that Sean Connery thing goin' on. Although you'd have to cut that fuckin' long hair and have it dyed. I don't think they've ever had a grey-haired grunge looking Bond. Or perhaps you could be the villain. What about that? Some super criminal type. Like that fat fuck who tried to rob Fort Knox. What was his name?'

The doctor's drowsy eyes met those of the big man. Why was he going down this line of discussion, he wondered? Did he know something? Was he toying with him?

The doctor must have looked puzzled because the leader said, 'Hey... you OK, Doc? This watch... it's not a rip-off, ya know? It's genuine. It's got a certificate of authentication and everything. Take a look inside.'

The doctor lowered his head, opened the case, and admired the Swiss timepiece.

Salvatore Vitalli nodded. 'Ain't that a thing of beauty?'

'Yes, it is. I don't quite know what to say.'

'You don't have to say anything, Doc. Apart from, why the fuck are you tryin' to rob me... you fuckin' rat bastard weasel!'

The doctor looked up.

There was the raised gun. His startled eyes saw the flash.

BANG!!

But he never heard the blast.

Chapter 10: Hide and Seek

A few days later, Doctor Lucas Roberts suddenly sat bolt upright in the middle of the night. His muscles and sinews were as tight as skin across a snare drum and his wide, stark eyes fervently searched the darkness for a clue as to where he was. For a moment he thought he was in Salvatore Vitalli's basement. He was breathing heavily, soaked in a film of cold sweat, and the sheets beneath him were damp.

Where was he?

He looked around. He was in bed. But not his own bed, another bed. Upon realising he was not dead, but had simply been asleep, the doctor exhaled a heavy sigh of relief, and his body climbed down from its heightened state of fight or flight, and he relaxed. He closed his eyes, buried his face in his hands and grimaced with umbrage, which seemed to mix with a growing sense of solace. Now it was all coming back to him.

What was this? A dream—another bloody nightmare?

Why now, after almost a week, was he still being plagued with night terrors over what he had stolen, and from whom?

'FUCK!' He spat the obscenity with uncharacteristic venom and thumped the palm of his hand against his temple. Would he ever sleep soundly again?

As he tried to recover from delirium, the nightmare's veiled images continued to loiter before his mind's eye, as if hiding in plain sight behind a translucent theatre curtain, beyond which was the final end-of-life act of a grotesque stage performance, in which he was the sole player. A player lying dead on the ground with a bullet through his head.

His mind continued to wrestle with the jumbled jigsaw of images until it finally managed to compartmentalise and separate the order of fantasy from the here and now, and then reality took president, and he fully realised where he was.

He was not at home in his apartment in Brooklyn, New York. Neither was he in the USA. He was in a hotel room three and a half thousand miles away in London, England, and as such was, for now, perfectly safe, despite what his nightmare would have him believe.

Yes—he had a lot of things to organise to ensure his continued safety and a fortune in hidden cash to consider. But that dream sequence involving him strangling the nurse, and the mob boss in the basement with the raised gun—and his execution?

My God! That had all seemed too real—frighteningly real! And why did he always wake just as the weapon was fired? It was almost as if the bullet triggered a spring mechanism in the bed, ejecting him into an upright sitting position. Damn nightmares! What the hell causes them, anyway?

If asked by a patient, he would have said acute stress disorder, or perhaps depression, or any number of things. And the cure? Well, most are based on cognitive-behavioural therapy. Some therapists would have you believe that if a sufferer writes down the complete dream sequence, but alters the part that leads to the nightmare scene. When the dream reoccurs, it might follow the revised path.

'Theoretical bullshit!' he muttered.

Should he just give back the money and free his conscience? Not a chance. He'd still get whacked. Besides, he liked the feeling of being rich. Although, that was not without its drawback. For over the past few days, he had noticed himself constantly looking over his shoulder, and he wondered how long that level of anxiety would last.

He checked his watch. It was four in the morning.

He shuffled across the damp bed sheet to a dry area and reached for his half-consumed glass of single malt whisky. He hadn't drunk for decades but had started again four days ago. In the semi-darkness, he savoured the last satisfying draft of Glen Moray '98, and then lay back into the soft pillows and tried to purge his memory of the dream's dreadful sequence of events.

So, there had been no confrontation with the nurse, or with 'Two Fingers' Tony whilst watching him devour chicken drumsticks in the kitchen. Neither had he followed Salvatore Vitalli to the basement to be gifted an Omega watch, moments before facing the business end of a gun. Although that part of his dream had perhaps been influenced by the watch he was now wearing on his left wrist, which was a new Carrera, a gift to himself, purchased only a few days ago from a Tag Heuer dealer in Oxford Street.

On the night of the theft, now almost a week ago, everything had run like clockwork for the doctor. It couldn't have gone much better. Opening the safe was easier than expected. And it took him just ten minutes to load the car with the bundles of banknotes. After which, he had driven sedately up along the winding drive towards the gates of the property, where there was just one last hurdle to overcome.

As he approached the gates, an elderly security guard rose from his seat within the warm confines of the small gatehouse and stepped out with a torch in his hand. 'Oh, it's you, Doc,' said the man. 'Kinda late, ain't it?'

'Eh, yes... hi, Bob. Yes, it is late. It's been a long day. How's the family?'

'Ah, so, so. You know how it is, Doc. Wife complaining all the time about having to be quiet whilst I sleep during the day. But we all need to earn a happy buck, don't we? And whilst I'm working nights, at least I don't have to listen to her snoring.'

'I could give her something for that, you know,' offered the doctor.

'Huh, so could I... a fuckin' black eye!' The security man hacked a smoker's laugh. 'Only joking. What's that saying about women? You can't live with 'em, and you certainly can't kill 'em. So, what do you do? Well, I'll tell ya. You get someone else to bump 'em off for ya! Ha!'

The doctor joined in the awkward moment as the security man meandered to the rear of the car, looking in through the blacked-out windows as he strolled. The doctor's worried eyes followed him through his mirrors. His vehicle was never checked. So, why now?

'Sorry for the inconvenience. What you got in the back here, Doc?' said the man flashing the beam of his torch. 'A couple of dead bodies?'

'No, just a fortune in used dollar bills,' said the doctor, forcing a smile.

'Oh, I'll take a share of that,' joked the security man. 'Mind if I take a look? Sorry, Doc… but we've been told to beef up security. Check everything in and out of the property, you know?'

The doctor could feel his face redden. 'Yes, of course, carry on. You've got your job to do, Bob,' he said, as he switched off the engine, stepped out from the vehicle and followed the man around to the rear of the car.

The security man was peering in through the rear window. As he spoke, his face contorted into an uncomfortable expression as he said, 'Eh… sorry, Doc. But would you mind opening it up?'

'It's just boxes of expired medication that's beyond its use-by-date,' explained the doctor. 'It's stuff that's been lying around in the house for months. I've been meaning to get rid of it for some time.'

'Well, if you got any morphine or opioids, you're trying to get rid of, Doc? I'll take those. They might help me sleep while my wife snores… ha!'

The doctor opened and raised the vehicle's rear door. 'Sorry, no. It's just boring everyday medication, out-of-date inhalers, tablets, antacids, creams, you know, that sort of stuff.'

The security man pulled back part of the blanket that covered the top of the crate that the doctor had used to carry the money. As he did, the doctor's heart rate peaked, causing him to intake a gasp of breath.

On top of the crate, beneath the blanket but covering the bundles of banknotes, were the stacked piles of medication boxes taken from the bunker, all of which were date stamped, and if checked, would have all been found to be well within their expiry date. The doctor had roughly piled them on top of the money, just in case, and was now glad he had. But how thorough would the man be?

The security man played the beam of his torch across the contents of the car and then turned his attention to the doctor. He eyed the doctor inquisitively. 'Hey, you look dead on your feet, Doc. Are you OK?'

'Yeah, I'm just tired, I guess, Bob,' said the doctor. 'I think there's a bed back home calling my name.'

Just then, the doctor's cell phone rang, which he had switched on only moments before. He pulled it from his pocket. It was the nurse's number. He also noticed he had a couple of missed calls and recognised both numbers to be that of Louie Marmarella.

'Huh... they don't leave you alone for a minute, do they, Doc?' grinned the security man as he pulled the blanket back over the crate.

'No, they don't, sadly. Eh, this is important. I do need to take it,' said the doctor, as he answered the call. 'Just hold for a moment, will you please?' he said to the caller, who sounded distraught. 'Sorry, Bob. You'll have to excuse me, it's the hospital. I really need to take this call.'

'Ah, we're done here. Go on, get yourself home, Doc. Go find that bed.'

'Eh, yes, I certainly will,' said the doctor, relieved as he climbed back into his car and gunned the engine to life. 'Thanks, Bob. I'll be seeing you.'

'Sure thing, Doc. Take care. Goodnight.'

And that was that. The gates parted, and the doctor drove seven million dollars in hard cash through them.

As he pulled away, his phone switched to the hands-free speaker system in the car, and he could hear the panicked nurse calling out. 'Doctor, he's coming round!' she said. And then more urgently, 'He's awake, doctor, he's awake please, doctor. Where are you? What shall I do?'

The doctor thought for a moment and then said. 'Greta, have you not listened to anything I have said? Keep him sedated!'

'OK,' said the nurse. 'But...'

As he accelerated, the doctor angrily picked up his phone and threw it out of the car's open window. To hell with it! He didn't need it anymore.

The cell phone landed on the road with a clatter and bounced into the grass verge. Even as the car drove on, the nurse's voice could still be heard through the car's speakers, asking more questions. But as the doctor distanced himself, the voice finally ceased—and then there was blessed silence.

Doctor Roberts did not sleep during that night, nor did he properly sleep the following three nights. After paying a quick visit to his apartment to collect a few personal things, he checked into a seedy-looking motel. He couldn't risk using his apartment; that would be the first place Vitalli would look for him, that is, if the theft was discovered quickly. So, for now, the motel would have to do.

His intention was to leave the country for a while using a false passport; all the Vitalli men had at least one. When travelling, the family members rarely used their own name. The doctor never had cause to use his false passport before. So, for him, this would be a first. However, on inspection of the passport, he found he had a problem. His passport photo, taken several years ago, depicted him with short brown hair.

He looked in the bathroom mirror and compared himself with the man seven years younger. The face staring back at him looked like a different person, which was the last thing he needed if attempting to leave the country under a pseudonym. The greying shoulder length hair which he had left largely unattended for the past few years would have to go, and not before time. After all, and he grimaced at his reflection—it made him look old.

Under cover of darkness, he left his motel room and walked the streets wearing a hoodie to conceal his face, and eventually found an all-night pharmacy a block away where he purchased a few items, including hair dye. Then, whilst back in his motel room, he applied the brown colour to his hair and tried to cut it, but gave up. He could see he would make a mess of it, so early that morning, after a restless night, he called into an old-fashioned walk-in barber shop close to the motel on the outskirts of Brooklyn where some guy called Franco attended to him.

The establishment was professional with a relaxed ambiance, and the doctor would find the whole experience therapeutic following his recent ordeal. The walls were adorned with pictures of celebrities that had frequented the salon over the years. There were pictures of actors, rock stars, and politicians of various levels of notoriety. There was an abundance of boxers. Mike Tyson was there, standing alongside a very young Franco. And there was a picture of Marilyn Monroe with her arms draped around Tony Curtis. Ironically, or perhaps purposely, either side of Marilyn, was a picture of JFK and Robert Kennedy.

The doctor was invited to sit and was given a catalogue to peruse. The catalogue had over one hundred different styles of haircut, and after some deliberation the doctor decided to go with a regulation high and tight style, inspired by the military, and not dissimilar to that of his passport photograph, inasmuch that the style comprised of shorter sides with a slightly longer back and top—which offered a more rugged masculine look to that of the lengthy, dishevelled 'Grunge' disaster that he had walked in with.

'Oh, my God... look at this,' groaned Franco, in his distinct Italian accent.

Franco was a thin, gaunt, middle-aged New York Italian in his mid-forties who was desperately trying to look twenty years younger. His lengthy, dark hair was subtly streaked with blue and red highlights, which somehow complimented his multicoloured waistcoat, which he wore open with a black short-sleeved shirt and flared velvet pants. Both arms were tattooed with a mishmash of Japanese psychedelic imagery. He wore bracelets, and his use of make-up and eyeliner applied in the style of a 1970s glam rocker should have looked garish, but somehow it all seemed to work. He looked disparagingly at the doctor as he picked through his lengthy locks. Hailing from Sorrento, Italy, his accent was rich and unmistakable. He spoke quickly, as if there was never enough time in the day to cater for everything he had to do.

'My God! What am I supposed to do with this?' he said, as if all hope had been sucked from the world. 'Sir, it's dull and horrible. Where have you been, on a desert island? Who are you, sir... Robinson Crusoe, or someone like that?'

'Sorry,' said the doctor. 'Yes, I admit, I have neglected it. It's been a few years since....'

'A few years? It looks terrible. Dry split ends. Look at all of this frizz and flyaway! I will need to wash and put some product on it.' Franco looked closely at the strands of hair. 'Sir, have you dyed this?'

'Eh, yes... last night,' said the embarrassed doctor. 'I tried to... eh, I was fed up with the grey.'

'Puh... it's bloody awfully bad. I will do it again properly. But trust me, sir. I will have you leaving looking wonderful.' Franco smartly clapped his hands and called out to an elderly bald assistant. 'Luigi, come... come, come! Luigi, I want you to colour this gentleman's hair, wash, condition it and prepare him for cutting.'

Thirty minutes later, the doctor, looking like a drenched sheepdog that had been out in the rain all night, was returned to Franco, who set about his task.

Whilst sitting there, watching, and listening as the snipping scissors went about their work, the doctor's mind wondered. If he was to leave the country and seek sanctuary abroad for a while, he would need money in his bank accounts, and a lot of it. When abroad, having cash in the USA was of no use, no matter how large the amount. He would need to find a means of converting as much of the cash as possible into cheques that could be deposited into his bank accounts without raising suspicion. But how could he do that?

Depositing sizeable amounts of cash at a bank was out of the question. So, he would need to find another method. And it would need to be quick, as time was against him. It wouldn't be long before Salvatore Vitalli discovered the theft and then his tracker dogs would be released. Word would spread all over the city and eyes would be alerted to look out for him. And Vitalli's web of influence was wide and invisible.

The doctor went over the same thought process again and again. How long did he have? he wondered? A few hours? Hopefully a few days. A week would be wonderful, but unlikely. So, what should he do?

As he sat there and watched the severed strands of his hair fall to the floor, his thoughts switched to the one hundred thousand dollars that he owed Louie Marmarella, money that he had recently used to fuel his gambling ventures—he refused to call it an addiction—but it was money he had lost, anyway. He thought of the casinos and the poker and blackjack tables, and then the essence of a plan materialised.

Yes. It was risky, and it would take time, and he had so little of that, but it might just work.

Franco was meticulous with his hair styling technique. He used various types of scissors, and was particularly fastidious when using hair clippers, almost as if the edges around the ears and neck had to be millimetre perfect, as if being measured by a laser rule. The interlocking teeth buzzed and teased the line of the doctor's cut to hairdressing perfection. The doctor thought Franco had finished but then the barber reached for an alcohol-soaked cotton ball which he rubbed into the skin at the back of the doctor's neck, after which he applied a dusting of powder which he then flashed over with a fine long-haired brush. Then he reached for the scissors once more, and began finessing his work, ensuring that not a single strand of hair was out of place.

When finally finished, Franco presented a mirror behind his client. 'You like?' he asked, admiring his work, as if he had just finished sculpting a masterpiece.

'Yes, that's quite a transformation,' replied the doctor.

'It is. But, please sir, do not leave it so long next time,' implored the barber. 'You have a good head of hair. If you treat your hair with respect and love, the follicles may remain with you all of your life. If not, you will be as bald as him.' Franco pointed to his elderly associate, Luigi, whose head was as smooth as a billiard ball. 'And who the fuck would like to look like that?'

After his haircut, the doctor declined the offer of ear and nose waxing, and certainly had no time for the singeing method of removing ear hair, whereby, a barber would wrap an alcohol infused cotton wad around his scissors, light it and then waft the flame against the edges of the client's ears. The doctor had experienced that once before but found the unpleasant fetid odour of burnt hair lingered within his nasal cavities for far too long. But he agreed to completing his grooming process with a hot towel shave, which followed the traditional Turkish method of applying hot towels to soften the skin, before being shaved with a straight-edged cut-throat razor, which made the doctor think of Sweeny Todd; the demon barber of London's Fleet Street, who used a cut-throat razor to slit the throats of his clients as he was shaving them. After which, in the blink of an eye, he would pull a lever, which released the seat of the chair, allowing the body to slide forward through a trapdoor and down into the cellar.

Then later, after he had closed the shop, Sweeney Todd would don his apron and black rubber gloves and descend to the cellar to dismember and butcher the corpse. He would later sell its component parts to a nearby shop, the meat to be cooked and used as filling for meat pies, and the blood to be used for black pudding, both of which, by all accounts, were very popular with the unsuspecting locals.

Just then, an old-fashioned telephone rang on the wall in the corner of Franco's barbershop, which was answered by Luigi. It was a call for Franco, who apologised and left the doctor unattended for a moment.

Was Franco on Vitalli's books wondered the doctor? Was he paying protection money from the proceeds of his business to the crime family Don? What if one of the Vitalli's or Sash called to collect whilst he was sitting there being restyled? The very thought shivered through the Doctor who suddenly felt vulnerable, as he glanced up and noticed a small security camera high on the wall in the corner, its red infra-red beam winking at him.

Christ! Why had he not noticed that before? Damn cameras—they were the bane of his life!

Who was watching? he wondered? Was anyone watching? No, surely not. It would be used for recording everyday footage in case of a burglary or perhaps an assault on a staff member.

He watched Franco through the mirror as he spoke quietly in the corner. Who would it be on the phone? he wondered. Perhaps just another client booking an appointment. Yes—of course it would be, and why would he think anything other than that? But why was he taking so long?

The call seemed to go on for far longer than that required to simply book an appointment, but then the receiver was replaced, and Franco returned to resume his task, and again the doctor felt the razor-sharp blade scrape and glide around the skin of his throat. He had seen many movies where mobster retribution was delivered with vicious finality using such an implement, and he sat motionless without moving his face for fear of being cut. He found himself lowering his eyes as he inadvertently glanced down at the floor, looking for evidence of what, exactly? A trap door? Don't be so bloody stupid, he urged himself. My God! His paranoia certainly was beginning to kick in.

Franco leaned forward. 'Are you comfortable, Doctor Roberts?' he asked as he continued to manipulate the cut-throat razor like an artist applying paint to a portrait.

Suddenly, the doctor felt dread wash over him as if doused by a bucket of iced water. Doctor Roberts? How did Franco know his name?

The camera! The phone call! Who was that on the phone? Was it Vitalli? Had he tracked him down already?

'How do you know my name?' blurted the doctor.

'The register,' said Franco simply. 'You signed in when you arrived.'

'Oh, yes. Of course,' spluttered the doctor.

'Are you alright, sir?'

'Eh, yes.' The doctor felt like a fool. Was his life really about to end sitting there?

No, it would not.

Once shaved, moisturising cream and cologne were applied by Franco with a characteristic flair to complete the process, after which the doctor thanked him, paid with cash, leaving a healthy tip, and walked out into the morning sunshine feeling like a new man.

After that, the doctor got busy.

Over the next three days and nights, he repeatedly visited a dozen casinos in and around New York state, where he exchanged various amounts of his stolen cash for casino chips. Then in each casino he would play the roulette for a short time, after which, he would cash in all the chips back to the cage cashiers, requesting each teller make payment back to him either by way of a banker's draft cheque, or directly into one of his three bank accounts.

Whilst working his cash conversion scam, he was careful not to exceed the casino's ten-thousand-dollar daily threshold which he knew would trigger a CTR—a Currency Transaction Report required by the IRS whenever the casino's monetary threshold was exceeded by an individual within a twenty-four-hour gaming period. Hence, him leaving a full day before returning to the same casino. He also needed to avoid an SAR—a Suspicious Activity

Report, which again would draw unwanted attention. But being the regular player that he was, most of the cage tellers in the region knew of him. He had won and lost thousands over the years and he was familiar enough with the gaming environment to stay well on the right side of being wrong. He visited each of the twelve casinos three times during those three days and nights. In between casino visits, he criss-crossed the state, depositing numerous cheques into his three bank accounts, beginning with his Citibank account. But instead of using his local branch, to which he had sent an electronic transfer of $9,850 from the Empire City Casino earlier on the first morning, he called in at a Citibank branch on 7th Avenue in Brooklyn.

'Lucky night at the casino,' he said to the miserable-looking woman Teller who, as it was a casino cashier's cheque he was depositing, never raised an eyebrow, or for the matter of that, never even raised her head all the time he was there. Had the nine thousand six hundred dollars been in cash, she most certainly would have had to show some modicum of interest. Large cash deposits are usually questioned and are often referred to higher authorities, and in some cases might even attract the attention of the US Treasury. Hence the reason why he couldn't simply deposit the stolen cash bundles at a bank.

The doctor repeated the process during those hectic three days at various branches of Bank of America, beginning with the one on 13th Avenue, again in Brooklyn, before paying a visit to the United Overseas Bank near the Rockefeller Center on 5th Avenue in Manhattan. Then, he deposited cheques at affiliated banks further afield.

Whilst doing all this, there was only one notable incident of concern, which occurred during the afternoon of the final third day. Whilst cashing his chips at the Resorts World Casino on Rockaway Boulevard, he noticed Frankie Vitalli wondering around the poker and blackjack tables. He knew Frankie was not a gambler, so concluded that he and the others had been sent to look for him.

It was the first sign that he knew his theft of the money had been discovered, and he was glad that his dyed short haircut offered some level of disguise. He had been lucky not to be recognised, and he quickly picked up his cashier's cheque and left.

That had been too close. Enough of the casinos, he decided. It was time to leave.

He had hidden the remainder of the huge stash of money, in what he considered to be a secure location, after which, on the evening of that third day, and feeling exhausted by his efforts, he finally made his way to JFK International Airport, where he boarded his Business Class British Airways flight to Heathrow, London using his false passport.

After a satisfying, sleepy six-hour flight, he cleared customs at Heathrow and jumped into a black London taxicab and headed for Westminster. Now he could finally rest easy and breathe, and he felt somewhat elated - like a child, elated.

He had done it! My God, he had actually gone and done it!

Two days before, he had made a reservation at the prestigious Landmark Hotel on Marylebone Road. He had used his American Express black credit card for the reservation and booking, which had no spending limit, although it was required that the balance be paid off in full each month.

Having just deposited over two hundred thousand dollars in his various bank accounts, that would not be an issue thanks to the convenience of internet banking. He had also brought with him some loose change, just under twelve thousand dollars in cash, an amount just short of the UK ten-thousand-pound limit which, if exceeded, would need to be declared to Customs.

His reservation at the hotel was for the twelve-hundred-dollar-per-night Grand Central Suite. Well, he was now wealthy, so why the hell not?

The website stated the hotel was an oasis of luxurious sophistication and serenity, and so it turned out to be. And it was just what he needed.

Originally opening in 1899 when rooms used to cost a mere three and sixpence a night, the large reception area was elegant with its tall stone arches and elaborate maple wood-panelled walls adorned with stunning flower and leafy plant displays. But the hotel's most striking feature was its spacious Winter Garden Dining room, set within an expansive eight-storey glass-roofed atrium with towering palm trees and sweeping staircases leading to the floors and rooms above. It was situated just beyond the lobby, stunningly artistic, almost Venetian, and he found himself marvelling at it, as he span round, captivated by the giddy enormity of the room's cavernous void. It was cathedral-like. And there they were, people taking Afternoon Tea whilst listening to someone playing Rachmaninov's "Rhapsody on a Theme of Paganini" on a seriously expensive, highly polished, gloss-black Steinway Grand Piano, and all whilst penguin waiters quietly scurried around attending to their every whim, serving finger sandwiches on three-tiered silver platters, together with teapots of Earl Grey, scones, strawberry preserve, and Devonshire clotted cream.

It was elegance personified, decided the doctor. And it was all so—English.

The doctor selected the five-star luxury hotel not just for its opulence but also as it was conveniently situated only thirty seconds from Marylebone station. Any sign of trouble and he could quickly board a train and be spirited away to anywhere in the UK, and then out of the country if needs must, should the Devil arrive.

But his immediate intention was to lie low for a couple of weeks in London, and then perhaps spend some time in Austria, or the South of France, or maybe even chance his arm at the casino in Monte Carlo. His cash, or rather Salvatore Vitalli's cash, was safe, but he knew at some point he would need to return to New York and find a way to properly launder the hidden stash of banknotes.

Ah, well... what a wonderful problem to have, he thought. A thought which seemed to settle him as he finished his remaining glass of whiskey, lay back on his bed and drifted, for the first time in almost a week, into a dreamless sleep.

# # #

A few days earlier—six hours after the morning of the theft, whilst the doctor was busy cash converting at the numerous casinos, Salvatore Vitalli was having breakfast with some of his crew. The leader hadn't seen Doctor Roberts that morning and was concerned. Johnny, who had gone down to the bunker complex looking for him, stepped up from the basement huffing and puffing.

'No... he's not down in the Warehouse either,' he said, returning to the breakfast table. 'It's just the nurse down there. Funny thing though, she said Dino opened his eyes last night, but only for a few seconds. Then, he crashed out again.'

The leader looked up from his breakfast. 'Really? Tell her to let us know if he comes round again.'

'I did.'

'If he does, we need to keep him sedated.'

'I told her that too.'

The big man looked at him severely. 'I know I shouldn't have to ask this question, but is he secured?'

'Of course he is. His arm and leg are handcuffed to the bed. Although, I'd prefer it if we hung him from the ceiling with a rope around his neck. ' Johnny called out to the housemaid. 'Hey, Elena. Two eggs over easy, white toast, and have you got some of that smoked bacon we had the other day?'

The Spanish housemaid, a thirty-something, olive-skinned beauty from the Bronx, nodded, 'Si, senior,' she said.

Johnny held up three fingers. 'Three should do it... thanks.'

The shapely, long-haired married brunette crossed the kitchen to the large refrigerator door and removed a tray of bacon.

'The Doc's not in his bedroom either,' said Frankie, as he too entered the kitchen wearing a royal blue double-breasted Bouclé blazer from Valentino's 'Summer Collection', off white pants, and a light blue silk shirt with a gold neck cravat.

'What the fuck?' spluttered Johnny, upon seeing him. 'Where are you going? A fuckin' pimp's convention?'

Frankie ignored him but looked disparagingly at the man wearing scruffy black joggers and a grey distressed T-shirt, the fabric of which was really only suitable as a hand-wipe for the garage mechanics.

'Two Fingers' Tony raised his head from his plate, grunted something indistinguishable and continued to plough his way through a pile of pancakes smothered with maple syrup, his salutation sounding almost like a muffled good morning welcome, but could also have passed for a Komodo dragon's mating call.

'You know something,' said Johnny, who eyed Fingers with disgust. 'Anyone read that book Animal Farm? Because watchin' him stuffin' his face like that reminds me of those pigs in a fuckin' trough.' Immediately, Johnny held up an apologetic hand to the housemaid. 'Elena, sorry for using the fuck word!'

'Eh... hey,' muttered Fingers. 'How can you apologise, and whilst apologising, again say the very thing you were apologising for?'

'What?' frowned Johnny. 'Did anyone speak then? Cuz if anyone did, I don't think it was English.'

'You heard me,' said Fingers.

'Oh... that was you, was it? What are you on about now?'

'You said it again.'

'Said what again?'

'Fuck!'

'Did I?'

'Yeah.'

'That's unusual.'

'You said, sorry for using the "fuck" word. You said it again, and you know Elena don't like cussing at the breakfast table.'

Johnny leaned across the table towards Fingers. 'OK, I'll fuckin' stop sayin' fuck then if it makes you fuckin' happy, you dumb fuck.'

'Ah, go shit it ya hat!' grumbled Fingers, as he stabbed his fork into his six-storey stack of pancakes.

'HEY! You two!' called the leader. 'Will you take it down a notch? I'm tryin' to finish my fuckin' breakfast here!'

'Sorry Boss.'

Salvatore Vitalli, who had been first down for breakfast, finished his last mouthful of food and discarded his knife and fork, which clattered onto his plate. He wiped his mouth on a napkin and shoved the plate away. He turned to the housemaid to compliment her. 'Elena… gorgeous,' he said.

'She certainly is,' whispered Frankie.

'I was referring to the food,' said the big man.

'I was referring to her ass,' said Frankie.

The leader threw Frankie a look of disdain and then focused on the others around the table. 'So, where is he?' he asked.

The others shook their heads and the big man's enquiring look turned towards his son.

'Who, the doctor? I don't know,' replied Frankie, as he tucked a matching gold silk kerchief into his left breast jacket pocket. He got up and looked out through the French doors to where the doctor usually parked his vehicle. 'Well, he ain't on the premises, that's for sure,' he announced. 'Because look… his car's gone.'

The leader frowned angrily, smothered a profanity, grabbed his cell phone and speed dialled the doctor's number. 'Damn, answerphone!' he snarled. 'I gotta go to Chicago. I ain't got time for this shit!' He waited for the automated message to finish, and then said, 'Doc, it's me. Where the fuck are you? Don't you remember what we spoke about… our arrangement? You got that thing to do this morning. Call me as soon as you pick up the message.'

Elena had heard enough bad language for one morning. 'Why you men swear all the time?' scolded the housemaid, her arms and hands gesticulating like an orchestral conductor using a tea towel as a baton, the motion of which caused her ample bust to oscillate provocatively beneath the thin material of her white blouse.

'Look at that,' leered Frankie. 'Looks like two Indian squaws wrestling under a blanket.'

The Spanish housemaid continued her denunciation. 'Always with you men, the swearing.'

'And always with you, the teasing,' drooled Frankie.

The housemaid turned her back. She had heard Frankie's remark and chose to ignore it, but smiled to herself.

'Hey, Boss,' called Fingers, shaking both men from their thoughts. 'Why ain't the Doc having breakfast with us?'

'Fuck me!' answered Johnny on his uncle's behalf. 'Where you bin all morning? Ain't you heard what's goin' on? The Doc's AWOL.'

'AWOL?'

'Yeah. And before you ask, I don't mean a fuckin' brick wall. I mean AWOL. It stands for Absent without Leave. A bit like your fuckin' brain, which disappeared about thirty years ago... AWOL. Or, if that's too difficult for you to understand, it means he's fucked off somewhere, and we don't know where he is!'

'Ah, fuck you! Just so as you know, there's nothing wrong with my brain, it's sharp. It's just that I speak slow.'

'OK, you two... that's enough!' said the big man. 'Jesus!' Salvatore Vitalli lowered his voice. 'Johnny, I hear our patient came to for a moment last night, did he? How does he look now?'

Johnny glanced over at the housemaid and lowered his voice. 'Well, he's fucked up, ain't he, Boss? I mean, he looks the same to me, inasmuch that he's still breathing, but I don't know how the hell he's hanging on.'

The leader nodded. 'How's that nurse doin'? Is she OK?'

'Eh, she's lookin' a bit tired.'

Frankie raised his head. 'I think I should go down and help her,' he said, as he slid from his chair and left the kitchen.

The leader, Johnny and Fingers cast a knowing look at one another, but it was Johnny who muttered what they were all thinking. 'I know what he's gonna help her with,' he said. 'He's gonna help her out of that uniform. I know he's you son and everything Boss... but fuck me, he's a walkin' erection.'

The housemaid fired an angry look; not towards Johnny for his abusive language, but more a look of jealousy towards the door through which Frankie had just disappeared?

Just then, Sash sauntered in through the kitchen's French double doors. 'Morning everyone,' he said as he handed the family boss a fat envelope. He had been doing the rounds collecting protection money. 'Something smells good,' he said.

The leader slid the envelope into his dressing gown pocket and pushed a chair out with his foot. 'Sash, have some breakfast,'

'Huh, you'll have to be quick,' said Johnny. 'Before this truck stop here, eats the fuckin' lot, and then starts on the crockery.'

'Ah, shut up,' groaned Finger's. He downed a glass of orange juice and omitted a loud belch, which seemed to go on forever.

'Oh, Jesus Christ! See what I mean,' groaned Johnny.

'Hey,' said Fingers. 'In Egypt and China, burping after a meal is considered good etiquette.'

'What? Who said that? Was that you, Fingers? Did you put a full sentence together?'

'Ah, fuck off you!'

Hey, guys... he put a full sentence together.'

'He's right though,' said Sash.

'What d'ya mean, he's right?'

'About burping after a meal, considered to be good etiquette in other countries.'

'What? Get the fuck outta here!'

'Yeah, it's a fact. It's a sign of approval. It shows your appreciation for the good food you've eaten. It's considered the highest compliment you could pay to your host.'

'A compliment? That's absolute fuckin' bullshit! What do you think I am, stupid? He eats too much, anyway. Look at him... he's diggin' his own fuckin' grave with his teeth!'

'Hey... I hate to break up this intellectual discussion on foreign culture,' interrupted the leader. 'But I don't suppose you've seen Doc on your travels, have you, Sash?'

'No, sorry Boss,' said the tall black man. 'Ain't you got something planned with him this morning? Fuck me, what's that smell?'

'IT'S HIM!' announced Johnny, pointing to Fingers. 'It's his rotten fuckin' guts! He burps and then we have to put up with the stink. How the fuck's that a compliment?'

'Hey! Getting back to the important issue,' said the big man. 'Yes, I have something planned for the Doc this morning. But he's gone on walkabout and ain't answering his damn phone. And I need to get to Chicago.'

'That's unusual. It's unlike the Doc,' said Sash. 'He usually always picks up.'

Salvatore Vitalli had something on his mind. He suddenly looked quietly pensive. He got up from the kitchen table, removed the bulky envelope containing money from his pocket, and made his way down to the basement. He stood before the safe and then opened it.

A quick glance around showed nothing looked out of place. The three watch cases were still there and the three shelves containing the bundles of money looked untouched. He dropped the envelope into a box at the bottom of the safe containing similar envelopes and closed the safe door. He span the combination dial and began to climb the steps back to the ground floor, but stopped halfway. Something was not quite right. He couldn't immediately put his finger on it, but then something clicked.

The three shelves containing the bundles of money were neatly filled to the edge, yet he had removed five bundles the evening before and had given them ex gratia to the doctor, twenty-five percent down payment for the Blood Money deal. So, how was it that the shelves appeared full again? He turned and walked back down the steps to the safe, entered the combination, and swung open the door.

Yes, the shelves were full. But how could that be? He touched one of the bundles with his index finger and applied pressure. The bundle slid back, and as he continued to push, it slid all the way back to the full extent of his arm. 'What the hell?'

He pushed back a few other bundles from each of the three shelves. They also slid back into the void beyond. Then the full realisation hit him.

'MOTHAFUCKER!'

He raced up to the kitchen. He glared at Johnny, Fingers and Sash, and said, 'I want everyone in here right now, including Joey! Someone, go wake him up. Elena, take the rest of the morning off!'

Chapter 11: The Postman is Always Late

Six days later, just after 8am, Salvatore Vitalli was again having a breakfast meeting in his kitchen with Johnny, Frankie, Sash, and Fingers. Joey had prised himself off his mattress and had also joined them.

Elena, the housemaid, was once again busy at the cooking range and there was that familiar Mama Jo's smell of fried bacon, sizzling sausage, and eggs, to accompany a box of doughnuts that she had brought in from Leske's Bakery.

'So, the Landmark Hotel in London, you sure that's where he's at?' asked Salvatore Vitalli, referring to the doctor, as he took a drink from a tall glass of freshly squeezed orange juice.

'Yeah, he's been there for the last three days,' said Frankie Vitalli. 'Spending our dough and livin' it up.'

'So, how did you find him?' asked the leader.

'My guy at the CIA can find anyone, providing you grease his wallet. If that asshole George Bush had asked him to find Bin Laden in 2001, we wouldn't have had to fuck around for the next ten years.'

'Oh, no, excuse me, please,' pleaded the housemaid, who could sometimes be emotional and willful, 'Senior Frankie, no, no with the swearing today, please.'

'OK... OK,' called Frankie. 'So, what's he stolen, Boss? A few hundred bucks? A painting?'

The crime family leader had not yet divulged the full extent of the doctor's theft, but decided now to enlighten them, 'It's a little more than that,' he said. The men's eyes turned and focused on him, attracted by the scent of scandal. 'Our friend the doctor,' continued the family Don, 'has helped himself to around one hundred and thirty bundles of wrapped dollar bills.'

'Hmph...WHAT?' spluttered Johnny. 'Hard cash?'

'Yeah, bundles of hard cash.'

'Where from... the safe?'

'No... my fuckin' sock drawer!' said the big man. 'Of course, the safe. Where else would it be?'

'How did he get into the safe, Boss?' asked Sash. 'I thought only you knew the combination for that.'

'That's right. I don't know how he got in.'

'Eh, I don't get it. Bundles of cash? What do you mean... bundles of cash?'

'What I said... bundles of twenty-dollar banknotes wrapped in cellophane. Do I have to paint a fuckin' picture?'

The leader preferred them to believe the bundles contained wrapped 20-dollar bills instead of 100-dollar bills.

Johnny looked gobsmacked. 'What? I don't believe it. You're sayin' our Doc, Doctor Roberts, the guy we've known for fuckin' years, has taken money from our safe?'

'Yes, that's what I'm sayin' for the umpteenth time.'

'I don't believe it. One hundred and thirty-five bundles? How many banknotes in a bundle?'

'Five hundred.'

'Eh, what? That's almost... A LOT!'

Sash, who was good with numbers, leaned in. 'What's that, Boss? Around one and a half million bucks?'

'Yeah, about that,' said the leader, happy for them to believe that amount instead of the true figure of seven million.

'Christ!' said the three men, almost like a choir of archangels singing acapello.

'Look,' continued the leader. 'I'm not about to let him get away with this, am I? Especially as we now know where he is, and I'll come back to that in a minute. But for now, I have just one question. What's he done with it all?'

The men looked at one another, and then Frankie said, 'One hundred and thirty bundles? Well, he certainly ain't took it with him, has he? And in the same way, we couldn't bank that much money without alerting the Feds, neither could he. And he would know that.'

'He must have stashed the greens somewhere before he left the country,' said Sash.

'I'll buy that,' replied the big man. 'That's what I thought. So, where's he put it all?'

'Could be anywhere,' said Frankie.

Johnny nudged Sash's arm. 'Hey, he's a gambling man. Perhaps he went to the casino, played the Roulette and put the lot on black and lost.'

'Shut the fuck up, you!' snarled the leader. 'If you ain't got anything constructive to say, stop flappin' ya gums.'

Elena, who had had to close her ears to the profanity, had just plated breakfast. She brought the plates to the table and began distributing them. 'Enjoy, *gentlemen*,' she said sarcastically.

'Thanks, beautiful,' said Frankie, as he took the opportunity to slide his hand around the housemaid's waist as she leaned across. He gave her a squeeze. 'Hey, would you mind putting a couple of extra sausages on for me, darlin'?' he said. 'All that exercise earlier has made me a hungry man.' His hand slid down to the woman's behind.

She slapped it away and beamed a knowing smile at the debonair man, who in her eyes was not only handsome, but was charming with it. 'Certainly, Mr. Frankie,' she purred, as she shuffled sexily across to the cooking range and placed two extra links of Landi's sweet Italian sausage onto the grill.

Frankie's eyes seemed transfixed by the hour-glass shape and movement of the woman's body. He remembered the comment Jack Lemon's character made in the movie "Some Like It Hot", when watching Marilyn Monroe's ass gyrate in a tight dress as she walked down the platform at the train station, 'Look at that,' Jack had said. 'Look how she moves. It's just like Jell-O on springs.'

'Hey!' whispered the big man to his son. 'How about you focusing your attention on the problem we got, instead of every bit of fuckin' skirt you see?'

Frankie shrugged. 'I'm on it, Boss,' he said. 'Don't worry.'

The big man lowered his voice so that the others couldn't hear, the wisdom of life filling his dark, hooded eyes as he spoke. 'Let me give you some advice.' He gestured towards the housemaid. 'Leave her alone. Her husband's a mean sonofabitch, and a fuckin' big unit. Trust me, son, you don't wanna mix with him. You don't need the grief, and neither do I. So, go empty your ball sack elsewhere. Why not try your wife for a change? You haven't been home for a week. You'll have forgotten what she fuckin' looks like.'

Frankie smiled ruefully and shook his head. 'Boss, I know... I know. I did ring to tell her I'd be away for a few days on business. She understands, but... look at *her!* She can't take her eyes off of me. What's a guy supposed to do? She's fuckin' beautiful. And her body, my God! Have you seen the way her hips sway as she moves from that cooking range across the kitchen? She's been driving me nuts for weeks, ever since Ma died, and you took her on. Any woman who moves like that... Jesus! Any red-blooded man would just love to....'

'I know!' intervened the big man. 'And without wanting to desecrate the memory of you mother, God bless her, if I were twenty years younger... well, let's not go there. But take heed of my advice, son. On this occasion, I suggest you go dip your wick elsewhere. *She* could get you into a lot of trouble.'

Frankie, who rarely heard his father call him 'son', turned away and again nodded as if agreeing with his father's premise, but as he looked at the alluring figure of the Spanish woman, whose provocative eyes momentarily glanced up at him, he knew only too well, that the stirring in his loins was far more powerful than the resolve of his self-discipline.

Johnny, who was still flummoxed by the theft leaned in. 'Is that why you went over to his place yesterday, Sash?' he asked, referring to the doctor's apartment.

'Yeah.'

'Why is it that I'm always last to know what's going on round here? Did you find anything?'

'What... like a million bucks tucked down the back of the sofa?'

The family leader looked aghast. 'Of course he didn't!' barked the big man. 'The Doc ain't that fuckin' stupid, is he?' What do ya think he's gonna do, leave you a Post-it note telling you where the fuckin' cash is stashed?'

There was an uncomfortable pause for reflection as they all began tucking into their breakfast. They ate in silence for a while until the leader raised his head. He had come to a decision. 'OK,' he growled. 'Here's what we're gonna do. I'm gonna send someone across the pond.'

Johnny frowned. 'What? You gonna punch the Doctor's ticket?'

'No, idiot! How the fuck do I get my money back if he's dead?'

The men all glanced at one another. But it was Sash who asked, 'So, what do ya wanna do, Boss?'

They all leaned in. 'I wanna know what he's doing, and where he goes. I ain't yet figured out how he got the combination. He may have had help. Someone else might be involved in this. If so, I wanna know who.' He eyed them each inquisitively.

'Don't look at me,' muttered Johnny. 'If I'd been involved, do ya think I'd still be sitting here with you clowns? I'd be on a boat, fishing for Marlin off the coast of Bermuda, givin' mouth-to-mouth to several Pina Colada's.'

The big man snap-turned his head to face him. His look was one of indignation.

Johnny recognised the look and tried to defuse the roasting that was coming his way. 'Ha! I'm only kidding,' he said with a mischievous grin. 'It would be Tequila's. I ain't that keen on Pino Colada's... they're for pussies.' He turned to Frankie, who had not been listening. 'Hey, Frankie... what's your favourite cocktail?'

Frankie, whose focus of attention was still on the housemaid, turned his head. 'Eh, what... cocktails? Err... Pino Colada's. Why?'

Johnny shrugged. 'Ha! See what I mean?'

Joey, who up until that point had been quietly listening, was harbouring a secret. 'Boss,' he said, his voice trembling with apprehension, 'I... I overheard Doctor Roberts talking to Mr. Marmarella that night.'

'What? Where?'

Joey gulped. 'He was on his phone outside, sitting on the terrace, when you were in here with everyone in the kitchen.'

'He was talking to Louie Marmarella?'

'Yeah.'

'Are you sure?'

'Yeah... he, err... err...'

'Joey, calm down. This is fuckin' important! Are you sure he was talking to Louie Marmarella?'

'Yeah, he mentioned him by name. They were talking about money. A lot of money.'

'That two-faced bastard! Why didn't you tell me before?'

'He's fuckin' scared of you, Boss, that's why,' said Frankie.

Joey wanted nothing more other than to reverse back into his shell but continued. He said, 'Mr. Marmarella was asking him for medical advice, and if he'd seen Dino.'

'And what did he say?'

'He lied. He said he hadn't seen him.'

'But he was talking about money.'

'Yeah... it sounded like it.'

'Right!' The leader sat back and addressed them all. 'I need someone over in London ASAP.' He turned to Frankie. 'Is the Doc still at that hotel?'

'Yeah, according to my CIA guy, his reservation is for another week.'

'Good. It's about time that corrupt CIA fuck earned his payoff. OK, I need someone over there in London in *that* hotel. I want our doctor friend followed. I wanna know everything. An' I mean everything! If he speaks to anyone, I wanna know who. If he dines out, I wanna know what he had for dinner. If he takes a dump, I wanna know what toilet roll he uses to wipe his ass.'

'I use that quilted stuff,' interrupted Johnny.

The leader was ready to continue his instructions but shuddered to a full stop before his frozen, perturbed face turned to Johnny. 'Really?'

'Yeah. I know you don't have it here, Boss. So, I bring my own,' explained Johnny.

Fingers piped up, 'What... you bring your own ass wipes?'

'Yeah. It's worth paying a bit extra, Boss; for good quality loo roll, I mean. When you wipe ya backside, there's nothing worse than having your finger disappear up your asshole through cheap fuckin' toilet tissue, is there?'

A quintet of mildly astonished eyes turned to face Johnny. 'What's the matter?' he said. 'Don't tell me you haven't done that.'

Fingers stopped eating in mid-chew. 'Jesus! You really are fuckin' disgusting,' he growled. 'Have I ever told you that?'

'Yeah, you tell him every day,' muttered Frankie. 'But it don't make much difference, does it?'

Johnny continued arguing his lavatorial narrative. 'Don't play the fuckin' righteous with me,' he rasped. 'You've all done that!'

'Maybe... but we don't fuckin' discuss it over breakfast, do we, dipshit?' mumbled Fingers. 'And who carries their own bog roll with 'em, anyway?'

'Is it scented?' enquired Frankie.

'Is what scented?' queried Johnny.

'That quilted toilet paper you use. Is it scented?'

'His fuckin' finger won't be when he pulls it out of his ass,' snarled Fingers.

'Ah, go soak ya head!'

'HEY! What the fuck's goin' on?' complained the leader. 'Do I need to crack some heads? We got a serious issue here! So why the fuck are we talkin' about shit?'

'Good point,' said Frankie. He called out to the housemaid, 'Elena, hold those sausages, will ya? I've kinda lost my appetite for 'em.'

The pretty housemaid took a stance, placing both hands on her hips. 'I don't know,' she announced. 'Swearing, and now toilet talk? And at the breakfast table! You men, please. You forget your manners?'

The housemaid machine-gunned a mouthful of Spanish and then went about her cooking, mumbling as she did so.

The scolded men's attention returned to the point in question.

'So, who you gonna send to London?' asked Frankie.

'Hey, what about Layzee?' suggested Sash. 'Sounds like a job for him. And he's due out soon.'

'He's already out,' said Johnny.

The leader turned sharply towards him. 'What d'ya mean, he's already out?'

'He's out! I rang the prison last night to find out when I could pick him up. They said he'd been released early, a few days ago.'

'Well, why the fuck didn't you tell us?' snarled the big man. 'You're as bad as him!' The leader pointed to Joey, who cowered on his chair.

'What do ya think I'm doin' now?' countered Johnny. 'I'm tellin' ya, ain't I.'

'More's to the point,' interjected Frankie. 'Why didn't Dawson tell us he was coming out early?'

The room fell quiet momentarily, all but for the sound of sizzling sausages.

'Coconut!' announced Johnny.

The leader glanced at him. 'What?'

'Coconut. Frankie asked if the toilet roll I use is scented. It is... it smells of coconuts.'

'Not for long after it's been round your arse,' muttered Fingers.

'Ah, shut up you... ya sap!' sneered Johnny.

'So, I wonder what Dawson's been up to?' mumbled Frankie.

Sash raised his head. 'Maybe he's converted to the church and joined a monastery.'

'Who?'

'Layzee. Prison can do that to you, ya know.'

'We can all live in hope,' sighed Frankie, who couldn't help shield his dislike of the man. 'I told you he was a fuckin' psycho.'

'What? Layzee a monk?' pondered Fingers, a rare smile cracking his severe leathery facial features into an alien grin. 'Can you really see him repenting his sins?'

'No,' said Johnny. 'He'd be in the fuckin' confessional box for a year.'

'Hey, this ain't no laughin' matter,' remarked the leader. 'Don't forget Layzee's got a contract out on him.'

'Oh, yeah... so he has. I forgot about that. Sorry, Boss,' remarked Johnny. 'That prick "Cadillac" Tony DeVille's after him.'

'That's right. Remember him? The guy you should have rubbed out a week ago?'

'Yeah, we know we fucked up there, Boss,' said Sash morosely. 'And as we ain't heard from Layzee, let's just hope he ain't already wearing a wooden overcoat.'

'Anyone want that last doughnut?' queried Fingers.

'Perhaps that's the very reason we ain't heard from him,' suggested Frankie, harbouring a degree of hope for the man's demise.

The leader thought for a moment, contemplating the possible death of one of his favourite associates. Then he said, 'Nah... I can't see it. He knows how to look after himself. And he must have his reasons for not getting in touch. He'll show up soon enough.'

'If we could get hold of him, though, I think he would be perfect for London,' reiterated Sash, not wishing *himself* to be ordered to cross the Atlantic. 'And it would get him away from that "Cadillac" Tony threat for a while.'

'Perfect?' rasped Frankie. 'The guy's a fuckin' psychopath! Ain't anybody listening to me? Doc Roberts has rich tastes. Can you imagine if that sociopath had to blend in at the Ritz in London or Claridges? He'd stand out like a turd in a punchbowl.'

'That's why I'm sending him over with you, Frankie,' said the big man. 'Would be good for both of you. You could keep him in check, teach him some decorum, and if things got messy, you'd have the best right-hand man in the business alongside you.'

Frankie looked awestruck, then he began to smile. 'You're winding me up, ain't you, Boss?'

'Do I look as though I'm fuckin' kidding?' said the big man.

Frankie's smile slid from his face with all the speed of a fried egg from a non-stick frying pan.

'OK, if nobody wants it, I'll have it,' announced Fingers as he reached to grab the last doughnut.

'Oh, no you don't!' interjected Johnny, as he quickly plucked the doughnut from the box and stuffed it into his mouth.

'You fuckin' asshole!' grimaced Fingers. 'You've already had two!'

'Three actually,' spluttered Johnny. 'But who's counting? Oh, I forgot. You can't, can you? You get stuck at two.'

'Fuck you!'

Just then, the house phone on the kitchen wall rang. Elena answered it. The call was from the gatehouse entrance to Salvatore Vitalli's property. It was one of the gatekeepers who asked to speak with the big man. Elena handed the phone to him.

'Mr. Vitalli,' said the sentry man, hesitantly. 'Sir, I think you need to come up here.'

'I'm busy. What for?' replied the family leader.

'There's been a delivery.'

'A delivery? What kind of delivery? What is it?'

'Boss, please... just come over. You need to see this.'

\# \# \#

Six hours earlier, a few miles away, and as night ambled along, dragging its feet, Layzee Dawson peered through the tatty drapes of his darkened, empty living room and cursed. 'Why don't you go back to bed, you nosey fuckers,' he grumbled to himself.

Some of his neighbours were still peering like paparazzi through their bedroom curtains, awakened earlier by the blue flashing lights of Harvey's ambulance, and the subsequent late-night furore when Tony DeVille was arrested and taken away.

In the meantime, Layzee had been busy selecting a few familiar tools from his basement, and once the drapes of the houses opposite stopped twitching, he killed the house lights and stepped outside. He bypassed the pool of blood on his drive and went next door to Harvey and Hilda's house, the side door of which was unlocked.

Inside, the house had that musty old folk's care home smell of cheap sherry, boiled potatoes, and something else. What was that smell? wondered Layzee. Urine?

Yes, it was. Harvey's wife had been right. The house harboured the same confined smell of warm car park elevators from The Projects, where late-night drunken piss-heads would use their elevator as a urinal and empty their bladders. Layzee remembered those elevators, and the putrid stench.

'Dirty bastards!' he grimaced, sourly.

He looked around the drab, tired interior of his neighbour's house which looked as though it was stuck in a 1960s-time warp with its dated pine furniture, cheap bric-à-brac ornaments and stacked boxes of medication which cluttered pine shelves on a wall above a Liberace style mirrored sideboard. Where the hell had they got that from? he wondered? And why?

Over an electric fired mantelpiece, three brightly coloured ceramic ornamental ducks, ranging in size from large to small, were positioned flying up the wall as if startled from a pond somewhere. Layzee recoiled back, almost as if he was about to vomit—they were the same mass-produced dreadful ornaments his grandmother used to have.

He span round and almost fell over an oxygen cylinder and face mask, which sat alongside two old worn armchairs, the seat cushions of which sagged heavily, shaped for decades by the behinds and companionship of his two elderly neighbours. There were two television sets in the living room, each positioned a few feet in front of the two armchairs. Both had headphone cables trailing from them, an indication that the elderly couple could never agree on what television program to watch.

The place had not seen a fresh lick of paint for decades, thought Layzee. But despite its tired and dated appearance, unlike Layzee's house, this house *was* a home—Hilda and Harvey's home, and as such, he felt it deserved respect for being just that.

He soon realised there was nothing of any real value in the house, and even if there had been, he had no intention of stealing anything, anyway. He kinda liked the old couple and hoped Harvey would pull through. Besides, he had a better reason for being in their house.

In the kitchen, through which pine was still the dominant theme, he found the interior door to the spacious double garage, and he stepped through, and switched on the lights. Inside, the musty smell of oil and rust hung thick in the stale air of the dimly lit garage, cobwebs draped in every corner, collecting dust and debris across years of neglect. Against one wall stood a haphazard collection of shelving units overflowing with an assortment of tools, engine parts, cans of spray-paint encrusted with grime and other random oddities accumulated over the decades. Wrenches, hammers, pliers, and screwdrivers of every size and shape were strewn about across dusty workbenches.

An old rusty green Chevy pickup truck was parked to one side—Layzee remembered from their earlier conversation that Harvey had said he once owned one. Clearly, the old fool had forgotten he still had it. But it had seen better days and looked more like a reject from a demolition derby. It also looked as though it had not had Harvey's behind, or for the matter of that, anyone's behind on its bench seat for years. The two nearside tyres were flat, and the windows and green tarpaulin sheet, which covered the rear load area, were thick with dust and grime.

He lifted the tarp and had a quick look beneath. An old, worn tyre, coiled cables, bent conduits, ropes and frayed boxes filled half the truck's flat load bed space, the rest taken up by a long, rectangular metal toolbox which had been welded to the body. He guessed the cardboard boxes within it would be obsolete electrical parts, capacitors, insulators, and fuses. Junk now, but all harking back to when Harvey was a power line worker, one of the most hazardous jobs imaginable back in the day when health and safety was unheard of.

Layzee turned his attention to making space alongside the old Chevy truck and began moving garbage bins out of the way. He switched off the garage lights and opened the motorised exterior double door, which swung up, creaking along its rails as it settled into the ceiling space, revealing the deserted street outside like a large IMAX cinema screen.

He then sauntered out and went for a night walk beneath the golden glow of the street-lights. After two years of prison, it felt good to be able to do that, without having Officer Birch, or any of the other screws watching him, but still he couldn't help but look over his shoulder every now and again, a survival habit he had formed whilst in prison. He glanced up and down the street at the surrounding houses.

Was he being watched now?

If he was, 'Fuck you!' he said as he stuck his middle finger up at arm's length and waved it around, offering 'the bird' from a jailbird, to anyone still peeking from behind their bedroom curtains.

Layzee continued to walk the sidewalk. He was searching for Tony DeVille's white Cadillac Eldorado which he knew wouldn't be too far away, and which eventually he found parked beneath the moonlit shadow of a tree just out of sight at the end of the street. With DeVille having been arrested, Layzee wanted to move it before the police sent a tow truck to impound it, and figured he best hide it, not in his own garage, but in his neighbours' garage.

The white Cadillac looked immaculately clean but was locked.

Layzee found himself in familiar territory and got to work. Using what he had collected from his basement. He took a thin rubber wedge and delicately tapped it with a hammer to prize apart the door's frame, the intention being to thread a long thin strip of bent metal that had a shaped hooked end through the gap to unlock the door from inside. After carefully manoeuvring it for ten seconds or so, Layzee's patience got the better of him.

'Fuck this!' he snarled, as the gentle tapping ceased and he went to smash the hammer through the driver's window. As he drew the hammer back, he kerbed his annoyance and stopped short of the destructive motion as his eyes quickly surveyed the street.

'No,' he muttered to himself. Awakening the neighbourhood and triggering the twitching curtains through which curious faces would again peer out, was the last thing he needed. He continued manipulating the strip of metal and then, after thirty seconds of surgical dexterity, the hooked end caught the locking mechanism and he was in. He jumped inside and quickly immobilised the alarm, and then hot-wired the car using the battery, ignition and starter wires within the steering column; skills he had learned as an adolescent car thief whilst working for a chop shop in Brooklyn, an enterprise which, until it got busted, used to double as an Auto Body Repair Shop, its main source of revenue coming from illicitly disassembling the parts from stolen cars and selling them via on-line marketing websites not dissimilar to that of eBay. With the engine running, Layzee suppressed an urge to gun the accelerator and tear off down the street, but instead drove quietly out of the neighbourhood.

Twenty minutes later, now sure that his neighbours would have lost interest and returned to their beds, Layzee returned as sedately as he had left, and reversed Tony DeVille's car slowly into Harvey and Hilda's double garage, parking it alongside Harvey's green Chevy pickup truck. He closed the double doors and switched on the garage lights. Then he went about checking the Cadillac's interior.

Unsurprisingly, the glove compartment relinquished a handgun and a box of ammunition. But it was after he climbed into the back of the car and checked within the structure of the front seat where the greatest find was revealed. Hidden there, within the seat's rear panel, which dropped down when pressure was applied to a telltale well-worn patch of fabric which triggered a release mechanism, was situated two racks onto which were secreted a small armoury of weaponry. Dawson's eyes widened and a thin smirk materialised on his face. Christmas had come early.

Positioned on the racks was a sawn-off shotgun, a Heckler and Koch USP semi-automatic pistol, a broken-down sniper rifle with telescopic scopes of various magnification, and a lightweight MP9 submachine gun.

Layzee sat back in the seat. 'Mary, mother of Jesus!' he whistled, as he ogled the collection of die-hard weaponry. It was not unusual for mob vehicles to be kitted out in this manner, but this vehicle had been pimped to the extreme. It had been professionally customised and with meticulous attention to hiding the detail of its criminal treasure trove. Dawson slid across the rear seat and checked the rear door cards. Situated in the panels of each door, he found similar quick release mechanisms which revealed further concealed compartments. Hidden inside the frame of the doors were ammunition clips, a couple of knives, a compact pair of binoculars and a medical case which contained various chemical vials for use with syringes which were positioned alongside.

Layzee's brow concertinaed into a frown. What the hell were they for? His frown morphed into a smile as he opened a smaller compartment, and out dropped a set of car keys. 'Thanks very much, Tony,' he mouthed.

He fixed everything back into place, got out of the car and took a quick look in the trunk, which revealed a further Pandora's box of surprises. Inside was a wardrobe of clothing. He rummaged through the items. There were uniforms of various types—NYPD police uniforms, an FBI jacket, security guard and military uniforms. There was even the tunic and robe of a clergyman.

'Looks like this guy raided a fuckin' fancy dress store,' he muttered to himself. He had been wondering where DeVille had acquired the paramedic's uniform, and now he knew. It seemed DeVille was prepared for every eventuality and, as he dug deeper into the trunk, Layzee was surprised to find women's clothing too. There was a suitcase containing wigs, makeup, false breasts, hip pads and high heels. 'Fuck me!' he said. 'Talk about guys in disguise. Looks like this arsehole's a fuckin' faggot!'

Layzee's bigoted brain had jumped to the wrong conclusion, but then he got to thinking straight, and he abruptly stood upright.

'No... no, he's not,' he said, suddenly feeling inferior. 'He's fuckin' clever.' It was almost a Eureka moment for Layzee; for DeVille was everything Layzee was not. DeVille was a technician, a highly competent killer. And by comparison, Layzee realised *he* was just a blunt instrument—a short-tempered sledgehammer. Unlike himself, DeVille approached *his* deadly line of work with the skill and precision of a neurosurgeon.

Dawson realised that his wife, Maria, had been right with what she had said when visiting him that one and only time in prison—Tony DeVille wasn't just good at his profession, he was a walking clinic, a grandmaster, a perfectionist. And tonight, Layzee had been lucky. And the police officer had also been right. Had the cop not returned when he did, DeVille would certainly have succeeded in his task of killing him, and he, Layzee Dawson, would now be lying in a morgue with a tag on his toe.

# # #

It was now six hours later. Following a security alert at his house, Salvatore Vitalli, still wearing his white monogrammed terry towelling dressing gown, stood with his crew outside the gatehouse to his property. They were all staring at something on the ground. Just beyond the open gates, where the block paved drive met the road, lay a highly polished, piano black coffin.

'Who's in it?' enquired the big man.

'I don't know,' said the gatekeeper. 'I haven't touched it.'

'Who delivered it?'

'I don't know, Boss. It must have been placed there sometime during the night. I don't know who delivered it.'

'Huh, well... it wasn't exactly the fuckin' postman, was it?'

'Eh... no.'

'And you heard nothing?'

'No, Boss.'

'No?'

'I've only just come on shift, Boss. When I arrived, that's when I spotted it.'

'Who was on the night shift, then?'

'Bob... but he heard nothing, either. I asked him.'

'He wouldn't,' blurted Johnny. 'Not only is he fuckin' blind, he's mutton deaf, too.'

Fingers intervened 'So, why the hell are we employing a gatekeeper who's as deaf as a fuckin' post, and as blind as a bat?'

'Hey, you... drop it!' said the leader. 'Don't go bustin' a fuckin' blood vessel, Fingers, or we'll need to get another one just like it for you.'

Sash stepped forward as if in a daze, almost as if he'd been hypnotised. 'It must have been delivered by the undead,' he said solemnly, his mind drifting elsewhere. 'They do that, you know.'

'Do what?' asked a petrified Joey.

'Send a coffin to someone before they need it.'

'Really?'

'HEY! Don't you give me none of that fuckin' Voodoo bullshit,' snarled the leader. 'I've told you before, Sash... all that stuff's total bollocks.'

Contrary to what his Boss believed; Sash harboured a deep fear of anything remotely linked to the occult. He firmly believed in the powers of Black Magic and its voodoo rituals, and that when subjected to sorcery, people could become seriously ill, or even die.

All of them stared at the black closed casket with its polished brassware and swing bar handles. There was not one of them who expected to see anything else other than the corpse of Layzee Dawson lying within.

'Those fuckers!' grunted Fingers, whose face had found a new level of morose.

'Shut up!' barked the big man. 'Frankie... open it!'

Fingers, who was clearly upset, wiped his bald head and face with a cloth.

'Sash said he'd arrive wearing a fuckin' wooden overcoat, didn't he?' he muttered forlornly. 'That bastard Tony DeVille! No matter how far he runs, it'll never be far enough to get away from me.'

Frankie knelt and tapped the casket with his fingers as if expecting it to emit a highly charged electric shock. He then applied a little upward pressure to the half casket lid, which was loose. He winced, expecting to see the face of a dead man as he lifted it open inch-by-inch, to reveal inside— NOTHING!

There was a collective gasp of relief over the lack of a body as Frankie opened the lid fully. The coffin with its luxurious, soft, white crepe lining was empty.

Joey, who was standing behind the others, and who was quietly reliving his Chamber of Horrors nightmare, peered over their shoulders, and looked with dread for evidence of scratch marks on the inside of the lid. But it was unmarked, its black gloss lacquered interior as perfectly polished as the exterior. He raised a finger. 'What's that?' he said, pointing.

Within the folds of the casket's lining was a small white envelope. Frankie reached in and took it. Still kneeling, he slid out a white card from within.

'What's it say?' enquired Johnny.

Frankie raised his eyes to meet the expectant gaze of the others. 'It says, *now who's thinking outside the box?*'

The men looked at one another, perplexed.

'What's that?' spat Johnny. 'Some kind of cryptic bullshit?'

'There's also something written on the back,' said Sash.

Frankie flipped the card and frowned. Written on the back were just four words.

'Well?' said the leader.

Frankie looked bemused. 'It says... it just says... *Fill in the Blank.* And the words have been handwritten in red ink.'

Johnny screwed his eyes up. 'Fill in the blank? What's this... a fuckin' crossword puzzle? What's that supposed to mean?'

'Hey, look!' said Frankie, as he eased the coffin lid shut and pointed. 'The name plate!'

Johnny, Fingers and Sash crouched and leaned across the casket, their elongated faces staring back at them from the black lacquered paintwork, distorted by the curvature of the coffin lid. On the lid was a shiny brass plaque where the name of the deceased would normally be engraved. It was difficult to make out the detail against the glint of the morning sunlight, but the name was only partially completed. On the plaque were a line of dashes before the Vitalli family surname, which was beautifully etched into the metal.

'Fill in the blank?' repeated Fingers.

'Yeah,' said Frankie as he ran his fingertips across the engraved letters of his family's name. 'It just says "Vitalli", but there's no Christian name before it, just a space where a Christian name should be.'

'That's the blank bit,' announced Johnny.

'Oh, fuck me… obviously!' huffed Fingers, as he threw his eyes to the Heavens.

The men stared in frozen astonishment, their mouths agape.

'Oh, my God! This casket is meant for one of us,' added Frankie morosely.

'OH NO!' sighed Joey.

Sash looked possessed as he took the card from Frankie and inspected it. 'It's a message from the Dark Lord,' he said, gravely and with demonic dread, his mind failing to shake off the vagaries of voodoo-ism. 'Look, he continued, his eyes wide as if accepting the inevitability of his demise. 'This ain't red ink. These words have been written in blood.'

'Will you knock it off, Sash!' said the big man.

'Those fuckin' bastards!' raged Johnny. 'I'll tell you what. Let's put Dino in it and send it right back to where it fuckin' came from!'

'We don't know where it came from,' said Frankie.

'It's from Marmarella!' intoned Johnny. 'It's gotta be!' Johnny looked at his Boss for affirmation.

'Maybe,' said the leader. 'But let's not get too excited. This is just someone sending their regards.'

'Sending their regards?'

'Yeah. It's a message… that's all.'

'I'll send them a fuckin' message!' said Johnny. 'One they'll never forget!'

Just then, the group's attention swung around towards the roar of a speeding car five hundred yards away, which had just appeared above the crest of the otherwise quiet suburban road. The car was approaching them at terrific speed.

It was a white car!

'Jesus Christ!' yelled Johnny. 'Ain't that Tony DeVille's Cadillac?'

'Yes, it is!' cried Frankie, who pulled a gun from a holster.

Johnny, Fingers, and Sash also pulled weapons and took cover behind the coffin, their arms extended, aiming down the road towards the car like a firing squad waiting to despatch a resident from Death Row.

In the heat of the moment, Johnny's finger involuntarily twitched on his trigger, firing a single shot… *BANG!!* *A* negligent discharge, which miraculously hit the windscreen of the car. The white car veered. It hit the kerb of the road, and amidst a flurry of flying dirt and grit, screeched to a halt sideways on, broadsiding a tree some two hundred yards away from where the men stood.

'Godamn it! HOLD YOUR FIRE!' yelled the crime family leader, who still had his hands in the pockets of his dressing gown, and who had not moved an inch from his standing position as if impervious to any threat.

Following the impact of Johnny's bullet, the men waited; guns poised, absorbing the next few eternal seconds, which seemed to last for hours, all eyes and guns focused on the white car—waiting for what?

There was no movement from the car until eventually, the driver's door swung open as if kicked. A figure clutching his upper left arm fell out onto the grass verge.

'No shooting!' ordered the big man.

'Ha! That's Tony DeVille!' bawled Johnny, triumphantly. 'I fuckin' got him! See... you gotta leave this shit to me!'

Everyone peered into the distance, scrutinising the shape of the man. 'That's not Tony DeVille,' said Fingers, as he lowered his weapon and took a step closer. 'I recognise that guy. I'd know him anywhere. He's lost a bit of weight, but...'

'What do ya mean it's not DeVille?' screeched Johnny, his emotional high disappearing like vapour into a cloud of mist. 'It's his fuckin' car, ain't it?'

'Yeah, it's his car alright,' said Salvatore Vitalli. 'But it ain't him.'

'Who is it then?'

'It's... Oh no, Jesus Christ!' gasped Fingers, as realisation arrived late to the party.

'What's up?' said Johnny. 'Eh, what's going on?'

'Shut up, idiot!' snarled Fingers. 'That's Layzee! You fuckin' shot Layzee.'

Frankie was already busy brushing himself down as the others all rose to their feet. 'Nice one, Johnny,' he said ruefully, as he holstered his weapon. 'Maybe this coffin will come in useful after all.'

Johnny's disbelieving eyes were on stalks, his gun now lying limp in the palm of his hand. 'Layzee Dawson? WHAT?! I've shot Layzee Dawson!

How the hell should I know? I mean... what the fuck's he doin' in DeVille's Cadillac?'

'Who cares? He's alive, ain't he. So, you're in the fuckin' shit!' glowered Fingers, the smile still on the move across his face.

'Well, he is for now,' muttered Frankie.

'So, where's Tony DeVille then?' flubbed Johnny.

Fingers gleeful look vanished in a microsecond at the mention of the man. 'Dead in a ditch somewhere, I hope,' he growled, his facial expression now back to matching the tone of his voice.

'Huh... well, well, well,' intervened Salvatore Vitalli, *his* face filling with admiration. 'I told you he'd show up, eventually, didn't I? Now, will somebody pull Joey outta that fuckin' hedge?'

'S... sorry, Boss.'

'And for Christ's sake, someone go and help Layzee!'

In the distance, Layzee Dawson raised his head from the grass verge and peered towards the men now running towards him. His vision was blurred from where his head had struck the car window. But he noticed something lying next to him, almost buried by the lengthy blades of grass. Although in pain, he reached out and picked it up. It was a cell phone; a cell phone flung from a speeding car a few nights ago.

It was Doctor Roberts' cell phone!

Chapter 12: A Woman's Will

ebbie Vitalli emerged from unconsciousness, opened her eyes, and tried to lift her arms, but found she couldn't. Her immediate impulse was to twist to free herself and stand, but she then realised her legs, arms and torso were roped to a wooden chair.

A knot of dread twisted her stomach.

'You bastards!' she muttered pitifully, her voice echoing bluntly in the gloom of the hot, stifling room, which seemed to be filled with the smell of oily machine parts and stale sweat. 'Where am I?' she murmured.

The question was more for herself to figure out, as she thought she was alone. Then she shuddered, as someone out of her line of sight responded.

'Lady, you're at the docks,' grunted a voice from somewhere behind where she was sitting. 'It's an old workshop. But don't worry, it's abandoned. So, we won't get disturbed. Now, SHUT UP!'

Mrs Vitalli recognised the voice as being that of one of the twin brothers, the one with rotting teeth and breath to match. Her heart sank as she struggled against the ropes binding her wrists and ankles to the chair. She could feel her parched tongue sticking like Velcro to the roof of her mouth. Her face was still wet with beads of perspiration, which dripped and ran down her forehead from her wet dishevelled blonde hair and into her bleary eyes, which stung from the salty rivulets.

'I need some water,' she gasped, her voice croaking as if she was being strangled by invisible fingers.

Rocco Capelli chuckled. 'Yeah, we all need things,' he drawled, with not a single ounce of empathy as he came from behind the chair.

Even though the room was hot, he was still wearing a suit, a black suit with patches of moisture beneath the armpits where his sweat had permeated the various layers of cloth. She guessed the rancid smell was from him, but it could have been from her too.

'They roughed you up pretty good, didn't they, lady?' said the brute of a man, referring to his brother and Louie Marmarella, and seemingly oblivious to the fact he had raped her the night before. He grabbed her face and twisted it one way, then the other, surveying the damage.

Mrs Vitalli snapped her head away. 'Get off me, you monster!' she snarled.

The man sneered at her.

She watched him as he unscrewed the top from a bottle of water and swallowed a long, satisfying draft from it. Her mouth would have salivated had it not been so dry as she watched the man drink, knowing nothing would be offered.

She tried to peer through the semi-darkness but was almost delirious from the humidity, and the relentless, stifling heat, which was less severe than the sauna but still so oppressive. She could feel the beat of her heart as it endeavoured to cope with the perpetual exertion of re-routing blood to her skin to cool her body. She was now dressed, but not in her own clothes. She was wearing an oversized white shirt and khaki shorts. But the shirt was drenched and lacked the wicking ability to disperse moisture, and as such, her body was still dangerously hot.

The man stood before her, finished off the water and threw the empty plastic bottle into the corner of the room. It bounced off the wall and landed with a hollow clatter onto a pile of other discarded bottles. He wiped his wet rubbery mouth with his hands, then flicked the residue from his fingers into Mrs Vitalli's face.

She glowered at him. Although exhausted, she still had an ounce of energy left to fire up the embers of raw hatred that smouldered deep within—hatred mixed with fear, loathing and the sinking feeling of hopeless inevitability.

'What is this place?' she gasped.

The man holding all the winning cards paused and then said impatiently, 'I ask the questions! I've already told you, it's a workshop. We use it as a place of safekeeping for troublesome people.'

'Troublesome people? What, like a prison? You can't keep me here.'

The man was now back behind the chair and was busy tightening Mrs Vitalli's restraints. 'Oh, yes, we can,' said Capelli, as he tugged at the rope, causing her to yelp. 'And we will until you tell us what you know about the disappearance of Mr. Marmarella's son.'

'I don't know anything.'

Mrs Vitalli could feel her heart racing. Her eyes were slowly acclimatising to the darkness, and she looked around. The walls of the room were flaked with petals of peeling sky-blue paint, and where there was no paint, the bare brick was exposed like the brittle bones of a withered corpse. Parts of the room and ceiling were shrouded with complex veils of cobwebs, which sagged heavily under the burden of miniscule dust and grime particles. The windows of the room were blacked out. There was a pungent, feral smell of stabled animals that hung in the air, which contributed to the stinging sensation in her eyes; ammonia, she guessed—or was it urine she could smell?

The cement floor was filthy and stained with—Lord knows what. It looked like a smeared cocktail of dried blood and perhaps other bodily secretions. Human bodily secretions, she guessed, horrified at the thought, as the realisation that she was perhaps sitting in a kill room finally registered with her—a room used for interrogation, torture and murder.

'Oh, my God,'she whimpered.

Dread rose from Mrs Vitalli's bare feet and filled her heart. She looked up. Above her hung the stationary blades of a rusted ceiling fan—it too was covered in a complex yarn of dirty silk strands, long since abandoned by the spiders that had spun them. She looked around the filthy room and thought of the horrors the walls had witnessed over the passage of time.

'It's so damned hot in here,' she rasped. 'Does that work?'

The Capelli twin looked up at the ceiling fan. 'It's busted,' growled his bored voice. 'Everything here is busted. Just like you're about to be... *busted!*'

'What do you mean?'

'Huh? What do you think I mean? I ain't exactly preparing to pitch you a line if beauty products, am I? So, let's get down to business, shall we? And sort out this mess you've got yourself into.'

Capelli leaned in front of her, his face only inches away, the rotten splinter of tooth hanging from his upper gum, the vile smell of halitosis causing her to wretch. She looked into the eyes of the brute. 'Oh look, stop it! You don't have to do this. I honestly don't know where that man's son is?'

Capelli tilted his head and ran his slathering tongue across his lips. 'Of course, that's what I would expect you would say.' He moved closer. 'But we don't believe you. *I* don't believe you! I think you're lying. But don't worry though, I'll help you arrive at the truth. So, I'll ask again. Where is Mr Marmarella's son? Your family must have him. Is he even alive?'

Mrs Vitalli began to sob but tried to hide it. She forced herself to meet his piercing gaze and swallowed hard. 'I... I don't know. I swear, I don't know anything about this.'

The man's eyes burned with fury as he again leaned menacingly towards her. Then, he exploded with rage. 'LIAR!' he yelled as he swung a heavy hand at the woman's face.

Mrs Vitalli's head jolted hard under the blinding impact. There was a sickening *'crack'* and for a moment, she thought her neck had been broken. The pain was intense, and stars flittered across her eyelids as she tried to regain her vision. She slowly levelled her head and glared up at the man who could so easily have killed her.

The eyes of the brute fell on her, and then he smiled a soft, fat smile and said with sadistic clarity. 'Now, do you understand? You were told things would get rough if you didn't comply.'

She watched as the man circled the chair as if consumed in thought.

He removed his suit jacket and turned to face her. 'I don't have time for this!' he barked, his few remaining rear molars grinding against his ulcerated gums in a fit of annoyance. 'But as we are here, we might as well enjoy ourselves!'

In the dim light, Mrs Vitalli couldn't see him clearly—just the silhouette of his frame. Her eyes followed him as he switched on a wall lamp and opened a canvas bag that was on a nearby table. Then the man's face turned towards her and was suddenly illuminated.

Mrs Vitalli's resolve, which had reached the lowest depth of rock-bottom minutes ago, found another lower level in which to reside.

'You fucking whore!' sneered the man gleefully. 'I think I'm going to enjoy our time together, like last night. And yes, I do like beating the sluts I fuck... just before I snap their necks!'

It was as if the man was about to seek retribution for all those women who found him repulsive. He began taking items from the canvas bag, placing them meticulously on the table. Horrified, Mrs Vitalli watched him in the semi-darkness. There was no sense of urgency about his movement. The oaf had all the time in the world to revel in his task and had probably spent many days in this dreadful place inflicting pain and suffering on his victims. He took out a plastic envelope and from within pulled on to his hands a thin pair of latex gloves. He snapped the fingers in place.

He looked almost bored—robotic, as if this was just another mundane day at the office. Or for that matter, it had perhaps never been an office for him, decided Mrs Vitalli. No, he wasn't the type for clerical work. More like the man from the local slaughterhouse. She remembered, a million years ago, that her husband had once mentioned that the Marmarella family owned an abattoir. Perhaps this brute would be the one satisfying his sadistic thirst for death by manning the captive-bolt pistol used to slaughter cattle. Mrs Vitalli could see him doing that. Yes—perhaps he started there; on that particular production line of death, this man; this murdering bastard!

He would enjoy the look of terror in the eyes of each beast as he raised the pistol and placed it mid-forehead. Then, after pausing for a cruel second or two, he would fire the bolt into the animal's brain and revel in the sight of several hundred pounds of flesh sent crashing to the stone floor by a single twitch of his index finger.

And then what? What then when that too becomes mundane? Where would he look to further satisfy his taste for killing? When slaughtering animals loses its appeal, where then does such a person go to get his killing fix?

People?

Yes, thought Mrs Vitalli. He would eventually arrive there, at the very top of the victim 'food chain'. For him, killing humans would be the premier league of murder. Only that would satisfy *his* demonic appetite—the bastard!

She watched him. And knew that the events of the next hour or so would be very unpleasant; for she had nothing to offer. By now, if she knew anything, she would have told them. This was going to be bad for her—very bad indeed.

The man walked over to her.

'Now, where shall we start?'

There was the merest hint of garlic on his wretched breath as he spat the words from his ugly mouth. He checked the bindings holding her to the chair and with a sharp tug, he tightened each rope that held her arms to the armrests and tied them off. The fibres bit into Mrs Vitalli's flesh like a hundred simultaneous mosquito bites and although she grimaced, she tried to suppress her reaction so as not to show any sign of weakness to the evil bastard who was preparing to lay into her. The man then did the same with her bare legs.

He said nothing, but again searched through his bag. He selected several instruments and placed them on the table.

Mrs Vitalli twisted in the chair and tried to see what they were. One was a riding crop which looked well worn. Another was a bottle containing some liquid. There was a smaller bottle; about the size used for women's nail varnish. Then there was a piece of lint and a hypodermic needle with a small vial containing a yellowish solution.

She wished she hadn't looked.

As a child, when visiting her dentist, she would always try to avoid catching a glimpse of the instruments. She had a particularly vivid imagination and could always imagine the most horrendous things; perhaps much like the man before her with his obvious dental phobia. Tears ran down her face.

'Please don't do this...'

Suddenly, with a metallic 'clank', the room was plunged into darkness. Then, in the cold blackness, there was a hissing swish and a loud... *CRACK!* A sudden explosion of pain tore through Mrs Vitalli's body like a savage charge of electricity as the riding crop made contact with her exposed shins.

She cried out and writhed as the fusion of agony ripped through her. She tried to absorb it—tried to swallow it down. Then came another, a loud whistling sound heralding its arrival as the snap from the riding crop cracked against her naked shins again. This time she had a chance to grit her teeth and stifle her agony cry.

Then, the next blow was harder, as if her refusal to cry out angered her aggressor, who quickly followed in with another blow, and then another.

Mr Vitalli squirmed in the chair, her body contorting like a dying snake in its final agony throws. The brief onslaught ended. Then, as she dared to open her eyes, another crack sounded. This time she prepared herself for the blow, but it never came. The sound was somewhere to her left. She tried to look round. But it was hopeless. She couldn't see a damn thing in the blackness. Another swish and the sound of impact, but nothing—no pain.

Then another. This time there *was* pain—terrible pain as the sharp leather rod found her shins with a savage... *SNAP!* And she cried out in agony.

'Argh... *YOU BASTARD!*' she yelled out loud, viciously, at the top of her voice as her body arched in an involuntary spasm against the grip of the unyielding coils of rope.

Then, as her muscles relaxed.... *SILENCE.*

The man had stopped asking questions. Why? Then she realised. It was because he was enjoying this.

Breathing—throbbing breathing. Her own breathing. It was the loudest thing in the room. She tried to control it, tried to listen for the man between gulps of air.

Her body had become taut, like a cat waiting to spring on some unsuspecting field mouse. She tried to relax, preserve energy. She tried also to gauge the movements of the man, sense his presence, anticipate the next strike, but she couldn't tell where he was. There was nothing. No sound. No motion. It was as if she was being flogged by a ghost.

She waited for whatever was coming next.

In the dimly lit, square room, the heavy, expectant silence filled the stale air and weighed on her. She knew it would all start again, but when? She could feel the throbbing welts on her shins swell like individual running veins of red-hot lava. But then the dull, pulsing ache seemed to subside, and the numbness of her nerves began to cloud the pain like an anaesthetic.

This man was a professional alright. She knew little of the intricacies of pain administration. Only that something she had once read stated that pain and the onslaught of torture can merge to such a point that the victim becomes confused, can't tell the difference. Pain becomes oblique. Almost acceptable to such an extent when it refuses to even exist. The beating continues, but pain refuses to register.

Then the hiss of the raised crop sounded again. There was the snap of impact and a scream of agony. But it was not Mrs Vitalli who screamed. Her heart was thumping in her chest—trying to get out.

But she hadn't been hit. She hadn't cried out. What the hell was going on? She was confused.

Where was he? Was the man thrashing himself? It was an almost absurd notion although the lunacy of the moment almost caused Mrs Vitalli to grin inwardly, but then another swish of the riding crop ended with contact on her shins and she cried out and squirmed in the chair under the terrible jolt, as pain ravaged her body and exploded in her head.

'OK.... last chance, you fuckin' bitch!' said the man with evil emblazoned across his face as he leaned in towards her. 'Now, tell me where he is. Is he alive... or have they killed him? Where are they holding him?'

'I don't know! Honestly, I don't know. If I knew, I would tell you!'

Capelli reached for the items on his table. 'OK, if that's how you want it, he said quietly. 'But know this... in time, everyone breaks. And you will too!'

He circled the heavy armchair and cracked his horrible instrument of torture hard against the wooden upright. He came around and leaned forward, his gaze intense and contemplative. He studied her, his eyes sharp and thoughtful. Mrs Vitalli raised her head and looked into them and, try as she might, all she could see there were watery pools of raw evil, magnified by the slightest smirk on the man's lips.

He turned away, and then quickly span back towards her, his face so close Mrs Vitalli could see every bead of perspiration.

'Now this is what we're gonna do,' he said, as a droplet of sweat meandered down the ridge of his hooked nose, formed a plump pear-shape and then fell and splashed onto the skin of Mrs Vitalli's bosom. 'I'm gonna give you some time to think about pain. And on a scale of one to ten... we're only at two. So, think hard! Because next time I come back... I won't be so fuckin' kind!'

'No, please. I don't know anything....'

In the final seconds of consciousness, above her, Mrs Vitalli saw Capelli was holding a syringe. She felt the sharp prick of a needle plunge into her neck. Then, blackness descended, and blessed oblivion softly welcomed her shattered body into its silent caress.

# # #

Sometime later, in the darkness, Mrs Vitalli came too. She felt as though she had awakened from a long sleep, that is, until the aching pain of her shins reminded her of the beating she had taken. Once again, she was sitting in a chair, but this one was more robust, heavier and was bolted to the floor, her hands, legs, and body again tied to it with rope.

She opened her heavy eyes and looked around. There was no sign of the Capelli brother. She was sitting in what looked to be a metal room. Grey walls surrounded her on all sides. But in the darkness, the room felt cooler and had an unfamiliar smell to it. Had she been moved?

She uttered a single, tired word of obscenity that hardly had the energy to pass beyond her dry lips as she wondered how much more of this she could take. Suddenly, as if prompted by her question, a beam of light came on and shone on her face.

The whip of the riding crop whistled through the air and again struck her shins, the sudden shock startling her as the searing sting brutally transported her back to reality from her dreamy, pain-free world of melancholy.

The blistering impact made her cry out as her body again writhed in a rictus of excruciating agony.

'Argh... you ASSHOLE!' she yelled at the top of her voice, her eyes wide like a tormented animal, the words ejaculating from her hoarse throat like spewed bile.

The damned riding crop was back in business.

The light went out and, in the darkness, she could just make out the fleeting shadow of someone.

CRRACK...!!

Several more strikes followed in quick succession, and she cried out again and again as she writhed against the thick coils of rope that held her tight to the wooden frame of the chair. She screwed up her face and clenched her teeth in readiness for the next searing impact—but it didn't come.

Her shins were burning, throbbing. She could feel the beat of her heart pulsing through the swollen welts. She gulped heavy quantities of air and then sat slumped, the remains of her energy all but expired. Once again, she was saturated, soaked in her own sweat and drowning in despair.

There was a click, and again she was blinded by the beam from a flashlight. She expected to hear the swish from the riding crop again, but through the glare in front of her, was the same face, the same ugly, snarling mouth with its single black tooth hanging from its yellow, diseased gum, and the stinking, rotting egg stench of halitosis emanating from it. The mouth spoke three words.

'WHERE IS HE?'

Mrs Vitalli raised her weary, beaten head, which had dropped to her chest, and looked up at the unshaven face of her torturer. 'Look,' she pleaded. 'Honestly, I don't know.'

'I see. So, that brief rest period didn't help much, did it? So, let's backtrack for a minute, shall we? Your husband decided not to come home last night on the very day that Dino Marmarella disappears. What a coincidence. Did he not call to say why he wasn't coming home? I need to remind you it is very important you answer these questions.'

'Yes. He said he had some business to attend to.'

'Did he? And did he say what kind of business?

'No.'

'So, he mentioned nothing about Dino Marmarella?'

'No.'

'You're lying. I don't believe he would not have told you. I think that conversation would have gone something like, I'm not coming home, darling... does he call you that? I'm not coming home because we've got Louie Marmarella's son and the shit's about to hit the fan. Or, he may have said, I'm not coming home, because we've killed Marmarella's son and the shit's about to hit the fan. It would have been one or the other, wouldn't it!?'

'No, he never said anything like that?'

'No?'

'No.'

'So, he made no reference at all to Dino Marmarella?'

'No.'

'You see, that's what I find difficult to understand.'

Rocco Capelli lowered himself and leaned in, his hangdog face only inches away from that of Mrs Vitalli. The single remaining black tooth at the front of his mouth hanging prominently like the lone survivor of a tragedy.

'I really want to believe your husband is not involved in Dino's disappearance, Mrs Vitalli,' he continued, 'but I can't. Especially when it was discovered that your husband was in possession of Dino Marmarella's cell phone.' He paused and gloated, as if revealing a magical trick, his eyes widening, waiting to gauge the poor woman's response.

'Yes, how do you explain that one?' whispered the brute. 'Dino's cell phone dropped out of your husband's pocket in the restaurant on the very day Dino went missing. Is that not coincidental?'

Mrs Vitalli's look of bewilderment deepened. 'I don't... I don't know,' she stammered.

'So, how do you think Dino's cell phone got into your husband's pocket? Did Dino accidentally drop it somewhere and your husband, being a good Samaritan, found it and picked it up, with every intention of handing it back to him? Or was Dino ambushed by your husband and his phone taken from him?'

Mrs Vitalli sobbed quietly as the man laid before her what he considered to be the only two plausible scenarios.

'He said nothing about a phone, or that man's son.'

'I wish I could believe that. But you're lying, aren't you? Admit it. Admit it, and I will let you go. Tell me what I need to know, and you can go home to that useless fuckin' cocksucker of a husband. Why are you tryin' to protect him, anyway?'

Mrs Vitalli eyed him suspiciously, knowing full well the offer of release was nothing but an insincere and pathetic ruse.

The man continued, 'He's worth nothing. He doesn't give a shit about you. Do you know that? He likes to sleep around. But there again, so do you. We had a nice time last night, didn't we?'

Mrs Vitalli glared at the man who had raped her, and then rage surfaced from the core of her soul as she remembered his heaving body on top of her, his animalistic, contorted face grunting as he savagely satisfied his sexual urge, before his brother took his turn.

'Ah, now I see anger in your eyes. Well, forget yesterday and concentrate on today!'

'FUCK YOU!!' snapped Mrs. Vitalli.

'Ah, there you go.' The man eyed her with contempt, as if eyeing a scurrying cockroach before stepping on it. 'You might live in a fancy house, and have nice things, nice clothes, a nice car to run around in, but you'll never escape your past, Mrs Vitalli. Once a whore, always a whore! And I could tell you were enjoying it last night. I could hear you moaning and groaning with pleasure...'

'I was crying in pain, you fucking ASSHOLE!' declared the distraught woman.

Again, surprised by her outburst, the Capelli brother paused, as if evaluating his position. Then, he said, 'You're not going to tell me, are you?'

'No. Because I don't know!'

The brute stepped forward. With his lips curling into a snarl, the man reached across and seized her throat, his grip like iron. 'You're running out of chances, sweetheart! This is your last opportunity to save yourself a world of hurt!' Capelli grabbed the riding crop and thrashed it across her face.

The woman screamed.

'Where are they hiding him? WHERE IS HE?'

Mrs Vitalli shook herself from the impact. 'Where is he?' she repeated defiantly. 'You tell me, you rapist, dumb FUCK!!'

The Capelli brother leaned in and again grabbed her by her throat. *There* was the overpowering wretched breath, his body wreaking of body odour. 'You'd better wise up, woman!' he snarled, the mouth of a rabid dog showering her face with spittle. 'Because I can make this last for fuckin' days!' His eyes turned black as he said, 'I've had enough of you!'

His other hand reached out towards her, and Mrs Vitalli felt the choking power of the man's two-handed grip around her neck. It slowly intensified, as if he had every intention of strangling her. She choked against the pressure of his fingers. Then the brute released her and backed off.

'FUCK YOU!' she spat, unable to contain her fury anymore, her resolve, and any hope of self-preservation all but gone.

He turned and faced her.

'Yes, that's what I said... FUCK YOU! And whilst you're about it, why don't you use some mouthwash, you dirty PIG? Your breath stinks!! The government should weaponize it and use it against the Russians!'

Upon hearing the woman's defiance, the thug, in his own wild frustration, yelled some obscenity and lashed out his right leg in a Taekwondo style kick. His boot impacted Mrs Vitalli's chest with such force it wrenched the chair from the flimsy bolts which anchored it to the floor and sent it careering across the room. It landed on its side and slid a few feet, Mrs Vitalli still tethered to it like a fighter pilot to an ejector seat. The man yelled something at her, threw down the riding crop in a fit of rage, grabbed his canvas bag and stormed off towards the door. He turned, growled something back at her, tore open the door and slammed it shut behind him.

Amidst the rictus of pain to her ribs, Debbie Vitalli's primal drive for survival fought with the temptation to just give up and let oblivion claim her. But somehow a flicker of hope still burned that she might find a way out. But how? The feeling of utter helplessness was suffocating.

She had watched him leave through the mirage of her own sweat soaked eyes, and then once again, she slipped into unconsciousness.

# # #

It felt like only seconds had passed when Mrs Vitalli opened her eyes, but it had been longer than that, and she could tell it was now nighttime.

She was still strapped to the heavy chair which was lying on its side in the featureless room, empty all but for a table against the wall. She was alone and wondered whether her torturer had finished with her for the day. The maelstrom of anger and hatred had left with him, and now everything was peaceful—quiet. But for how long? When would he be back?

She looked around the shadowy blackness. Although the windows were covered with sheets of fabric, a chink of light shone into the room from a lamp somewhere outside. The narrow triangular wedge of light bathed part of the floor in a golden glow. She could see very little, apart from a sliver of something which shone from the floor a few feet away, illuminated by the beam of light.

What was it? she wondered.

It looked like a silver coin. She tried to focus on it. Then she realised—it wasn't a coin. It was a twisted piece of metal, one of four U-shaped brackets that had been drilled into the floor, onto which the legs of the chair had been bolted. What had caught her attention was that one of the brackets was bent and, although still attached to the floor, had been split, its jagged edge now sitting upright and clean where the metal had sheered. It glinted in the darkness, its serrated vertical finger almost beckoning to her.

Slowly, an idea began to emerge. Yes, she decided, if she could just somehow drag herself along the floor, she might be able to use the bracket's exposed sharp edge to fray the coils of rope holding her arm to the chair.

But could she?

It was a crazy idea, and any minute the man might return, but what other choices were there? She knew she would never be released. She would be disposed of, never to be found. Without a body, any blame associated with her disappearance would be easy to refute. That's how it would be.

Immediately, she got to work. She began to jolt her body back and forth in a frantic see-saw effort to move the damned chair, which was solid and similar in heft to those used to execute death row prisoners by electrocution.

The chair moved, but not by much. From where she lay, her orientation to the metal shard was all wrong. So, she spent the next frantic few minutes trying to turn herself. It took every ounce of what little strength she had left, but eventually she manoeuvred it so that she was level with the shard of broken metal a few feet away. Then, using her right foot, she endeavoured to crab the chair over to where the broken bracket lay. Her foot could barely reach the floor, but it did, just, and allowed her to lever the chair along the floor inch by agonising inch.

It must have taken some twenty minutes of exertion, but she got herself into a position where her tethered arm was adjacent to the sharp edge of the damaged bracket. Then she rocked to and fro in the chair. Sweat from her face dripped and pooled onto the filthy floor, mixing with the dried blood and filth. The foul soup stank and filled her nose with the vile stench of a sewage farm, which made her wretch. Nonetheless, her rocking motion was working. The sharp piece of metal began to fray the fibres as it rubbed against the rope... YES!

Buoyed by success, she kept on. It was a painfully slow business and occasionally, the shard of metal cut into her forearm. But she was now oblivious to the pain. The sensation of pain, dulled by adrenalin coursing through his veins, had become oblique and she was amazed at what her body could endure. The rope was now stained with blood from her lacerations. She grimaced with the effort but worked at it, praying that the man would not return.

It took her about half an hour, but the last twisted fibre of rope gave, and the tight coils around her arm immediately relaxed. A feeling of blessed joy replaced her despair. She scrabbled with the chair until she was able to pull her arm out from the corkscrew of rope. Two minutes later, she was free. She stood upright.

Her body was shaking from her exertions. She rubbed the feeling back into her arms and legs—her poor legs. The welts on her exposed shins looked horrendous, but inside she felt elated.

What now?

She limped across the room to a circular window and peered through the narrow gap in the fabric sheet, which had been used to block out daylight.

What she saw surprised her. Water—all she could see was water—seawater. Then she realised she was on a ship. She frowned and tried to work out what had happened.

So, she had been moved!

She quickly made her way to another porthole window, which again was unopenable, and moved aside the cloth covering it. From what she could tell, it appeared the ship was moored along a quayside.

What in heaven's name? Her mind raced. Where was she? She must be at one of New York's ports, maybe Port Newark, or more likely Red Hook in Brooklyn. But what ship? Whose ship? And why was she aboard? And how did they get her on board? Is it not the responsibility of the U.S. Coast Guard to oversee security operations? Perhaps a few of their employees were on Marmarella's payroll, thought Mrs Vitalli—bribed to look the other way as and when required.

Judging by the size of the room, Mrs Vitalli's intuition sensed that the ship was large. It would be a container ship or some other large cargo freighter of some sort.

She tried to gauge her surroundings. The room was in the bowels of the vessel, just above the waterline. But that was all circumstantial. It didn't matter where she was. Although she was out of the chair, she was still in captivity—still a prisoner. A prisoner with a death sentence, no doubt. She knew the capabilities of these men. She had been around these people all of her life and knew that once they realised she was of no value, they would dispose of her. And as she had been moved to a ship, she knew it would be at sea, and it would be the very next time the ship sailed. 'Huh, sleeping with the fishes,' so the colloquial expression goes. Was that how she was to meet her fate? 'You assholes!' she muttered to herself.

She had to find a way out!

She moved across to the door, put her ear against it, and listened.

There was nothing. She twisted the door handle, not expecting much, but then, by some miracle, it opened.

'Oh, my God!'

She immediately closed it and then realised that in his anger, the brute of a brother must have forgotten to lock it, or assumed she couldn't escape from the chair. She needed to act quickly. She looked around the room for anything that could be of use.

She picked up a small flashlight which had been left on the floor next to the discarded riding crop. She switched it on and danced the narrow beam around the room, but there was nothing she could use as a weapon—apart from the damn riding crop.

She put the flashlight in the pocket of the shorts she was wearing and picked up the instrument of torture that had caused her so much pain. It was heavier than she had expected. It was thicker at one end, where it formed a handle. The other end, where it tapered, was finished with a leather tongue. It was almost two feet in length and wound with red braided leather. Or was the red the blood from her shins?

She went back to the door and gently eased it open again. She peered around and down what turned out to be a long, empty passageway. She stepped outside and then quietly moved along to the end of the corridor, where a stairwell descended further into the bowels of the ship.

She listened for a moment and then tiptoed silently down the stairwell into another narrow passageway and peeked around a corner.

She froze. 'CHRIST!'

Rocco Capelli was standing some thirty feet along the passageway smoking a cigarette beneath a sign that said, 'No Smoking', and he was looking directly at her.

She slowly turned.

'HEY!' yelled the brute.

She climbed back up the steps of the stairwell.

Damn it! She'd given herself away. 'You bloody fool!' she urged. She hobbled the length of the passageway as best she could, but then felt disorientated.

Which way?

At the end, she turned a corner and waited.

Which way—damn it?

The ship's corridors and stairwells were like a maze. She looked around. Her options were few. She could hear the man muttering and cursing as he climbed the stairwell. The brute was coming after her.

She found a door to a maintenance storeroom and opened it. But it led nowhere, and she closed it. There was a shadowy partition opposite where two bulkheads met. Rather than be trapped in the storeroom, she preferred to be out in the passageway where she could run—or try to. She stepped into the dark partition and hid, pressing herself flat against the wall. The man stopped halfway along the corridor and opened a locker door and pulled something from it. Mrs Vitalli chanced a look and could see that the man was handling something heavy.

Oh, God—this would not end well. But for whom? All she had was the damn riding crop.

'WHERE ARE YOU? You fuckin' SKANK!' called the damned brute as he made his way along the passage. 'Your time's up! We've heard enough of your bullshit!'

Mrs Vitalli stood as still as death, hoping that the shadow of the partition was sufficient to hide her from the man coming up the corridor.

He drew level with her. And then he too stood listening. 'I can smell your fear,' he growled. 'How did you get out of the chair?'

He was close—too close. So close, she could smell him too.

He lifted a heavy wrench. 'I could shoot you, but where's the fun in that?'

Then, without any warning, the man turned and with a grunt, shouldered the heavy wrench upwards with all the force his powerful arms could muster. Mrs Vitalli saw it only at the last second and ducked. The wrench smashed into the wall where her head had been a moment earlier and jammed tight. So, they had decided to finish her.

Whilst the brute snarled to free it, Mrs Vitalli heaved her knee up into the man's gut with all the force she could summon. The man grunted, but the blow had little effect other than to force him to release the wrench.

Mrs Vitalli was stunned. On the insistence of her husband, she had, many years ago, attended self-defence classes. Any normal man would now be grovelling on the floor. She clawed her nails into the man's face and again brought her knee up hard into his gut with every ounce of strength she possessed. The man's stomach muscles were as solid as pack ice and instead of falling to the floor, he simply smiled, his grin exposing his single black tooth at the front of his mouth.

He laughed at her.

Mrs Vitalli saw an opportunity and whipped the riding crop across the brute's face and then slammed a right-hook into his jaw which almost broke her hand. The man winced at the contact. He had hardly flinched but instead was now coming after her, lumbering up the passageway like some demented rhino, accelerating as he ran.

'Come here, you fuckin' BITCH!' he yelled.

Mrs Vitalli backed off—and backed off fast. She glanced behind. She was trapped. Behind her was a lattice wall of pipes. To her left, a bulkhead. To her right, a door. However, in front of her was this charging dinosaur of a man, hell-bent on demolition. With no time to check whether it was open, the door won. At the very last second, she twisted the handle and crashed through into a narrow cupboard. Like a raging bull fooled by a Matador's red cape, the man, far from being agile, had no time to correct his momentum and bludgeoned himself head-first against the metal pipes, a sickening crack preceding a heavy landslide of flesh and bone as the brute slid down the wall and slumped to the floor like some slaughtered Minotaur.

Panting for breath, Mrs Vitalli stepped out and waited, fully expecting the man to climb to his feet. But he didn't move. She took a step forward and hesitantly leaned over the crumpled body with the riding crop raised and ready to strike. But there was no sign of movement—he was quite still. The sole discoloured tooth that once hung from his upper gum lay on the floor alongside his face.

She hesitated, perhaps for half a minute, and then tentatively reached forward and placed the index and middle finger of her other hand on the man's neck in the hollow area beside his windpipe. There was no sign of a pulse.

The man was dead. Broken neck surmised Mrs Vitalli.

Then she realised. Oh, my God...! She had killed him. No, she corrected herself; he had killed himself! 'Good riddance, you ASSHOLE!' she hissed as she spat into his face.

But now, she had to think quickly. She didn't know who else might be on the ship. Perhaps his brother was there somewhere, or maybe some members of the crew.

She had the presence of mind to realise that it would not do for the body to be found too soon. So, where could she put it? The cupboard was too small to hide it, so she grabbed the man's foot and, whilst still holding the crop, dragged his cumbersome bulk down the corridor the few feet towards the maintenance storeroom.

She wondered how long it would be before the man was missed. Then, just as she was about to grab the door handle, the brute suddenly lashed out with his trailing leg. She doubled up in pain as his boot landed hard in her solar plexus.

She yelped.

The man yelled something guttural and struggled to his feet. 'You fuckin' WHORE!' he yelled, his tongue, oddly, searching his mouth for his lost tooth. He grabbed her with one hand around her neck and punched her in the face with the other.

Mrs Vitalli screamed.

Then, his thick, powerful fingers were around her throat again, squeezing the soft flesh, choking her as she fought to break the man's hold.

She grappled with the man's hands, which were the size of dinner plates, but she could do nothing to prize his fingers apart.

The pressure intensified.

'SEE... you're weak!' gloated the killer, as he homed in on his latest victim. 'Look at you, all banged up. You need to fix your face. But don't worry... I'll fix it for you!'

Mrs. Vitalli felt her knees buckle and with all her strength gone, she loosened her grip on the riding crop which fell to the floor.

She was spent!... Done!!... FINISHED!!!

As she slumped against the storeroom door, a calmness seemed to descend on her. She felt oblivion beckon as she slowly slid down the outside of the storeroom door. Then, unexpectedly the door handle was in her hand, and instinctively, she twisted it.

Under the intense pressure and weight of both bodies, the door swung inwards and slammed hard against the wall as they both crashed through the aperture and landed heavily side-by-side on the floor.

The man's hands lost their grip on Mrs Vitalli's throat and as he tried to twist and restore his hold, she saw an opportunity and punched the battered face as hard as she could.

The punch did little to immobilise the man, but as they grappled, it bought Mrs Vitalli a split second to reach up and grab the handle of something above. It was a 5-litre tin of paint, and she dragged it from the shelf overhead. The heavy tin crashed down onto the side of the man's head, which also had to endure the secondary impact of the floor as his face smashed into it.

Mrs Vitalli looked behind. The riding crop was just within reach. She grabbed it.

As the man tried to lift himself, she jumped onto his back and hooked the crop over the bullet shaped head and pulled it down past his chin to the thick muscular neck. The man collapsed forward and was now pinned face down to the floor by the weight of her body. She forced her knees into the crease of the man's spine, and her hands pulled as hard as she could on the thick end of the crop which strained against the trachea and windpipe of the man's bulging neck. There was a terrible gurgling sound as he spat out some obscenity. Then the purple tongue appeared from the gaping mouth as foam collected between his yellow, bleeding gums, and saliva showered the floor and drizzled down and over the braided leather of the crop that was choking the life from him.

The man gargled, bucked, and writhed as his hands scrambled to grab something—anything. But Mrs Vitalli hung on—her Herculean effort fuelled by an ocean of adrenalin.

The brute's arms thrashed about like the tentacles of an octopus, but they were trapped as if tethered—just as Mrs Vitalli's arms had been tethered earlier!

'How do you like it—YOU BASTARD!' grunted the woman.

She mustered every last ounce of strength she had left, and with her knee hard against the middle of the man's shoulder blades, heaved a final, urgent tug on the crop.

'Die—you BASTARD!' she grimaced. 'Die! Die!! DIE!!!'

There was a double, hideous... *CRRAACK!* as the crop split in two at exactly the same moment the man's neck finally capitulated and fractured with a sickening, sharp *SNAP...!* somewhere around the fourth or fifth cervical vertebrae. And then, the taught, thrashing body beneath Mrs Vitalli ceased its wild gesticulations—its fight gone—the body now flaccid and lifeless as if a plug had been pulled and all power to the brute had been lost.

Mrs Vitalli rolled away, panting, her lungs gulping vast quantities of air. She quickly sat up and kicked herself backwards and looked on in astonishment. Her heart was beating fast, and her breathing was laboured, but with every exhaled gasp, her heart rate and her breathing slowed.

What had she done?

She had saved her life, and probably the lives of other women. She had killed a rapist and a murderer—that's what she had done!

She guessed the man's spinal cord had been severed. She pulled out the flashlight. Then, for the second time, she tentatively leaned across the body and shone the beam into the open glazed eyes. The pupils were fixed and dilated, and there was no reaction whatsoever to the bright light.

This time, the man really was dead.

She fell back against the wall and breathed a single heavy sigh of relief.

My God, she had killed him. The very shocking thought of that terrified her. But then, he was hell-bent on murdering her, so why the concern?

'STOP IT!' she urged herself—this was far from over.

She picked up the remains of the now impotent broken riding crop from the floor, looked at it, and tossed it aside. She sat for a moment, gathering her thoughts whilst scrutinising the silence. Had anyone heard the commotion?

She listened hard.

No, there was nothing, apart from the thumping beat of her heart as it continued to recover. She glanced at the body and savagely kicked the gaunt face of the man who had almost ended her life. Yes, those months of self-defence classes she had attended all those years ago had certainly been worth it. And her husband's insistence that she complete the course had probably just saved her life.

She slowly got to her feet and quietly closed the door. She dragged the dead body further into a corner of the storeroom and covered it with a plastic sheet. She then positioned some boxes around the corpse and, once satisfied that she had done all she could to conceal the body, she pressed her ear against the door and listened.

Still nothing.

She eased the door open slowly and peeked outside. The corridor was dark. She was scared. As scared as she had ever been.

Now what?

Chapter 13: Black Fingernails and Red Wine

Following the drama of the empty coffin delivered to Salvatore Vitalli's residence that morning, Sash left the close family members to reacquaint themselves with Layzee Dawson and took it upon himself to call and see a friend.

He hadn't seen her since the Dino Marmarella incident a few days ago, and after driving for about twenty minutes he pulled up outside the impressive colonial home of Mr. and Mrs. Francis Vitalli whose house was in a residential neighbourhood between Bay Hill and Bensonhurst, considered by many to be the main Little Italy of Brooklyn and home to the largest Italian and Neapolitan speaking communities outside of Sicily and Naples.

At the front of the property, situated in the affluent region of Dyker Heights, was a small, well maintained lawned area. Spanning the width of the house was an impressive white painted porch from which hung a wooden slated three-seater roped swing seat. A couple of grey rattan chairs and a matching side table were nearby.

A black wrought-iron gate led to the rear yard which again was laid to grass with a quaint wooden pergola in the far corner alongside the detached separate garage, which was rarely used; their cars were usually parked on the drive, as was Mrs. Vitalli's white Ford Mustang convertible, which sat gleaming in the bright sunshine—suggesting she was at home.

The rear garden of the property was a riot of colour, the borders filled with herbaceous bushes from amongst which several ornamental Roman statues on stone plinths peeked out, their placement influenced by the statues of Piazza della Signoria in Florence, Italy; where the original statues relate to stories of religion, murder, and mythology. It was where the couple honeymooned a decade ago.

Frankie always wanted to visit the home country, but it was his wife who returned emotionally touched by what she had seen and experienced there; the wonderful food and wine served beneath the heat of the midday sun in the open-air restaurants of the cobble-stoned piazzas, where large fans blow misty water vapour to cool its diners.

The joyous time was made even more special by the warm and welcoming nature of the local people, and the sheer beauty of the Renaissance architecture that adorned every corner. And there was so much to appreciate; the medieval Ponte Vecchio three-arched stone bridge over the Arno River with its iconic shoebox row of brown and coffee-coloured shops and houses spread across its span, which makes it look top heavy and almost on the verge of collapse. And then there was the beautiful cathedral of Santa Maria del Fiore with Brunelleschi's famous terracotta tiled dome, the largest masonry dome in the world.

And you could go on, the Uffizi Gallery containing ancient sculptures and paintings from the Middles Ages through to the Modern period by names such as Di Vinci, Botticelli and Caravaggio. And, of course, not too far away, Pizza's famous leaning tower.

Mrs. Vitalli loved it all and her house and garden were adorned with reminders of her visit.

It was not unusual for Sash to call at their house. Normally, it would be to drop off money or contraband, a routine which had sparked his friendship with the gorgeous blonde wife of Frankie Vitalli. In the early days, when Frankie was not around, Mrs. Vitalli would offer him coffee and sometimes even breakfast when he made his drops. And whenever he called, whatever the time of day, she would always appear fresh, made-up, and attractive.

'Hello darling,' she would say, a greeting she habitually used when meeting people.

She had a soft, easy-going demeanour about her, some would say bordering on provocative, and Sash would agree with that. She was funny, had a dry, edgy sense of humour, and he liked her. He liked her a lot. He always looked forward to seeing her and began scheduling his drop-off's mid-morning when he hoped Frankie would be out on business, or more likely, on his way to meet some young 'filly' somewhere.

Sash knew Frankie had long since lost interest in his wife, and Sash could never understand that, but she appeared to have lost interest in him too. Theirs had become a marriage of convenience; a habitual lifestyle played out without drama or incident, and all whilst Frankie was busy reliving his youth, much of which was spent chasing women and finessing his ability to charm them into bed.

But what Sash and her husband were unaware of was that Mrs Vitalli was of a similar disposition, in that she too was promiscuous and had her own secret circle of friends—many of which came with benefits.

Sash had always admired Frankie's confidence. He wished he could communicate with women as well as Frankie, but he was at the opposite end of the social spectrum. Whilst Frankie possessed natural charm and was forthright and openly flirtatious, Sash was a private person. He was an only child who never knew his father and whose mother died whilst giving birth to him. Raised by multiple foster parents, Sash had become an introvert—a loner who found small-talk difficult and felt uncomfortable when in the company of groups of strangers, and even when with friends of which he had few. Some would say he was socially inept, but he just thought he was a little shy; a shyness that disappeared completely once he was in work mode, dealing with the roaches with whom he shared the darker side of his everyday world.

Sash, his full name Alexander Jackson, was a former soldier in the Army. Despite his many misdemeanours, he had somehow avoided serving any jail time whilst a civilian and had never been arrested or even cautioned. He did not know his date of birth but put his age at around thirty-two. He liked to keep himself fit, had a lithe athletic frame and would visit the local gym three or four times a week, and would often be seen jogging around the hiking trails of Van Cortlandt Park, of which half is forested and home to the largest freshwater lake in the borough; a lake he sometimes used for disposing of criminal evidence.

Sash had never been married and tended to flit between women. His relationships never amounted to much. They were brief, idle affairs. Usually, he would pick up some woman in one of his speak-easy jazz club haunts; the 75 Club or Showman's in Harlem, which would inevitably lead to some brief sexual encounter somewhere, usually in his car or a motel room. He would never take anyone back to his apartment—he didn't want to risk the aftermath of a confused woman turning up on his doorstep day after day. After the physical gratification had concluded, for Sash, that would be that. Emotional ties never materialised for him. He was never around long enough for anything meaningful to develop—that is until he met Mrs. Debbie Vitalli.

His friendship with her started simply. He was hired as a driver for the Vitalli family a few years before and had immediately clicked with Frankie and his father. Salvatore Vitalli liked his work ethic. He was dependable, had a methodical, non-nonsense approach to his duties, demonstrated unwavering loyalty and soon became a confidante, someone they trusted, and he was proud of that.

His early role, which involved simply chauffeuring the principal family members around, evolved to include some of their business interests, collecting money and handling goods, although his relationship with Frankie had recently soured for reasons of conjecture associated with rumours linking him to his wife. But Sash was thick skinned, a tough, quiet man, who thought nothing of putting a bullet into the head of any lowlife who crossed him or crossed any of the family members for the matter of that. And after all, rumours were just rumours, idle talk or opinion often disseminated with no discernable source.

Over time, things moved on and Sash found himself noticing Mrs. Vitalli more and more. For him, friendship turned to attraction, which had always been there but an attraction that intensified as he got to know her, and he would intentionally seek opportunities to be in her company. He almost found himself yearning for her. Oddly, even when he was with her it never seemed to be enough—something was missing. A genuine relationship, maybe? For he always seemed to be looking forward to their next encounter.

He felt almost like a stalker and was uncomfortable with that, and for the past few weeks had purposely distanced himself in an attempt to shake himself free of the emotional tie that had begun to encroach on his persona. But still, he found himself thinking about her. He thought about her a lot—too much, in fact. And often, when alone at night, the devil on his shoulder would fill his thoughts with fantasies of how things might be with Mrs Vitalli, should something untoward happen to Frankie.

Then, three months ago, as providence would have it, he arrived at their house late evening on a snowy Christmas Eve to drop off her husband, who had been on an all-day bender. Dyker Heights, where they lived, was famous for its Christmas decorations, erected each year by its residents, and the street was awash with festive pageantry further enhanced by a recent dusting of snow.

When they arrived, and whilst supporting her inebriated husband, Sash knocked on the large oak door. 'Are you alright?' he asked Frankie.

'No, not really,' said Frankie. 'I've drunk too much.'

'I'll say,' said Sash.

Upon opening the front door, Mrs. Vitalli's eyes widened at the sight of Sash supporting her blind drunk husband, his body swaying unsteadily as he hung on to Sash, barely able to stand. She fired Frankie with a disparaging look of scorn as he staggered in and stumbled past her, without even a 'by your leave'.

Sash remained standing outside on the porch. Then his eyes met those of the gorgeous blonde woman, and for a few seconds there was a peculiar moment, not dissimilar to that, when divorced couples happen to meet accidentally.

They smiled unsurely at one other, as if they had just met on a blind date. Mrs Vitalli hadn't seen the handsome, tall black American for weeks. Then she seemed to gather herself. 'Sash, please come on in out of the cold,' she insisted. 'You must be freezing. I'll make you some coffee.'

Sash hesitated.

There are times in life when a decision has to be made when one arrives at a crossroads. Do you continue straight on along the path of safety and mediocrity, or turn left or right? Left might lead you along a trail to opportunity, wealth, happiness and long life, whereas right might send you down a dark back alley to your demise.

On that evening, Mrs. Vitalli was wearing a stylish, off-the-shoulder ruched black dress which looked expensive. Although, far from being a connoisseur of female fashion, Sash knew of Frankie's preference for designer clothes, and guessed his wife would have similar expensive tastes.

He had never seen her dressed for a social engagement before and was taken aback by her Hollywood film star appearance. She had also been out with friends that day, a 'girl's only' Christmas Eve lunch at a fine dining restaurant, the Honey Badger in Fenimore Street.

Mrs Vitalli's hair had been coloured ash blonde and was immaculate. She usually wore it long, but it had been a few weeks since he last saw her, and she had since changed her hairstyle to a neat bob cut, which hung heavily to her shoulders. She looked stunning and Sash had to check himself in order to stop his jaw from dropping to the floor.

After being invited in, and whilst still standing there drinking in the vision of her beauty, all those feelings of unrequited desire that Sash had tried so hard to repress, bubbled up from the dark recess in the corner of his mind where they had been folded up and stowed.

Her eyes sparkled as she took the initiative, and almost before Sash had a chance to kick the snow from his shoes, she took hold of his large, cold hand and pulled him indoors. His heart leapt at her touch, and for some obscure reason, he noticed the tips of her long-manicured fingernails had been painted gloss black to match the colour of her dress and shoes.

She looked fabulous.

At the crossroads of chance, Sash had deviated from the straight path, but had he taken the left or the right turn?

Mrs Vitalli quickly closed the front door and then turned and looked up at the tall black man now standing in her hallway. 'Well, hello stranger,' she whispered.

'Good evening,' said Sash, noticing the switch from her usual 'Hello darling' greeting. He liked her new look and said so. 'Mrs. Vitalli, you look stunning tonight,' he said, and then added quickly and awkwardly, 'that's not to say you don't always look stunning. I mean...'

She smiled at his awkwardness, allowing silence to settle between them and thanked him, and commented that, in all the time she had known him, she had never seen him wear anything other than a suit.

Sash felt a little embarrassed that she would even notice such a thing. Which meant she would also have noticed that, unlike the tailor-made suits Frankie wore, his were simple off the peg affairs and bared little resemblance in quality to the fine cloth and cut of her husband's suits; no doubt hand made by Sartoria Gallo, reputed to be one of New York's finest bespoke Italian tailors.

They stepped through to the living room where Frankie was lying face down unconscious on the sofa, his head buried between two cushions. They helped him upstairs, and as he groaned and complained, dropped him on his bed, leaving him fully clothed to sleep off his excesses. Sash then followed Mrs. Vitalli downstairs and sat at the breakfast bar in the retro-styled kitchen which seemed to have every modern-day gadget anyone could wish for. There was a stainless steel De'Longhi coffee machine, alongside which was placed a matching Kitchenaid Stand Mixer, which he knew were expensive; he remembered once seeing a line of them in Macy's department store.

A large stainless steel Smeg American style four door fridge freezer was recessed in amongst the neat, white kitchen units, beneath which, along the expanse of the polished black granite counter-top, were reflected images of a line of copper saucepans which hung above from a rack suspended from the ceiling. The cooking range was a replica of the one in Salvatore Vitalli's kitchen, and he guessed they were once part of a seized shipment from Europe which the family had helped themselves to.

It was all a far cry from the scant kitchen in Sash's Woodlawn Heights apartment, which comprised little more than a two-ringed cooker and a battered white fridge.

'So, how have you been keeping, Sash?' asked Mrs. Vitalli as she opened a carton of milk.

'Eh…busy, Mrs Vitalli,' he said, as he looked around, re-familiarising himself with his surroundings.

Mrs. Vitalli's house was dressed for Christmas. The overhead kitchen spotlights were dimmed warm white, and soft jazz was playing in the background through integral ceiling mounted speakers. It was a cosy, warm environment and Sash could feel his heart racing. After all, it was late evening, and here he was, alone with this beautiful woman.

He had never been at her house so late in the day and this moment was almost too big for him. He had longed for such an opportunity, but it had arrived unexpectedly, and he felt ill prepared. Huh…after all, he was still wearing his everyday suit, for God's sake.

Mrs. Vitalli sensed he was uncomfortable. She wondered if he found her attractive at all. Yet, she had often caught him looking at her in the way men often looked at her. Perhaps he was shy or more likely afraid of jeopardising his job should her husband or anyone suspect him of something inappropriate. It was a shame, she thought, as he was handsome and had a youthful Luther Vandross look about him. But as she had not seen him for weeks, and she thought perhaps she was just not his type.

She could not have been more wrong.

For Sash, it was far more than just a physical attraction that he held for the married woman. In his eyes, she was the embodiment of womanly perfection. Yes, she was shapely, bordering on voluptuous and perfectly proportioned, but it was her demeanour that attracted him so. She was unlike any woman he had ever known and nothing like those ill-mannered skanks with whom he had casual flings. It was the way she carried herself; her sparkling personality and all those little idiosyncrasies about her that he had come to love.

Love?

What the hell was he doing using that word? What was he thinking? He was torturing himself. She was and always would be, out of reach. He had to keep reminding himself of that. So why the hell did he step through that front door tonight?

He watched her as she moved around the kitchen, swaying back and forth to the piped music playing in the background as she busied herself preparing them coffee.

'Jesus Christ!' thought Sash. This was sheer agony!

The music changed to a soft ballad, and Mrs. Vitalli's eyes lit up. 'Oh, I really do love this track, don't you?' she said, referring to "I See Your Face Before Me" sung by the deep, melodic voice of Johnny Hartman.

She smiled. 'Now, this is more like it,' she said. She suddenly stopped what she was doing and raised a questioning finger in the air. 'Oh, Sash, this was from that movie. Oh, you must have seen it. I can't recall the name of it. What was it called?'

Sash was mesmerised by her movement. Her new look was sharp, salacious, and she looked innately sexy. Her black dress was figure-hugging, with a long, central slit along its length, which ran almost to the crutch, and such was its tight fit; he could have been forgiven for thinking she had been sown into it. He shook himself from his hypnotic trance. Sash was a film buff—there was little worth watching that he hadn't seen.

'Err... I know this movie,' he said with a frown. 'Eh, it's a beautiful film. Of course... it's from "The Bridges of Madison County".'

'Ahh, yes, that's right,' beamed Mrs. Vitalli joyfully. 'Meryl Streep and Clint Eastwood.' She continued, swaying as if dancing with an invisible partner.

The style of her dress allowed Sash to see the entirety of her bare shoulders which appeared slender and vulnerable, and when she turned to face him as she silently danced, the square cut of the fragile garment hung loosely just above the swell of her cleavage, the material of which only just managing to the protect her modesty.

'Oh, I so love that film,' she said, dreamily. 'A married woman who meets a handsome man whilst her husband's away, and invites him into, of all places, her kitchen... and they fall in love. How wonderfully romantic.'

'Yes,' said Sash, as he watched her, taking stock of every facet of the beautiful woman. He noticed her face had only a light dusting of rouge, although her lips, which were full and luscious, wore a deep, glossy red which is, as is so often the case in the animal world, a sure sign of imminent danger.

'That scene in the film,' she continued. 'It's not dissimilar to our situation tonight, don't you think?' She smiled that lascivious smile as she slid the coffee cups across the breakfast bar. She came round and sat next to him on one of the highchairs.

'I guess so,' said Sash. 'It's certainly a romantic movie, yet tragic too.'

'Yes, but at least they had those few wonderful days together. It's one of my favourite movies. Whenever it comes on TV, even if it's part way through, I always end up watching all of it.'

There was a swish of nylon as Mrs. Vitalli crossed her legs provocatively; her thigh purposely exposed by the V-shape of her dress, perhaps for him to appreciate? And he did.

'I know what you mean,' he said. 'Some films have that effect on me too.' He glanced down at her legs; he couldn't help himself.

She noticed him look and said, 'Yes, but with you, I guess it would be something manly like "Goodfellows" or some James Cagney film, wouldn't it?'

Sash had lost the thread of the conversation. 'Eh, what do you mean?'

Mrs Vitalli smiled wickedly. She knew very well what she was doing, and the effect it was having. 'A film that you catch part way through that you have to watch to the end,' she explained, her eyes blazing with intent.

'Eh... yes, but not always that genre,' he replied. 'I like romantic movies too.'

'Do you, Sash? Name one.'

Sash noticed she was wearing a diamond studded white gold flower-lace pendant necklace. He remembered her telling him once that it was a gift from her husband purchased years ago from Van Cleef and Arpels on 5th Avenue; back when her husband gave a damn. 'OK,' he said. 'A romantic movie? Let me think.'

While she waited, Mrs Vitalli delicately sipped her coffee and continued swaying to the music whilst studying him. 'What a lovely voice he has,' she said, referring to the velvet tones of Johnny Hartman. 'It's a little like yours.'

Sash felt her eyes all about him. They seemed to carefully scrutinise every line and crease of his leathery face in an intense holocaust of careful and measured assessment. The initial flame softened, but the look of fire in the woman's eyes lingered—still probing the semi-darkness as she looked at him, and through him, almost as if stripping away the various layers of his clothing.

'So, come on, Sash. What *is* your favourite romantic movie?'

'There are a few, but one in particular stands out. And it's one you're gonna really like.'

'What is it? Is it an old or a new film?'

'Well, that's an interesting question,' said Sash. 'It could be perceived as being both.'

Mrs Vitalli frowned. 'OK. Are you referring to the storyline or the year of its release?'

'I'm referring to the timeline within the story.'

'Oh, I see. But is it a modern film?'

'Eh, no.'

'Is it a black and white movie?'

'No.'

'But it's a romantic movie?'

'Yes.'

'Err... Patrick Swayze and Demi Moore "Ghost",' ventured Mrs Vitalli.

'No.'

'OK, let me think. Err... is it "Pretty Woman"?'

Sash shook his head. 'Go back another ten years.'

'What? Back to the eighties?' Mrs Vitalli looked bewildered.

'I tell you what... I'll put you out your misery,' said Sash.

'Is that a clue, Sash? Is it "Misery" with James Caan and Catherine Bates?'

'No! That was a horror flick,' smiled Sash. 'We're talking about a love story… a romance that transcends time.'

'Mmm… I know… it's that movie, "Always", isn't it? That film with Richard Dreyfuss and Holly Hunter. He's a pilot and a firefighter. He dies and comes back to her as a ghost. I love that movie. Is it that one?'

'Eh, no, no, no… but it's a similar kinda premise.'

'Really. I can't place it.' Debbie Vitalli's eyes rose to the ceiling in thoughtful contemplation. Then she glanced at him. 'But I do like this game,' she said.

'OK, I'll tell you. But you're gonna kick yourself.' Sash looked across his shoulder at the vision of loveliness sitting so close beside him, her eyes wide in anticipation. A mischievous smile formed on her lips, those highly kissable lips just a few tantalising inches away. He looked into her eyes. 'What if I were to say, "Somewhere in Time"?'

Mrs. Vitalli's hand flew to her mouth. 'Oh my God, yes,' she said breathlessly. 'Sash, you've surprised me. Now, there's a love story. That look on Christopher Reeve's face when he sees Jane Seymour's portrait for the first time in that hotel's museum of memorabilia. Do you remember that scene?'

'Of course,' smiled Sash, pleased with his choice. 'Quite a moment.'

Mrs. Vitalli was already reliving the scene in her mind's eye and grasped his arm. 'And then he realises the picture was taken fifty or sixty years ago but felt somehow that he knew her. The very thought of it is sending shivers up and down my spine right now.'

Her touch was sending shivers up and down Sash's spine, too.

'That movie was filmed at The Grand Hotel in Michigan; I looked it up. Do you know they still hold "Somewhere in Time" weekends at that hotel for fans of the movie?'

Sash frowned. 'Oh really, do they? I never knew that.'

'Yes, apparently every year; Jane Seymour attended one. I remembered seeing a video once; I think it was something on YouTube. She was wearing her costume from the movie. And during that weekend, the hotel guests also wore period costumes too. I would have loved to have been there.'

'Me too,' said Sash.

'Perhaps when they have another one, you can take me.'

There's only one place I'd like to take *you*, thought Sash.

Mrs. Vitalli seemed to get excited and then said, 'Sash, fancy something a little stronger. I prepared some mulled wine earlier; it's warming on the stove.'

'Sure,' he said. 'Is that what I can smell?'

'Yes, it's infused with cinnamon and fruit. Have you not tried it before?'

'No.'

'Oh, you must. It's delicious.'

'Oh, bugger,' groaned Sash.

'What's the matter?'

'Eh, I forgot, I'm driving.'

'Oh, come on, Sash, it's Christmas, and one won't hurt you. Anyway, most of the alcohol will have boiled away by now.'

Whether or not alcohol was present, it would make little difference to Sash. He was already drunk, his senses stupefied by just sitting alongside this beautiful woman.

Mrs Vitalli slid from the chair, crossed the kitchen, reached up to a cupboard and selected a couple of thick glass tumblers, the type often used for hot liqueur coffees. Sash watched her, again teasing himself, admiring the lines and shape of her bare shoulders, the curve of her back, the pinch of her waist, and the wonderful swell of her rear. Oh, how he longed to walk over to her, slip his hands around her waist and hold her close.

She took a ladle and poured the warm drinks and as she drew near with their glasses; she looked at him across the breakfast bar and smiled. 'Here we are then', she said. 'Let's share a toast.' She thought for a moment and then said, 'Here's to secret liaisons, love, and romance,' She leaned across the breakfast bar towards him, and there was the clink of glasses as she fixed him with a smouldering look before taking a sip of her drink—all the while gazing into his face.

Her wide almond-shaped eyes were deep pools of blue, weapons of mass emotion, realised Sash, and he wondered how many men had fallen into them only to drown deliciously. His poker face never budged an inch.

She was beautiful and knew it—and for women with such obvious beauty, perhaps it doesn't always pay for a man to appear too interested. The push and pull of flirtation can sometimes be difficult to interpret, and it was that that seemed to cloud his judgement.

Was he mistaking her warm friendship for something he had long hoped for? Or was she just being friendly? He couldn't tell. He found her impossible to read. He so wanted to take her in his arms, hold her and kiss those full lips. All the signs, fuelled by innuendo, seemed to be there; they were dripping from her, but what if he was mistaken? What if he had misread those signs? If he acted on them and she recoiled in horror, then he would be damned. She would inform her husband he had made a pass at her, and that would be that. He would be exiled from the family business, and that would be the most favourable outcome he could hope for. And the repercussions of such an indiscretion might even be worse than that—it was a dangerous game he was playing.

'So, tell me, what have you been doing with yourself lately, Sash?' asked Mrs. Vitalli, her face only a few tantalising inches from his, as she delicately sipped from her glass, and then ran her finger around its rim.

Such was her position, the cut of her dress above her cleavage afforded Sash the most delicious glimpse of her bosom. She certainly knew how to use her body as a canvas, he decided; and he so longed to be the artist to paint her.

'By the way, I haven't seen you for a while,' she said with a frown. 'Have you been avoiding me?' She smiled as she posed the question, her face once again alive with mischief.

Those eyes, thought Sash. He tried hard to avert his own as she leaned further across, but failed dismally. 'No, of course not,' he said, lying through his teeth. 'Just busy with work. You know how it is.'

He was surprised by her direct approach and felt slightly embarrassed, but also confused. 'Mmm... this is good,' he said, nodding his appreciation of the warm wine whilst trying to sidestep her question.

'Yes, isn't it just? I'm glad you like it,' she said.

Her attention momentarily switched to her husband upstairs. 'So, where has he been all day?' she asked.

'He's been with the guys at Bamonte's,' he said, referring to the old-school retro style Italian restaurant in Withers Street, Brooklyn.

'With you?'

'No, I've been busy.'

'Busy with a lady friend, Sash?'

Again, those wide precocious eyes, the flutter of eyelashes, the fullness of her blonde hair framing the soft skin of her perfect face, and that petulant smile as her look of enquiry endeavoured to probe a little further.

'No, not on this occasion,' he said. He hadn't the courage to say that he had lost interest in other women. His emotions had been, and still were, too deeply invested in the woman before him, and this wasn't helping matters. In fact, he felt like a caged beast robbed of the freedom and right to exercise and act on his feelings. He felt he was spiralling into a black hole, one from which he might never escape.

The expression in Mrs Vitalli's eyes widened. 'Tell you what,' she said breezily. 'Let's go to the living room and continue our chat about movies.' Without waiting for a response, she slipped off her heels, grabbed her glass and quickly skipped around the breakfast bar and headed for the lounge.

Like an obedient puppy dog, Sash followed her and was invited to sit on the sofa. Mrs. Vitalli could have occupied the adjacent armchair, but instead sat alongside him.

Now she really was close. Too close!

Oh God, thought Sash. That perfume, its subtle scent, was intoxicating, and over the weeks and months had become synonymous with everything about her. Sometimes when walking the busy streets of New York, he would catch a hint of someone wearing the same perfume and think she was somewhere amongst the crowd. His eyes would scan the faces, but she was never there.

Sitting next to her now, and feeling the warmth of her body, he felt his heart race. Now what? He was fearful of the repercussions if things escalated and felt like a naughty schoolboy playing truant, but it was that sense of jeopardy that fed the intensity of that moment for him. But would it for her too?

They sat and talked about their favourite movies until after midnight. They found they shared a passion for old classics, "Casablanca", "Psycho", and in particular Jack Lemmon movies, "The Apartment", "The Odd Couple", and "Some Like it Hot" with Marilyn Monroe and Tony Curtis. They covered many films, everything from the 1944 film "Double Indemnity" with Barbara Stanwyck, Edward G and Fred McMurray to "Shawshank", "Forest Gump" and, of course, everyone's favourite Christmas film, "It's a Wonderful Life".

Mrs Vitalli said she had missed their conversations. Sash felt that at that moment it would be so easy to drift beyond the boundaries of friendship. But venturing into that realm of intimacy was dangerous. Especially given the fact that she was a married woman, and worse, married to the son of the family Don; married to the man who was asleep upstairs, or so he thought.

'Sash, do you like my dress?' she asked, out of the blue, changing the subject and the mood of the moment.

'Yes,' he said, glancing down at her exposed leg. And then he couldn't believe what he said immediately after. 'I like what's in it too.'

Mrs. Vitalli turned her face towards him, and her eyes widened as if outraged. Sash felt anxious.

Damn it! Had he overstepped that invisible boundary? He felt everything sink within him, as if he had traversed the sudden drop of a roller-coaster speed bump. He fully expected to feel the slap of a hand across his face.

But then, Mrs. Vitalli's look of surprise softened as the merest upward slant of a smile appeared across her lips.

'Do you?' she whispered.

Sash felt her hand touch his thigh.

Suddenly, with a bang and a clatter, the door to the living room burst open and there was a clumsy groan. 'Argh... Jesus!'

It was Frankie Vitalli, falling through the door onto the floor of the living room.

He got up.

Hanging on the door handle in an effort to remain upright, he said drunkenly. 'Oh... are you still here, Sash?'

Mrs Vitalli quickly removed her hand from Sash's thigh.

'Eh, yes,' said Sash, awkwardly.

Frankie stumbled and then pointed at him with a shaky finger. 'You shouldn't be messing with her,' he said unforgivably. His finger moved a couple of degrees and pointed to his wife. 'Huh, you don't know where she's been. What time is it?'

'It's one o'clock in the morning, and you should be in bed,' advised Mrs Vitalli, showing little sign of any empathy. 'Look at the state of you!'

Frankie tried to brush himself down. 'What's the matter with me?'

Sash quickly rose from the sofa. 'Eh, I was just leaving,' he said.

'Eh, why?' said Frankie as he collapsed into an armchair. 'Sit down, have another drink. And Debs, get one for me too, would you?'

'Oh, Lord. Haven't you had enough?' said his wife.

'No... of course not. You know what they say, alcohol might well be man's worst enemy, but the Bible says, "love your enemy". So, I'd love another drink... so, I'm gonna have one. What are you two drinking?'

'Mulled wine. It's Christmas!' said Mrs. Vitalli, who eyed her husband with contempt.

Frankie was having trouble stringing a sentence together. 'Ugh, I ain't havin' that shit. Eh... I'll have a brandy and soda.'

'Will you?' said his wife. 'Are you sure? Do you think that's wise?'

Frankie chuckled. 'Oh... I'm in trouble. Come on, Debs. Where's your Christmas spirit?'

'It looks like you've drunk it all.'

'Oh, that's funny. She's a funny girl, Sash. Come on, beautiful, get me a drink. Don't you think she's beautiful, Sash? I'm gonna love her up tonight.'

Mrs. Vitalli was getting increasingly annoyed and embarrassed. 'You're not coming anywhere near me!' she said.

'Ha! Oh dear, that's done it. Come on, Debs, one for the road. And get one for Denzel. Don't you think he looks like Denzel? I do.'

Mrs. Vitalli reluctantly rose from the sofa, sashayed across to the drinks cabinet, and fixed a weak drink for her husband. Sash stole a couple of glances at her and exhaled a sigh of relief. Or was it disappointment at her husband's intrusion at that key moment?

Frankie took a sip of his drink. 'What the fuck's this? Tastes like rat's piss.'

'That's all you're having,' said Mrs. Vitalli.

'Ah, fuck it. Thanks for dropping me back, Sash,' slurred Frankie. 'You're a good guy. I've always said that. He's a good guy, Debs.'

'Yes, a good guy. I know.'

'And do you know what I know?' garbled Frankie, continuing his drunken monologue. 'I know you can't get fat drinking alcohol; did you know that? It's a myth. Alcohol makes you lean... lean against a wall, a table, a chair, and ugly people. Oh... we had a good session tonight, didn't we, Sash?'

'Well, you certainly did, by the looks of it. I wasn't there.'

Frankie looked confused. 'Oh yeah, that's right. Where the f... where the hell were you?'

'He was with... his lady friend,' replied Mrs. Vitalli, in an attempt to deflect any curiosity her husband might foster over her and Sash's close encounter of the sofa kind. She glanced a look at Sash, who caught her drift and played along.

'Eh, yeah... a lady friend,' he said.

Frankie's finger again pointed at his associate. 'Ah, good for you! I bet he's got a woman in every port, and a woman in every apartment block, too. He's a dark horse, this guy. Sex God of the Bronx... that's what they call him!'

Sash fired an embarrassed look at Mrs. Vitalli.

'Really,' she said, her blue eyes widening to accommodate a glint of fascination as she smiled at the tall black man.

'Yeah, that's right. Apparently, he's hung like a fuckin' horse, too. Ain't that right Sash?'

Mrs. Vitalli glanced across at him. 'Oh,' she murmured, with an upward inflection and a smile of intrigue. 'It's all coming out now.'

'And don't you get any ideas about takin' in out either, Sash,' garbled Frankie. 'Leave it where it is.'

Sash, realising it was definitely time to leave, placed his unfinished drink on the fireplace mantle. 'Well, it's time I said goodnight,' he said. 'Thanks for the drinks and your hospitality, Mrs. Vitalli,' he nodded his appreciation. 'Both of you, enjoy the holidays. Have a great Christmas!'

'Yeah... you too. Have a good one,' slurred Frankie, as he tried to get up but fell back into his armchair, spilling some of his drink on his was down.

Sash made his way through the living room and into the hallway.

'I'll see him out,' called Mrs. Vitalli, who followed him through.

Sash turned to say goodnight but found Mrs. Vitalli to be standing very close. She looked up at him with those big beautiful almond eyes, and he suddenly knew he was about to drown in the irresistible deep pools of blue.

'Sash, here's your Christmas present,' she said softly. She reached up, held his face, and kissed him full on the mouth.

Surprised by her action, Sash wrapped his arms around her and held her tight, a year of longing finally released into a few seconds of heavenly bliss as the chains of pent-up restraint were finally cast aside. Mrs. Vitalli seemed to fit perfectly within his orbit of reach. He could feel the heavenly swell of her breasts pressing against his chest, and there was not a single ounce of resistance in her as his hands slid to her waist and deliciously explored her shapely physique, his hands moulding to her curvaceous hips and then round and down.

During that sublime moment, Sash felt unbelievably alive. The kiss went on as if transcending time, until eventually, somewhere in time, they parted. They looked into one another's eyes, both surprised by the intensity of the moment.

'Goodnight,' said Mrs. Vitalli, her breath but a whisper. 'Don't be a stranger.'

'You try to keep me away,' said Sash, as his hand delicately touched her face.

And with that, he left.

Mrs. Vitalli watched him as he pulled up the lapels of his jacket and trudged through the snow, the golden glow of streetlights painting a romantic Christmas card image of a lone soul trying to find his way home.

Chapter 14: Torment

Once back home in his fifth storey apartment on that Christmas morning three months ago, Sash found himself sitting in his living room, alone in the darkness, lost in his thoughts. It was two in the morning, or was it closer to three?

Either way, it didn't really matter.

The room was pitch black apart from a few chinks of moonlight shining in through the slats of his living room blinds, the narrow translucent beams of light almost replicating the bars of a prison cell as they inched across the grey walls of the room, fuelled by the dawdling passage of time.

Sash had done many bad things over the past two years since he joined the Vitalli outfit, but all in the name of, and sanctioned by, the head of the family. He had watched men dig their own graves in the woods and he had then shot them dead and buried them beneath the dirt they had dug. Others, he had thrown to their deaths from the roofs of apartment blocks. Some he had weighed down and tossed over the side of a boat, whilst they were still alive. But they all had one thing in common: none had been innocent civilians, and he was somehow able to take solace from that. They were all rival mobsters or gang members, low life soap scum, murderers and rapists of innocent women and children, who had crossed the line in the wrong region of New York and unfortunately for them had appeared on Salvatore Vitalli's radar.

If the police could not handle the dregs of society, or if the courts, when given the opportunity to administer justice, had failed in their duties and released them back amongst the populace, then so be it; there was little doubt street justice would prevail. And if a Mob family member had been a victim, then doubt would not even enter the equation—the perpetrators would get their comeuppance, and usually in the most horrific manner. And when it came to that, there was only one rule: don't let anyone survive; they will only come back later and put you down.

Sash gazed up from his sofa at the prison bar shadows on the wall. Were they the shadows of a prison built for the ghosts of those he had killed, he wondered? Ghosts that were loitering in the afterlife, waiting in perpetuity for payback, waiting for when he would eventually arrive their side of the ectoplasmic fence.

Sash grimaced. 'Fuck 'em!' He never killed anyone who hadn't got it coming.

Sash never had an issue with separating the good from the bad in his life. He found it easy to compartmentalise. So, why was he now even thinking about the scumbags he had dispatched? He had better things to think about. He had just spent a wonderful hour with the world's most beautiful woman.

He realised it was three o'clock. He knew that by virtue of the fact that he had sat there many times in the early hours, and when the first shadow cast by the moonlight crossed the corner where the ceiling met the wall, it was three o'clock. He smiled and realised that some might consider him to be a sad bastard. Well, whatever. He didn't care.

He shook all the thoughts of death and doom from his mind and replaced them with the happier events of the evening.

A peculiar perplexed glazed look appeared on his face, which seemed to hover somewhere between mild satisfaction and bewilderment. He was unsure whether to be pleased about what had happened with Mrs. Vitalli—obviously he was—he was delighted. But what came with that was an overwhelming sense of uncertainty which grated on him. He liked things to be organised in his life. He preferred clarity. He was not one for flying by the seat of his pants. He liked belt and braces. His inclination was towards order and predictability. And if proof were needed, his apartment echoed that sentiment; it was bland and sterile, a veritable, grey-walled bachelor pad unbesmirched with frills compared to what many would consider a proper home, like the one an hour away from which he had just returned.

There was not one piece of Christmas décor anywhere to be seen in Sash's apartment, not even a tree or a Christmas card from someone. But although devoid of much in the way of fancy furniture and those little homely touches that make a house a home, what he had in his apartment by way of possessions, he kept immaculately clean and tidy.

His living environment had the minimalistic appearance of a one-man army barracks which harkened back to a previous existence, back to when Sash was an infantryman in the U.S. Army, which he joined in his late teens.

The living room, although sparse, had a state-of-the-art TV and a music system, alongside which was his precious collection of vinyl records. The wardrobe in his bedroom was organised, filled with freshly laundered and pressed shirts, which were regimentally lined up, as were his casual clothes hanging alongside his suits. His shoes, which were placed on a rack at the foot of the wardrobe, were always polished to a parade gloss shine. Even his trainers, after being used, were always wiped clean. His sock and underwear drawers were similarly neat and tidy; the only unusual item in his wardrobe being a narrow metal gun safe which contained his legally owned weapons and associated ammunition.

His kitchen cupboards contained little by way of items of food; he tended to eat out, or had food delivered. There were just a couple of boxes of cereal, a jar of decaffeinated coffee, and a few cartons of milk in the fridge. The only counter-top appliance was a kettle, and unlike Mrs. Vitalli's expensive De'Longhi machine for making coffee, his was far simpler—a spoon for stirring.

But there *was* a type of counter bottom appliance in his kitchen. Out of sight but easily within reach was a quick release gun holster attached beneath the counter-top, containing a fully loaded Glock—the safety switched off in case he needed it quickly. And within the wooden structure of the kitchen door was something else unusual to his apartment block. There was a hidden system of ballistic plates—not the sort of plates you would see on a dining table; these were a defence system; although light, they were five times stronger than steel and capable of stopping almost anything fired at them, short of a bazooka. He also had the same arrangement in his bedroom and front doors. When Sash joined the Vitalli family organisation, and when it became apparent that the nature of his work could attract undesirables to his home, it was the first thing he did. However, it did not go unnoticed.

When installing the bulletproof panels, his small framed, arrogant grey-haired landlord, Mr. Goldschmidt, arrived on the scene, dragging a chip which, by the time he spoke to Sash, was firmly embedded on his shoulder.

'Hey! What the fuck are you doin'? snarled the short, elderly man, looking down at Sash, who was kneeling on the floor dismantling his front door with spanners and a screwdriver.

Sash looked up at the small man with the larger-than-life attitude. He said, 'I'm upgrading my front door.'

'What d'ya mean upgrading your front door?' snivelled the arrogant landlord. 'That's my fuckin' door. What's it doin' in pieces?'

'I'm just adding these panels to the inside of it.'

'What d'ya mean, panels?'

'These... they give the door extra strength. Don't worry, it'll look the same when I've finished.'

'HEY! You leave my fuckin' door alone! Put down that fuckin' screwdriver. In fact, you can pack ya shit and get out!'

Sash stood up. 'What do ya mean, get out?'

'You've just violated one of my strict house rules: decimation of property.'

'Err... but, but...'

'Shut up and listen! It clearly states in your Let Agreement, that's if you've ever learned to fuckin' read, that if a tenant damages anything related to their apartment or the building, he or she will be evicted. And from where I'm standing, you've violated that condition one hundred and fifty percent. So, pack your bags and fuck off!'

'Look, Mr. Goldschmidt,' said Sash. 'I ain't destroying the door, I'm reinforcing it.'

Just then, the elevator arrived at the fifth floor and out stepped Two

Fingers Tony Vitalli, who had come to lend Sash a hand.

'You stay right there,' said the landlord to Sash. 'I'm calling the cops.'

'Hey... what's going on here?' queried Fingers upon seeing the fracas.

'None of your fuckin' business. Who the fuck are you?'

Fingers looked down at the old, balding landlord with his grey-haired comb-over who was now standing between him and Sash, and whose head was at least a foot below their shoulders. 'What's your problem?' he asked.

'Huh, not that it's got anything to do with you, but look, his door's on the floor in fuckin' pieces.'

'Yeah, I can see that. What are you, his neighbour?'

'No. I own the fuckin' place.'

'Oh, you're the landlord.'

'Yeah, that's right.'

'Oh, I see.' Fingers looked around. It was the first time he had seen Sash's apartment. 'Eh... nice place you got here.'

'What d'ya mean 'nice place'? It's a fuckin' shithole!'

'I was just trying to be polite,' said Sash. 'But yeah... you're right, it *is* a shithole.' He eyed the small man with curious intrigue. 'Hey, man, why are you so fuckin' miserable? You look as though you should be retired. How old are you?'

'Huh, old enough to know when someone's fuckin' me over. What's it gotta do with *you*, anyway?'

'Hey, look guy, nobody's fuckin' you over... OK? You should be happy you're still alive in this fuckin' neighbourhood. Huh, how old are you? You gotta be in your sixties if you're a day.'

'What's the hell's that gotta do with it? I'm sixty-seven. How old are you?'

'That don't matter. Look, mister, if you wanna see sixty-eight, you'll calm the fuck down.'

'Hey, big fella. Don't you fuckin' start that with me? I've bin here since the fuckin' seventies, since I inherited this dump. So every day I'm above ground's a fuckin' bonus. I've seen it all, from gang violence and druggies to hookers and robbers, so don't think you're gonna step into my place and intimidate me.'

Fingers, realising they had got off on the wrong footing, stepped back. 'OK… OK… Sash, go put the kettle on. Let's have a coffee with this guy and tell him what we're doin'.'

'I don't want a fuckin' coffee!' grunted the landlord. 'But I do wanna know what's he doin' with my door.'

'What's the matter with you?' asked Fingers, exasperated by the old man's demeanour. 'Why are you such a fuckin' grinch?'

'He's busted my fuckin' door!'

'No, he ain't. I've told you. We're upgrading it. Making it better. There are some mean fuckers around here with guns. Sometimes they'll come to your fuckin' place and try to shoot their way in. This'll stop that. And if you like, once we've done fixing Sash's door, we'll fix yours too. Give you a bit of extra protection. How d'ya fancy that? All courtesy of the Vitalli family.'

'The Vitalli family. You're with the Vitalli family?'

'I *am* the Vitalli family. Well, one of them.'

The landlord looked puzzled, almost as if royalty had stepped across his threshold. He said, 'Christ! Which one are you, Frankie Vitalli?'

'No, I'm Tony Fingers Vitalli. Pleased to meet you.'

'Huh, Fingers… I've heard of that name. Well, what do ya know, a real-life gangster standing in my property?'

'Hey! Watch ya fuckin' mouth,' growled Fingers. 'I'm a businessman.'

The landlord folded his arms. 'Yeah, right… and I'm a ten-cent millionaire. So, what's with you and this eggplant?' he said, rudely referring to Sash.

Fingers eyed the short man disparagingly. 'Eggplant? See what I mean. You really need to work on your people skills, mister. Sash works for us; he's a valued member of our business organisation, and we like to protect our people, and where they live.'

Sash intervened. 'He's just told me to pack my shit and get out,' he said with a heavy look of concern.

Fingers again looked with disgust at the landlord. 'Ahh… you did, huh? And why's that?'

'Because he looks as useless as tits on a boar hog and, besides, he's destroying my property.'

'No, he ain't. He's improving his place.' Fingers turned to Sash. 'You up to date with your rent, Sash?'

'Yeah, Boss. Err… what am I? Err… I'm six months in front.'

Fingers nodded as if impressed. 'What? You're six months up front with your rent?'

'Eh, yeah.'

Fingers again looked down and eyed the bigoted landlord. 'Look mister, you got no reason to have a gripe with Sash, and certainly no reason to evict him. Now here's what you're gonna do. You're gonna disappear and come back in thirty minutes. By which time this door will be finished, back on its hinges, and will look as good as new. Then, if you want, we'll fix *your* door up the same, so *you* get some extra protection from the scumbags out there on the street. And then everyone's happy. Have we got a deal?'

The landlord eyed Fingers with suspicion. 'What are these panels?'

'They're level four ballistic plates. Similar to what the cops use for body armour.'

'OK. In thirty minutes, I'll be back to inspect it. But if that door ain't fixed and back in place…' the landlord pointed to Sash. 'He packs his crap up and leaves.' Then he turned and shuffled off down the corridor, muttering as he went.

'Hey!' called Fingers. 'I didn't get your name.'

The landlord stopped and turned. 'That's cuz I never gave it ya.'

Sash filled in the blank. 'His name's Donald Goldschmidt,' he said quietly.

Fingers frowned. 'Mr. Goldshit?' said Fingers.

'No, it's Goldschmidt!' called the landlord.

'That's what I said!'

'No, you didn't, you said 'shit'… Goldshit. It's not Goldshit, it's Goldschmidt. There's no shit in Schmidt.'

'Well, there should be,' mused Fingers beneath his breath. 'Cuz mister… you're fuckin' full of it.'

The landlord, who was now out of earshot, continued on his way. Fingers turned to Sash. 'Christ. What a mean, grumpy fucker. Sash, you need to find somewhere better. Get outta this dump.'

After that episode, the landlord couldn't do enough for Sash and even offered him a two-bedroomed apartment for the same rent, which Sash turned down, as the bedroom window of his current apartment led directly out to the fire escape ladders on the building's façade—a useful getaway should he ever need it?

# # #

Sash's time in the U.S. Army did not pass without controversy. He learned much, but two things stuck with him and became his mantra: one; you can never be too careful, and two; good things happen to those who carry an Uzi.

Sash poured himself a drink and decided it was a waste of time going to bed. He couldn't stop thinking about the beautiful woman who had been in his arms only an hour or so before. Now he knew how the man felt in that film he and Mrs. Vitalli had discussed; the man who was impossibly separated from the woman he loved by a quantum shift in time. But for Sash, he was separated not by time but by circumstance; that, and Mrs Vitalli's wedding ring.

Over the years, he had had many passionate moments with other men's wives. He preferred married women. He felt they were less of an emotional burden. They knew what they wanted and afterwards they would usually just return home to their husbands. But with Mrs. Vitalli, it was different; with her, there had been no sexual altercation, just a powerful emotional one, and he could not quite fathom why he was so drawn to her.

Sash's taste for married women began whilst in the Army, where he had had a brief affair with the wife of a deployed Sergeant First Class, who was assigned to 15th Special Forces Group. Sash's looks and powerful physique rarely failed him. He met the woman at a spin class she was teaching at the cycling studio at his army base. But their three-week affair was soon discovered, and Sash was arrested under the Uniform Code of Military Justice, Article 134 for adultery, now called Extramarital Sexual Conduct.

Whilst only a few U.S. States still criminalise civilians for extramarital affairs, the U.S. military maintains a strict stance regarding infidelity amongst its service members. Punishment bestowed upon Sash would have been a year in the brig had he not laid out the Sergeant when accused of the allegation. That indiscretion was costly and resulted in him being found guilty of assault as well as adultery. And his penance? The forfeit of pay, his allowances, and a hefty sentence of ten years confinement, which he served at Leavenworth.

After being dishonourably discharged, Sash was released around his thirtieth birthday. But his army experience had certainly been of use and would stand him in good stead. He had learned how to keep his body in shape, and how to defend himself. He had become proficient at mixed martial arts and had become an efficient marksman. Up until his arrest he had designs on becoming a Green Beret and undertook some of the training, completing the three-week SFAS training course at Fort Bragg—SFAS being an acronym for "Special Forces Selection and Assessment"—although its participants replace the words with their own, "School for Advanced Suffering". But it was just before starting the next phase of his Green Beret training, the Q Course, when his hopes were dashed after allegations of his infidelity came to the fore and Sash was court martialled for violation of the adultery rule. But that was almost thirteen years ago. After his jail term and once back on civvy street, Sash soon fell into a life of crime dealing drugs in and around Harlem and the Bronx, that is until an intermediary arranged for him to meet Salvatore Vitalli, who was looking for someone reliable who could drive, but also someone who could handle themselves, provide close personal protection and was not afraid to use a gun when required.

The money was not great but sufficient, and the job had its perks, but crucially, it got him away from dealing drugs and out of the spotlight of New York's finest, and of the DEA, which inevitably would have led to further jail time. So, all of that and everything he had ever done in his life had brought him to this very moment, right here and right now, staring at the wall in his apartment, still in his suit, sitting in the darkness on his well-worn leather sofa—alone, and with a woman very much on his mind.

The living room window of his apartment was open and every so often a soft breeze brought with it the delicious aroma of Mrs. Vitalli's perfume, the essence lifted and riding the draft from the cloth of his suit jacket, which had been impregnated with the scent of her fragrance during their embrace. Proof, if any were needed, that it had not all been a dream.

Sash did not feel tired at all. How could he sleep after what had happened? He slipped off his jacket but kept it close, folding it and laying it with great care on the arm of his sofa, as if handling it harshly might somehow disperse and cause the precious aroma to disappear.

He was suddenly hit with a flashback. 'Here's your Christmas present,' she had said, and she kissed him. And it was the best Christmas present he could have; it was the *only* Christmas present he would have.

As the minutes turned to hours in the darkness, he would periodically raise the sleeve of his jacket blindly to his face and breathe in her essence, replenishing his senses with the luxurious scent of her body and the memory of her soft lips. And when he did, he would close his eyes and, like the man in the movie, he would instantly be transported back in time, back to her house, back to the hallway, back to the moment of that kiss, and the feel of her wonderful body in his hands.

'Don't be a stranger,' she had also said.

Well, he wouldn't be. And this was not just sexual chemistry running rampant now—for Sash, it was how he imagined a full-blown romance to be. Not that he would recognise it if it was—this was a first for him. But whatever it was, he knew he would not be able to just banish this to the closet in his mind reserved for discarded emotional baggage, like he had so many times before—this was too big.

Tonight, the flames of desire that he held for Mrs. Vitalli, and which he had tried so hard to extinguish during the weeks he had kept away from her, had been rekindled. And then during that kiss, desire had been elevated thirty thousand feet up to the stratosphere. But at least he had some clarity now. He was no longer blind. Gone was the ambiguity. He now knew how she felt about him. The fog of doubt that had hung around clouding his vision had vanished. When they kissed and he held her, he saw it all, the willingness in her eyes, her mouth, her passion, the shape and feel of her voluptuous body as he took her in his arms.

He closed his eyes once more and was delivered an essence of scent courtesy of the breeze, and again he relived that moment. Already he was wondering when he would see her again, and how they would react with one another? But his was a preposterous situation, filled with jeopardy but driven by reckless excitement.

Sash prided himself on being a well-disciplined, careful man, but these thoughts and feelings seemed to cut straight through that secure barrier he had fashioned for himself and were now beyond control. Perhaps his emotions were intensified by the fact he could never properly have her. But then, he could never properly have those other married women either, and that never bothered him. So why was this different?

He allowed the frustrated hiss of a whispered obscenity to pass between his lips as he fought to work out where he stood in the grand scheme of things. And how would she be feeling? he wondered. He wondered about her throughout the night until the moon disappeared, and the sun rose on that Christmas day and bathed his apartment with dappled shafts of morning sunrise.

Bottom line was this, he decided—it was a hopeless predicament. And whichever way he played it out, it all came back to the simple fact she was married to the son of a mafia Don, and as such, would never leave him— would she?

The devil on his shoulder prodded him with his three-pronged blivet, reminding him that Frankie had many enemies, any one of which might rise up and take him out at any time.

What the hell was he thinking? He shook himself free from his demonic thoughts and brushed the Devil from his shoulder.

He had read somewhere that unrequited love is the worst kind, the most powerful and hurtful kind. If this was the stirrings of that 'L' word he had always avoided; if it *was* that that he was feeling, he hated its damned, painful intrusion into his simple life. It felt like a virus coursing through the foundation of his soul, running rampant with no fear of succumbing to a cure because a cure would never be found for this.

Again, the red demon reappeared and prodded him with his trident, injecting a further evil serum of murderous intent, which seemed to twist and turn and dissolve in on itself, eventually manifesting as a question. What if Frankie was to become the victim of a tragic accident?

'Yes, that would do it, wouldn't it?' whispered the devil on his shoulder. 'Then she would be all yours.'

Oh, God—yes, thought Sash.

Oh, that kiss.

Again, the memory swept over him, and he bathed in its glorious afterglow, clinging to it, never wanting it to fade.

After the scene played out, once again, he shook himself free of the murderous notions that were swimming through his thoughts. But somehow, they remained, but distant now, and diluted almost to nothing.

Almost.

He wondered what she and her husband were doing now. It was unlike Frankie to drink to excess, but Christ—he really had been wasted. He was usually the most focused of the Vitalli family. But by now, he guessed, Frankie would certainly have a raging hangover *and* a mouth like the bottom of a birdcage.

And what of her, Mrs. Vitalli—Debbie? Had he won the right to call her by her Christian name now? He never had before. What would she be doing now? he wondered. Would she be alone, too?

Perhaps she would now be up and sitting in the kitchen sipping something hot, courtesy of that expensive coffee machine; sitting there alone with her thoughts too, staring out at the Roman statues in the garden—statues that would be eyeing one another, as if knowing everything but saying nothing.

Unbeknown to him, just twenty miles away, Mrs. Vitalli was doing just that; she *was* sitting in her kitchen, gazing out at the leafless trees now peppered white with last night's dusting of snow.

Her husband was still out of it, asleep in bed. She had got up early that morning after just three hours of sleep on the sofa and had been for a walk in the snow through the park.

Her thoughts were all about the handsome, tall black man who spoke little but to whom she was so attracted, yet she realised she knew nothing personal about him. He was so secretive. Where did he live? How old was he? Had he a woman or a girlfriend? And what of his family?

There was an aura of mystery about him. He was so unlike the other men she knew, the men to whom she would occasionally make love. With them, for her, it was just a physical fix for an itch that needed scratching, and she suddenly realised she didn't want to see them anymore. But with Sash, now she knew he had feelings for her. She just wanted more of him, and only him. She wanted to be with him now.

Talking to him the night before and sitting on the sofa next to him, she found incredibly erotic. And kissing him and feeling his strong arms around her and the urgency of his embrace for that brief moment was all the confirmation she needed. What would have happened, she wondered, had her husband not been there?

She bit her lip and smiled wickedly.

She remembered back to her husband's drunken ramblings. 'Sex God of the Bronx', he had called him. Again, she smiled and then thought, perhaps it was right what they say—there *is* no smoke without fire? But a fire had certainly been lit within her.

And that was how it all began for them those few months ago. But unbeknown to anyone, Mrs. Vitalli was now missing, and Sash, who was sitting in his car outside her house, was soon to discover that awful truth.

Chapter 15: A Bird in the Hand

After the drama of the empty coffin delivered to Salvatore Vitalli's house that morning, and following the unexpected arrival of Layzee Dawson, Sash excused himself from the family gathering, saying he had a personal issue to sort out. The others, including Frankie Vitalli, were so consumed with Dawson's account of what had happened since his release from prison, they had not bothered to enquire what Sash's personal business might be, and he had no problem slipping away.

It was three months since Sash and Mrs. Vitalli had first kissed on that Christmas Eve, and now here he was again, sitting in his car outside her large, detached house, in the leafy suburb of Dyker Heights. He had not seen her for a while and as Frankie would not be returning home for a few days, Sash was hoping to surprise her. Especially after the disappointment the night before, when they had arranged a night of passion at her house. That is, until Salvatore Vitalli's late call for a family meeting had scuppered that plan; a meeting which had extended into the early hours, after which, on the insistence of the main man, they had all stayed overnight at his residence.

Sash got out of his car, walked up the porch steps, faced the solid oak door of Mrs. Vitalli's house and rang the doorbell. He rang it a further three times before deciding to let himself in via the side kitchen door—Mrs Vitalli had secretly provided him with a key. He thought perhaps she was in the bathroom taking a shower.

The side door was unlocked, but even before he stepped into the house, his sixth sense prickled—something was wrong. There was an awful aura about the place.

He walked silently through the kitchen, across the hall and into the living room, and then saw the aftermath of something horrific.

What the hell had happened here?

The place was a mess. It had been trashed. It looked like a home invasion, ransacked by burglars, or so it appeared—or was that how it was meant to look?

He pulled a gun from his cross-draw hip holster, took off the safety, and strode through the downstairs rooms, calling Mrs. Vitalli's name. 'Debbie! Debbie, where are you?'

He climbed the stairs to check the bedrooms, dreading that he might find something unthinkable. A body perhaps—her body?

Oh, God! Surely not!

He quickly checked every room. But she was not there, and he exhaled a breath of relief, and upon realising the house was empty, holstered his weapon. Perhaps she was out shopping, and this had happened whilst she was away. Yes—that must be it. But her car was there in the drive, and she would certainly have used it to get to the mall.

Sash felt rage build within as all sensible options for her safety seemed to ebb and then perish. 'You bastards!' he muttered beneath his breath. 'If ever you've laid a finger on her—I'll kill you!'

Mrs. Vitalli and Sash's arrangement was that they would never contact one another via their cell phones. That would be a dead giveaway and easily discovered. He knew Frankie had some corrupt CIA official whom he sometimes used and should he or Salvatore Vitalli find out that something was going on between them—perish the thought of the consequences. Despite his son's philandering, the family leader was a firm believer in the sanctimony of marriage. So, Sash and Mrs. Vitalli had to remain aloof, and had devised other methods of contact when they wanted to get in touch and meet one another.

If they had not spoken for a while, they would leave written messages at obscure preordained locations. They would be brief messages with just a time, date and place, but as a precautionary measure, in case the message was found and read by someone, they had agreed that the time stated in the message be incorrect by two hours. So, if the message stated 10pm, then the actual time for their rendezvous would be 8pm.

One such place for leaving a message was beneath a stone statuette on the front porch of Mrs. Vitalli's house. Another was in the crevice of a stone wall located nearby in Dyker Beach Park, in the shadow of the Varrazano-Narrows Bridge. And as he had a key to her house, and if not at home, Mrs. Vitalli had even joked about placing a message inside the pink folds of her favourite decorative ornament—a Tutufa Rubeta conch seashell, which she kept on the vanity unit in her en-suite bathroom.

Sash had only one secret place local to where he lived where she could leave a message, and it was less clandestine. If she called round to see him and he was not at home, she would simply post her note in his mailbox in the lobby at his Woodlawn Heights apartment in the Bronx. Sash had not provided her with a key, as he was too embarrassed about his modest apartment.

They would both check these pigeonhole locations regularly. The messages, however received, would appertain to a meeting place two or three days later, which would be out of town somewhere and would lead to a night of "dirty food", music, slow dancing, and later—passionate lovemaking.

But what Sash did not realise was that, such was the nature of Mrs. Vitalli's sexual appetite, he was not the only one with whom she was intimate. Mrs. Vitalli was aware of her husband's infidelities, and as such, she too would flirt. Her sexual desires had evolved from a young age, perhaps as a result of her days working in the shady dives of Las Vegas. Sexual encounters for her were nothing to be ashamed of—she had no inhibitions. She had had many sexual partners in her lifetime. And like Sash, all had fallen under her spell, seduced by her charms and her propensity to act on her desires. But for Sash, it was not just the act of sex that drew him to the beautiful woman. Whether or not he liked it, he had become emotionally invested in her, too.

He had never been in love. Perhaps now he was. But it was not like a switch that could be turned off; it lingered painfully, and forever she seemed to occupy his thoughts.

The master bedroom in Mrs. Vitalli's house was a war-zone, and it appeared an almighty struggle had taken place there. The dressing-table mirror was smashed, and items were strewn across the floor.

So, what happened here?

Sash looked around. The door to the en-suite bathroom was damaged too, hanging from a single hinge as if kicked in. He dashed downstairs and checked the statuette on the porch in case there was a note, but nothing was there. And of course, there wouldn't be. Then he was back upstairs in her bedroom at what appeared to be the epicentre of the struggle. He checked the cupboards and drawers, looking for what, exactly? He didn't know.

His mind was reeling. And then he remembered the damn Conche seashell on the vanity unit that she had joked about. She said that if ever she and Frankie had a big fight, as a last resort, she might leave a message there. She said it was the nearest thing to a message in a bottle thrown out to sea. He remembered them laughing about it. But she said it was unlikely that it would ever come to that, as she and Frankie rarely argued about anything. But something significant had happened here. But what?

Sash's mind was in a whirl. Frankie was due to go to London with Layzee, but had he been back during the past week, he wondered? Had they had such a row? Frankie had spent the past few days at his father's house, but had he been home? Had such an argument ensued? And if so, why? Perhaps Frankie had learned of their affair, and if he had, and had confronted her, had their row escalated to something more sinister?

Had Frankie attacked her? And if so, what had he done with her, and when? And how far had he gone? Sash had been with him only an hour ago, and Frankie's demeanour didn't look out of sorts. He seemed his usual self, flirting with the housemaid and the nurse as he usually did.

Sash approached the battered door of the en-suite bathroom and pushed it open. He hadn't checked the bath. Was her body lying in it?

A shiver of dread washed over him as he walked over to it. But it was empty. He noticed the curved glass screen of the adjacent shower cubicle had multiple cracks—further signs of a struggle.

Although absurd, the seashell now became his focus of attention, and he looked around for it. He noticed the large wall mirror was smeared red with something. Was it blood? His fingertips brushed the glass. No—it appeared to be lipstick. It seemed she might have written something on the mirror, but whatever it was had been wiped off and the red smears provided no clue.

But the shell? Where was it? It was usually on the counter-top, but it was missing.

In his frustration, Sash tore open the door to the vanity unit, reached in and scooped everything out. There was a small cosmetic travel case. Perhaps there might be a message there. He snatched it and opened it. But it was empty, its contents scattered across the floor.

Then he saw it!

The damn shell was lying partly broken in the corner, almost hidden by the door. He slid across the floor, grabbed it and twisted his fingers around its corkscrew of folds.

YES! There was something tucked inside—a crumpled tissue. He teased it out and quickly unfolded it, almost tearing it in his haste.

On it, written in what appeared to be black eyeliner, were a few scrambled words; 'TAKEN TWIN BROS' is all it said—the letters jagged and rushed—the final 'S' of the abbreviated word for 'brothers' hardly formed.

What? Oh God! The poor woman. So, this wasn't Frankie's doing after all.

Twin brothers? They would certainly be the Capelli brothers. There was no doubt about that now. And there was no doubt who had sent them, either. Louie Marmarella would have sent them to snatch Frankie.

Sash knew of the brother's reputation—they were evil, callous psychopaths, both of them. And if you got in their way, they would not discriminate; be it a man or a woman, they would hurt you—the bastards!

He pictured the scene and could envisage the framed motion of Mrs. Vitalli and the two brothers, almost like ghostly silhouettes—Mrs. Vitalli running up the stairs and through her bedroom and locking herself in the bathroom pursued by the two men.

She would have only had a few seconds to scrawl a message on the mirror. But she had been clever. She had had the presence of mind to also grab something and scribble a note and hide it in the shell before the door was smashed in. The brothers would have wiped the mirror, thinking that was the only message. Perhaps she had tried to fight them off as they did. From where he stood, Sash could visualise it all; the door kicked in, the scuffle, the melee as they fought, the impact of struggling bodies causing the shower screen to crack.

Then, after overpowering her, they would have dragged her out kicking and screaming. He knew she was feisty. She was strong for her size and would certainly have put up a fight. But Sash would know nothing of the violent sexual abuse she had endured.

He looked around, his eyes scouring the floor for clues. Amongst the strewn bottles, lotions and make-up paraphernalia, he caught sight of a used syringe. He picked it up.

So, they had sedated her—the bastards! What had they done with her then? What would he have done in that situation? He followed his train of thought. They'd have bundled her into a car, but where had they taken her?

He stared at the note, his face taut and fierce with rage as he ground his teeth. What was this—retribution for Dino Marmarella?

Louie Marmarella had put two and two together and slam-dunked the total, arriving at the obvious conclusion that the Vitalli's *were* responsible for his son's disappearance. Well, he was right about that!

And would Mrs. Vitalli have known about what had happened to Dino Marmarella that day? Did she know he had been shot and taken to Salvatore Vitalli's house? Probably not. Frankie had always said that he never discussed business matters with his wife. But when had all this happened? How long had she been missing?

If this had occurred on the night of Dino's disappearance, she could have been kidnapped four or five days ago. And as Frankie had been staying at his father's house all that time, he would know nothing—the useless idiot! Did he ever call her and check to see if she was OK? Obviously not! And Sash couldn't—they had agreed not to use their cell phones. Sash cursed him.

Christ, why was there no security here? There was only one reason—the Vitalli's had become sloppy, complacent. And Sash was livid with himself too. Why hadn't he checked in on her before? Yes, he had a particularly heavy schedule that week, but what about her bloody husband, for God's sake? Wasn't that down to him? No, he was too busy seducing that nurse and flirting with the housemaid.

'Huh, sonofabitch!' said Sash. If Frankie hadn't been chasing pussy, he would have been at home! He'd have been there to protect her! And the brothers would have taken him, NOT HER!

Wickedly, Sash wished they had. Perhaps that would be the ideal solution, and he remembered the Devil on his shoulder, who had once whispered to him, *with Frankie out of the way, that would leave the path clear for him.* That is, if she was still alive.

That thought hit him hard. No, they wouldn't kill her. Not yet. If that was their intention, her body would be here in her house. No—with Dino missing, they would use her as a bargaining chip, surely.

Now what was he to do?

His relationship with Frankie had soured—soured over the growing rumours of his relationship with his wife—but they were just rumours. He and Mrs. Vitalli had been very careful about their affair and had left no evidence.

But how the hell could he explain finding what he had found this morning? Why would he even be at Mrs. Vitalli's house? There were no planned drops today. And he, being there, would almost certainly cement those rumours. He would need to find an excuse for calling at her house. Or should he just walk away and leave? Let Frankie find the shambles when he eventually returned home.

No! He couldn't do that. He thought too much of her, and she was in trouble, wherever she was. What a mess! The Vitalli's had Dino Marmarella, and now the Marmarella's had Debbie Vitalli. And all Sash could hope for was whilst Dino was being afforded medical care, they would treat her with the same respect and solicitude.

Sash's thoughts turned to the empty coffin delivered that very morning to Salvatore Vitalli's house. Christ—thank God she wasn't in it! Everyone expected to see Layzee Dawson lying within, his corpse sent as a message.

But with what he had discovered this morning, that message could so easily have been the body of Frankie's wife—*that* didn't bear thinking about.

Sash wandered through to the bedroom and sat on the bed.

He was stuck in a corner. But what should he do? He needed to think of something. Then he realised what was required. The solution was a deal; he decided. A straight swap—Dino Marmarella for Debbie Vitalli. Could he broker such a deal? Such an arrangement was above his pay grade and would need to be sanctioned by the family Don. But how could he go to Salvatore Vitalli with this?

He needed to find a solution.

# # #

Meanwhile, on the other side of town, Salvatore Vitalli was sitting with his family around a large table on the terrace in the rear garden of his house.

'So, Layzee... how the fuck did you end up in Tony DeVille's Cadillac?' asked Fingers.

The nurse who had been watching over Dino Marmarella had been summoned to attend to Layzee's gunshot wound. The bullet fired by Johnny had impacted the windshield of the white Cadillac and had struck Dawson's left arm but had embedded in the car's backrest of the front seat. Layzee had been lucky; his injury was just a flesh wound which had only torn the skin. Although it had left a gash across his 'New York Yankees' tattoo on his bicep. Thankfully, the laceration only required cleaning and a few stitches.

Whilst they continued talking, the nurse injected anaesthetic around the area and with shaky hands; she set about stitching and closing the wound. Layzee grunted as the small, curved suture needle pierced his skin.

'Sorry,' said the young nurse anxiously.

'Just hold on a minute,' grumbled Layzee. 'What's your name, darlin'?'

'Greta.'

'Greta, that juice you just pumped into me ain't kicked in yet. Give it a minute, will ya? Have you ever done this before?'

'Yes, but not on a real person.'

'What's that supposed to mean?'

'I attended a workshop once.'

'A workshop?'

Johnny Vitalli leaned in. 'Yeah, she's a dab hand at changing oil filters, but give her a needle and thread... I bet she couldn't sow a button on a fuckin' overcoat.'

'Hey you... shut up!' snapped Layzee. He fixed Johnny a hard stare and pointed at him. 'Johnny, you're on thin ice as it is. Don't you fuckin' wind me up anymore!' He turned back to the nurse. 'What sort of workshop, darlin'?'

'It was part of our training. It was a suture training workshop. We practiced on synthetic skin.'

'Huh...synthetic skin? OK, that's fine. Don't worry, I got no problem with that.' He turned to Johnny. 'See... she's qualified. Everyone has a first time, Johnny.' He turned back to the nurse. 'Just relax, darlin', do ya best, and don't take any notice of that fuckin' douchebag.'

Layzee Dawson again fired a look of scorn at Johnny and then continued to relate how he had thwarted "Cadillac" Tony DeVille's attempt to kill him, and how DeVille had been arrested and was now in custody. He finished relating his story with, 'and after surviving all that shit, I get back here...' he pointed to Johnny. '...and that asshole shoots me!'

Johnny, who was sitting next to Joey but opposite Dawson, again leaned in. 'Look, I'm sorry I shot you. OK? It was a mistake anyone could have made. What would you have done? I see "Cadillac" Tony's car coming at us at three hundred miles an hour. What do you expect me to do? Let it hit us? So, yeah... I took the shot.'

Layzee glared at him again. 'You've always been a trigger-happy bastard,' he growled.

'Well, it least it's only a graze,' added Johnny.

Fingers, who was sitting next to Frankie, decided to contribute to the conversation. 'Yeah, but the bullet could have hit his head, and he'd be fuckin' dead!'

'Hey, you!' yelled Johnny. 'Will you shut up? What are you tryin' to do? Stir up shit again! OK, I shot him, but at least it ain't as bad as what Joey did?'

Layzee frowned. 'What d'ya mean, what Joey did?'

'What... ain't you heard? Joey went and shot Dino Marmarella the other day.'

'Huh...what?' It was the first time Layzee had heard of the shooting. He turned to Joey. 'Fuck me... I'm impressed. Nice one, Joey.'

Salvatore Vitalli, who had been reading the New York Post, intervened. His eyes appeared over the pages. 'Yeah, but he didn't mean to.' The big man folded his newspaper and placed it on the table, and reached for his coffee. 'He put two slugs in Dino Marmarella when they should have been in Tony DeVille! We were tryin' to protect your ass.' The leader shuffled frostily in his chair and explained. 'I got word that your wife had put a contract out on you, so I decided to take out that cocksucker to whom she'd given the job before he had a chance to get to you. If these useless mothers hadn't fucked up, then none of this shit would have gone down. DeVille would now be on ice with a tag on his toe, and you'd still be in one piece.'

'Just for the record,' added Frankie. 'I wasn't involved. If I had been, we wouldn't be having this conversation, because the job would have been sorted.'

'So, where were you?' snarled Johnny.

'Taking care of fuckin' business,' snapped Frankie.

'Yeah, your business being fuckin', I suppose.'

'HEY!' growled the leader. 'Have some respect! What's done is done. Now leave it!'

There was a pregnant hush, but Frankie wasn't about to let that comment drop. 'Huh... how do you like that?' He pointed his finger at Johnny. 'You cheeky fuck! For your information, I was at the docks organising the movement of a batch of watches.'

Counterfeit watches had become big business. It is said that for every genuine Swiss luxury watch made, the fake watch industry puts out two.

Extrapolating that equation equates to forty million fake watches every year—a one-billion-dollar industry, and one in which the Vitalli's wanted a slice.

'I don't care what anybody says,' continued Layzee Dawson. 'Putting a couple of slugs in Dino Marmarella has to be a good day in anyone's books. Is he dead?'

'No,' said Joey. 'He's fighting for his life. But I hope he fails!'

All eyes swung round to where Joey was sitting. With the exception of Frankie, they all looked at one another, surprised at Joey's sudden lack of empathy for the man he had mistakenly shot. Up until then, he had been full of remorse. So, what had changed with him? Only Frankie knew.

'Ahh... well, that's not so good, Joey,' said Layzee. 'What's the matter with you guys? Can't anybody shoot straight around here?'

Sitting outside in the warm sunshine around the table on the raised terrace seemed to dampen everyone's resolve. The question remained unanswered. It was too perfect a morning to argue.

Elena appeared through the kitchen's French doors and provided a delightful moment of intermission as she replenished everyone with coffee. She smiled a look of appreciation. 'Not much swearing this morning,' she said.

'No... but stick around,' said Johnny. 'With us sitting outside, I don't think you've heard all what's been said. So far, we've had nine 'fucks', two 'shits' and a handful of 'mothafuckers'. So, how much do we owe the swear box now?'

The housemaid glared at Johnny. 'It's full!' she said, as she poured Frankie a coffee. 'Perhaps next time we make it bigger, we get an oil drum!'

'Ha... that's a good idea,' said Frankie. 'Thanks, gorgeous.'

Elena acknowledged Frankie's commendation with a smile before making her way back to the kitchen, her hips swaying within the tight confines of her short skirt. All eyes were drawn to her as she left, with each of the men entertaining the same thought, although only one passed comment.

'Christ!' whispered Frankie, as he buried his face in his hands, fighting to temper his testosterone-fuelled cravings.

Salvatore Vitalli brought Layzee up to speed. 'So, bottom line is this' he began, leaning towards him. 'We've got Dino in the bunker's medical room downstairs with a gunshot wound, far worse than yours, might I add. He was in the care of Doctor Robert's. You remember him?'

Layzee looked thoughtful. 'Yeah, I remember him. The guy with the long grey hair?'

'That's right. I trusted him. We all did, didn't we?'

The leader looked around for affirmation. The others nodded.

'We treated him like family,' continued the big man. 'As you know, he's been our physician for ten years. Well, you're gonna love this ...' Salvatore Vitalli's tone became menacing. 'Imagine my surprise a few days ago when I found out our doctor friend had disappeared with a fortune in dollar bills. MY FUCKIN' MONEY!!'

'What d'ya mean a fortune?' asked Layzee.

Fingers leaned across the table, a fresh scowl sitting atop the permanent one that forever occupied his face. 'Doc Roberts has fucked off with over a million from our safe,' he growled from the corner of his mouth. 'He's shacked up in some swank hotel in London. He thinks he's safe, but we know where he is.'

'Excuse me, sir,' said the nurse. 'I've finished. The wound just needs dressing and a bandage.'

Layzee looked at the knitted line of stitches across the tattoo on his bicep. 'Hey, that's not bad, babe,' he nodded as he wiped away some blood that had seeped from the wound.

Finger's brow concertinaed itself into a frown. 'Yeah, but from where I'm sitting, it don't look right,'

Layzee looked puzzled. 'What do ya mean, it don't look right?'

'Your 'New York Yankees tatt' don't read right any more.'

'What d'ya mean?'

'Well, look at it. Now it's been stitched, that 'Y' on 'Yankees' is twisted. It now looks like a 'W', and that last 'E' looks more like an 'R'.'

Johnny leaned over and looked. 'Oh yeah... he's right. It don't say 'New York Yankees' any more... it says 'New York Wankers'!'

'Hey, dipshit! You're going the right way for a punch in the head. Now, shut your noise!'

All the men leaned over and peered at the misaligned tattoo, including the nurse. 'Oh, I'm sorry, sir. I couldn't do anything about that,' she said worriedly. 'That part of the skin was too damaged.'

'Ah, don't worry, darlin',' shrugged Layzee. 'Who gives a shit?'

'Yeah,' said Johnny. 'They've been playing crap this season, anyway. So at least it reads right now... ha, hee!'

'HEY! You got a fuckin' death wish this morning, Johnny?' said Layzee. 'You just keep pushing my buttons and see where it gets ya.'

Salvatore Vitalli had heard enough. 'OK... can we get back to business now?'

Layzee Dawson pulled something out of his pocket. 'Oh, by the way, anyone lost a phone?' he said, placing it on the table.

The big man frowned. 'Where did you get that?'

'I found it down the road. It was laying in the grass verge. Does it belong to anyone?'

'Yeah, it does,' said the leader. He picked it up. 'This is Doc Roberts' phone.'

'Boss, pass it to me. I'll take a look,' said Fingers.

The big man handed the phone across and pointed to Frankie and Layzee. 'You two, I'm giving you twelve hours to get to London. I want you both in that fancy hotel where our doctor friend's hiding. And Frankie, don't even start to moan and whinge about this. You're going... and that's final!'

Frankie, whose jaw had dropped, looked at the family leader in astonishment, and then at Layzee Dawson. He knew by his father's demeanour that now wasn't the time to complain. 'OK. But I ain't sharing a fuckin' room with him!' he said, pointing to Dawson.

'Don't worry,' said Layzee. 'You ain't my type.'

'Enough!' snapped the leader. 'Now both of you, sort out your grievances, pack a case and get going!'

'Hey,' said Fingers, who had a quick look at Doctor Roberts' cell phone. 'Boss, look at this. Do ya wanna know how the Doc got into the safe?'

Salvatore Vitalli frowned and leaned over. The others all gathered around too. Fingers played the video, and they all watched the grainy footage of the leader entering the safe's combination.

'Run it again!' growled the big man.

The video played again and when it finished, Frankie said, 'Huh... so, what do ya know? Looks like the Doc didn't have an accomplice after all.'

'Crafty bastard,' mused Fingers.

'Didn't you notice him filming you, Boss?' enquired Johnny, who then bit his lip and wished he could redact his question.

'Yeah,' growled the big man, as Johnny winced. 'I grew a pair of eyes in the back of my fuckin' head and then said, why don't you film me opening the safe, Doc? And then, when we're all asleep, you can come down and help yourself to the fuckin' dough. Of course, I didn't know he was filming me, you dumb-assed mother-head!'

The big man looked up and eyed each of them severely, and then said, 'So... it turns out our doctor friend's not just a thief, he's a lyin' bastard too! He fed me a load of baloney about Dino having rare blood. Told me he needed a transfusion or else he'd die. Now it appears that scumbag's on the mend and don't need any blood. I've told the nurse to keep him sedated until we sort this shit out.'

Salvatore Vitalli glanced down at his hands. He looked, dispirited. He nodded as if recalling some memory, and then said, 'And to think I trusted him.'

The others, realising now was not the time to pass comment, lowered their heads.

The big man gathered himself. 'Right! Frankie, those airline tickets to London, make it three. I'm coming with you.'

'You can't, Boss,' said Frankie. 'Haven't you got that meeting in Chicago?'

The leader thought for a moment and then cursed, 'Oh, yeah... fuck! I can't miss that. OK, you two go. Frankie, we'll talk before you leave.'

Just then Sash arrived on the terrace, and all eyes turned towards him. He had just returned from the devastation at Debbie Vitalli's home, knowing she was missing. But before anyone had a chance to speak, Salvatore Vitalli's cell phone rang.

'Boss, I need to speak to you,' said Sash.

'Just give me a minute,' said the leader, who eyed his cell phone suspiciously. Although the caller's number was withheld, he answered it anyway.

'Salvatore Vitalli, I presume?' enquired a voice.

'Who wants to know?'

'Don't you recognise my voice?'

The big man frowned. 'Louie Marmarella? How the fuck did you get this number?'

'That don't matter, does it? Does it really matter how I got it? I don't think so. Fact is... I have got it! And that's all that fuckin' matters, right?'

Salvatore Vitalli stepped away from the table and distanced himself from prying ears. 'What do you want, Louie?' he asked.

'I want the answer to a simple question, Sal. Where's my son? Is he at your house?'

'No. He's not at my house. He's probably playing with his toys at the crèche.'

'LOOK! Don't fuckin' lie to me. Where have you got him? I know you have him. Either you have him, or your fuckin' son has got him locked up somewhere. Where is he?'

'Hey! I told you, he's not in my house.'

'I don't believe you.'

'Well, to be honest, I don't really care what you believe, Louie.'

'He's at your house, ain't he?'

'I'll tell you what I'll do for you, Louie. Why don't you come over? I'll give you the two-bit guided tour, and you can check every room for yourself.'

'Just tell me if he's alive?'

Vitalli paused. 'OK... he's alive. Happy now? And I got a question too. Did you send a fuckin' coffin to my house today, Louie?'

'Yeah, I did. A nice big one. Does it fit? It comes in three sizes, dead, almost dead, and soon to be fuckin' dead, unless I get my son back.'

'Unless I'm mistaken, that sounds like a threat, Louie. Are you threatening me?'

'You catch on quick, don't you?' Marmarella took a moment to think and then said, 'Have you looked around lately, Sal? Have you noticed if anyone's missing?'

'Yeah, my brother's missing. He's been missin' for months. You wanna talk to me about him?'

'No, not particularly. I'm wondering, though, whether you got anyone else missing.'

'What do ya mean? What the fuck are you on about? What have you done, Louie?'

'Let me put it this way, Sal. If you take one of mine, I'll take two of yours.'

'HEY! This has to stop, Louie, before someone gets hurt. We need to arrange a sit down.'

'Yeah, maybe. See, I bought myself a banker's card, Sal. Something precious that belongs to you. Well, not exactly you. But someone close to you.'

'What have you done, Louie? You fuckin' dirtbag!'

'Me, a dirtbag?' Hey... you colossal prick! You fuckin' started this when you took my son. And if you fuckin' hurt that boy...'

'NO! You started it when you kidnapped my brother Sam.'

'Ahh... I don't know anything about that.'

'...and then took a contract out on Layzee Dawson.'

'Oh, you heard about that?'

'Damn right, I did!'

'Well, it wasn't me who took a contract out on that asshole. That was his fuckin' wife. Can you believe that?' Marmarella chuckled. 'His own wife took a contract out on him. That's fuckin' priceless!'

'Yeah, but you allowed it to happen, didn't you? And it's your guy who's been given the contract. And I understand he tried to fulfil that contract last night, but failed, didn't he? Layzee was too smart for him.'

'No, he ain't smart. He just got lucky. DeVille got interrupted, and he's been detained for a day or two, so what? But he's persistent. He'll be released soon enough, and then he'll finish the fuckin' job.'

'You're an asshole, Louie.... always have been. And don't forget. I know what happened ten years ago with Joey's parents. So, I suggest you take my advice and call off your dog.'

'Hey, that's got fuck all to do with me. If you wanna cancel that contract, you'll need to talk to Dawson's wife. And good luck finding her.'

'You ain't listening to me, Louie? I asked you nicely to call off your dog! You can do that.'

'You ain't in any position to ask me to do a god-damned thing. If you want a war, Sal... I'll bring it direct to your fuckin' door. Let me show you. Just keep an eye on Joey and watch this.'

Salvatore Vitalli looked bemused but turned to face his family, all of whom were still sitting at the long table on the terrace. At that exact moment, there was a sharp, whistling sound like the whip from a taught branch of a tree, then a single dull 'whap' sounded out, followed by the crack and the distant thump from a rifle that had just been fired.

Joey, who had been sitting on a wooden bench at the table on the terrace with his back to the lawn, was suddenly flung up and forward across the tabletop as if he had been on the business end of an invisible left hook from Sonny Liston. A brief spray of crimson seemed to burst from his shoulder blade as everyone around him jumped up. Then, upon realising Joey had just been shot, the men all threw themselves to the ground and scrambled for cover.

Salvatore Vitalli had turned just in time to catch the fleeting glimpse of Joey's body as it jackknifed up and landed in a sprawl across the table. 'JOEY!' he yelled, dropping the phone.

Joey lay crumpled on the table like a contorted zombie, the back of his suit jacket covered by an obscene liquid smear of red.

Everyone froze. Was he dead?

There was an awful period of silence that, if it continued, would provide the answer. But then, miraculously, Joey's still body twitched, and he began to crawl across the table. He was still conscious and looked bewildered but scrambled to the table's edge. Frankie reached forward, grabbed him and pulled him onto the ground behind the cover of a nearby chair.

Then Frankie raised his wet hand to his face, horrified at what he saw.

It was daubed red with something sticky, but he soon realised it was not blood—it was paint!

Yes—it was red paint! What the Hell?

The others regarded Joey with the same look of shock and horror.

Frankie called out, 'Boss, I think he's OK!'

Joey groaned, more from shock than bodily damage.

Salvatore Vitalli bent and picked up the phone, his face ravaged and contorted with rage.

Marmarella was still on the line, waiting for him. He said, 'See how easy it is to get to you, Sal? Have I got your attention now? You think you're safe in your big fancy house behind your fuckin' walls, your trees, your bodyguards, and your bulletproof glass. Well, you're not. Let that be a warning. Unless I get my boy back, next time it might be you, and the bullet will have an explosive tip and a full metal jacket for company.'

'You fuckin' asshole, Marmarella!' snarled the big man. But he was wasting his breath.

The line was already dead.

# # #

In the minutes that followed, chaos broke out at the Vitalli family home. Something Marmarella said to Salvatore Vitalli suggested someone may have been kidnapped. Which was confirmed when Sash informed the group that he had called at Frankie's house to drop off a few crates of whiskey, only to find it trashed and no sign of Frankie's wife. And as there was no reply from Debbie Vitalli's phone, it appeared *she* was the one missing. Sash avoided mentioned anything about the note he had found. It was in his pocket. How would he ever explain that?

Understandably, Frankie went crazy. He was due to fly to London that afternoon with Layzee and insisted he stay and look for his wife. But his father had other ideas. He pulled Frankie to one side and told him he would fix a meeting with Marmarella and arrange an exchange—a straight swap, Dino for Frankie's wife. Despite the situation, he urged his son to maintain his composure and keep his proposed meeting with Marmarella under wraps. He told Frankie not to worry, but insisted he still go to London with Layzee Dawson. The family leader decided it would be better all-round if Frankie was out of the way for a few days whilst he straightened things out. The last thing Salvatore Vitalli needed was Frankie and Louie Marmarella in the same room together, and besides, he knew Marmarella wouldn't take the meeting if Frankie or Layzee were present. Frankie objected, but his argument fell on deaf ears. And so later that afternoon, he and Layzee reluctantly left for the airport.

Meanwhile, upstairs, Joey stood alone, angry and stripped to the waist in his bathroom. His mind was racing. His suit jacket, daubed in blood red paint, was lying on the bedroom floor.

He approached the bathroom mirror and winced as he inspected his back. The projectile that had hit him on the shoulder-blade had struck with considerable force. During that terror-filled moment, Joey truly believed he had been shot with a genuine bullet.

But what kind of projectile was that? he wondered. It was certainly not a standard paintball rifle that had been used. He knew a little about those. He had fired them as a teenager and had been hit with a few paintball rounds when taking part in recreational team events. Weapons used in those open-air combat arenas were limited to a muzzle velocity of around 300 feet per second. They could hurt when they hit—especially on unprotected areas of the body. Which is why participants wear armour. But whatever hit him today seemed to strike with the force of a 9mm bullet.

It must have been a 'First Strike' projectile or something similar, he decided. He had heard of those—high velocity non-lethal rounds that can cover greater distances with improved power and accuracy. But whatever it was, it had hit hard and caused a hefty bruise and swelling. But it so easily could have been a real bullet though, thought Joey. Next time, it might be.

So, what was this? A mock execution? The bastards!

No! What he had just experienced was a harsh wake-up call.

At twenty-one, Joey knew he was floundering in the criminal underworld. Surrounded by a family of hardened men who would kill without hesitation and then sleep soundly at night, Joey knew he was in over his head. He recalled the mocking looks from the past week, the whispers about his weaknesses, his inexperience, his mistakes. And his stomach churned. He felt he had failed his family. He felt he had failed himself.

As he gazed into the mirror, images of his childhood flashed by—a gentler time, when his father and mother were alive. Oh, how he missed them. And those wonderful days growing up. Those were great times, great years.

Vivid scenes flickered across his mind's eye—warm summer afternoons spent climbing trees in the backyard, the comforting aroma of his mother's freshly baked bread wafting through the kitchen window into the garden. Those years had been filled with fun and adventure. He remembered lazy days spent exploring the bluebell woods near their home, family picnics, fishing by the river, and the thrill of riding his first bicycle down the neighbourhood streets. Evenings would be spent gathered around the warmth of the fireplace watching old black and white movies, his father recounting fantastic stories of famous people he had met. But, and he smiled at the recollection, talking once a movie had begun was very much frowned upon by his father, who insisted on silence whilst watching his favourites—Humphrey Bogart, James Cagney and the like.

His father would re-tell stories of how, as a kid, he would sneak into the cinema with his friends. Someone would pay, and then when inside, once the lights were dimmed, his friend would allow half a dozen of them in through the emergency exit door at the side of the cinema screen. They would crawl in, find a seat, and watch both movies over and over. Back then, a low-budget film, a B-movie, would be shown as part of a double bill alongside the blockbuster main movie.

A wistful, smile fought its way through Joey's glum expression and formed at the corners of his mouth as he recalled those simpler times, when the weight of adult responsibility and mob life had yet to settle on his shoulders. Back then, his parents wrapped him in kid's gloves. He felt protected, a source of strength and security that he'd always taken for granted. Now, with both his mother and father long passed, their absence left an ache that time had softened but had never really healed. It had been a car accident—ten years ago. Their car had left the road and crashed over a nearby mountain precipice, his mother thrown from the wreckage before it plunged down an embankment onto railway tracks before being hit by a freight train. His father never stood a chance and died at the scene, his mother—a day later.

The subsequent enquiry concluded accidental death. On that fateful night, Joey had not been in the parent's car. He was on a sleepover at his friend's house and ever since then he had lived with his godfather, the family patriarch, Salvatore Vitalli, that is until six months ago on his twenty-first birthday when Doctor Roberts found him an apartment in the same building where he himself lived.

Oh, how he longed to hear his mother's gentle laughter once more and feel the reassuring weight of his father's hand on his shoulder. What would his father's advice be? he wondered. The memories of their faces, voices, and mannerisms had begun to fade, like old black and white photographs losing their clarity. He so wanted to impress his Uncle Vitalli, Doc Roberts, Frankie and the others—especially Frankie, who seemed to stroll through life as easy as 1, 2, 3.

As his flood of reminiscence began to ebb, Joey found himself anchored once more in the present standing in his bathroom—a young man gazing in the mirror, as a once freckled-faced boy looked back at him.

He pushed the cosseted thoughts aside. He needed to focus on the here and now, and he needed to focus on survival too. The last few years had certainly been the steepest of learning curves. But the landscape had changed over the past few days. It appeared Frankie's wife had disappeared, and his friend, Doctor Roberts, had fled to London. What the hell was going on? But it was the day before that Joey would never forget.

It was about this time the day before, when Frankie found Joey in the medical wardroom in the bunker complex. Joey was down there checking to see if Dino Marmarella was OK. He was still sedated, but Greta said his condition seemed to be improving, and it was then when Frankie suggested he and Joey go for a drive.

Out of curiosity, Joey agreed, and Frankie drove them to the cliff road high above the train track where his parents' accident occurred ten years ago. Joey had often been there, but always alone.

As they drove up, Frankie was unusually quiet as if his mind was wrestling with something. Once at the top of the escarpment, they parked the car on the edge of the road and got out. It was a warm day; the skies were clear and there was the chatter of birdsong in the air. They walked over to a bend in the road where a crash barrier was situated.

'It was here,' said Frankie, 'This is where your parent's car left the road.'

'Yes, I know,' said Joey. 'But why are we here?'

'This wasn't there back then,' continued Frankie as he pointed and then stepped over the crash barrier towards the precipice. 'Back then, it was just a wire fence.'

Puzzled, Joey followed him.

'And all these bushes... they weren't here either,' said Frankie. 'I remember it like it was yesterday. It's not something you forget. It was nighttime. From a distance, the accident looked like a freight train had exploded down there on the tracks. But then it became apparent a car had left the road and had careered over the edge down the embankment and came to rest on the tracks, seconds before the train hit it. By the time I got here, the place was crawling with cops. There was an ambulance parked just over there where that lay-by is. That wasn't there then either.'

Frankie stepped back over the barrier onto the road.

'It had been raining that day. The road was damp, but I remember seeing tyre marks. Two sets of converging tyre marks. The cops didn't seem interested. They put the crash down to driving fast, speeding, a dark road, poor conditions... ya know, the usual bullshit. They seemed to be more interested in the train. But I distinctly remember seeing those two sets of tyre skid marks... just about here.' Frankie knelt and pointed to a spot on the road.

Upon hearing what was being said, Joey was dumbstruck. Frankie continued, 'And there were shards of coloured glass just there.' He pointed to another areas of the road. 'That's when I got to thinking this was no accident. Why would there be glass all the way back there when the car went through the fence over there? My guess, and I still stand by it, was the glass was from the back of your parents' car where a second car hit your father's rear fender and smashed the indicator and rear brake lights, forcing the car over the edge. You could see the tyre tracks in the mud. But then it began to rain again, heavy. I tried to explain what I found to some police officer... some asshole from the local precinct, but it was soon apparent the cops had already made their mind up. As far as they were concerned, it was clear cut... "single vehicle accident" they called it... decision made. No further investigation required. Huh... less paperwork for those assholes to complete, I suppose. I came back up here the next day, but the rain had washed the tyre marks away. But on the night it happened, I saw those tyre marks. Two sets of tyre marks, converging... just there.' Frankie stared down at the tarmac. 'I can still see them now. But at the time nobody wanted to listen.'

As he recalled the events of that night, Joey could feel Frankie's pain. Frankie's pain matched that of his own. It was the first Joey had heard of Frankie's account of that tragic night. He had no idea that he had been there. 'Where did they find my mother?' he asked.

Frankie let out a heavy sigh. He pointed. 'Over there, kid. She was flung from the car, but she was in a bad... well...' Frankie shook his head.

'Did you get a chance to speak to her?'

'No. It was mayhem. Sirens were sounding, and she was surrounded by paramedics. They loaded her into the ambulance and took her off to the hospital. Well, the rest you know. But what you don't know, Joey, is this...' Frankie rose to his feet, hesitated and then his demeanour changed. With vitriol in his eyes, he said, 'A couple of years later, and this is what I wanted to tell ya. Dino Marmarella was in some bar in Brooklyn. Back then he was about your age now, perhaps a bit older, twenty-three, twenty-four maybe. He was with his buddies. They were drunk and swapping stories. Bragging about stuff they'd done. Ya know, burglaries, car thefts, fights they'd been in... the usual adolescent shit. Then Dino, being the big-headed fucker that he is, mentioned the cliff road accident. A barmaid I knew told me what she'd overheard. She remembered Dino gloating, saying he'd chalked up his first kill. And that it wasn't just one kill, it turned out to be two kills... mother and father. He laughed. They all laughed.'

Joey looked astonished and dazed. 'And he was referring to my ma and pa?'

'Yeah.'

'He said that?'

'So, I was told. And I believe it. It fits with what I know about him, and what I saw that night. I'm sorry, kid.'

Joey looked stunned and began to shudder. 'So, they were murdered? But why?'

'I don't know. Who does? How can you second guess the mind of a psycho?'

'No. I mean, why wasn't I told before?'

'The Boss wanted to protect you.'

'But can't we go to the police?'

'Joey, it was ten years ago. Where's the evidence?'

'But he admitted it. And the barmaid heard him?'

'And if he was challenged now, he'd deny it. The legal eagles would put it down to 'heresay'. And hearsay's not admissible as evidence, kid.'

'So, who knows about this?'

'My father and me... and now you.'

'So, after all this time, why did you tell me?'

'I dunno. Perhaps seeing you full of regret and feeling sorry for that piece of shit got me riled up.'

Joey turned away and looked down at the embankment as he had so many times before. After a few thoughtful moments, he came back and shook Frankie's hand. 'I'm glad you told me, Frankie. Thanks!'

'You'd have found out sooner or later, kid. And by the way, that barmaid. She's dead.'

'Dead? How?'

'She was fooling around and fell off the Verrazzano Bridge, so the papers speculated.'

'Really?'

'No. I mean, no, she wasn't fooling around and fell off the bridge. My guess is someone threw her off the bridge. They found her a few days later, washed up on Rockaway Beach. She'd been raped and strangled.'

'Who did it?'

'Nobody knows. It was years ago. Case went cold, unsolved. Although, if it happened now, I bet a DNA sample would match that bastard we got lying down in that medical room back home.'

On the way back home, Frankie continued to relate stories of the Marmarella's. Although the Vitalli's were no angels themselves, the Marmarella's rap sheet was a father and son catalogue of crime an inch thick and with not a single reprimand or conviction associated with any of it.

'It was as if they had a free pass to commit any heinous act imaginable,' said Frankie. 'From drug trafficking, abductions, sexual assault, and even the killing of innocents completely unrelated to organized crime. They must have a guardian angel, right?' mused Frankie cynically, as they pulled into the driveway of the Vitalli home. 'Probably the Police Commissioner himself, who knows?'

And that's how the day ended yesterday for Joey. And now after that revelation, here he was, standing in his bathroom, wondering why he had ever felt guilt for Dino Marmarella. He had no feeling of guilt now. He wished him dead. He hated the Marmarella's as fiercely as Frankie. But unlike Frankie, he feared them, too.

He exhaled a sigh, 'I can't take another day like this', he muttered to his reflection in the bathroom mirror.

Perhaps he should get away for a week or two. Yes, a vacation. Get away from New York for a while. He always wanted to go to Europe. Perhaps he should go to England, perhaps London. Yes, London. He would go to London. And he wondered if he should try to locate Doctor Roberts. He remembered the doctor once told him his favourite hotel in England was 'The Land Lark', or something like that—it was in London.

Again, he looked at the face in the mirror. A defeated face lined with dread and foreboding stared back at him. He didn't recognise himself anymore.

But his reflection seemed to, and it began speaking to him. 'Time to man up!' said the freckled-faced boy, looking back at the young man. 'You can't keep being soft. They'll eat you alive. You gotta toughen up, or you're finished. Shape up or ship out!' said the voice. 'Or you'll end up dead in an alley somewhere!' And then the voice became more visceral, '... and in a grave, next to your mother and father!'

The words shook Joey to his core, and he turned away. But even as he attempted to find his resolve, doubt found a conduit of weakness and crept in like it always had. Could he really harden himself enough to survive in this merciless world? Or was he destined to become just another cautionary tale of the streets?

Time would tell.

Chapter 16: Force Majeure

According to legend, Poseidon, the King of the Seas, sculpted magnificent white horses that resemble crashing waves. When ocean winds are strong, the waves arch and mimic the flowing manes of these mythical creatures, the thunderous crash of surf resembling the sound of their galloping hooves as they race towards the shore.

Today was such a day. The prevailing winds blowing in from the ocean off the east coast of New York had strengthened to Force Six, gaining momentum partly as a result of the concrete and glass canyons, created by the city skyscrapers, through which the winds are compressed and forced through the thoroughfare of streets and boulevards like air through jet turbines. Yet, it wasn't the rocking motion of the ship in the harbour that awakened Debbie Vitalli, but rather the sudden distant cry of a voice somewhere.

She opened her eyes. 'Where was she?' she asked herself. She found herself to be lying on a metal floor in pitch darkness.

She sat up.

Wherever she was, it was cold, and she was shivering, but perhaps more through stress than the lack of warmth. She felt the tube-like shape of a flashlight in her hand, her thumb resting on the button. She pressed it, and sharply turned her face away from the bright conical beam, which momentarily blinded her. Then, once again accustomed to the light, and with wide, anxious eyes, she shone the beam up and around the small, boxlike storeroom, fearful of what she knew it would reveal.

On the grey racked shelves were stacked tins of paint, coils of rope, electrical cables of various colours, and rows of boxes containing spare parts. She played the shaft of light up, down and across the racks until eventually it illuminated the dead body of Rocco Capelli lying a few feet away. Although she was expecting to see it, the body's close proximity still startled her, and she was only just able to stifle a scream as realisation fully dawned on her and her heart sank. So, the nightmare that she had lived through had not been a dream.

She looked at the dead man. 'You murdering, rapist, bastard!' she said.

Next to the body was the large tin of paint she had dragged from the overhead rack, which had struck his head during their death struggle.

Now she remembered—she remembered it all.

Yes, she was still in the small maintenance storeroom onboard the ship. And yes, she had somehow killed this man. A man who would have killed her had it not been for that moment of luck when her fingers touched the handle of the door, which slammed open, breaking his hold on her throat. She would have been strangled by the brute lying next to her; of that—she was sure. Now, fully conscious, and without the veil of adrenalin to mask the pain, her face, legs, and hands ached with a throbbing heaviness. But at least she was alive. She remembered being told by her husband that the dead man lying alongside, and his twin brother, were notorious killers, and many who had crossed swords with them had not fared well. What he failed to tell her was that they were both rapist psychopaths, too!

Again, she glanced across and her face grimaced. It could so easily be her lying there, dead on the floor.

The sheets of plastic which she had used to conceal the corpse reminded her of scenes from crime documentaries—all that was missing was the entanglement of yellow and black police barrier tape that warns; "Crime Scene Do Not Cross".

Only this was a crime scene yet to be discovered, she told herself. But then, it wasn't a crime scene at all, was it? It was self-defence. It was either him or her, and it was as simple as that. She had been in the fight of her life to save her life. And it was this evil thug who was the cause of it, and the cause of his own death.

She began muttering to herself—rehearsing an interview she might someday have with the police, her whisperings arguing that she had been raped, beaten, and tortured by this man, and he would have killed *her* had she not somehow turned the tables.

But what was she to do now? How could she escape this damned place? She was trapped in a viper's nest, trapped in the enemy camp. She felt overwhelmed and scared and began to tear up. She wiped away the wetness from her eyes as the severe and authoritative side of her persona ordered the softer, vulnerable side to 'GET A GRIP!'

Her eyes flashed towards the closed door, as again a single distant yell sounded somewhere far away, and she sat up on her haunches, which caused her to wince from the pain in her legs. Was someone else being beaten in this hellhole? she wondered.

She touched her shins—the welts felt like bulging varicose veins, and her face was aching from where the brute had punched her. The left side of her jaw felt swollen, and when she touched her lip, she could feel the crust of a wound where blood had coagulated.

Her fingers explored the contours of her face. On the other side, there was something similar just below her eye on the ridge of her cheekbone, another laceration, but far more pronounced.

God, she must look a fright, she huffed.

She reached for the tin of paint on the floor, upturned it, and, using the bottom as a mirror, she recoiled at her reflection. She didn't recognise herself. Her face was grimy black, with shadows of blue and purple from the cuts and swollen bruises.

Just then, a dull clang sounded somewhere and seemed to reverberate fast through the ship's metal structure like a voltage spike of electricity through copper wire. She quickly switched off the flashlight, plunging herself back into darkness, all her senses prickling on high alert.

She waited until the bangs and creaks abated, then tentatively she switched the torch back on, which flickered as if it were about to die.

'Oh, no!' she gasped. She tapped it, and it seemed to settle.

Again, she looked around. There was no window or porthole in the room for reference. So, she had no idea of the time of day, or even if it was day—it might be nighttime for all she knew. She just hoped the ship had not sailed, and that it was still in dock, and as she could not hear the rumble of engines, assumed that to be the case.

She tried to concentrate and consider her options, playing down the severity of her predicament. Other restless, metallic noises sounded throughout the ship's steel structure, squeaks and groans echoing, almost as if the vessel was stretching after a night's slumber. But then, there it was again—that faint yell. It sounded like a human voice. Was it the dead man's brother calling for him, she wondered? It might be. Or perhaps it was a crew member.

Before falling asleep, she thought she heard muffled voices, but could not make out whether they were close or distant, or even if they were on the ship. If they were in port, they might be voices from the dockside. Following her ordeal, she had succumbed to exhaustion and was unsure whether she had slept for minutes or hours.

So, what should she do? She couldn't just sit and wait in the hope she might be rescued. That would never happen. But if she tried to find her way off the ship, she might be captured and be back to square one. And besides, it wouldn't be too long before a search party was sent to find the missing Capelli brother.

She had no choice. Stay—get caught, and be murdered, or do something and try to survive this nightmare.

A shroud of calmness seemed to descend and envelop her like a warm, comforting blanket. But shouldn't she be filled with panic and dread? Yes, most certainly, but she wasn't. It was almost as if she was resigned to dying—had already died and was now resurrected. She had been so fortunate. Luck had been the deciding factor—nothing else. The pivotal swing of fate that often teeters between life or death as you live from day to day, on this occasion, had come to rest in her favour—not so for the man lying alongside.

The wrestling creaking of the ship subsided for a few seconds and in the pause that followed, again she could hear the faint sound of that distant cry. Was it the bark of an animal? The howl of a dog, perhaps?

She sat and waited until she could hear nothing. Then she stood, switched off the flashlight and gripped the handle of the door that had saved her. She inhaled a deep breath and slowly lowered it.

She peeked outside.

The corridor was dark and cold. It smelled of stale sweat and motor oil. She could hear herself breathing, which sounded loud. She bit her lip, steadied herself, and grimaced as she tentatively stepped out from the relative safety of the storeroom into the naked hostility of the passageway. Immediately, she was startled by the brilliant shock of overhead lights, which came on, triggered by her movement as she crossed an invisible beam of infrared. 'Damn it!' she hissed. 'Come on... pull yourself together!'

To her right was the ladderwell near the lattice of vertical pipes where the twin brother had almost bludgeoned himself to death. That way would lead to the room above on the next deck where she had been tortured. So, she decided to try the opposite direction; a long, narrow passageway painted grey with what appeared to be doors either side.

Slowly, she edged her way along the sterile corridor, triggering more overhead lights which came on and then switched off as she tiptoed through each zone as the detection beams found and then lost her.

At the end was a right turn and then a left turn leading to a similar passageway cloaked in near darkness with again what appeared to be more solid steel doors on either side—all of which appeared to be closed.

She crept on. Again, sections of the narrow corridor automatically illuminated as she moved. She looked back. The lights behind had switched themselves off—the time delay only being about fifteen seconds.

After twenty yards or so, a hollow clang startled her and caused the flashlight to slip from her hand.

'Shit!' she hissed, as it clattered onto the metal floor. As she kneeled to pick up the torch, she heard a noise to her right from the other side of one of the doors and she froze on her haunches. Her hearing intensified as if all bodily power had been rerouted to that particular sensory organ.

'You assholes!' mumbled a voice from the other side of the solid grey door. 'It's about time you brought me some food.'

Mrs. Vitalli froze rigid, half expecting the door to swing open. It was a man's voice—a man's voice that sounded somehow familiar. 'Come on, then. Let's have it, you bastard!' continued the voice from the other side of the door.

She frowned. Yes—she recognised the voice. It sounded very much like Samuel Vitalli—Spaghetti Sam—Salvatore Vitalli's brother, who had been missing for months, presumed dead. Almost blindly, she whispered, 'Sam, is that you?'

It went quiet. And then the voice, sounding like a ghoul on a ghost train, said, 'Who's that?'

'It's Deborah... Sam, is that you?'

Again, silence. She listened for a response but felt horribly exposed standing halfway along the empty passageway, bathed in light, talking to a door. If someone stepped out from one of the other doors now or appeared around the corner at the end of the corridor, there was nowhere for her to hide.

'Who is that?' enquired the voice. 'Playing games with me now, are you? You sadistic fuck! Just pass me the food.'

Mrs. Vitalli frowned in disbelief. Yes, it must be him, she decided. 'Sam?' she whispered, as loud as she dare. 'Samuel Vitalli? Is that really you?'

Again, there was a pause, and she was plunged into near darkness as the overhead lighting, unable to detect movement, switched itself off.

'Oh Christ,' muttered the voice in a disbelieving intonation. 'I must be dying. I'm hearing voices now. I don't know why...' The man chuckled. He sounded as if he had lost his mind. '...but I can even hear Deborah's voice now. Has the end finally come? Good. I've had enough... bring it on!'

Spaghetti Sam was the only one of the Vitalli family who called Frankie's wife 'Deborah'. Everyone else called her Debbie or Debs.

'Sam!' she said, elated to hear him. 'It *is* Deborah. I'm here!'

There was a pause, and then, 'Here? I'm finally going mad?' mumbled the voice, drunkenly. 'Either that or I'm already dead and I'm hearing spirits now. Makes a change from counting roaches, I suppose. But where are the angels? Aren't there supposed to be angels when you die? And what about the white light? Ain't I supposed to head towards the white light? I can't see any light.'

Mrs. Vitalli, who was still kneeling in the darkness, said, 'Sam, you're not dead and you're not dying! It's me, Deborah... I'm here!'

'Deborah... here?' said the man, as if conversing with a phantom. 'Impossible.'

'Sam, listen to me! I'm Frankie's wife. You remember me, don't you?'

'Frankie's wife? Deborah? Yeah, sure I remember. Great ass... nice boobs.'

'Sam, you're not thinking clearly. It *is* Deborah... I'm here. I'm on the other side of this bloody door. How do I open it?'

'You can't,' said the dazed voice, as if mumbling in his sleep. 'It's locked.'

'Sam, I'll prove I'm here. I'll activate the corridor lights. Watch the bottom of the door.' She stood up and stepped back. Immediately, the overhead lights came on. Then she heard the urgent shuffling of bodily movement across the metal floor on the other side of the door.

'Deborah?' The voice was now clearer. 'Is that really you? Or am I going nuts!'

'Sam, you're not going nuts, and yes, it really is me. I'm here. Believe me, I'd rather be anywhere else, but I'm here. Wherever here is.'

'Am I hallucinating? My mind's not fuckin' with me... is it?'

'No... of course not.'

'OK, I'll believe you. But, if you're fucking with me...'

'Sam, listen to me. You've been missing for months. We'd all given up hope. We all thought you were...' She paused as if she had stumbled into a verbal cul-de-sac.

'Dead... is that what you were going to say?'

Mrs Vitalli winced. 'Oh, sorry.'

'Yeah, I thought I was dead a minute ago. And I will be if I stay here much longer. Deborah, if that really is you... what the Hell are you doing here? And where are the boys? Are they with you? For Christ's sake, tell me they're with you!'

'No, they're not, unfortunately.'

'Well, what are *you* doing here?'

'It's a long story. I was abducted.'

'You too?' The voice sounded concerned and then it said angrily, 'What is this? A new fuckin' ploy of Marmarella's? Kidnapping family members. What's he trying to achieve?'

'If I had to hazard a guess, I would say leverage. It gives him leverage, should he need it.'

'Yeah, maybe. Was it the Capelli brothers who snatched you?'

'Yes.'

'Bastards! They ambushed me too, right outside my fuckin' home. How's my wife?'

'Katherine's fine. Devastated, obviously. She's clinically depressed. She's on prescription medication. But she's OK.'

'She's a strong woman.'

'Yes, I know, and everyone has been there for her.'

'Good. Did they hurt you?'

'Yes, they did.'

'Oh, no! You poor thing. But why did they take you?'

Just then the corridor lighting again switched itself off and Mrs. Vitalli was once again grateful to be shrouded in darkness.

'Deborah... are you still there?'

'Yes, of course,' she whispered. She continued to explain. 'I think the reason I'm here is that Louie Marmarella's son is missing. The brothers broke into my house. They were after Frankie, but he was away on business. So, they took me. They think I know where Marmarella's son is being held.'

'Well, that asshole has had too many birthdays already,' said Sam. 'So, let's hope he's lying dead, rotting in a dumpster somewhere. But do you know where he is?

'No.' Mrs. Vitalli could not hold back what she had done any longer. 'Sam,' she said, hesitantly. 'I've killed one of them.'

'Eh... what do you mean, killed one of them? Killed who?'

'I've killed one of those twin brothers.'

'What? How? Who? Which one? No, shh... it doesn't matter. Killing either of those assholes is great news! But... are you sure?'

'Yes.'

'OK. Well, that's one less shit stain we need worry about. I could have sworn I heard one of them yelling last night. I thought I was dreaming. Was that down to you?'

'Probably.'

'Jesus H Christ, Deborah. And he's really dead?'

'Yes.'

'How did you manage that? He's twice the size of you. I hope it's the one with the black teeth. I hope it's Rocco.'

'It *is* Rocco. Was Rocco.'

'Really?'

'Yes.'

'Good! He's put me through hell, that sadistic bastard. He used to use a riding crop on me, across my fuckin' shins.'

'Yes, he used it on me too.'

'Evil mothafucker! And you've killed him?'

'Yes... with the riding crop.'

'Huh...ha! With the riding crop? Christ! If we ever get outta here, woman, remind me never to take you anywhere near a stables. By the way, I'm sorry about the ass and boob comment earlier. That was outta line.'

Mrs. Vitalli smiled for the first time in days, her bruised and split lips quivering as once again her eyes welled up with tears, amazed that even now and despite everything Sam had been through, he somehow still had his faculties, and had retained his dry sense of humour. It felt good to hear his voice. 'Sam, what is this place?' she asked.

'Well, apart from it being a floating prison, it's a cargo freighter of some kind. From what I can tell, they use it for drug running to San Juan in Puerto Rico. Since I was ambushed and brought here, we've put to sea a couple of times. I thought they'd throw me over the side, but after beating me up a few times, I think they've now got bored with that and have decided just to keep me alive, for entertainment.'

'Yes, like I said, probably for leverage.' Mrs. Vitalli again felt tears welling up in her eyes. She wiped away the moisture.

Deborah,' continued the whispered voice through the door. 'Listen. It goes without saying, we gotta get outta here. As soon as they find that brother's body, we're dead meat. See the letterbox in this door?'

'Yes.'

'It's an old jail cell door. They lock that letterbox. But that's how they deliver food to me, which is due soon. I need you to find something hard, Deborah, hard and heavy that you can hit someone with. When they pass me the food tray, I'll try to grab their hands, and you can hit them... but hard, I mean really... HARD! Then you can unlock the door, and we can get outta here.'

Mrs. Vitalli thought for a moment and then remembered the wrench that Rocco Capelli had swung at her; the wrench that had got stuck in the bulkhead wall.

Sam asked. 'Deborah, where have you put that asshole's body?'

'It's in a storage room, back there. I covered it with a plastic sheet to try to hide it.'

'Good. Did you search it?'

Mrs Vitalli grimaced. 'No.'

'Deborah, he may have a gun on him, and a phone. We could use them.'

'Yes, damn it, of course. Why didn't I think of that?'

'Deborah, go back and search him.'

'OK.'

'But be careful. Don't get caught. As we're still on port, I don't think there's much in the way of crew on this ship at the moment, but there are a few of Marmarella's wise guys about. They tend to come and go.'

'Right... OK. I'm on my way.'

She took off down the passageway, the zoned lighting again betraying her presence as she quietly made her way back to the storage room. She closed the door, looked at the dead body and felt a moment of nausea at having to touch it. She moved a few of the boxes and pulled the plastic sheet away.

The body was still warm, but stiffness and the onset of Rigor Mortis had begun. She reached into the jacket pockets and pulled out two cell phones, one of which was hers. There was a gun in a hip holster which she also removed, together with its sausage-shaped silencer, which she screwed onto the barrel. She was thinking clearly now and was just about to set off back to Sam when she had an idea.

Both phones were switched off. She switched hers on. There was hardly any battery power left on it, and she quickly dialled Frankie's phone. She noticed there was only one bar on the signal scale, but it rang.

'Pick up!' she urged.

It rang a dozen times and then the signal was lost. 'Damn it! Why are you never there for me?' she scowled. She tried again, but the single bar of signal reception had gone. She tried switching on the dead man's phone, but like him, its battery had completely expired.

She had another idea. She checked the settings on her phone and switched on its GPS tracking facility, which would enable anyone with access to her phone's number to locate its position, usually with pinpoint accuracy; that is, if the signal reception improved before the battery completely died.

She quickly typed a text message which read: '*Help! Debbie. Kidnapped. On ship. Trace phone. Be quick.*'

She sent it to Sash's cell phone number, hoping somehow the message would eventually get through, but with poor signal reception, owing perhaps to all the surrounding metal, and the weak battery, it was a long shot. Having done that, she was then back in the passageway, with the gun in her hand pointing the way. She got to the elbow along the narrow corridor and peeked around the corner.

She froze in her tracks.

Around the turn, along the narrow passageway, beyond the dark zoned area where she stood, was a man at Sam's door. He was illuminated by the overhead lights in that section of the corridor, and she was horrified to see it was the other twin brother—Ricco Capelli. He was wearing the same matching black suit as his dead brother. And such was their likeness, it was a surreal moment for Mrs Vitalli, as it seemed as if Rocco Capelli had been resurrected. And it was *he* who was unlocking the letterbox slot in Sam's door.

She watched as he passed a tray of food through the opening. Sam was cursing loudly at him, probably to forewarn her of his presence, but Capelli was saying nothing.

As she had not yet returned, Sam had not grabbed his wrist as he had planned.

Then the Capelli twin taunted Sam. 'This will be you last meal, before I finish you,' said the brute, who then hacked a laugh.

'Damn it!' mouthed Mrs Vitalli. Had they missed their opportunity?

The Capelli brother locked the letterbox slot. He pocketed a ring of keys, and began walking, but not walking back to where he had come from, he was walking towards her, sauntering along the narrow passageway as if he hadn't a care in the world.

Mrs. Vitalli had little time to think as panic paralysed her. She fought to suppress her fear as she spun back around the corner and threw herself flat against the bulkhead wall. She stood rooted to the spot, wide-eyed. Her calmness had forsaken her. In her shaking hand was the gun with the cylindrical silencer protruding fatly from the barrel.

It was now or never; she decided. Either live or DIE!

She felt a rivulet of sweat stream from her brow, and she wiped it away before it stung her eyes. Her breathing was now the only thing she could hear.

COME ON! she urged herself.

Fuelled by the awful memory of the past thirty-six hours, and without allowing another thought to cloud her judgement, she quickly released the gun's safety and cocked the hammer. She could hear the brothers' echoing footsteps getting closer. She lowered the weapon, pointing it at the floor in a two-handed grip.

She took a deep breath.

Then, in a determined, fluid, almost balletic motion, she stepped smartly around the dark corner, which immediately triggered the lighting, and knelt to one knee. She raised her arms and levelled the gun down the passageway directly at Ricco Capelli, whom upon seeing her, stopped walking.

He was some thirty feet away. He frowned and began slowly raising his hands above his head, almost as if in mock surrender.

'Ah... hello, baby,' he said, pretentiously, his face breaking into a beaming smile, showing perfectly the pearlescent whites of his DaVinci veneered teeth. 'There you are. What are you doing on walkabout?'

His smile broadened as he lowered his hands and grabbed his crutch. 'I get it. You've come looking for me, haven't you?' he said confidently. 'You wanna say hello to my big stack again, don't you? Come on, honey, put that down. Let's have some fun.'

Mrs. Vitalli's eyes narrowed, and her lips tightened, as she mouthed the word, 'Fun?' as images of rape and torture flooded her vision like a chequerboard mural of snapshot memories. 'You think... that was fun for me?'

Her hands started to shake, and her pursed lips tightened. Probably at the same rate, Ricco Capelli's sphincter muscle began to contract.

His smile drained from his face.

Again, Mrs. Vitalli could feel the whip of the riding crop, the stench and blistering furnace of the sauna from the day before, and the grunt of the man now standing before her, as he savagely took his turn as he raped her, pounding her relentlessly in her own house, and in her own bed as he stifled her screams with his hand across her mouth.

Ricco Capelli must have seen something unexpected in her eyes, as he said, 'Hey, take it easy.' He began slowly backing away. 'Come on, baby. You know you liked it.'

Mrs. Vitalli lowered her face and grimaced at the arrogance of the petulant brute. The pressure of her finger on the trigger intensified until the corridor lights suddenly died and the raised gun spat a single, muffled word.... *PHUT!*

In the darkness, there was a bright flash of fiery orange as the bullet exited the weapon's barrel and the cocky twin brother instantly buckled to his knees, clutching his stomach, a look of pure astonishment replacing his smarmy smile as his mouth babbled incoherently.

'UGH... err, what are ya doin'?' He raised his head. 'No! Don't... Don't...!'

How many others had likewise pleaded for their lives whilst staring down the barrel of this brute's gun, thought Mrs Vitalli, as she stood before him?

'No...no... NO!!!'

Those were to be his last words as Mrs. Vitalli stepped forward.

'Go meet your brother!' she snapped coldly, the man's puzzled eyes widening as her words registered with him.

'YES...that' right, you twisted fuck! This is your brother's gun. He's DEAD! And so are YOU!' She again squeezed the trigger... *PHUT!*

The final bullet struck Capelli just above his right eyebrow, whipping his head back against the floor, killing him stone dead, the rear of his head now smashed open, brain matter spattered and strewn across the floor like an upturned bloodied bowl of pig's innards.

Mrs Vitalli gasped and began to heave at the awful sight. She turned her head away, astonished by the extent of the ghastly mess. She knew a little about ballistics and surmised that the gun must have been loaded with dumdum bullets; bullets with a hollow point designed to mushroom and expand on impact, inflicting massive damage. She winced at the sight of the expanding pool of blood, but then quickly gathered herself.

Samuel Vitalli was unable to see what had happened but had heard it all, his ear pressed hard against the door. His mouth was agog, fearful of who had shot who. 'Jesus Christ!' he called. 'Deborah, tell me you're OK.'

'Yes, I'm OK,' came her nervous voice.

'Thank God! What's happened?'

'I've shot him.'

'Is he dead?

'Yes.'

'Oh God, I can't believe it. You're a fuckin' superhero. How did you do that?'

There was a pause as Mrs. Vitalli surveyed the body at her feet. 'Well, I suppose you can't be married to an underboss for ten years without picking up some of his traits,' she said, as she knelt and began checking the body for keys.

'I guess not,' said Sam. 'Godamn it, woman! Remind me never to cross you. Have you found his keys yet?'

'Yes.'

Then, quickly, she was outside Sam's door, grappling to find the correct key amongst a bunch of keys. 'God, which one is it?' she snarled, as she tried one, then another.

'Calm down,' said Sam. 'Take your time.'

'We haven't got time.'

'Yes, we have. More time than you realise. Nobody ever comes down here, only to bring food. Now, take a deep breath. But for God's sake, hurry up! No, no, I'm joking. Deborah, take your time, please.'

'Damn it, there must be a dozen keys here.'

'OK... but take it easy. You'll get there.'

She tried one after the other as Sam Vitalli quietly grimaced with every failed attempt.

'Deborah,' he said. 'Before you open that door, and you will when you find the correct key, I must apologise for the smell in here. It's a bit funky, to say the least. I wasn't exactly expecting guests today.'

'Sam, how can you joke at a time like this?' she said, as she continued to try each key.

'It's how I get through the day. It's how I protect my sanity, I guess. How are you doing?'

'None of these seem to work,' she said, annoyingly, as she continued to struggle with the ring of keys, as again the lights died, her fumbling fingers shaking in the darkness as if the keys were red hot.

'Calm down,' said Sam. 'One will fit. Just keep trying.'

Having gone through every key, Mrs. Vitalli slid the last one into the keyhole, paused and then turned it. The lock snapped open, and the door sitting on heavily greased hinges swung inwards, revealing her long-lost relative.

For a moment they both stood staring at one another disbelievingly, each appalled by the vision of the other.

For as long as she had known him, Sam, who was in his late forties, always looked portly—a bruising silverback of a man. He was an outdoors type, always tanned and healthy looking. He had dark brown hair peppered with grey, but the man now standing before her looked pale, scrawny and old for his years. Sam was always clean shaven but now he had a full beard, which, with the addition of his lengthy, untidy hair, seemed to add a decade to his already aged look. Such was his appearance, Mrs. Vitalli realised that if she had passed Sam in the street looking the way he did, she would never have recognised him.

She stepped into Sam's prison cell, and they hugged one another. 'My God, Sam,' she said, surprised at how thin and bony he was. 'You've lost so much weight,'

'Yeah, ain't that a thing, but I gotta be careful what I say to my wife now. She'll be heavier than me. And you know what they say, women who carry a little extra weight live a lot longer than men who mention it.'

Mrs. Vitalli smiled. 'It's so good to see you, Sam.'

'Yeah, you too, babe. But see what I mean about the smell in here? It stinks, don't it? Sorry about that. It's the maid's day-off, I'm afraid.'

'How inconsiderate of her,' said Mrs. Vitalli. 'And with you expecting company too.'

'Yes, I'll see to it that she's fired straight away.'

'Sam held his sister-in-law at arm's length and looked her up and down. 'Beneath this I'm fine, really,' he said, 'but, Christ, sis... look at you!' He grimaced. 'And your legs! Those fuckin' animals!'

Flashbacks of the horrors of the last 2 days, or was it 3, 4 or 5 days, again flitted across Mrs. Vitalli's subconscious like a trailer montage for a horror movie? 'It's nothing they haven't paid for,' she said severely. 'I'll mend.'

'You will, providing we get out of here,' said Sam. 'Shit's fucked six ways till Sunday, but at least we've got a weapon now.' Sam thought for a moment and then his demeanour changed. He said, 'Deborah, I haven't seen myself for a while. I've not been feeling too good. How do I look to you?'

Mrs. Vitalli tried to smile, but her reassurance emerged more as a pitiful wince. She felt like crying but somehow stemmed the flow of tears—just. She hugged him and said, 'Sam, you're malnourished. Anyone can see that, but otherwise you look good. You look... great actually.'

'Nice try, Deborah,' he said thickly, with a roguish grin. 'You're lying. I know I needed to shed a few pounds, but this is ridiculous.' He pulled the waistband of his trousers, which were now three or four sizes too big. He turned his head and looked down the passageway at the contorted body and bloodied mess of Ricco Capelli.

'Jesus! I can't believe you've killed both of them,' he said. 'Right, let's get him in here and try to clean up the mess out there. Grab that bucket and towel, would you?'

Just then there was a noise, and the ship seemed to shudder. The two captives looked aghast at one another. It was the deep, mechanical, rumbling drone of diesel engines. Was the vessel preparing to leave port?

The ship's public address system suddenly crackled to life amidst the initial shrill of loud feedback and then came an announcement spoken in a strange accent. 'Attention everyone. We'll be underway and about to thirty minutes. Sea's gonna be rough, so those wimps with weak stomachs, don't forget to take your fuckin' pills. And Ricco, Rocco! Where the fuck are you two? Get your arses back to the Bridge!'

A static click marked the end the of blunt announcement. Horrified, Sam and Mrs. Vitalli looked at one another.

'Oh, no!' Now they really were trapped. 'Who was that?' asked Mrs. Vitalli.

'He's the ship's Captain,' said Sam. Mrs. Vitalli sensed a tone of disapproval in Sam's voice. 'A particularly nasty all-round piece of dog shit,' he continued, his face contorted as if the stench and proximity of dog shit had assaulted his sense of smell. 'He's Russian. There's a few Russians onboard. He goes by the name of Vladimir Mashkov, although I guess that's not his real name. I had the displeasure of meeting him the night they brought me here. He's another asshole. It seems like they've rounded up all the assholes in the world and stuck 'em on this ship. I heard some of the crew talking. They seem to think he was a former battleship captain in the Military Maritime Fleet, the naval arm of the Russian armed forces, if you will. He's a personal friend of Louie Marmarella and certainly someone we need to avoid. Your husband knows him though.'

Mrs Vitalli looked surprised.

'Frankie did a deal with him. He bought five thousand high-quality counterfeit Swiss watches from him a while back. Marmarella didn't want them. He prefers to peddle his drugs. So, Frankie caught wind of it and bought the complete batch.'

Deborah Vitalli frowned. 'Well, if he knows Frankie, he'd let us off the ship, wouldn't he?'

'Not a chance. His affiliation with Marmarella is far stronger than the one he has with your husband. But at least we have this now.' Sam raised the gun. 'And I bet there's one just like it on that dead fucker out there. And clearly, there's no point in asking you if know how to use one. Huh, Jesus! Deborah, you're some kind of dark horse. There's bound to be another gun on that body out there. Two guns are better than one. So, I'll go check his body, and then let's get the fuck outta here.'

Chapter 17: A Different Perspective

At London's Landmark Hotel, beneath the vast glass roof of its eight-storey atrium, where soaring palm trees tower within the elegant cavernous void of the Winter Garden Restaurant, dinner service had just finished, and many of its guests who had filled their fancy with fillet mignon with a lobster tail or perhaps had plumped for the loin of venison served with a parsnip puree, were retiring for the night, including Doctor Lucas Roberts, who had hoped to be dining with a friend who had made the trip all the way from America. However, just before seven, he had received a message saying that his friend had been delayed and was unsure when they would arrive.

After dinner, he sat alone in the bar for an hour or so, had a couple of drinks, and then retired to his room. At eleven o'clock, there was a knock on the door of Suite 601 and Doctor Roberts, who was still wearing a royal blue shirt and grey chinos, opened the door.

Standing there was a beautiful woman, looking stylishly affluent, yet apprehensive. 'Oh, I do beg your pardon,' she said, with a frown of confusion. 'I think I've been given the wrong room number. Sorry to disturb you.'

She turned to walk away.

'Maria?' called the doctor.

Layzee Dawson's estranged wife froze in mid-stride and turned her head. She regarded the man with a puzzled look of astonishment, and then recognition finally dawned. 'Lucas?' she enquired.

'Yes. Hello Maria,' said the doctor. 'Eh, sorry... it's the hair. I should have warned you. I called in at a barber shop before I left New York.'

'So, I see,' said Mrs. Dawson, as she regarded his short haircut with intrigue. 'Good grief! Is that really you? The grey has gone too.'

'Yes... I needed to change my appearance,' said the doctor.

Her eyes appraised him as if scanning a sculpted statue in a museum. 'You look like a different man,' she said. 'It... it suits you.'

'Do you think so?'

'Yes, I do,' she nodded appreciatively.

'And you, heaven above,' said the doctor, as he stepped forward. 'You look incredible.'

The doctor reached out and hugged her; but not as he would hug a close friend or a family member he had not seen for a while. He took her in his arms and embraced her as he would a lover. And then he passionately kissed her. 'Thank God you're finally here,' he said as their lips parted. 'It's so good to see you. Maria.' He placed her at arm's length. 'Let me look at you.'

She was wearing a Moschino ribbed casual two-piece outfit, a cream V neck long sleeve top with matching wide leg slacks. He was surprised to see that she was now a brunette with long, flowing hair. She was carrying a copper pink Radley shoulder bag, and her oval Prada spectacles, the lenses tinted with a hint of brown, conveyed a countenance that many might associate with that of a legal secretary, or a perhaps a civil servant.

'And you,' he said. 'If I'd have passed you in the street, I would never have known.'

'Well, likewise with you,' she said. 'But isn't that the idea? Appearing unrecognisable becomes second nature when you've been in the Witness Protection Program for two years. Anyway, how are you, Lucas? You do look well.'

'I'm fine,' he said. 'But more importantly, how are you?'

'I'm OK now, but I have to admit to being a little overwhelmed by all of this globe-trotting.'

'I know. But don't worry,' he said, a gleam of excitement in his eyes. 'Maria... we did it! We finally did it! Come on in... let's talk. I'll arrange for your luggage to be brought up.'

Mrs. Dawson stepped through the hall entrance into the suite's elegant lounge with its tasteful décor, twin sofas, dining table and windows which overlooked the huge expanse of the hotel's glass atrium. 'Good grief, this is rather nice,' she said, looking around.

'Yes,' said the doctor. 'Only the best for us now.'

Next to the lounge was a spacious bedroom with its en-suite bathroom and dressing area. 'I love the high ceilings and décor,' continued Mrs. Dawson, her eyes wide as she drank in the opulence of her surroundings. 'Those white panelled walls with the gold flourishes on the cornices, and those apricot drapes with the swags and tails... they're gorgeous. Lucas, everything's so grand. This must be very expensive.'

'Eh... yes, it is,' he said. 'But Maria, we're rich.'

'Are we?'

The doctor nodded, bemused by the fact that the gravity of what they had accomplished together had not yet fully registered with her.

He took her in his arms. 'With what you endured, Maria,' he said, looking into her eyes and reaffirming his appreciation. 'You deserve this. And this is only the beginning.'

She snaked her arms around his neck and kissed him. 'Thank you. And I do like this,' she said as she ran her fingers through his new hair. 'But right now, there is something I must do.'

'What's that?' he asked. He suddenly realised she might be hungry. 'Oh, do forgive me. Have you eaten? I can order some room service.'

'No, no, thank you. I had a late supper on the plane. I just want to wash off the dust of travel.'

'Oh, of course, help yourself. The bathroom's just through there.'

Twenty minutes later, Mrs Dawson emerged wearing a soft white Egyptian cotton bathrobe. She looked fresh, as if she had just returned from the Spa, and the sparkle was back in her eyes.

'Ah, the blonde's back,' said the doctor.

'Yes, it was a wig,' said Maria, referring to the brunette that had arrived earlier. 'I have several in different colours. Which do you prefer?'

'I prefer your natural look,' he said, as he fixed them a cognac and joined her on the larger of the two deep sofas. Whilst she had been away, he had dimmed the lights and there was now soft music playing low in the background.

'OK.... a toast,' he said, looking into her eyes. 'Here's to the wings of liberty. May she never lose a feather.' They clinked glasses.

'I like that,' smiled Maria. 'But given our circumstances, perhaps something along the lines of "may fortune favour the brave" might be more appropriate.'

'Huh, yes, or should that be may a *large* fortune favour the brave.'

They both took a sip of their brandy, to which the doctor had added a splash of peppermint cordial.

'When I was given the message regarding your delay,' he said. 'I was fearful you might have had passport problems... you know, having now to travel under your new name.'

'No, it was just a delayed flight,' replied Maria, as she repositioned a cushion and snuggled into the doctor's embrace on the sofa. 'We had a two-hour delay in New York,' she explained. 'And then, after landing, they held us on the plane for twenty minutes before we disembarked. And to add insult to injury, it was then almost forty minutes before our luggage began to appear on the carousel. But there was no problem with my passport.'

'Good,' said the doctor. 'But it will be me that will be the problem. I don't think I'll ever get used to calling you Tilly Jacobs.'

Maria smiled. 'Well, you don't have to. Maria's fine. If anyone ever queries you calling me that, I'll say it's my second Christian name, which I prefer you to use.'

They briefly discussed Maria's transition across London and the idiosyn-crasies of a talkative, elderly London taxi driver who provided a forensic account of the hotel's history. Mrs. Dawson recalled his monologue.

'So, it's the Landmark Hotel, ain't it?' began the taxi driver with a mild Cockney accent. 'Proper five-star gaff that. 1899 it opened... designed by Sir Robert Edis. Originally, it was called the Great Central, but in the 1920's it stopped being used as a hotel. Know why? The economy went tits up. Just like today. It was a convalescent home during the second world war, when it was a used as a military office for years, then it was headquarters for the British Railways Board. Staff used to call it "The Kremlin." Huh... fancy that. Then the Japs got hold of it in the mid-eighties, restored it and then it reopened as a hotel in the early nineties. It was called "The Regent" then until it was flogged to a Thai company who re-opened it later as "The Landmark". See... foreigners have taken over London town. Now we got Japanese, Thai's, Indians, Chinese, Arabs, dodgy Russian oligarchs and every other colour and creed known to man, plus all those illegal immigrants swimmin' the fuckin' Channel to get here for free health care, a roof over their head and a few quid off the social. They all want to come here. Soft touch, ain't we us British? It's all down to diversity, see. Multiculturalism's the buzzword in the city, sad really cuz, it ain't the London I remember. Ah, here it is look... The Landmark looks proper fancy now though' don't it? OH, fuck me! Look at this geeza!' The driver gave a blast of the car horn. 'Watch where you're goin', you fuckin' idiot!'

Maria Dawson smiled. Although she had given him a generous tip, she was unsure what to make of the outspoken, opinionated driver. Were all Englishmen like this? she wondered.

It had been cold and foggy outside, but cosseted within the warmth of the hotel suite, she and the Doctor began reminiscing about how they had met ten years before, and what they had been through.

Their relationship began whilst Mrs. Dawson was still living with her husband. The young doctor, as he was then, had been caring for their elderly neighbours who lived immediately next door, Hilda and Harvey Bernstein, the couple who, unbeknown to Maria had had an altercation with Mrs. Dawson husband only a few days ago following his early release from prison—an altercation that resulted in Harvey Bernstein being accidentally injured in a firearm incident and hospitalised.

Owing to their advancing years, the doctor had, for many years, frequently visited the elderly couple on medical grounds, and a friendship developed between himself, his two patients and Mrs. Dawson, as Maria would often run errands to the local pharmacy collecting medication for her two ageing neighbours.

'Do you remember me doing that?' she said, as she reflected on those days many years ago.

'Yes, I do,' said the doctor. 'Sorry to bring him up in conversation, but wasn't it about then when I first met your husband?'

Maria nodded.

On occasion, when visiting the Bernstein's, the doctor would chat with Layzee Dawson, who, owing to his association with the Vitalli crime family, eventually introduced him to Salvatore Vitalli, which led to the doctor becoming the family's trusted physician, a relationship which strengthened through the years.

The doctor shook his head as memories returned. 'Oh my God, do you realise it's been ten years since I first met Mr. Vitalli?' he said. 'Back then he was in the process of having that large house of his renovated. Do you remember?'

Maria looked thoughtful. 'Yes, I do remember.'

During those ten years, Mrs. Dawson and the doctor would talk often when he visited Hilda and Harvey Bernstein and their friendship evolved into one of mutual attraction. In time, Mrs. Dawson felt she could confide in the doctor and began talking about her unhappy marriage, and how miserable she had become living with a mafia enforcer who had lost all interest in her and was openly pursuing other women. She said she was trapped and wanted to get out of the marriage but couldn't. It was then when the doctor's friendship with her escalated beyond attraction to something more intimate.

'But isn't life full of peculiarities?' he said, thinking back to that time. 'Had I not become involved with the Vitalli's when I did, we might never have got together.'

Maria, who was now lying in the doctor's arms, squeezed his hand. 'Yes, you were my rock back then,' she said. 'You still are.'

'You see, we were falling in love, Maria. And we knew something had to be done about your husband. It was just a matter of what, when and how.'

It was then when ideas began to surface regarding how Maria could end her marriage. Her husband's purpose in life seemed to revolve around his philandering and his criminal activities, most of which would involve the disposal of rival mobster and gang members. Sometimes, she would watch the news during the evenings and see scenes of murder and destruction, knowing full well that her husband had been involved, although it was never admitted.

She feared him. And knew he would never grant her a divorce. Although he had never hurt her, she knew that if she just up and left he would hunt her down and then violence would certainly ensue. And as neither she nor the doctor had the stomach to kill the man, they knew they needed to find a more legally acceptable solution to his problem.

So, under the guidance of the doctor, they set in motion a sequence of events that would take her husband completely out of circulation. And that was when they hit upon the notion of framing her husband for the brutal assault of his wife. And as violence was in his nature, making that stick should be simple, provided they planned it carefully. They considered numerous ways in which to achieve that objective, but only one appeared to carry enough weight to succeed in a courtroom. And it was a drastic measure, especially for Mrs. Dawson.

'You were so brave, Maria,' said the doctor. 'Tell me if you want me to stop talking about this.'

'No. It's OK, go on. It all seems so long ago now.'

For their plan to succeed, they decided that Maria would need to appear as though she had been severely beaten by her husband, who would then be arrested for assault. Despite the doctor's apprehension, Mrs. Dawson was adamant she wanted to go ahead with the plan and insisted that it would be worth the pain and suffering, but it would need to appear genuine.

It was decided that the doctor administer the drubbing as scientifically as he could, and in such a manner that it would not endanger her life but would look convincing enough to hopefully secure a guilty verdict in a court of law.

If found guilty, her husband would be imprisoned for many years and the threat of any reprisal would be gone.

They decided to arrange Maria's 'assault' on a day when Layzee Dawson would not be expected home until late evening. They did not have to wait long and when the day arrived, the doctor prepared Maria Dawson by applying anaesthetic to various regions of her face and upper body. Then, whilst fighting back tears, the doctor undertook the awful act of beating her, making sure her blood was smeared across a baseball bat, that she would later say her husband had used on her. The doctor purposely cut shallow lacerations on areas of her face, shoulders, and arms, but in places that he knew would heal perfectly.

'Oh God, I'd rather not talk about what I had to do to you,' said the doctor, his voice faltering as the memories returned.

'Darling, had you not done that, we would not be here together now. Please...' Maria checked herself and then smiled. 'I was going to say, please don't beat yourself up over it. But I guess that's a bad choice of words.'

The doctor glanced at her, horrified, and then they both laughed. But there was no getting away from the fact the process the doctor had to undertake was horrific and sickened him. He recalled being amazed at her courage and determination, even when she insisted he continue when he felt he had damaged her enough.

She was adamant that she had to look dreadfully beaten, in order for their scheme to work, knowing the police would photograph her, and that the photographic images would be used as evidence and shown to the jury along with the bloodied baseball bat during the subsequent trial.

Then, after the terrible physical act was over, the doctor, racked with remorse, recalled venting his angst when he trashed the downstairs rooms of her house as if an almighty struggle had occurred, again something they had planned in order to further reinforce their story - her story.

The doctor looked at the woman he loved. All signs of the terrible beating had long gone, and she now looked gorgeous as she lay relaxed in his arms.

'I remember then,' he continued solemnly. 'That I had to leave you.'

'Yes. That was the worst part,' said Maria, sipping her balloon of cognac.

'I remember telling you to call the police immediately you heard his car pull into the drive.'

'Yes, and I did.' For a moment, Maria was lost in thought as memories of that night came flooding back. 'The police arrived very quickly.'

'Eh, yes they did,' agreed the doctor. 'I remember. I was sitting in my car down the street, watching it all play out. I felt so bloody helpless. I saw your husband pull into the drive and stagger drunkenly into the house. Then, I tried to imagine what was going on. You alone with him. Then, as you say, the police arrived, and I had to watch as you were put into an ambulance and taken to hospital, longing to be with you. But knowing I had to stay away.'

'But the plan worked, Lucas,' said Maria. She grasped his arm. 'I can see that it still hurts you. But Lucas, it worked!'

She was right, thought the doctor. Layzee was arrested and taken away, although he did not go willingly and fought like a trojan. The police had to call for backup, and it took four of them to finally cuff and wrestle him into the police vehicle, a contributing factor to him later being refused bail on account of the risk of repeated violence, especially as he was also facing charges for another incident of assault that, at the time, neither Maria nor the doctor were aware of, the stabbing of a prostitute, who had mercifully survived his attack.

Then, Mrs. Dawson began a drastic regime to further reinforce her case. A physical change. She felt she needed to look like an abused woman. So, under the watchful eye of the doctor, who ensured she was taking sufficient vitamins and supplements, she shed three stones in weight—almost twenty kilos—in just ten weeks.

Then, two things happened. Layzee was found guilty and sentenced to four years' incarceration, which they both felt was ludicrously insufficient punishment. Then, immediately after the trial, Mrs. Dawson entered the witness protection program to become Matilda Jacobs. After which, they set about the next phase of their plan—a scheme to con the Vitalli family leader out of a large amount of money, large enough for them to start a new life together somewhere. And that was where the doctor's expertise would be put to good use. He planned to anonymously frame and bribe one of the Vitalli's, ideally Johnny—who he perceived as being erratic and easy to fool.

Things remained quiet for a while. The doctor continued working and would visit Maria most weekends. But that was far from the life they wanted, and whilst the doctor waited for an opportunity, almost two years flew by. Then, they received some news—disastrous news. After only two years into his sentence, they heard Maria's husband had become eligible for early parole and might be released.

All the doubt and fear returned. The doctor and Mrs. Dawson were desperate. They knew if released, Layzee would hunt her down looking for revenge. And it was then, blinded by desperation and running out of time, when Doctor Robert's suggested Mrs. Dawson take out a contract on her husband's life to finally put an end to the threat of him finding and killing her.

The doctor knew Louie Marmarella. So, risking their combined savings, Mrs. Dawson met and struck a deal with Marmarella's chief enforcer, Antonio DeVille—"Cadillac" Tony DeVille, to kill her husband.

Maria recalled the conversation. 'Actually, he was a real gentleman,' she said. 'I was surprised, considering he was Marmarella's equivalent of Layzee. I thought he would be a brute. But he wasn't. He was businesslike. I remember he was proud of his impeccable record. One hundred percent success rate, he said. Even though he was a ruthless killer, talking to him was almost like talking to a bank manager.'

Maria decided not to mention her visit to the Elmira Correctional Facility just before Layzee's parole hearing. She hoped visiting her husband in prison would trigger an adverse violent reaction from him, which would jeopardise his early release, resulting in him serving his *full* four-year sentence—buying them a bit more time. But it did not. The doctor was unaware of that visit, and Mrs. Dawson saw no reason to trouble him with it.

During those difficult two years, the financial part of their scheme failed to materialise—that is, until the day Joey Vitalli shot Dino Marmarella, mistaking him for "Cadillac" Tony DeVille.

It was then when the doctor was called upon by Salvatore Vitalli to save the life of Dino Marmarella in order to prevent the two crime families from going to war. And that was the opportunity the doctor had been waiting for. His eyes glazed over and for a moment, he was back in the room talking to the crime family boss once again. He explained his thinking to Maria. She had heard it before, but she liked to watch him as he re-lived and revelled in his ingenuity.

'I formulated the wildest of schemes,' he began. 'A scheme so fantastical it might just work. I went to Salvatore Vitalli and advised him that Dino Marmarella had an extremely rare blood type. A blood type so rare, blood banks had no supply of it. And if it could not be sourced, Dino Marmarella would die. Of course, it was not true. It was a complete fabrication. I made out the first bullet had caused massive damage, but it hadn't, really. The operation to remove both bullets was straightforward, and Dino's life was never in danger... he was always going to recover. I just had to keep him sedated for as long as possible.'

Maria enjoyed watching his excitement. 'Then what?' she said, encouraging him to continue.

'Well... I then explained to Mr. Vitalli that I had searched the database and only one living person was listed as having the same rare blood type variant as Dino, and that person was you.'

'I wish I could have seen his face,' said Maria. 'And he believed you.'

'Yes... every word. I also fed him a yarn about you trafficking human organs. He swallowed that story too.'

Maria's salacious smile beamed wider. 'My God!'

'I told him that you were well aware of the value of your rare blood type and had been selling it on the black market via the Dark Web for years, using me as an intermediary.'

'I can't believe he fell for *that*.'

'Well, he did. You have to remember, Maria... he has the mind of a criminal. But please, give me some credit for my acting ability. I was proud of it. It was certainly up there with your performance two years ago when you were on the stand that day in court. Although it was surreal, sitting next to Salvatore Vitalli watching you being questioned, and marvelling at your performance. Wow! I was in awe. What was it your husband yelled out?

Something about Meryl Streep couldn't play it better. Christ! I almost cried out in laughter. But the other day, at Salvatore Vitalli's house in his study, it was crunch-time. I *had* to convince him of the Blood Money deal.'

Maria squeezed his hand. 'But you did!'

'Yes, thankfully. He knew if Dino died, and Louie Marmarella found out it was as a result of his son being shot by one of the Vitalli's, then an all-out war would ensue. Marmarella's Floridian contingent would be called to arms, and all hell would break loose. So, he wanted to believe in what I was telling him. He *needed* to believe in what I was telling him. I led him down the path. And he followed me.'

'See... he trusted you,' said Maria. 'And hates me.'

'Yes. I'm afraid so. I'll never forget the look on his face. He was almost salivating at the prospect of you losing your life. But you see, Maria, his hatred of you is what made the plan work. That's all he could see. But don't worry, you're now part of the Witness Protection Program, and we're thousands of miles away, and don't forget we're now rich.'

Whilst Mrs. Dawson looked uncomfortably apprehensive, the doctor went on to explain about the one-million-dollar blood money proposal and how he sold it to Salvatore Vitalli.

'It was so easy,' he said. 'But what I didn't expect was for him to offer twenty-five percent of the agreed payment up front. I asked for half of that.'

Maria frowned. 'Why do you think he did that?'

'To lock me into the deal,' said the doctor.

'Yes, that makes sense. Nevertheless, he must really trust you.'

'Well, maybe. But he was still really thinking of himself. You see, he didn't want to leave a paper trail, so he insisted he would provide the upfront payment in cash. That's when he took me to his safe in the basement where I managed to film him dialling the safe's combination. Then he handed me the money. Five packets of fifty thousand dollars.'

'That was so clever of you,' said Maria. 'And then you realised how much more was in the safe.'

'Yes, millions. A fortune in hard cash. It was somewhat fortuitous I had my phone with me.' The doctor shrugged. 'Well, the rest you know.'

'And you stole it all.'

'Yes, most of it.'

'It was the perfect opportunity. I hated the thought of trying to bribe one of the family. That would have been fraught with danger. Then, once I got the money using the casinos, I exchanged as much cash as possible over the next few days and nights, hid the rest, and now, here we are.'

'And to think, if you had not been Hilda and Harvey's physician, we might never have met all those years ago. By the way, how are they?

'Oh, my God, yes,' said the doctor. 'I'm sorry... I meant to tell you.'

Maria looked aghast. 'Oh no! What's happened?'

'There was an accident a few days ago,' began the doctor as Maria's hand flew to her mouth, 'But don't worry, they're both OK. It was something to do with the accidental discharge of a firearm. Harvey's own shotgun, so I understand. Eh... he's in hospital. He's injured, but he's OK... he's OK!'

'Oh, my God! How did that happen?'

'I don't know. The details are unclear. When I called at their house, it was empty. I wanted to see them, but visiting the hospital was obviously too risky at the time. So, I rang the hospital and spoke to them both.' The doctor forced a smile of reassurance. 'Hilda was a bit vague, but I think it was her doing. She said she dropped the gun, and it went off.' The doctor smiled again. 'You know how she is. She's a real stalwart. She refused point blank to leave Harvey's side. She had left the house unlocked, so I told her that I had been and secured everything.'

'But Harvey's, OK?'

'Yes.'

'What on the earth was she doing with a gun?'

'I don't know. Although, she did mention something about intruders in your old empty house next door.'

Maria looked worried. 'But they are, OK?

'Yes.'

'Hilda's wonderful,' said Maria. 'She's so protective of Harvey. Are you sure he's going to be alright?'

'Yes.'

Dr. Roberts was aware that, as Hilda and Harvey had no immediate family, and as a result of Maria's many years of kindness, the elderly couple recently amended their Will, appointing Maria as the sole beneficiary, betrothing her their house and all their worldly possessions. The doctor mulled over that for a while, and a quiet grin of satisfaction appeared. Then, as it was just after two o'clock, they decided it was time for bed.

Although tired, they made love, but afterwards, as the doctor lay and contemplated the day whilst Maria slept, something was playing on his mind, and a sudden unnerving feeling of foreboding shivered through his neural apparatus when he realised what it was.

Talking about the events that had led them to this moment had triggered the memory of a colossal error of judgement. When re-stacking the packets of banknotes to form a false front in Salvatore Vitalli's safe, the doctor realised he had forgotten to leave five gaps where the family Don had handed him his five fifty-thousand-dollar packets.

'Oh, my God!' thought the doctor. Would that have been noticed, he wondered? And if so, when? Maybe, but what difference would it make now? Both he and Maria were safe. Nobody knew where they were. And with that comforting thought, the doctor settled with his arms around Maria and drifted off to sleep.

# # #

A few hours later, just after 5.30 that same morning, Frankie Vitalli and Layzee Dawson's New York flight broke through the damp fog of a dreary London morning and, with a squeal of tyres, touched down at Heathrow Airport. The two men, who despised one another, had hardly spoken during their journey, and had even sat rows apart on the aircraft. They cleared customs and then hailed a taxicab to take them to the Landmark Hotel. They were both charged by Salvatore Vitalli with apprehending the doctor but knew nothing of whom he was with.

After pulling away from the airport's taxi rank, the cab driver, who was just finishing his long shift, turned his head slightly to address the two men in the back of his cab and began a well-practiced and familiar monologue.

'So, the Landmark Hotel, yeah?' he said.

'That's right,' said Frankie Vitalli. 'How far is it?'

'About twenty-five minutes, sir. Proper five-star gaff that.'

The driver, against all probabilities, was the very same taxi driver who had driven Mrs. Dawson to the Landmark Hotel seven hours earlier. '1899 it opened. Designed by Sir Robert Edis. Originally, it was called the Great Central, but in the 1920's it stopped being used as a hotel. Know why?'

Layzee Dawson leaned forward.

'HEY!' No, I don't know why,' he growled from the back of the all-black London taxicab. 'Because frankly, I don't give a shit! What is it with you fuckin' cab drivers, always yackin'? Why is that? Why do you insist on feeding us this bullshit? You tryin' to endear yourself to get a decent tip? Well, listen up! We've just had a long flight, and we're dead beat. So, here's my tip... shut the fuck up, and drive the cab!'

Surprised, but not totally astonished by his associate's outburst, Frankie Vitalli glared across at his partner. 'You done?' he asked.

Layzee settled back into his seat. 'Yeah, what's it to you!'

'Well... unless you reign in that bad attitude of yours, we got no chance of getting this job done. We're on our way to a fancy hotel. You start beating up the bellboy cuz he scuffed your suitcase, and we'll be in jail within an hour. I knew it was wrong bringing you on this job.'

Layzee eyed him as if scrapping away dog dirt from his boot. 'Huh... that so? Well, fuck you... an' the horse you rode in on!'

Chapter 18: Half Cut

After breakfast, Johnny Vitalli walked down the lengthy corridor from the grand hall and knocked on the door of Salvatore Vitalli's study and leaned in. 'Boss, can I have a word?'

Salvatore Vitalli's eyes rose from his paperwork. 'I'm busy... What is it? Is it important?'

'Eh... Well, yes and no. But mainly, eh, um... Yes.'

'Christ! What's the matter with you?'

'You know that barber guy, Franco?'

'The hairdresser?'

'Yeah.'

'What about him?'

'I had a call from him late last night. He said some guy called at his salon and threatened him yesterday.'

'Threatened him... why?'

'Yeah. The guy said he wanted money from him in exchange for personal protection services and to ensure the security of his business.'

'Hold on... ain't that barber shop on our books?'

'Yeah. He pays us to look after his interests. That's why he called. Boss, we had this shit a few months back, remember? Last time, it was some jerk-off trying to shake-down that high-end car dealership that was also on our books. Turned out that guy had no mob connections, just a gang member who needed to be introduced to a piece of four-by-two.'

'You think this is one of Marmarella's guys?'

'I don't know. If it is, he's trampling on our toes again, Boss. Maybe he's forgotten where his territory ends and ours begins. It won't be the first time. Anyway, Franco said the guy demanded money... five large and gave him twenty-four hours to find it.'

The big man emitted a sigh and leaned back from his desk. 'Jesus! Johnny, look, I'm busy preparing for this damn Chicago meeting. This don't sound like Marmarella to me, more likely some crack-head. Just go sort it out, will ya?'

An hour later, the skies over Brooklyn had darkened and torrential rain was falling like stair rods across the East Coast. Johnny pulled up and parked outside Franco's barber shop. The salon's tinted window was sheltered by a faded green awning and a red neon 'Open' sign blinked steadily from within. He dashed through the downpour, cursing the weather, and entered through the narrow door which was set back from the rain-slicked sidewalk. Once inside, he was met by the pungent aroma of pomade, talcum powder, and a faint trace of cigars mixed with lavender and citrus notes from aftershave products. 'Jeez... smells like a fuckin' brothel in here,' he said, as he shut the door on the bad weather.

'Ahh... Mr Johnny,' said Franco, enthusiastically in his quirky Italian-English, his arms outstretched as if accepting applause from an audience in a theatre. He was still sporting his trademark multi-coloured waistcoat, although his long brown hair had had lost its blue streaks—the blue replaced with strands of purple. 'Thank a God, you're here,' he said.

There was a brief exchange of hugs and then Franco said, 'Luigi, come, come, come! Luigi don't mess about. Get Mr Johnny a cup of coffee. How would you like your coffee, Mr Johnny? Black with a sugar or no sugar, or white with a sugar or no sugar?'

'Black... hold the sugar,' said Johnny, as he looked around, and then added. 'Although, I'll take a drop of scotch if ya got any. That'll get it on its feet?'

'Ah, an aristocrat,' said Franco, nodding his approval. 'An Irish coffee. I like that. Of course, personally I prefer brandy, but whiskey works too. Luigi, get the whiskey. And not the fucking cheap shit! The good stuff. It is in the safe.'

Johnny frowned. 'You keep your scotch in the safe? Why's that?'

'It's Luigi. He drinks like a drowning fish. Leave the whiskey out, he cannot help himself. A nip here… A nip there. Next thing you know, there are no more nips, because there is no more whiskey! It's too much of a temptation for him.' Franco leaned to one side and called out to his associate, 'And it is a not for you to drink!' he blurted, as his short, bald-headed, elderly assistant scuttled through a plastic curtain of multi-coloured beads to the back office. 'And Luigi, remember, you have a blue rinse booking later, and Mrs Papadopoulos will not thank you for breathing boozy breath all over her.'

Johnny looked on bemused. 'So, let's get down to it, shall we? What's going on?'

Franco turned towards him and grimaced. 'Oh, Mr Johnny, I've a big a problem. It's err… it's this guy. I never seen him before. He was here yesterday.'

'Yeah, so you said on the phone. What was he like?'

'Tough-looking guy, maybe Slovakian, but Russian I think, or from somewhere horrible. He had dark hair, a mess, dandruff, oily scalp split-ends. Looked as though it hadn't been washed for a month. Lord knows what was living in it. Probably moths, I think.'

'OK, I got that, Franco, I got that. He's got shit hair. Get to the point!'

'Of course. At first, I thought him a Libra. But then, as he spoke, I thought, no, definitely Capricorn. Or maybe Taurus. He could have been Taur…'

'Hey… hey, hey, look! I don't need to know his fuckin' star sign, do I? Did he have a weapon or anything with him?'

'He came in carrying a box.'

'A box?'

'He said things had changed, and that I was to pay him five thousand dollars, and that I had twenty-four hours to get the money. I mean, what does he think this business is, a fuckin' stockbroker Wall Street kind of place? Five K… that's more than we take in a week!'

'Alright, alright… take it easy! Slow down. Then what happened?'

'I tried to make a joke. I said, I liked his hair. How did he manage to get it to come out of his nostrils like that? But he did not see funny side. He said it was my choice.'

'Your choice?'

'Yes. The money, or else.'

'Or else what?'

'He opened the box.'

'And?'

'There was a severed head in it. He said it needed a haircut. Well, I could see that. The hair was lank, scruffy, a tangled mess and soaked in blood. But I said... NO! Unless it has a body attached... I am a not touching it.'

Johnny's eyebrows had knitted themselves into a frown. 'Jesus Christ! Then what?'

'He then said I get money, or else he break my finger. This one... And that one... And this one too. I said, how could I create hairstyling perfection with a broken fingers... fucking idiot! I told him I was a friend of Mr Vitalli.'

'Oh right. And then what did he say?'

'Oh, Mamma Mia! He said, fuck, Mr Vitalli. He said *that* arrangement had expired, and that I now pay him. He got angry and said he would be here to collect money today, or else... broken fingers. He also wanted a free haircut... cheeky fuck! Or he would destroy all of my precious photo pictures.'

'Did he?'

'Yes.'

Johnny looked around at the walls crammed with dozens of photos of famous personalities—so many, he could hardly see the colour of the paint on the wall. 'He threatened to destroy all these?'

'Yes.'

'What a fuckin' asshole,' said Johnny.

'Yes, that's a right, Mr Johnny. I said to Luigi. Luigi, I said. The man's a fucking asshole. Stronzo! And do you know what Luigi said?'

'No.'

'He said nothing. He doesn't speak much.'

Franco turned toward his office at the back of the salon and yelled, 'Luigi, fare presto! Why is the coffee taking so long? You're not drinking my best whiskey, are you? Pezzo de merda!'

'Hey, steady,' said Johnny. 'Why are you calling him a piece of shit? He's just doin' his job, ain't he? He's helping out.'

'Yes, you're right. I'm just stressed, Mr Johnny. Last night... *NO SLEEP!*'

'Ah, alright, I think I've got the picture. And you've got fuckin' hundreds. Look at all these things?' Johnny glanced across the plethora of framed photos on the walls.

'Yes, And I would like to keep them.'

'OK. Do you know when this douchebag's due to arrive?'

'Of course, we are a professional business. Luigi booked him in for his... *free haircut.* He's due in at 11.30.' Franco glanced at the clock on the wall. 'About thirty minutes... but I do not have the money, Mr Johnny. He will destroy me, Luigi, and my pictures. I'm not so bothered about Luigi, but my pictures? Yes, I am bothered.'

'Don't worry,' said Johnny. 'We'll sort something out.'

Johnny left the salon, and a few minutes later, returned and gave Franco a bundle of dollar notes.

'What is this?'

'It's five thousand dollars,' said Johnny. 'Counterfeit dollars. Prop money. They use it in movies.'

Franco took the wad and inspected. 'Ahh... it looks a real.'

'Of course it does. It's good, ain't it?'

Franco frowned and then began to panic. 'Che cazzo! Mr Johnny, I cannot give him this. When he finds it's a fake money, he will break my fingers, and my legs too, and burn my place to the ground.'

'Just hold on,' said Johnny. He pointed to the wad of fake banknotes. '*This* is just to buy us some time. I have an idea. We need to put the fear of God into this guy. Have you got a spare apron?'

'Of course, why?'

Punctually, at 11.30, a man stepped into the salon.

Johnny was now Federico, a new member of staff wearing the same barber's apron as Franco and Luigi.

Johnny could tell the man was the Russian by the fact Franco's facial skin had paled to the same shade of white as the ceramic sinks used for back-washing hair. The man was mid-forties, smaller in stature than Johnny had expected, but the underlying threat of aggression on the man's hard face was clear to see. His face was weathered through years of hard living. It was an insensitive face. A face that had perhaps witnessed much violence and had grown immune to the consequences of its use over the decades. One thing was for sure though, thought Johnny. This man was no druggie.

Once again, the man was carrying a box. The man's shift eyes surveyed everyone in the shop. 'Well?' he said, his thick Russian accent betraying his place of origin.

Having Johnny there, Franco looked bullish. 'Ah, you're back. What? No 'good morning', or how are you? Don't people greet one another in your country?'

'Shut the fuck up!' said the man. The man's disinterested eyes looked at Johnny, then Luigi, and turned back to Franco. 'Now... my money?'

'OK...OK,' said Franco, who then couldn't help himself. His curiosity got the better of him. 'But I have to ask. What is in the box?'

'Ah, the box? There is nothing in the box. But there might be if I do not get my money.'

'OK. I have it,' said Franco. He opened the till on his reception counter and took out the wad of counterfeit dollar bills.

The man sneered a grin and said, 'Ah, good. This will be a regular thing, five hundred every week.' He snatched the bundle of notes and riffled through them. 'Is it all here?'

'Yes,' said Franco.

'I will count it later. If not, I will return. And it will not be pleasant for you.'

'It *is* all there,' said Franco. 'I do not want any trouble. But my friend Mr Vitalli is not happy.'

'I told you yesterday... FUCK, Mr Vitalli! Now, my haircut. And don't try anything cute. I do not want it too short, just tidy.'

'Of course,' said Franco. 'But first, we wash. Get the filth out of it.'

Annoyed by the insult, the man seized Franco by the wrist, then released him.

'What is the matter with you?' snapped Franco. 'You are getting a free haircut, are you not?'

Franco draped a black hairdressing cape around the man, fastened the clip, and directed him to a washbasin that was shaped to comfortably accept the nape of a customer's neck. The man sat and leaned back against the basin as Franco carefully tried to position a towel over the man's face. The man snatched it and tossed it aside. '*NIET!*' he sneered.

'What is the matter?' said Franco

The Russian glared up at him. 'I want to see.'

'As you wish, sir. But the soap... it might get in your eyes. Don't blame me if it stings.' Franco turned and beckoned Johnny with his fingers. 'Federico, please come.' Johnny stepped forward and pulled on a pair of latex gloves. 'Federico,' said Franco. 'Wash, condition and prepare this gentlemen's hair for cutting.'

'Certainly,' said Johnny.

Johnny's eyes briefly met those of the man. Yes, he thought. There was a calculating calmness about this man's demeanour. A slow, controlled confidence in the grey eyes, and not a hint of a smile-line anywhere on his face. He guessed there was little that would phase this man.

For the next two minutes, Johnny lathered and washed the man's hair, resisting the urge to grab him by the throat and punch his face. The man seemed to relax under the flow of warm water as his hair was then rinsed. Johnny then applied another product—a lot of product, careful to conceal the bottle's label on which was written: 'Hair Removal Cream'. He rubbed vigorously at the man's scalp. After thirty seconds or so, bits of the man's hair began sticking to his gloved fingers. 'Just a few minutes for that conditioner to take full effect, sir,' he said as he stepped away.

Luigi, Franco and Johnny watched from a distance. Then Johnny returned with something in his hand. He placed the item out of sight and began to rinse the man's head, tufts of hair coming away, falling into the sink as if the man's head had been sheared, leaving areas of exposed scalp.

The man must have felt a cool sensation of loss as he suddenly sat up and whipped the cloak away. His hands went to his head, and as he lowered them. They too were filled with swathes of his hair. 'What the fuck!'

Johnny was on him in a heartbeat. He grabbed the item, which was a trouser belt, shaped into a noose, and hooked it over the man's head, pinning his neck behind the headrest of the chair. He pulled it tight. The man had no time to react, other than to choke, and as Johnny fended off his flailing arms, he grabbed his chin and forced the man's near bald head hard back, smashing the back of his skull against the sink with such force the ceramic bowel fractured with a dull... *CRUNCH!*

The man lay dazed.

'Ah... sorry about that,' said Johnny. 'I thought that bottle was conditioner. But we all make mistakes, don't we? Your mistake was stepping foot into this establishment yesterday. Now, tell me, who you are working for... Louie Marmarella?'

The man appeared to quickly recover, and his piercing eyes stared up at Johnny. Oddly, he did not struggle. Neither was there panic in his voice.

'What is your name?' he asked coldly.

Johnny's intention had not been to kill the man, merely to teach him a lesson and scare him off but by virtue of the fact the man had asked that question, and the relaxed manner in which it was asked, Johnny realised this man was hardly a crack-head, as his boss had suggested, he was professional, and Johnny knew trying to deter him would never be enough. He had seen that look many times before. He remembered the old mob adage, *"never let them walk, they'll only come back and kill you"*.

But what Johnny had not seen was the man's dangling arm, his hand reaching down to his boot, his fingers extending, searching, reaching for something. Then the man suddenly jerked violently in the chair and Johnny howled in pain. The man had pulled a fixed blade knife from a concealed boot sheath and stabbed Johnny in his left thigh, the short, razor-sharp, stubby blade embedding in the fleshy muscle almost to the hilt.

Johnny screamed.

He forced his full body weight hard against the man's chin. The man released the knife and fought against the belt restraint, his hands grappling to free himself, his legs thrashing wildly. But Johnny bared down with all his strength, and then adrenalin found him another gear, and with a final jolt, a single sickening snap sounded.... *CRAACK!* And the man's body suddenly lost all motor functionality and slumped in the chair like a passed-out drunkard.

Franco's eyes were wide, and his hands flew to his mouth. 'Ma che cazzo!' he said. 'Luigi, don't look!'

Johnny staggered back and yelped as he quickly pulled the short, stubby blade from his leg.

Franco remonstrated, 'Is he dead?'

'FUCK HIM!' said Johnny. 'Look at my leg! He fuckin' stabbed me!'

With a look of a man about to vomit, Franco surveyed the river of blood running down from the wound over Johnny's shoe. 'Oh, Mamma Mia! Oh, my God!' he gasped. 'Luigi, quick! Get a mop... the floor. Look at the floor... the blood! My expensive travertine tiles...quick! Fetch a mop!'

'HEY!' said Johnny. 'What about my fuckin' leg?'

'Oh, of course, Mr Johnny... Sorry!' Franco grabbed a towel and rushed over to assist. He wrapped it around Johnny's leg.

'Oh, Jesus Christ! ...Steady!' winced Johnny. 'That fuckin' hurts! Christ... fetch me that belt!'

Franco looked around. 'Oh...! Which belt?'

'MY BELT! The one round his fuckin' neck!'

'Oh... I don't think I can touch him... ugh! Luigi, fetch the belt!'

Luigi released the belt from the man's neck and passed it to Johnny, who wound it around the blood-stained towel on his thigh, using it as a temporary tourniquet. Franco backed himself into a chair and began fanning himself with his hand. Johnny also found a chair and a few minutes later, his wound was being properly bandaged by Luigi.

As he did so, Johnny looked down at the kneeling man and said curiously, 'You know something... I can see my refection in Luigi's bald head.'

'Yes. I think he must polish it with beeswax every day,' said Franco, who quickly got up and who was now standing by the door, making sure no one entered until the mess was cleared up. Luigi finished what he was doing, got up, and proceeded to mop the blood from the floor.

'You will need a stitches for that,' said Franco, still fanning his face.

'I know. Don't worry, I got someone who can fix me up. Although I'm taking these as a souvenir.' Johnny gestured to the Russian's short-bladed knife and sheath. He got to his feet and grabbed hold of Franco by his shoulders, supporting himself. 'Ah... it's not too bad,' he said. 'Look... this was never gonna end any other way. You know that, don't you?' He pointed to the slumped body in the chair. 'If he had walked outta here, trust me, he'd have been back.'

Just then, the salon door opened and a woman in her sixties staggered in out of the pouring rain. 'Oh, the weather, the weather!' she scowled, as she fought to get her open umbrella past the door. Luigi rushed over to help and between them they collapsed the umbrella, which had limbs like a struggling lobster.

'Oh, thank you, thank you,' said the woman. 'It's deathly out there.'

'It's deathly in here too,' muttered Franco to himself, who then turned and then switched on the charm. 'Ah, Mrs Papadopoulos. Welcome, welcome... come... come, come. How are you today?'

'Oh, not too bad,' said the woman.

'Ah, as beautiful as ever. Right... let me look. Blue rinse and a trim. Yes?'

'Yes, but not too much off.' The woman looked inquisitively at the man slumped in the chair. 'Good grief. Is he all right?'

'Ahh... he's half cut. Too much to drink,' said Johnny. 'He's fallen asleep. It happens a lot.'

'But his hair...'

'Yeah, there's no accounting for taste, is there? He wanted one of those skinhead cuts. It's all the rage over there in the Bronx.'

Franco intervened and busied himself with the woman, deflecting her curiosity, whilst Johnny put a call into his boss.

'Boss,' said Johnny. 'I've got a pest control problem. That vermin infestation we talked about earlier. I could do with some help cleaning-up.'

Johnny must have been asked how many; for he replied, 'Just the one.'

Twenty minutes later, whilst Mrs Papadopoulos was having her hair baked—her head stuck in a noisy, free-standing hood dryer—a van arrived and parked at the rear of Franco's emporium. Fingers and Joey stepped out, both men wearing white overalls.

Johnny was waiting for them, leaning against the wall smoking a cigarette. 'How ya doin' guys?' he said. 'Joey... You, OK?' Joey nodded. 'Ah, Fingers, I like the white. Makes you look like a big fuckin' fluffy marshmallow. What's the matter with your face, though?'

Fingers grimaced. 'What do ya mean?'

'You got a face like a bag of smashed crabs. What's the matter with you?'

'Well, if you must know, I was having a quiet morning. Now I gotta sort *your* shit out again. How do ya expect me to look?'

'Well, let me put it this way, Fingers,' said Johnny. 'If you wanna know what sexual position spawns the ugliest kids... Go ask ya mother!'

'Fuck off you!' grumbled Fingers.

'Now, now... joking apart. Count yourselves lucky, you guys. At least you didn't get stabbed today.'

'What?' said Joey. 'You've been stabbed?'

Johnny explained the events of the morning as his two cousins loaded the body into a plastic zip bag and then drove off, leaving him with Franco.

'Now, if anyone comes asking questions about that guy,' said Johnny. 'What do ya say?'

Franco looked at Luigi and then shrugged. 'I tell them he came, took the money, had his haircut, and left.'

'No, no. If anyone asks, you tell him he was a "no show". He never arrived. OK?'

'Of course, yes, he never came. I was left with an empty chair. That's what I will a say.'

'And what about him?' asked Johnny, pointing to Luigi.

'Well, if you have another bag. Yes, please take him. No, no... I am joking. What would I do without him?'

'Yeah, exactly. Anyway, the Russian... any idea who he is?'

'You mean who he was? Luigi booked him in. Let me see.' Franco checked his large appointment book and ran his finger down the names. He turned to his assistant. 'Luigi, where is his name? Sometimes, I cannot read your writing. The page looks as though a spider dipped in ink crawled across it with five broken legs.'

Luigi pointed.

'Here?' queried Franco. 'This is his name... Gorbachev? You booked him in as Mikhail Gorbachev? He told you his name was Gorbachev... and you believed him, Luigi? You idiot! Get outta my sight! Mr Johnny... if you have another bag? Take him!'

'Jesus!' said Johnny. 'Let me see.' He span the book round and placed his finger beneath the name. 'Gorbachev. Well... that's just about as useful as deodorant to a cab driver? But hold on, what's this?'

Johnny noticed another name on the facing page. 'Franco. This guy here,' he said. 'Doctor Roberts?'

'Yes, what about him?'

'What did he look like?'

'Eh... yes. I remember. Slender guy. Spoke nice. He had long shoulder hair. It was grey, and he tried to dye it, but it was awfully bad. So, I do it again. He wanted a shortcut. Which suited him. He left looking like a proper gentleman and gave a big tip.'

Johnny gave a knowing nod. 'Yeah, I bet he did.' He pressed for a description and by the time Franco finished, Johnny was left in no doubt who it was—Doctor Lucas Roberts had called in to disguise himself. Once again, he spoke to his boss.'

Ten minutes later, a call traversed the Atlantic Ocean and was picked up in London by Salvatore Vitalli's son.

'Yeah, that's right,' said the big man. 'Short brown hair. Now find him! And bring him back. How's Layzee?'

'How is he?' said Frankie. 'Huh...I told you it was wrong sending him. How long you got?'

Chapter 19: The Clean-Up Crew

As the sun rose over London, Doctor Lucas Roberts stirred from a good night's rest in his luxurious hotel suite. Ever since arriving in London, he had been plagued with nightmares. But not last night. Had the presence of the woman lying alongside him banished those night terrors?

He hoped so.

For a moment he lay still, listening to the distant hum of the city awakening. He yawned and stretched. Gone was the weight of worry that had burdened his shoulders for so long. In its place, an eagerness to embrace the day and all its possibilities.

He checked his watch—it was just after 7am. He leaned over and tenderly kissed the forehead of Maria Dawson, who was still sound asleep. For the first time in his life, he felt complete. He had everything he wanted; freedom from his life as a crime family associate, wealth, and the woman he loved. Fulfilment was his. But by God—he had had to fight for it.

After a refreshing shower, he donned his white bathrobe and stood in front of the window overlooking tree-lined Marylebone Road and admired the view of the bustling city below.

His mind wandered back across the ocean to New York and the ramifications of what he had done. How persistent would Salvatore Vitalli be in trying to find him, he wondered? No doubt, his apartment would have been torn apart already, in their search for the money or a clue to where it might be. But that hardly mattered. He had left nothing of value, just a wardrobe of clothes, furniture, a TV, and a few kitchen appliances. And the personal documents from his study? Incinerated—he had burned everything of a sensitive nature. He found it surprising how little he needed to take with him. People hoard so much junk throughout their lives. And when it comes down to it, as a single man with no wife or siblings, what do you really need to take with you to start over? Your passport, driving license, money, bank account paraphernalia, and that's about it—isn't it?

With a sense of purpose, his thoughts turned to his agenda for the day, and his excitement grew, knowing Maria would be thrilled with what he had planned. However, unbeknownst to him, two men had recently arrived at Heathrow Airport with sinister intentions that might soon disrupt those plans.

After shaving, he ordered breakfast to be sent to his suite and twenty minutes later, there was a knock at the door.

'Room service,' announced a muffled voice.

'Shouldn't that be suite service?' called Mrs. Dawson from the bathroom.

'Maria, don't be such a bloody snob,' replied the doctor with a smile. There was a squeak of laughter from the bathroom as he answered the door.

After exchanging good morning pleasantries, a waiter wearing a white tunic and white gloves, his head lowered, wheeled in a heated trolley with an elevated sense of pride and care. The cloches covering the plates of food were arranged in a precise and organised manner. And the waiter had a confident demeanour as he momentarily lifted the lids off the plates, revealing the perfectly cooked food beneath, the aroma filling the room with wonderful smells of bacon, sizzling sausage, golden toast, and everything else one would associate with a traditional full English breakfast.

The doctor nodded his head appreciatively. 'Thank you, that looks delicious,' he said.

The waiter replaced the cloches, gestured towards the dining table near the window that looked down and out to the busy atrium restaurant, and asked, 'Would you like to dine here, sir? Or would you prefer to enjoy your breakfast in the comfort of your bedroom?'

'Eh... on the table just there's fine,' said the doctor, who, after the waiter had finished laying everything out, pressed a ten-dollar banknote into the palm of his hand.

'Oh, thank you sir, that's very kind,' nodded the waiter as he left. 'Enjoy your breakfast.'

Whilst waiting for Maria the doctor sat and continued reading his copy of The Telegraph newspaper, the headlines focusing on the recent troubles in the Middle East, the results of a by-election, and the latest Royal family scandal, allegedly involving a senior member of the Royals with a midget.

After her shower and still wearing her bathrobe, Maria Dawson joined the doctor.

'Oh, this looks wonderful,' she said.

The doctor poured her coffee from a cafetière, which she took black, and then poured himself a cup of Earl Grey tea. The view down to the restaurant within the hotel's stunning glass roofed atrium was as spectacular beneath the morning sun as it was elegant beneath the moonlight the night before.

As Maria gazed out, she looked melancholic as her thoughts drifted out and down to where hotel guests were also dining, surrounded by an indoor oasis of tall palm trees that seemed to reach up to the sky as if in search of freedom.

'Isn't it sad?' said Maria, pensively. 'Although they look majestic beneath that glass dome, don't you think it's sad, Lucas, that those palm trees will never feel a warm breeze or the heat of a desert sun, or even the occasional downpour of rain on their leaves?'

'Here, take this,' said the doctor, failing to acknowledge Maria's wistfulness, his mind very much focused on the mechanics of the day. 'I bought us a couple of new cell phones,' he said. 'Or mobile phones, as they are called in England. We should use these from now on. I've programmed the numbers on fast dial for each of them.'

'England... that has such a nice ring to it,' said Maria, her train of thought momentarily diverted. 'OK,' she said, as she blindly took the new phone and then shook herself from her daydream. 'So, what's the plan for today, Lucas?' she asked, like a giddy teenager. 'I've never been to London before.'

The doctor folded his newspaper and placed it neatly on the side of the table, the edges of it aligning perfectly with the desk.

'Well, first... let's not be tourists today,' he said, with the merest hint of a cunning frown. 'We've plenty of time for the Tower of London, Buckingham Palace and all of that.' He looked at her severely. 'As your physician. What I prescribe for your current condition, Mrs. Dawson, is a two-pronged course of treatment. The first part of which will be a trip to Knightsbridge and a visit to Harrods.'

Maria's eyes widened in anticipation. 'Oh, God. Do you feel I need of retail therapy, doctor?' she mused.

The doctor nodded. 'Afraid so.'

'Well, if that's your diagnosis and your recommendation, who am I to object? On the contrary, I feel I have no choice but to accept.'

'Good, I'll grab my prescription pad and write it up for you,' said the doctor. 'But I have to insist we return here to the hotel after lunch for the second part of your treatment.'

Maria fired a question mark smile at him. 'And what's that?'

The doctor dropped the flirtatious pretence, his face serious as he pointed out of the window and down to the restaurant. 'Maria, you really must experience Afternoon Tea down there later. It's such a beautiful thing.'

'Must I?'

'Yes, I insist.'

'Oh, OK... agreed,' she said, after which she added flirtatiously, 'And will there be a third part of my treatment when we get back to our room?'

The doctor's face broke into a grin but was unable to match the lascivious smile etched on Maria's face. 'I'll see what I can do.'

They finished their breakfast and within half an hour; they were dressed and in the elevator, heading for the ground floor. But as Maria and the doctor hurried through the crowded lobby area, fate intervened and saved them from an unexpected encounter that would have ruined the course of their day.

Little did they know Frankie Vitalli and Maria's husband, Layzee Dawson, were standing at the head of the queue at the busy reception desk. Had either of the two men turned around, the couple's presence would have been immediately apparent, and all hell would have broken loose. Fortunately for them, on this occasion, the doctor was walking with a woman on each arm, Maria and Lady Luck, as he exited the hotel unnoticed.

In the meantime, at the check-in desk at the hotel, Frankie Vitalli found himself in the midst of a fiery dispute with a male receptionist and one of the hotel managers. The manager was tall and stood proudly in his smart uniform, exuding an air of superiority not dissimilar to that of a proud cockerel sitting atop a hillock at sunrise overseeing his clucking hens.

The tension was palpable as the men exchanged heated words, voices raised and hands gesturing wildly, causing heads to turn and curious glances to be cast in their direction.

'Now listen, you're not hearing me, are you?' argued Frankie Vitalli. 'How many times do I have to go over this? When I rang and made the reservation yesterday, it was for two double rooms. The jerk-off on the phone, who might have been you, I don't know... confirmed the booking. So, it's you guys that made the mistake, not me. I was very specific about my requirements. I booked two separate double rooms! Now, this is a large hotel, so I'm sure you can fix your error.'

'You mean fix their fuck up!' mumbled Layzee beneath his breath.

'I'm sorry, sir, but we do not have any record of your booking,' said the manager in a dismissive, matter-of-fact tone. 'And we are fully booked.'

His assistant agreed with him. 'Yes, we are very busy, sir. The hotel *is* full.'

'Well, that's just not good enough,' said Frankie. 'Try again!'

The manager, with a visible expression of displeasure, tapped away at his computer. After a brief pause, he said reluctantly, as he frowned at his computer screen, 'Eh... I suppose I could offer you the vacant standby staff room on the sixth floor.'

Bored with the situation, Layzee muttered, 'Whoopie fuckin' do!'

'Sorry, sir, I didn't quite catch that,' said the manager, raising his nose in the air and turning to face Layzee. 'Did you say something, sir?'

Layzee, who had left Frankie to handle the indiscretion, decided it was time to add his opinion. He glared at the hotel manager.

'Huh, I know what's goin' on here,' he growled. 'I get it. Is it cuz of these?' He pointed to the cluster of tattooed daggers prominently displayed on the side of his neck. 'Is it that I don't fit your ideal customer profile that you're being such a dick?'

'I'm sorry, but I find your tone to be quite disrespectful,' stuttered the manager. 'It's important for you to know that we strongly believe in treating everyone fairly and equally, regardless of their race, skin colour, or religious beliefs. Discrimination of any kind is simply not acceptable.'

'I agree,' said Layzee. 'I treat everyone equally, too. Everyone gets the same measure of contempt from me... YOU included!' Layzee turned his back on the man, also averting his eyes from Frankie Vitalli, who was shaking his head with disdain.

The confusion over the room booking had now been going on for fifteen minutes, and Layzee Dawson's blood pressure valve, which had so far withstood three atmospheres of suppressed anger, was about to fail catastrophically, as it exceeded the fourth.

'So, getting back to the staff room, it's not a large room, sir,' said the manager, switching his focus of attention back to Frankie. 'In fact, it's quite small, and not to the high standard of our guest rooms, but it does have a double bed; if you don't mind sharing.' He glanced at Layzee, and then winced as if there was a bad smell under his nose.

That was the tipping point for Layzee. He shoved Frankie to one side and leaned across the reception desk, his face inches away from that of the manager. 'A staff room with a double bed, you say. A fuckin' double bed? Is that all you got? What do you take us for, a couple of fuckin' shirt lifters? Although, judging by the look of you pair of gumps. I wouldn't put that...'

'HEY... Enough!' interrupted Frankie, turning towards Layzee and pulling him to one side. Frankie lowered his voice. 'Do you remember what we spoke about in the taxicab on the way over?'

Layzee snorted. 'Look, *Boss!*' he said, emphasising the word "Boss" in a mocking, derogatory manner. 'This is a clusterfuck! I ain't staying in no two-bit room... especially with YOU! I ain't that keen on your aftershave.

An' I certainly ain't sharing a fuckin' a double bed with ya! You heard what that dipshit said. He said it was a small room, it'll be a pokey hole no bigger than a fuckin' shoebox, and I've been banged up in one of them for two years, so fuck that!'

'I ain't particularly keen on the idea either,' said Frankie. 'And you're right, on this job, I am your boss. But regarding the accommodation, it seems we don't have much choice, do we?'

'Yeah, we do. You stay in the shoebox. I'll be at The Ritz!' Layzee turned to walk off.

Frankie grabbed his arm. 'Oh no you don't!' he said, pulling him back and lowering his voice to a whisper. 'You know why we're here. We got a job to do. We got to find out where our doctor friend's hidden our million bucks before he blows it all.' The two men were still unaware that the true figure stolen was seven million dollars. 'Now, we know what room the doctor's in,' continued Frankie. 'So, let's find him, sort out what we need to sort out, and then we can get the fuck outta here.'

The growing queue of impatient people behind, witnessing the fracas, suddenly regarded one another uncomfortably, as if someone amongst them had passed wind and each was suspicious of the other. Judging by a few with crimped noses, it appeared someone had, which was as welcome as a rattlesnake at a square dance.

One man in the line, a hefty, red-necked American from Willow Park, Texas who was wearing stonewashed Levi's and a native western suede cowboy jacket with a row of fringe suede tassels hanging beneath each arm, and who was perhaps everyone's main contender for the phantom fart, decided he was big enough to intervene. He stepped forward in his hand-stitched alligator skin cowboy boots, his eyes beneath the brim of his buffalo leather Stetson narrowing as he focused on Layzee.

'Hey, come on buddy,' said the Texan. 'What's the friggin' hold up there?'

Layzee turned towards him. 'Oh, Christ, look at you. You got something you say, Clint?' he growled. 'Who rattled your fuckin' cage?'

'Hey! No need for you to raise ya bristles there, man,' drawled the Texan, his body language displaying all the signs of impending conflict. 'How dare you speak to me like that!' He took a step closer to Layzee.

'Oh, I see,' said Layzee, recognising the signs. 'Have I upset your precious sensibilities, sidebusta?'

'Sidebusta?' repeated the Texan, his mouth forming a Robert DeNiro scowl. 'Hey fella, you best pull in ya horns and shut ya big mouth, you got no right airing ya lungs at me.'

The man, who was clearly angered, approached Layzee. Both men were about the same height and squared up to one another like prizefighters at a pre-fight weigh-in.

Layzee decided it was time to clarify his intentions. 'If you don't wanna lose those nice teeth, mister,' he said. 'I suggest you go take a walk. Now fuck off!'

The Texan had no intention of moving. 'Huh… You lookin' to kick up a row?' he said. 'You back off, buster! Or I'll beat ya so ugly, you'd back a buzzard off a gut wagon!'

There was a collective intake of breath from those present. For a moment, the two big men continued to glare at one another—a stand-off— a showdown, almost like a scene from Fred Zimmerman's famous western "High Noon". All that was missing was tumbleweed blowing across the pristine marble of the hotel's lobby.

People in the queue slowly backed away, not wanting to get caught in the crossfire, should fists fly, but most were keen to see if the big Texan had the kahunas to lash out and put one on the heavily set, tattooed New Yorker from the Bronx.

Frankie Vitalli closed his eyes in exasperation, his worst nightmare materialising. 'I knew it was wrong bringing you,' he said beneath his breath as hotel security arrived at the scene.

'OK, we'll take the room!' called Frankie to the receptionist, his words immediately defusing the stand-off, as Layzee turned to face him.

'Are you fuckin' kiddin'?' said Layzee.

'Very well, sir,' intervened the manager. 'And of course I'll discount the room.'

'Discount the room?' intoned Layzee, turning his attention back to the manager. 'You should be payin' us for the fuckin' inconvenience.'

Meanwhile, as the doctor and Maria stepped outside, the doctor wearing a blue blazer and grey trousers, whilst Maria was stylishly garbed in a red Gucci dress; they were met with a bustling scene. The hotel's covered entrance was teeming with people. A plethora of taxi cabs were lined up, their engines humming, ready to whisk passengers away to various parts of the city. The hotel's prime location meant that the cabs catered not only for the hotel guests but also for those arriving or departing from nearby Marylebone train station.

A hotel porter beckoned over a taxicab for them, and as Maria and the doctor climbed in, the porter leaned in through the open window. 'Harrods please driver,' he said, and the cab sped away.

On this occasion, there was no en-route commentary. No mention by the cab driver that back in the 19th century Harrods began life as a one-room shop selling tea. Neither did he mention that the store was the first to introduce escalators to the world in 1898. Nor was there any talk of Harrods' famous motto, "*Ominia Omnibus Ubique*"—a Latin phrase, the translation of which is, "All things, for all people, everywhere". None of those facts were disclosed. The driver simply went quietly about his task of passenger deliverance, until the couple eventually alighted the taxicab and stepped into Harrods' world of exquisite décor, its famous store filled with goods of the highest quality and, arguably, with prices that would bring tears to the eyes of most people.

Back in the hotel, the heated exchange between the hefty Texan and Layzee Dawson had dissipated for now, but Layzee being Layzee had marked his card.

They had both checked-in and were handed a key to the spare staff room. But instead of an electronic key-card, as was the norm, it was an old-fashioned key, an omen which smacked of what was to follow. And as sure as night follows day, when they entered room 624, it was, as expected, cramped and sparse. To add insult to injury, the bed was not a double bed but narrow, bunk beds, one on top of the other, and the room was situated at the side of the hotel with views of skid row; a narrow, dark alleyway crammed with garbage skips and crates of empty bottles.

'Perfect!' snarled Layzee. 'It's a fuckin' cupboard! I'm back at the penitentiary. Look at this dump! I ain't staying here. I wouldn't spend a night here if I was fuckin' homeless. I had a better cage at Elmira.' *Cage* being a term sometimes used by inmates when referring to their prison cell.

Frankie had no words. 'OK,' he said. 'Let's pay the doctor a visit.'

Ten minutes later, the two men were walking the corridors checking room numbers. Their room was on the same floor.

'*WHAT?* Is this it?' asked Layzee Dawson, firing Frankie a look of outrage. 'He's in a fuckin' suite? And not just any suite... *The Grand Central Suite?*'

'Looks like it,' said Frankie, glancing over his shoulder. The hallway was empty except for a housekeeper's trolley a few doors back.

'OK, step aside,' snarled Layzee. 'Fuckin' Grand Central Suite. He pulled out a compact device from his pocket—a T-shaped portable card read/writer that could decipher information from the lock. He slid the black plastic card into the slot and pressed a button to activate it. The device emitted a soft whirring sound as it cycled through thousands of possible key codes, looking for one that matched.

'I love this James Bond shit, don't you?' said Frankie.

Layzee glared at him. 'No!'

'You mean no, as in Dr. No?'

'Shut up! And keep an eye open for that maid.'

Thirty seconds was all it took for the light on the device to flash green— it had cracked the code. The lock mechanism clicked open and Layzee withdrew the device and pocketed it. He gently pushed the door ajar and peered inside. They quietly entered into a narrow hallway and closed the door behind them, sealing off any noise or traces of their illicit entry.

'Jeez! Look at this!' whispered Layzee, the shapes of the luxurious furnishings appearing as they crept along the hallway. Then the room opened up, revealing its opulence.

'Sonofabitch! Look at this!' said Layzee as he glanced back at Frankie. 'You gotta be fuckin' kiddin' me! And we're stayin' in a fuckin' shoebox? Are you taking' the piss?'

'Shh... keep your voice down.'

The two men crept around the lounge, but it appeared the large suite was empty. Frankie made his way to the bedroom, and then a noise from the bathroom made him freeze in mid-stride. The shower had just turned on.

'Doc?' he said.

A voice called out. 'I've almost finished, sir.'

Frankie pushed open the door and saw a pretty young maid. She was busy cleaning.

'Hmm... nice,' he said. 'Take your time, honey. I'll just stand here and observe, if you don't mind.'

He leaned against the wall and watched her as she finished polishing the glass shower screen to smear free perfection, his experienced eye appraising the shape of the young woman. A lewd thought materialised in his mind's eye and he explored it for a moment as he watched her ample breasts oscillate within the tight confines of her uniform.

'Jesus, that's beautiful,' he mumbled to himself, mesmerised by her action. 'There's an awful lot of pressure there. If that top button was to just pop open.' He threw his eyes to the heavens. 'Lord, please don't strike me blind... not now.'

He gestured to her. 'You know, you remind me of someone,' he said as she kneeled and continued to polish, his view of her womanly assets now significantly better.

'Really?' she said.

'Eh... yes. We got a maid back home in New York. Her name's Elena. She looks like you, from the neck down... I mean. From the neck up, she's beautiful, but even there I think you have the edge on her. You're an absolute Ten... gorgeous.'

The maid finished what she was doing and got to her feet. 'There... all done,' she said as she brushed herself down.

'Ah, that's a shame. I could watch you do that all day.' Frankie reached into his wallet and pulled out a twenty-pound note.

'Oh, that's not necessary, sir,' said the maid.

'Oh yes, it is. It was worth it for the show.'

'I beg your pardon.'

'Oh, take it. You girls work hard and for not much money. Go on, take it.'

The maid hesitated. She rarely took money from men whom she considered lechers. But this was twenty pounds, and the man was right about poor pay. She was on minimum wage. 'Thank you,' she said.

Never one to miss an opportunity, Frankie said, 'This is my friend's room, but if you want some company later, I'll be in room 624 tonight.'

Frankie always worked on his ten-to-one premise—that being, that if he was to offer such a proposal to ten women, four would ignore him, three would polity decline, two might slap him, but one might just take him up on his offer.

The maid frowned. 'Room 624? That's a staff room,' she said.

Layzee appeared on the scene. 'Yeah, tell me about it! It's a shithole, right?'

The maid chose the second option of Frankie's ten-to-one scheme and quickly collected her cleaning kit and left.

'Well, she had a lucky escape, didn't she?' said Layzee. 'Now tell me. Are you sure this is the right room?'

'Yeah... why?'

Layzee pointed to a line of dresses hanging alongside men's clothes in the wardrobe. 'What the hell's all this shit, then?' he grimaced. 'The Doc's either shacked up with some broad, or he's a fuckin' cross-dresser and he's one of them transvestical types. And if he is... he's kept that quiet over the years, ain't he?'

Frankie shrugged. 'Well, either way, he ain't here, is he? So, let's go.'

Layzee wandered over to the window overlooking the restaurant below, where patrons were enjoying Afternoon Tea. 'Hold on,' he said. 'What the hell?'

Frankie joined him at the window. 'What's up? Did you spot him?'

Layzee's expression hardened. 'No. But there's someone else down there I recognise.'

Frankie squinted and peered out. 'Who?'

'That fuckin' bitch there!' mouthed Layzee, his jaw clenched.

'Which bitch? Who is it?'

Pointing down, Layzee growled. 'That woman down there at that table.'

'Which one?'

'The one in the red dress with the green Harrods bag.'

Frankie studied the scene, then recognition flashed across his face. 'Oh shit! Ain't that...'

'YES, IT IS!' said Layzee grimly.

'Your wife? What the hell is she doing here?'

They watched as a man approached her table. He had a neat short haircut. 'And that's Doc Roberts joining her,' said Layzee.

'Oh God! Now that makes sense,' said Frankie. 'The dresses in the closet?' A tense silence fell as the implication and the gravity of the moment sank in. 'Doc Roberts and your missus?' queried Frankie.

'Yeah, looks like it,' Layzee said through gritted teeth. 'Well, what d'ya know? The Doc and my wife... ha, ha...'

# # #

Down below in the tranquillity of the restaurant, a piano was playing a piece of classical music—Mozart's Allegro Sonata No.16 in C.

'So, how do you like London so far?' asked Doctor Roberts, as he and Maria sat at their table amongst the busy ensemble of people enjoying the relaxed ambiance.

'I love it,' said Maria, as she looked around, taking in her surroundings.

A young foreign-looking waiter arrived at their table dressed impeccably in a white tuxedo, wearing white matching gloves. He placed a three-tiered silver platter filled with finger sandwiches and scones on the table.

'So, what do we have here?' enquired Maria.

The waiter who spoke very little English frowned. Another waiter who was passing noticed his colleague's predicament and stepped in to assist. He leaned forward and gestured with his white gloved hand.

'Madam, you have finger sandwiches made with various breads, rye, malt, brown, white and granary, with fillings consisting of smoked salmon with crème cheese, egg with cress, beef with a horseradish cream, prawns with a dill mayonnaise and Wiltshire ham with chutney. Then you have warm scones with strawberry preserve, Devonshire clotted cream and various pastries and petit fours. And, of course, your choice of teas. If you have not tried it yet, may I recommend Peach Oolong? It's a very nice speciality tea from China, fragrant and sweet, delicious with your vanilla petit fours.'

The foreign waiter standing alongside nodded his thanks to his colleague. 'Molte gratzie,' he whispered.

'That's wonderful. Thank you both,' said the doctor. He looked at Maria. 'See what I mean?'

'Yes. It's amazing,' she said, her eyes devouring the beautifully presented morsels of food laid out like hors d'oeuvres on the tiered platter.

Sitting at the adjacent table was the big Texan cowboy with his wife. 'Hi guys,' he said with a southern drawl, leaning over. 'Couldn't help notice a couple of friendly Americans here. Where are you guys from?'

'New York,' said the doctor. 'Arrived a few days ago. How about you?'

'Checked in only this morning. We're from Willow Park, Texas. Quite a mixture of people staying here. Beautiful hotel. Nice to see a couple of friendly folk from the States, though.'

Maria smiled. 'Well, aren't all us Americans friendly?' she said.

'Huh... funny you should ask, mam, but no. Met an ignorant New Yorker when I was checking in this morning. In fact, talk of the devil... there he is. That guy there, see?' The Texan hesitated as he saw Layzee Dawson heading towards him. 'Oh Lordy, have I spoken out of turn?' he said. 'Heck, he's not with you, is he?'

Maria turned her head and gasped, her hand flying to her mouth as not one but two imposing figures wearing suits strode across the floor, their faces twisted into masks of fury as they made a beeline for her table.

'OH GOD!' she howled, horrified as she suddenly recognised her husband. Doctor Roberts' face paled, his fork clattering against his plate.

The two men arrived at their table and, for a moment, Layzee Dawson and Frankie Vitalli stood and looked down upon them.

'Look what we have here,' said Layzee. 'Nice little get together we got goin' on, huh?'

'Well, well… and if it ain't the good doctor himself,' said Frankie, his eyes narrowing. 'Thought you could skip town with our money, did ya, Doc? Mind if we join you?'

The two men did not wait to be invited. They pulled out a couple of chairs and sat down.

Doctor Roberts stiffened. 'Gentlemen, Maria had nothing to do with what happened,' he said. 'This is just between you and me. Surely, you and I can discuss this like civilized men.'

Frankie snorted, his hand disappearing into his jacket pocket. 'Oh, we're way past discussing, Doc,' he said. 'We're well past discussing.'

The doctor was half expecting to see a gun or some other weapon. But Frankie pulled out the doctor's old cell phone found on the grass verge.

He touched the screen.

The video recording that the doctor filmed of Salvatore Vitalli opening his safe began to play. Frankie turned the screen so the doctor could see. 'This was clever?' he said with a nod of appreciation.

The doctor looked on disbelievingly as he watched the dull video footage. He remembered angrily throwing the phone from his car and cursed his moment of carelessness. 'Look, guys,' he said. 'Can't we just…'

'SHUT the fuck up!' snarled Layzee. 'We got just one question. Where you hid the money?'

It was at that moment that the young foreign waiter unwittingly returned and offered menus to the two new arrivees.

Layzee looked up at him. 'Get lost!' he said. Again, the waiter looked confused. 'Beat it!' said Layzee.

The waiter remained, his face fixed with a frown of incomprehension, the two menus still in his hand.

'Do you speak English?' asked Layzee. 'Leave. Go. Auf wiedersehem, au revoir, arrivederci, bonna vista.' Having exhausted his foreign language repertoire, Layzee could feel Frankie's eyes on him. He turned to face him.

'WHAT?'

'Bona vista means "*nice view*",' said Frankie.

Layzee eyed the waiter again, who still appeared nonplussed. He tried the universal language of, '*FUCK OFF!*'

That did it.

The waiter scuttled away, as the burly Texan, still wearing his Stetson, leaned across from his table. 'Hey, buddy!' he said. 'Curb your language in here, will ya? I heard enough of your bluster this morning.'

Layzee turned to him and pointed a finger. 'HEY YOU! Keep out of this. It's none of your fuckin' business!'

The Texan's wife, a full-figured brunette with worried eyes, glared at her husband. 'Jake... please,' she said.

The big Texan grimaced but backed off.

Frankie pocketed the phone, lowered his voice. 'Mind if I have one of those?' he asked. 'They looked delish.' He reached past the silver teapot and plucked a crustless rectangular smoked salmon sandwich from the second tier of the silver platter. 'Didn't think you'd mind,' he said, as he stuffed all of it into his mouth, 'Especially as it's being paid for outta the money stolen from our safe.' They watched him as he consumed the fancy sandwich. 'Hmm... these are nice. After all these years, I never saw that one coming, Doc. Clever. But the boss ain't too happy.'

Doctor Roberts said, 'Frankie, look, we can talk about this.'

'Damn right we can. We can talk about it right now!'

Layzee had his eyes trained on his wife, but could not contain himself any longer. He slammed his fist on the table, rattling the silverware. 'And how are you doin', darlin'? I told you I'd find you. And this time, there's no glass screen separating us, is there?' You fuckin' BITCH!!'

Outraged, and elderly, grey-haired English gentleman also sitting close by with his wife turned his head and said, 'Excuse me, sir.'

His accent was standard British upper/middle class, often referred to as 'received pronunciation', the posh dialect usually associated with people who live in the southeastern part of England. 'Do you mind, sir? I find your aggression and use of profanity most unacceptable!'

'Oh, listen to you with a plum up ya ass!' said Layzee. 'Do I mind, old timer? No! Now, wind ya neck in, Gramps. And mind your own fuckin' business. And what are YOU looking at?' said Layzee to his wife, who appeared shocked at the affront, her eyes wide with outrage.

'Good grief, sir,' said the man. 'How dare you speak to my wife in that manner?'

Once again, the Texan was getting agitated. 'Which is exactly what I said to him this morning,' he said.

'Oh, you wanna start on me again, do ya, cowboy?' said Layzee.

The elderly gentleman stood up. 'Sir, such uncouth behaviour is quite unacceptable in an establishment of this calibre.'

'Quite unacceptable?' queried Layzee. 'How is *quite unacceptable* different to just *unacceptable*? Christ, you fuckin' British are so stuck up your own asses.' Layzee gestured to the man's wife. 'I bet you been stuck up hers a few times.'

'My God, sir, I am not standing for this.'

'Well, sit down then.'

'Sir, I'm afraid I shall have to report you to the management.'

'Ah, go knock yourself out. In fact, why not go the whole nine yards and just call the fuckin' cops?'

'I bloody well will!' said the gentlemen.

'Henry!' snapped his wife. 'Language, please.'

'Yeah! Listen to your old lady. Sit the fuck down, Henry, and stop swearin'! You know something, Henry? Some folk die when they get to twenty-five, but don't get buried till they reach ninety. Does that ring true for you two? Did you both stop living when you got to twenty-five and have bin treading water ever since? Fuckin' coffin-dodgers!'

'How dare you, sir! I have never, ever, been so insulted in my whole life.'

'Well, should get out more often,' said Layzee. 'Seems like knob jockeys like you have nothing better to do than sit in your castles, counting your millions.'

'Knob jockeys?' frowned the man.

'HENRY!' snapped his wife. 'I'm leaving!'

Layzee looked bemused. 'Huh... now see what you done, Henry? She's leavin' ya! Just like this tramp here left me two years ago!' He pointed to Maria.

'Hey!' snarled the doctor. 'That's enough!'

'Yeah, what you gonna do?' growled Layzee.

The elderly woman rose from her table and grabbed her coat.

'Henry, be careful, she's goin'. I warned ya! If she walks out on ya for good, you better hope she's got no shit on ya... I tell ya. If she has, you could end up doin' a stretch in prison, like I did. And come chow time, I don't think you'd approve of the menu.'

Recalling years of marriage, Maria Dawson fixed her husband with a withering glare, vividly remembering the countless times he had displayed such aggressive rhetoric to her. Her heart sank. Would she ever be rid of this man?

Frankie said, 'Layzee! Have you quite finished? Shut up and let me handle this, will ya?'

'No! I guess I'm gonna sort this out!' said the big Texan as he got to his feet and stepped over to where Layzee was sitting.

Layzee said, 'Oh... here we go.'

The Texan pointed his finger at Layzee's face. 'Buddy, I don't think I've ever met anyone as rude as you. Now you either apologise to these fine folk or I will personally put you down.'

The doctor looked up at the big Texan cowboy and was grateful for his intervention; it gave him time to think. Whilst the men berated one another, his mind raced, adrenaline pumping through his arteries. To get them out of this mess, he had to think fast, but knew their only real chance of escape was to run.

With a trembling hand, he reached for the hot silver teapot. In one swift motion, he swiped it towards Layzee Dawson and upended the table, sending plates and crockery crashing to the floor. Layzee yelped as hot liquid showered his face and chaos erupted as terrified patrons nearby scattered, screaming in panic like monkeys fleeing a falling tree.

'Maria, come on!' he shouted, as he grabbed her hand and bolted towards the hotel's kitchen. They weaved through the tables and then crashed through the kitchen doors, dodging flailing pots and pans and frantic staff until they reached the back door. They burst into an alleyway lined with garbage skips and crates of empty bottles, the same skips and crates Layzee has seen from the window of his room six floors above.

'This way!' called the doctor.

'Lucas, wait!' said Maria as she slipped off her heels. She picked them up, and they both ran down the alley hand-in-hand, hearts pounding.

Upon reaching the street, they made a break for nearby Marylebone train station across the road from the hotel's rear entrance, their only hope, to lose themselves in the crowd and board a train—any train!

Amidst the rumpus in the hotel, the sound of chaotic yelling behind them had faded, but Layzee and Frankie were after them. They had followed them through the kitchen, down the alley, and were hot on their heels, Layzee leading the way, screaming obscenities as he ran.

Lucas and Maria fled for their lives, the doctor's footsteps slipping and sliding against the damp pavement as they raced towards the train terminal. They shared a fleeting glance back, their eyes filled with fear and exhilaration.

The two men had not given up—far from it. They were still in pursuit, some fifty yards behind, but closing fast, their faces twisted in determination.

The desperate couple ran into the busy, cavernous terminal, blending into a sea of commuters. They looked around.

'This way!' said the doctor.

'NO...! The platforms are over there!' urged Maria upon seeing the signs. But the doctor pulled her back to where a bank of storage lockers was situated.

Behind, Layzee and Frankie had lost sight of them. 'Where the hell are they?' snarled Layzee.

'FUCK IT! I don't know,' said Frankie. 'You go that way!' They separated, picking their way amongst the crowd, their necks straining to see.

Meanwhile, kneeling out of sight, the doctor punched a code into the keypad on a locker and pulled out his Gladstone medical bag. He glanced up at the huge overhead train information board looking for departures. 'COME ON, there's a train about to leave Platform One... let's GO!' He took Maria's hand.

Layzee spotted them. 'There they are!' he yelled. He took up the chase. Frankie heard him, span on his heels and followed.

'Maria, RUN!' yelled the doctor.

As they both forced their way through the bustling throng heading for the same platform, people cried out in annoyance, the doctor offering hurried apologies but without breaking stride as he reached into his jacket pocket.

'Here,' he said. 'Tickets!' With his usual pragmatism, as a contingency, he had purchased them a few days before.

Maria looked confused. 'Which way?'

'This way!' he said as he pushed through a funnel of commuters queuing to get through the ticket gates. 'Sorry, I'm a doctor!' he called authoritatively, lifting his bag. 'I have a medical emergency. PLEASE... make way!'

Amidst the bustle of jostling bodies, they inserted their tickets into the slot at the platform ticket gate and quickly followed one another, Maria pushing first through the three-pronged chrome turnstile.

Chasing them down, Layzee was the quicker of the two and was close. He was less apologetic as he shoved people aside, yells of complaint sounding as he reached out across the barrier.

He grabbed the doctor's sleeve. 'GOT YOU!' he snarled; his mouth contorted; his teeth baring a grin of loathing.

Maria halted in her tracks. 'Damn you, Layzee!' she yelled. She stepped back, grabbed the doctor's free hand holding the bag and pulled.

'HEY, asshole!' bellowed a stranger who, in Layzee's parlance, was built like a brick shithouse. He grabbed Layzee's arm. 'Let him go! There's an emergency... He's a DOCTOR!'

As the man tackled Layzee, Lucas yanked himself free, and they continued to run down a flight of stairs onto the platform where up ahead the train was readying for departure, its engine's low hum reverberating through the station. The platform assistant, wearing a high-vis jacket, blew a high-pitched whistle.

'NO!' yelled the doctor. 'COME ON, MARIA!'

As fast as they could run, they reached the first carriage, but it was packed. 'MARIA! Next ONE!!' yelled the doctor.

They reached the second carriage as the doors were just beginning to close. They leapt through the narrowing gap, falling onto the floor in an undignified heap as the doors slid shut with a hiss of compressed air.

They untangled themselves as passengers eyed them curiously. 'Christ! That was close!' said the doctor.

They scrambled to their feet and began picking their way along the carriage, searching for a hiding spot amidst a line of other passengers looking for vacant seats.

'Where are they?' gasped Maria. 'Did they get on?'

Lucas was behind her. He gripped her hand. 'I don't think so!' he said.

'Are you sure?'

'No!' Their eyes scanned the faces behind, and then they found a window seat.

'LOOK!' said Maria, as she wiped condensation from the glass. 'Outside!'

Having no tickets, Layzee and Frankie had quickly vaulted the platform ticket barriers, alerting armed security guards who were soon after them, dashing down the flight of stairs and onto the platform where the two men were quickly apprehended, their arms gesticulating wildly as they were grabbed and thrown to the ground just below the window where the doctor and Maria were watching.

The two men were promptly cuffed and upon being searched, one of the guards pulled out the key card cloning device from Layzee's pocket. He held it up and exchanged words with a colleague.

Frankie glanced across and then, upon seeing what they had found, dropped his dismayed face to the ground, cursing inwardly at his father's insistence that Layzee accompany him on what was now a failed venture.

With half a dozen size twelve boots pinning him to the floor, a struggling Layzee looked up at the window of the carriage only to see Maria's fist raised, her middle finger extended as the train inched away from the station, gathering speed with an escalating rumble. He yelled something, but the obscenity was lost, drowned by the noise of the diesel engines.

Inside the dimly lit carriage, Maria and the doctor huddled together, their breath mingling in the cool air as they stole fleeting moments of respite from the pursuit.

'So, how did they find us, Lucas?' asked Maria.

'I don't know,' said the doctor. He thought for a moment and then said, 'When booking the room, I foolishly used my credit card. Perhaps it was that.'

Maria's wide eyes stared into his face. 'Could they have traced *me?*'

'Highly unlikely,' said the doctor. 'Besides, the look on your husband's face was one of surprise. You were the last person he expected to see in London. No... I'm sure it was me they found. We'll need to be more careful.'

Through the window, a panorama of the city's gritty urban landscape began rolling past, the train's steel wheels clacking rhythmically like a heartbeat over the rails as it accelerated.

Maria and the doctor watched blindly as their train carried them further from the salubrious veneers of London's tourist havens, graffiti-covered brick facades and crumbling warehouses whipping by in a kaleidoscope of colour and decay. Gradually, the dense city buildings began thinning out, vacant lots and overgrown parks appearing amidst the urban sprawl. Then finally, the clustered housing developments and shopping centres of the suburbs rushed by in a blur of motion, signalling London's outer edge.

As they looked outside, they had no idea where they were going.

A black hole appeared and swallowed the train whole. and then spat it out into blinding daylight, revealing a vast expanse of open countryside stretching out before it. Lush rolling hills and patchwork fields of vibrant green meadows extended as far as the eye could see, punctuated by the occasional copse of trees. Eventually, the setting sun painted the rural landscape in rich golden hues, a stark contrast to the dreary concrete greys of the city.

With each passing mile, the memory of the city's skyline faded into the distance. Be it north, south, east or west, only one thing was for certain. They had narrowly escaped the snarling wrath of New York's Vitalli crime family—at least for now. But even as they hurtled towards an uncertain destination, Maria and Doctor Roberts knew their escape today was only the beginning of their journey. For in the shadows of the train's flickering lights, relief was replaced by uncertainty.

'Where are we going?' asked Maria.

'Tonight, I don't know,' smiled the doctor, 'It doesn't matter, anywhere. But, well… we'll find a hotel for the night somewhere. But tomorrow… we'll be going to Austria!'

'Austria?'

'Yes.'

Maria gasped. 'OK… but my passport!'

'Don't worry, it's with mine in here.' Lucas tapped his Gladstone medical bag. 'All our valuables are in here.' He had secured his bag in the locker earlier that day, as he had every day since his arrival in London. A "go bag" ready for such an occasion—ready in the event a quick exit was required.

Maria looked at him and smiled. 'You think of everything, don't you?' She squeezed his hand. 'So, the plan is to go to Austria?'

'Yes, that's always been the plan. I wanted to surprise you. There's a place I know, high in the mountains. We'll need some warm clothes, but we'll be safe there.' The doctor thought for a moment and then asked, 'Maria, have you ever skied?'

'No.'

'I'll teach you.'

'OK, but I have a question.'

'What… about skiing?'

'No.' She looked at him pensively. 'Lucas… where did you hide seven million dollars?'

Lucas smiled. He realised if anything untoward was to have happened to him; if Layzee had access to a gun, and if Layzee had pulled the trigger, and if the bullet had found its target, he might now be dead, and Maria would never know where to look. He leaned closer and whispered the location in her ear.

Maria gasped. 'NO! Really? Oh, my God!'

The doctor nodded. 'Yes... and we must retrieve it someday soon.'

Maria huddled into the warm embrace of her man, happy in the knowledge that no matter what darkness awaited on the horizon, or what secrets they fled from, their fates were now inextricably intertwined.

But now they had each other, and that was all that mattered.

Chapter 20: Needle in a Smokestack

To buy themselves some time, should anyone come down to the bowels of the ship, Debbie and Samuel Vitalli quickly dragged Ricco Capelli's body from the corridor into the ship's prison cell, which had been Sam's home for the past six months. They then set about cleaning the corridor floor of blood and brain matter, using Sam's frayed T-shirt as a mop, which they rinsed into the small sink in the dark room before repeating the ghastly process until the corridor floor was clean. The faint rumble of the ship's engine continued to drone and there was a shimmering vibration of the deck plates beneath their feet as Sam exchanged the remainder of the rags he was wearing for the dead man's black shirt and suit.

'Not exactly a tailored fit, is it?' he said.

Debbie looked at the thin man with his full beard in the oversized clothes. 'It looks OK,' she said. 'At least the shoes fit.'

'Now, we gotta get you fixed up,' said Sam.

'How?'

'His brother.'

Debbie cringed. 'Oh no!'

Sam looked sorrowfully at his sister-in-law garbed in someone else's filthy, oversized white shirt and grimy khaki shorts. He shook his head as he pursed his lips. 'Deborah, it's the only way. You'll look less conspicuous. You can't possibly go out wearing those, especially with that storm howling outside. How long before we leave port?'

Debbie looked down at herself and knew he was right. 'The announcement said thirty minutes. But that was ten minutes ago.'

'Oh shit... OK. We need to move. Gimme a hand... help me lift this asshole.'

Between them they hauled the dead body onto the bunk bed and draped it with the rags Sam had been wearing and covered most of the rest of the body with the single bed sheet, adjusting everything so that, to a cursory look through the door's letterbox, it would appear Sam was asleep.

Sam regarded his fellow captive. 'Look at you,' he said as he touched Debbie's face, which was swollen red along her jawline, the rest of her beauty now a patchwork quilt of purple and blue bruises. 'And look what they did to you...those bastards! Come on, let's go home.'

They locked the cell door and then made their way back to the maintenance room, where they also removed Rocco Cappelli's body of its clothes.

Sam stood back and regarded his sister-in-law, who had now exchanged her shorts and shirt. She, too, looked buried in the black shirt and suit of the dead twin brother. She had turned up and folded in the legs and sleeves of the suit to fashion a better fit. 'Well?' she asked.

'Huh! We look like a couple of extras from "Men in Black",' said Sam. 'But it will have to do. At least we got these.' He raised the Glock handgun.

'Yes,' said Debbie, who also raised the gun in her hand, hers fitted with a suppressor. 'And we have the element of surprise too,' she added. 'But time's running out. Come on, Sam, let's get outta this nightmare.'

They took off down the corridor.

Meanwhile, outside in the dockyard, a car screeched into the main car park and skidded to a stop in a parking bay.

Sash had received Debbie's text message, but had been unable to speak to her, or trace the phone's location. The message mentioned a ship, and he guessed if it was still in New York Harbour, it would be at the local docks.

On a hunch, he had plumped for Brooklyn's Red Hook Marine Terminal, mainly because it was the location of Louie Marmarella's abattoir business. He hoped he had made the right choice, but now he had arrived, a familiar pang of doubt gripped him as he wondered if the tenuous text would lead to a dead end, or worse—a dead woman.

A knot of dread twisted his gut as he pondered how he could extrapolate even a single spark of hope from the labyrinth of darkness shrouding her disappearance. Yet, at that moment, the question gnawing at his resolve more ferociously than any killer's intent was the damning exodus of her husband? Why in hell's name would a man flee the country when his wife's safety hung in the balance? For Frankie, the recovery of the stolen money clearly outweighed any value he placed on his wife's existence. Could it be that, to him, Debbie's life was negligible… discardable… meaningless?

Even though his father had insisted Frankie go, there was no other way you could call it. But that was the difference between Sash and Frankie Vitalli. Whilst Frankie appeared not to give a damn about his wife; to Sash, she meant everything. He realised her life now hung by a frayed thread, a faint whisper in the abyss of probability; for he knew, given the Capelli brother's depraved minds, that if she was alive, it was an inconsequential 'if'. The twin brothers' reputations preceded them. To them, death was their national language, and lives—mere currency to be traded.

As hatred's bitter bile burned his throat; for he had no idea of events unfolding on board the ship, Sash opened the door of the car, his heart pounding as he stepped out, his confused senses instantly assaulted by a cacophony of clanging steel and diesel engines from forklift trucks as they dashed across the harbour like oversized go-karts. In the distance, four towering gantry cranes appeared above the buildings, giant steel spiders plucking containers off the decks of moored ships, redistributing their brightly coloured metal boxes across the yards, where hundreds more shielded the Manhattan skyline.

The terminal was a full-service container port and handled many commodities, including fresh and frozen produce which were temporarily stored in the huge warehouses spread across the sixty-acre site, before being distributed across New York state and beyond.

Sash scanned the dizzying landscape as he made his way into the familiar security building and up to the empty counter. The dockyard was a regular locale for both the Marmarella's, and the Vitalli's, so, some of the employees he knew. He recognised the sentry man on duty.

'How's things, Sash? It's been a while,' said a gruff face full of hair and beard who appeared from a back office.

'How's it goin', Jerry?' said Sash. 'How's your wife and family?'

'Yeah, good thanks,' nodded the man. He did not ask after Sash's family. He remembered Sash had no wife or kids.

'Jerry,' said Sash. 'I have an urgent problem that I need to resolve, and, eh... I think you can help. Take a look at this.' He showed the man the text message: *Help. Debbie. Kidnapped. On ship. Trace phone. Be quick.*

The man frowned. 'What the fuck?'

'Yeah, exactly,' said Sash. 'Any ideas?'

The security man scratched his head and read the message again. Then his eyes beneath his thick, bushy monobrow rose. 'Oh, Lordy! Damn... are we talking about Frankie Vitalli's wife here?'

'Yes, we are.'

'Jesus, Sash! Are you sure it's this terminal?'

'No. I've just a gut feeling it might be.'

The man wrestled with options and then said, 'But surely, this is a job for the cops, Sash?'

'No, it ain't. That's the last thing I need?'

The man emitted a heavy sigh. 'Well, if she's on a ship and it's here, it could be any one of half a dozen. Eh... let me think.'

Sash pocketed the phone, raised his eyes and looked up at the man. 'Jerry, do any of those half dozen ships have links with Louie Marmarella's outfit, by any chance?'

At the mention of Marmarella's name, the security man stiffened uneasily, which suggested to Sash the man knew something. But Sash then wondered if the man might have a stronger alliance with the Marmarella family and might withhold the information he so desperately needed.

'Oh... eh... I dunno, Sash,' said Jerry.

The air thickened with tension as Sash laid his cards on the table. 'Jerry,' he said. 'Point me in the right direction and I'll make it worth your while,' his words carrying an unmistakable undercurrent of bribery. He leaned towards the man. 'And Mr. Vitalli will not forget you helped him.'

The guard's face paled, beads of sweat betraying his internal tug-of-war. He had the look of a man who wished he hadn't turned up for work that morning. This was the last thing he needed. 'Eh, look, Sash,' he said, anxiety edging his tone. 'Listen... I appreciate that, Sash, and I wanna help but I need this job, see... and if ever word got back to...'

'IT WON'T!' said Sash , raising his hand to silence him.. 'Who's gonna know? All you need to do, Jerry, is just point a finger. That's all I'm asking.'

With deliberate nonchalance, Sash reached into his jacket and withdrew a thick wad of crisp one hundred-dollar bills. With a deft flick of his thumb, he peeled off five before his eyes met those of the guard again. 'Here,' he said. 'Take 'em!'

Jerry looked at the money and wet his lips, conflict playing out on his features. 'Oh, Sash, look... Christ! I really wanna help, but...'

'STOP!' said Sash.

The sound of more bills separating from the wad was ominous, like the click of a shotgun's breech being racked in a tense stand-off. Ten more crisp one hundred-dollar bills joined the five on the counter as Sash extended his offering. 'Look, there's fifteen-hundred bucks there, Jerry. If I were you, I'd take 'em.'

The gravel in Sash's voice now carried the unmistakable timbre of a sense of a threat, thinly veiled in his revised offer. The man's eyes narrowed.

'Could you put another five on there, Sash?'

'Don't fuckin' push it, Jerry.'

The security officer's Adam's apple bobbed in a reflexive gulp, as Sash's piercing stare bored into him. 'Go on... take 'em!'

The guard hesitated, his hand reaching, hovering. Then he snatched the money, a guttural 'Fuck!' escaping his lips as morality took a backseat to greed. With a furtive glance over his shoulder, he pointed towards the window.

'Right... Sash, look... listen! The cruise terminal is over there on the left— Pier 1. But you go right—Pier 7. There's a big fuckin' cargo ship there. And take these!' A yellow hi-visibility vest and white hard hat changed hands.

Sash spotted a clipboard lying nearby. Memories of his army days came back to remind him that a man carrying a clipboard always seemed to move with impunity. 'I'll take this too,' he said, already reaching for it.

'Err, OK. But you never got those from me!' said the man. 'And we never spoke, right?'

'Yeah... you got it,' said Sash as he also picked up a pen from the counter. Sash went to leave and then turned to face the man. 'I'm pretty sure Mr Vitalli will also show his appreciation,' he said.

'Eh yeah... give him my regards.'

Sash nodded and left the building.

He was immediately hit with a brisk wind. Above the stacked towers of containers, the skies were darkening from grey to a threatening black. A storm was on its way, blowing in from the ocean. It was getting late. He put on the safety attire and headed down the nearest lane between a line of rust-streaked shipping containers towards the smell of seawater, which hung in the air tinged with the acrid tang of marine fuel and grease so pungent, he could taste it. The wind was strengthening to the point where white-caps were showing across the waters of the harbour. To the left, he could see a cruise ship which Jerry had mentioned. As he said, it was docked at Pier 1.

He swung a right turn. Across the water, where ferries and tour boats criss-cross the East River, the grey, tall skyscrapers of lower Manhattan's Financial District came into view with Governors Island to the left. Owing to their height and density, the monolithic buildings appeared so close, Sash felt he could almost touch them. As he quickly walked, he noticed the skyline was punctuated by other famous towers; the Gothic marvel that is the Woolworth Building, the World's tallest structure until 1930, and in the distance the wedge-shaped Flatiron Building. The piers of the Hudson River and the Brooklyn Bridge stretched out to the north, while the Manhattan Bridge framed the view to the north-east.

Again, the gathering storm increased its wind-force, as *he* increased his fast walk. Dock workers wearing high-visibility jackets and white helmets went about their duties, paying him no attention as he strode on, every so often glancing at the clipboard as if he was hurrying in search of something—or someone.

He was. But where was she?

He arrived at Pier 7 where a metal gangway bridged the gap between the pier and the vast ship, the low hum of its engines rumbling. He looked up at the towering ship's funnel. Boiler steam and engine exhaust rose from the smokestack, and he realised the ship was preparing to leave. He checked the rusty red hull and made a note of the ship's name. It appeared the gangway was about to be pulled.

'Hey you, hold it!' he called out to a guy in a similar hi-visibility vest. 'I'm a representative from the Port Authority of New York and New Jersey. I need to find and board a ship.' He glanced at his clipboard. 'The Siberian Star?'

'What? That's this ship!' called the dockworker. 'But it's about to leave.'

'It'll leave when I say it'll leave,' said Sash, as he ran his finger across his clipboard. 'Yeah, this is the one.' He stepped onto the gangway. 'I have reason to believe there's someone onboard this ship who shouldn't be.'

'But it's due to disembark? We got orders to pull the gangway.'

Sash pulled a pen from the clipboard. 'What's your name?' he asked.

'Why?'

'If you interfere with an inspection, I'll need your name.'

The man hesitated and then said, 'I ain't interfering with nothing, mister.'

'Good,' said Sash. 'You've saved me some paperwork.'

Sash continued up the gangway and as he stepped onboard through the door below the top deck, a deckhand standing alone queried his presence. 'Who the hell are you?' said a short, stocky man with a thick Russian accent.

'Port Authority,' said Sash. 'I'm looking for a Mrs Deborah Vitalli.'

'Oh, that bitch,' snarled the man. 'Never heard of her. Where is your identification?'

Five seconds later, the man was lying flat out unconscious on the deck after finding himself on the business end of Sash's identification—a powerful straight jab to his chin providing the requested credentials. Sash lifted the legs of the unconscious body and dragged it away from the door.

Meanwhile, four decks below, the woman he was searching for, and Samuel Vitalli, whom he had no idea was onboard, were making their way up to the third deck wearing the Capelli brothers' black suits.

'Don't hesitate,' said Sam to Debbie Vitalli. 'We can't fuck around. If you see anyone and we're challenged… just shoot them.'

Two decks above, Sash made his way to a stairwell. 'Christ! This is gonna be like looking for a needle in a haystack,' he muttered to himself.

As the ship prepared to depart from the bustling port, Debbie Vitalli winced from the humming stench of having to wear Rocco Capelli's suit. Whilst elsewhere, the ship's bridge was humming with a flurry of coordinated activity.

Captain Vladimir Mashkov stood at the helm, his keen eyes scanning the array of instruments before him. He spoke into a handset, his baritone voice crackling over the intercom, echoing through the vessel's corridors. 'All hands prepare to depart. Winds are picking up, steady on deck.'

Debbie and Sam looked at one another.

'Oh, NO!' said Debbie, again sensing motion vibrations coursing through the deck plates underfoot. 'We're leaving port.'

'I think you'll find we've already left port,' said Sam, who recognised the sensation. He had experienced it a few times during the past six months.

'Oh, no! We're trapped!' gasped the desperate woman.

'So, it would seem,' said Sam. 'OK, let's go.' They climbed the stairs to Deck 3.

Onboard and taking temporary control of the ship's course and speed was a stranger to the crew, a Pilot from Sandy Hook Pilots Association, a man with local expert knowledge of the harbour's tidal flow, its depth, currents, and obstacles. Instead of the captain, once underway, he would issue commands to the helmsman and would guide the ship out of the harbour to open sea.

Sandy Hook maritime pilots had covered the comings and goings of large ships in and out of New York harbour for over 300 years. On this occasion, once safe passage had been negotiated through *The Narrows*, a tidal strait that separates the boroughs of Staten Island and Brooklyn, the Pilot would disembark, usually by helicopter, but owing to the bad weather, that would not be the case on this particular evening.

Having just boarded, Sash silently slipped down the staircase to Deck 3 and into a long, dimly lit corridor. Some distance away, he spotted two figures in black suits walking away from him. As they walked, overhead lights came on and off as they passed through each lighting detection zone.

'Well, what do ya know?' Sash muttered to himself. 'The Capelli brothers. Huh...they'll know where Debbie is.' He reached into his jacket and withdrew a handgun. His initial thought was to shoot and kill one of them and maim the other. He went after them.

On the bridge, the navigator, a fresh-faced ensign, had meticulously plotted the ship's intended course—cross-referencing charts and making precise calculations. 'Course laid in, Captain,' he reported crisply.

In the communications hub, the radio operator established contact with the harbour master and relayed the captain's intentions and receiving clearance for departure.

The helmsman, a weathered sailor with decades of experience, placed his calloused hands on the ship's controls, awaiting the order to engage the engines. The order was given, and the ship's bow thrusters gradually pushed the large vessel from the pier.

Just then, the men on the bridge looked up from what they were doing as two muffled bangs sounded below decks.

'What was that?' asked the Sandy Hook pilot.

'Nothing for you to be concerned about,' said Mashkov. 'Everything's in order. My men are carrying out repairs to a bilge pump. Just get on with your job.'

The pilot cast a sour glance at the Russian captain and then provided the helmsman with a directional heading. 'Dead slow ahead. Port 15,' he said.

'Dead slow ahead. Wheel on Port 15,' came the reply from the helmsman as, with a deep blare of the ship's horn, the vessel continued to inch away from the dock, its massive bulk cutting through the waters of the harbour.

The First Officer, a no-nonsense woman named Ramirez, who oversaw everything operational, leaned across to Mashkov with an enquiring eye.

Mashkov, referring to the sounds of muffled gunfire, whispered, 'It's nothing. I knew this was about to happen, but not so soon. Our over exuberant colleagues are putting paid to a couple of guests who have outstayed their welcome. I understand they received their orders from Mr Marmarella earlier.'

The formidable woman's acidic glare matched the frown etched across her forehead. 'Couldn't they have at least waited until we were out at sea?'

'Yes,' said Mashkov. 'That would have been preferable. Fuckin' Capelli brothers! I wondered where they had got to. They never answer their radios. Go check. Make sure everything's OK.'

Below on Deck 3, a scene of confusion had rapidly unfolded, like a sinister Bolshoi ballet. Seconds earlier, Sash had been moving with silent intent, his handgun raised, his footfalls muffled as he tailed the two figures whom he believed to be the Capelli brothers. But just as he crept closer, something seemed out of kilter. Something was not quite right—one was significantly shorter than the other and had blonde hair.

Debbie Vitalli, alerted behind by an overhead light coming on, sensed a presence and span round. Upon seeing what appeared to be a crewman wearing a hi-vis jacket holding a gun—she aimed to fire hers.

Sam's hair-trigger reactions outpaced even Debbie's lethal reflexes. He twisted a split second earlier, seized her arm and wrenched it skywards, as she fired off two rounds.

PHUT... Ting! PHUT... Ting!

The double tab bullets ricocheted off the corridor's metal ceiling in a torrent of sparks.

'Sam! What are you doing?' she gasped.

Sam pointed to the man whom she had tried to shoot. Then, she too recognised whom she had almost shot—who she had almost killed.

She dropped the weapon.

'Sash! Oh my God!' she cried, relief and horror intermingling as she propelled herself into his arms. 'Oh God, I am so sorry. Are you alright?' Her words tumbled out in a breathless rush before her lips crashed against his in a desperate, passionate kiss.

Sash returned the embrace, his heart rate beginning to steady. 'Yes, I am now,' he murmured. 'Thank God you're alive.' He glanced at the bearded figure standing alongside her who had just saved his life. 'Thanks Sam,' he said. And then realisation dawned. 'SAM?'

Sam cleared his throat. 'Hi Sash,' he said with a roguish grin. 'By the way, I didn't get that reaction when she saw me.'

Sash stared at the man disbelieving; his brow furrowed as he drank in the sight of... 'SAMUEL VITALLI?' he said. 'Huh... Sam, you're ALIVE!' His voice laced with astonishment.

Sam's smile widened a fraction. 'Yeah, ain't that a thing? How's it goin', Sash?'

'I don't know,' said Sash, shaking his head. 'What the fuck's goin' on? We're knee deep in shit, aren't we? But Sam... we all thought you were...'

'Dead! Yeah, I know. Deborah told me. But then, after six months, I'd have thought the same too.'

'Oh, it's good to see you, Sam. But Christ, you've lost a shitload of weight!'

'Yeah, that starve the fucka to death diet, works really well.'

Sash looked at the woman in his arms and brushed away a rogue strand of bloodstained hair from her bruised face. Then her battered condition registered with him. 'Jesus! What have they done to you?' he said, now horrified at her appearance.

'I knew you'd try to find me,' whispered Debbie, her eyes shimmering with a profound mix of love and gratitude. 'But don't worry, I'll mend.'

'You will, providing we get outta here,' he said. 'So, why are you two wearing these suits? Where are the Capelli brothers?'

Debbie Vitalli's eyes narrowed. 'DEAD!' she snapped. 'Sam's alive and they're dead!'

'She killed both of them,' said Sam.

'What? You killed the two Capelli brothers?'

'After what they did to me... Yes, I did!'

'Look,' said Sam. 'We'll catch up later. But right now, we need to get off this damn ship.'

'It's too late,' said Sash. 'We're already underway.'

Somewhere behind, they heard footsteps clambering down a stairwell.

'Quick, let's go!' said Sam. 'This way.'

Sash looked confused. 'Where are we going?'

Sam studied the two faces staring back at him. 'I've an idea. Follow me.'

A few decks below, the First Officer had reached Sam's cell. She hammered the door with her handgun, and upon receiving no response, she cursed and pulled out a set of keys, only to find inside what she thought was a sleeping body on the bunk.

'Get up, you PIG!' she snarled.

She cracked the head of the 'sleeping' man with the butt of her weapon, but there was still no response. She looked curiously at the weapon in her hand, which now felt slimy. She snatched the bed sheet away and found the naked dead Capelli brother, his head—or what was left of it—lying on a bloodied pillow.

She recoiled.

She had seen many dead men, but finding this one surprised her. With a gaping mouth, she radioed Captain Mashkov.

'WHAT?' snarled Mashkov, as he backed off to a corner of the bridge out if earshot of the Pilot. He lowered his voice into his handset. 'I cannot do anything now. I need to get rid of this damn pilot. How the fuck did they get out? The deck crew will be around. Get help and find them!'

The three captives gathered pace as they negotiated the maze of ships' corridors. Sam appeared to know where he was going.

'How do know your way around?' asked Debbie.

As they quickly walked, Sam explained. 'During the past six months, when at sea, and when they knew I couldn't escape, they would sometimes let me out for an hour or so, shackled and chaperoned, of course. I used the time to memorise my way round parts of the ship and tried to hang on to that memory, hoping someday it might help me get outta here. It was all I had to think about for months.'

Sam paused and looked around. At the end of the passageway, a ladder-well rose up to the next deck at an angle of about 45 degrees and then continued up to the deck beyond that. Sam closed his eyes and tracked his mental map. 'Hold on!' he said as he motioned left, right and then up with his hands. 'Ehm... yes, we need to go up here.'

'So where are we going?' asked Sash.

'Let me explain,' said Sam. 'Somewhere on deck will be a ladder that the harbour pilot will use to get off the ship and board his tender. I remember seeing that ladder. Some of the wooden steps were yellow to improve visibility, I guess. It was wound around a spindle. The crew lower the ladder over the side of the hull. Then, when the pilot's finished his job of steering the ship out of the harbour, he climbs down the ladder to a boat that comes in to collect him. I've seen it done. The ship doesn't stop, and it looks fuckin' dangerous, but...' Sam fired a glance at Debbie Vitalli, who looked horripilated at the suggestion. He continued, 'If we get to the ladder before he does, and before the boat leaves, we're home free. We simply climb down the ladder and board the boat.'

'Simply climb down the ladder?' repeated Mrs Vitalli, her face wracked with fear.

'But what if they don't let us board the boat?' asked Sash.

'They will... course they will! They won't let us drown, will they? But if the pilot gets off before we get to the ladder and the boat leaves, then we're really screwed. So, let's hope he hasn't already left the ship. Come on! Let's GO!'

Without waiting for Debbie to air her dissatisfaction with the plan, they climbed the double stairwell and finally crashed through a door on the ship's starboard side, stumbling out onto the open deck beneath the vast night sky as the huge vessel rolled from side-to-side.

The fresh, briny breeze enveloped them, and they all breathed in a deep, grateful lungful of cool sea air. Peering around the deck, their handguns raised in readiness, they realised they were no longer needed—there was no sign of anyone. The crew had sensibly sought sanctuary from the hellish winds below deck. And up there, the three captives had the entire breathing sea to themselves.

Sam grinned widely, savouring his hard-won moment of blissful libera-tion, momentarily forgetting he was still a captive, but glad to see they had not yet left New York Harbour. Which meant the pilot would still be on the ship's bridge, navigating passage through the waters.

'Wow! Look at Manhattan.' he said, lovingly.

The towering spires of Manhattan's cityscape pierced the inky black nighttime sky, its countless windows glittering a billion tiny jewels of light. 'Christ, I didn't realise it was so beautiful,' said Sam, a smile breaking across his sunken cheeks as the stiff wind whipped at his hair and riffled his ill-fitting clothes. 'I also didn't realise it was nighttime. I thought it would be daylight. But guys, smell that fresh air in this glorious breeze. Wonderful!'

Sash shot him an incredulous look. 'Sam, are you mad? That's no breeze! It's a damn gale out here!'

But Sam didn't care. He spread his arms out wide, relishing the lashing wind. 'Guys, I've been locked up in a six-by-eight box for months,' he said. 'Incarceration has a tendency to reset your priorities. Believe me, this is great!'

He turned his face up to the heavens, allowing the invigorating gusts to wash over him as if standing beneath a waterfall, as dark clouds raced across the canopy of sparkling stars. To him, it was like being reborn. After the stale, oppressive confines of his cramped quarters, this wild, open freedom was the ultimate relief. He bathed in it, and then refocused. 'OK...this way!' he said, his words lost in the strong wind as it snatched each syllable from his mouth, tossed them up, and fired them out to sea.

He led the way, heading across the blustery emptiness. He was looking for two bright yellow guide rails through which he hoped the ladder would be hanging, suspended over the side of the ship's hull. Then he spotted it!

'THERE!' he said. 'COME ON!'

The forty-foot roped ladder had been deployed. It looked like a narrow piece of ship's rigging composed of broad hardwood steps with a six-foot elongated plank—a spreader—positioned every eighth step, its function; to prevent the ladder from twisting against the rusting hull. But in the torrid conditions, the spreader was having little effect as the ship rolled from side to side.

Sam looked over and down onto the icy waters and saw the size and swell of the waves. 'Oh, Christ!' he grimaced as the ladder crashed against the hull. He couldn't fend off a feeling of dread. On a night like this, he knew it wouldn't be pretty, but this was ridiculous. Misjudge the roll of the ship or lose your grip, and death was a very real probability.

He looked further out. Yes—there it was! A Pilot boat illuminated by bright lights was closely following alongside the merchant ship, positioned fifty yards back, waiting to come in and collect the Pilot from the ladder.

Debbie crept to the edge of the deck, peered over the side, and yelled. 'Oh my God, you've gotta be joking!'

Sam placed a reassuring hand on her shoulder. 'Deborah, listen to me. This is our ticket off this tub. It's our only way out. If we don't get off, they'll find us, and we'll end up as fish food... simple as.' His hand squeezed her shoulder. 'You can do this!'

Sash stepped in close. 'Debbie, Sam's right. This *is* our only chance!' Sash slipped off his yellow hi-visibility vest and gently secured it around the terrified woman, pulling the straps snug in a protective embrace, as the roaring chaos around them muted for a moment, and their eyes met. 'You'll be fine,' he said softly, their faces inches apart. 'Sam will go first, then you follow, and I'll be right behind you.'

Debbie felt the very real tangible grip of fear as her heart rate quickened. 'What if I slip and fall?' she asked, her anguished words almost catching in her throat.

Sash's hand found hers, their fingers intertwining. 'Then I'll come in right after you. And I'll find you.'

Then Sam's gruff voice sliced through the tension. He cupped his hands around his mouth to project over the crashing surf. 'DEBORAH! Where's that damn torch?' he yelled. 'Come on! LET'S GO!'

Sash gave Debbie's hand one last reassuring squeeze before releasing it. But in that private moment, Sash wondered if that would be the last time he would ever touch her living body.

Debbie pulled the torch from her pocket and handed it to Sam. 'Do we need these?' she asked, raising her gun.

'No!' said Sam. 'Leave the guns and anything else that might snag on the way down.'

They each removed their jackets and dropped them, Debbie replacing her yellow hi-visibility vest, which Sash again secured. Sash pushed his wallet into his trouser pocket as Sam aimed the torch at the pilot boat and flashed it three times quickly, three times slowly, and then again, three times quickly. He repeated the sequence over and over.

Against the dark skies, through the murk, the skipper of the pilot boat saw the flashes of light in his peripheral vision.

He squinted.

'What the hell is that, he muttered?' Again, the same sequence of flashes. He brought up his binoculars. 'Morse Code?' he said to himself. 'What's going on?' The sequence kept repeating. Yes, it was the emergency signal S.O.S—Save Our Souls.'

The boat's skipper radioed his pilot on board the ship. 'Are you flashing a light up there?' he asked.

'No, I'm not. Why?'

'Are you on deck by the ladder?'

'No, not yet. I'm still on the bridge. This storm's a bitch. But we're almost out of the harbour. I'll be there in a few minutes. Why'd you ask?'

'Well, someone's already there. They're flashing an emergency Morse Code signal.'

'Alright, I'll check it out when I get there.'

One of the two men aboard the Pilot boat was tethered to the deck to assist with the recovery of the Pilot. He too had spotted the flashing lights and threw a searchlight beam up to the ladder, the conical shaft of light cutting through the unrelenting spray of saltwater. The skipper and the crewman then watched in astonishment as three figures one-by-one clambered over the side and began a precarious descent down the ladder, neither of them wearing life jackets.

'Jesus Christ! What the hell?' was the skipper's immediate reaction. Then concern gripped him. With a wind-force of 6 or 7, without lifejackets, if any of them were to slip into the rough seas, it would not be a rescue mission he would have to undertake, it would be body recovery.

He needed to act fast. He applied power, but steering was not so easy, It was like trying to stabilise a boat in a washing machine, but he fought the turbulent wake and brought the small Pilot boat towards the hull of the large merchant ship as it continued to roll in the heaving swells, salt spray lashing across the deck as towering walls of black water crashed against the ship's hull. Down the side of the ship, the slender pilot's rope ladder swung wildly, its wooden steps slick and treacherous, three bodies clinging to it with every ounce of strength they possessed.

Meanwhile, the Russian woman, First Officer Ramirez, was searching the corridors and decks. She had checked the maintenance storeroom and had also found the dead body of the other Capelli brother. She had radioed her find to the Captain, who was about to re-take control of his vessel as the ship was close to open sea, and the Pilot, who was just about to leave, had finished his task.

Back on the ladder, Sam's frozen fingers gripped the vertical ropes, his knuckles white. He glanced up at the two figures. Debbie was immediately above, and Sash was above her, holding on with grim determination.

Just then, a rogue wave broke across the ship's beam, dousing them all in frigid spray.

'FUCK!' yelled Sam, who, as he was the lower of the three, caught the brunt of the freezing deluge. He lowered himself another step, but each shift of his weight caused the hazardous ladder to buck and contort, threatening to fling them all into the churning abyss.

As they were close to open sea, and without the protection of the harbour, the waves had become monstrous.

'GO! GO!!' yelled Sash over the roar of the churning grey waters as the pilot boat butted against the hull.

With grim determination, Sam nodded and continued his descent, timing his movements between the violent rolls of the ship as the ladder swung out and then came crashing back against the ship's red wall of steel. Each wooden step to which he was clinging felt like a bar of ice. Twenty feet below, the pilot boat bobbed insanely, its deck awash in white-water as it endeavoured to hug the huge vessel's hull in readiness to receive the struggling bodies.

Sam focused on placing one foot down in front of the other, feeling for the next plank of wood, avoiding weight transference until he was sure of his footing—or as sure as he could be.

'Don't look!' he urged himself. 'Don't look DOWN!'

Once set, he then reached up with his free hand and helped position Debbie's foot as she, too, stepped down. Below, the pilot boat appeared to be a toy tossed about in a bathtub, its deck rising and falling erratically. Sam couldn't help but look down. Timing their jumps would be critical. But it looked IMPOSSIBLE!

Another huge swell lifted the pilot boat high, bringing it up towards them with horrifying speed before dropping it into a trough between waves, a funnel of spray rising like New York's Bethesda Fountain, the plume of water hitting the three clinging bodies with savage force.

Sam froze, his heart pounding. How the hell was he supposed to get onboard? Another wave slammed into the ladder, making it buck and twist.

Above, grimacing against the stinging spray, Debbie cried out as she too clung on after almost being thrown off, her right arm hooking around the vertical side rope as the ladder again crashed against the hull. 'I can't do THIS!' she screamed.

Sam grabbed her foot again and repositioned it. 'COME ON! Steady!' he yelled; his voice nearly drowned by the thunderous roar. With grim determination, he forced his stiff limbs to move again, half-falling, half-climbing down the last few steps as the ship ploughed through the waters.

The pilot boat surged up beneath him. It was NOW or NEVER!!!

He leapt at the last possible moment and landed heavily onto the rubberised platform of the pilot boat's heaving deck, his weak legs buckling, unable to support his weight. Again, the boat fell away into a deep trough between huge swells. The other two peered down and watched in horror as Sam slid across the narrow deck and almost disappeared off the other side. But just in time, the crewman reached out and grabbed him.

Sam scrambled and rolled to his hands and knees, and clutched a handrail before the next godforsaken wave rammed the boat. He cursed loudly. It was like riding a damn bucking bronco!

'COME ON!' urged the Pilot boat's crewman, shouting and beckoning down Debbie Vitalli, the next in line, as the boat rose up again. 'MOVE YOUR ARSE!' he yelled.

Buoyed by Sam's success, Debbie was almost at the bottom of the ladder. Silhouetted against the towering steel prow of the ship, she unhooked her arm and stepped down one step, then another. Then she slipped and lost her footing!

She gasped, her eyes wide with terror, her life hanging by a single hand gripping the rope as a curtain of water slammed into her dangling body, sending the ladder out and then crashing it back against the hull.

'NO ...!!' yelled Sash as he grimaced against the stinging spray, readying himself to go in after her, should she fall.

Debbie held on and scrambled to reach and managed to lift her left foot back onto a wooden step. She heaved her body up and then got her right foot back into position. She clung on and gathered her senses. She looked up at Sash, who sensed a presence above and raised his head.

A face appeared—it was the Pilot who looked over the side and down to Sash, who was about twenty feet below. 'What the hell are you doing?' he bellowed.

Many pilots over the years had lost their lives undertaking this dangerous manoeuvre. Would today claim another?

Just then, First Officer Ramirez *CRASHED* through the door onto the exposed deck. She looked around for the escapees. Where were they?

Halfway down the ladder, beneath the underbelly of the hull, Sash looked up. He called out to the pilot. 'We need to get off this damn ship!' he yelled. 'YOU need to get off it too! I'll explain later!'

Now was not a time to argue. As the Pilot swung his one leg over the edge, the Russian woman spotted him, and the pile of discarded jackets and guns. She dashed across to where the ladder had been deployed. She pulled her own weapon out and pointed it. 'HEY YOU!' she yelled, as she lost her footing and fell.

There was the sound of a gunshot which missed the pilot who was about to mount the ladder, but the woman got up, followed in and shoved him from his precarious perch.

The pilot fell overboard, his body whistling past the three escapees as he plunged DOWN and DOWN—and CRASHED into the white thrashing water below, where he disappeared beneath the foaming surface.

Debbie screamed; she thought it was Sash. She looked up. But no—thank God he was still there! She looked down at her feet. She had reached the last step. Again, the boat rose from the swell, but this time she felt hands grab her as the distant sound of ill-fired bullets rang out high above.

Debbie threw caution to the gale force wind and released her hold, allowing the crewman to pluck her from the ladder. He twisted and flung her like a rag doll across towards Sam, who caught hold of her. Shaking with raw relief, they both grasped and clung onto the railing supports on the tossed boat.

Sam, who had seen the pilot fall, turned his head and looked back. He could just see the head of the man, now some fifty yards behind, rising above the ebb and flow of the waves. His lifejacket had so far saved him, but he was fighting to clear the wash of the ship's eighty-ton propellers.

Then the Pilot boat hit a tidal surge of surf and lurched away from the ship, a wall of water crashing over them. Above, on the ship's deck, the Russian woman was again thrown from her feet by the rogue wave and was sent gambolling across the deck, her gun sliding across its steel plates as her head struck a steel stanchion and knocked her senseless.

The Pilot boat's skipper, who had been oblivious to the sound of gunfire, fought to correct his boat's line of motion and applied more power. The bow rose and closed the gap; the buffer again bumping and scuffing against the ship's hull, a squeal of rubber piercing the din of the storm.

Next was Sash.

For a moment, there was a brief welcomed respite from the slashing waves, and Sash was able to step almost lethargically from the last rung of the ladder onto the pilot boat's platform. He grabbed a support rail. Then a crest of white water hurled the bucketing boat upwards. Immediately, the boat's skipper engaged full power, and they were away, distancing themselves from the behemoth ship at an alarming rate of knots, a rooster tail of white foaming water extending behind them—the turbulent wake created by the propellers, and the water rushing back to fill the void left by the boat's passage.

Once out of danger, the skipper turned the boat and headed back to recover his pilot who was quickly pulled from the murderous surf. Then, once in calmer waters, the skipper throttled back and turned to face his three uninvited passengers. 'You bloody fools!' he said. 'What the hell was all that about?'

Now inside the Pilot boat's cramped bridge, the three cold and bedraggled escapees explained some, but not all, of their predicament to the three-man crew, who listened in astonishment to their tale of capture and imprisonment.

'Yes, there was something about that Russian Captain that appeared suspicious,' said the exhausted pilot. 'I haven't seen him before. And that First Officer? I'm sure she fired a gun at me.'

'No,' said the skipper. 'Surely not.'

Debbie, Sam and Sash exchanged knowing glances but said nothing as they watched the imposing cargo vessel escape the harbour's breakwater and merge into the open sea, fading into the inky darkness like a ghost ship, its hulking silhouette soon swallowed by the black abyss of the night.

Unbeknownst to them, with a flick of a switch, the Siberian Star's transponder was silenced, rendering the vessel a 'Dark Ship'—completely undetectable to satellite monitoring. Beneath its cloak of invisibility, nefarious deeds could now unfold unchallenged.

Five of the six watching from the pilot boat might have wondered what unlawful dealings awaited it at its mysterious destination? But one of them knew—Sam knew. During the past six months, he had been there. He was no stranger to the illicit activities taking place. Though unable to witness them first-hand, he was well-versed in the intricate process orchestrated by Louie Marmarella's brother. It was the reason he was abducted in the first place. Clandestine cargo would be offloaded, and a covert exchange of money for various substances would occur, the contraband sourced from small vessels lurking north of Puerto Rico—illegal cargo destined to evade the clutches of law enforcement, slipping through the net as it made its way back to the U.S.

Whether off the coast of Miami, Fort Lauderdale or New York, other small boats would collect the contraband from the clandestine merchant ship and transport it on to secluded coves and bays along the East coast where it would be spirited away.

While drug enforcement agencies might seize a portion of the shipments, for every one boat apprehended, nine others would navigate through—ten percent loss deemed an acceptable risk by the cartels in a global multi-billion-dollar market where there exists over twenty million users.

The skipper of the pilot boat remained curious and continued to ask questions of his unexpected passengers, but the three were evasive, sticking to their tale of capture, mistaken identity—purposely omitting to mention the name of the Marmarella family. With so much corruption about, they were unsure where allegiances would lie. As more questions were asked and batted away, suspicions between the crew of the pilot ship lingered like the salty spray in the air.

Then, once back on dry land, the three escapees embraced in a huddle, smiles now replacing their looks of terror, the shadows of which would be forever etched in their memories.

Of course, there would be paperwork and a report to be filed, but Debbie, Sam, and Sash were finally safe. All they had to do now was find Sash's car and escape the docks, that is, after security had spent some time interviewing them. But with them looking the way they did, Debbie beaten up, and Sam looking like a castaway from a desert island, what if awkward questions were asked?

Sash looked across the harbour from which he had recently departed. As expected, walking towards them was a security detail and, low and behold, there he was. Jerry was on his way over, already fifteen hundred dollars richer and no doubt ready to deflect—should that amount be doubled; any question of suspicion that might encumber the three Vitalli associates.

Sash smiled. 'I think we're gonna be alright,' he said, as he reached into his pocket and withdrew his wallet.

Chapter 21: Painkiller

Dino Marmarella's shifty eyes regarded the uniformed nurse with suspicion as he lay recovering from his injuries in bed. It was the first time he had been awake for almost a week. He watched her for a few minutes whilst trying to evaluate his situation and where he was. She appeared to be flummoxed, as if looking for something.

'What's your name?' he asked, his voice failing to shield an element of contempt for the woman looking after him.

'Greta,' said the nurse.

'And where am I? What hospital is this?'

'You're not in a hospital,' replied the nurse. 'You're at Mr. Vitalli's residence. You're in his private medical ward.'

'What? At the Vitalli's house? Which Vitalli... Frankie Vitalli?'

'No, his father. Although you're not actually in his house. It's a facility nearby.'

'A facility? MOTHAFUCKER!'

There was a sudden ferocious jewellery clatter of metal-on-metal as Dino tried to get up from the hospital bed, only to find his right wrist and right ankle tethered to the bed's side rail with handcuffs. He cried out in anger and then winced in discomfort as the wounds in his back and buttock showed just why he was lying in a hospital bed. An angry remonstration exploded from his snarling mouth. 'What the fuck's going on?'

'You need to rest,' said the nurse, her voice now hesitant as she became suddenly wary of the man for whom she had cared for the few days. She explained, 'You've been shot and have been recovering from your injuries.'

'SHOT? Shot by who?'

'I don't know. I think Mr. Vitalli senior found you and brought you here to be treated. That's all I know.'

'Treated? Why here? Last thing I knew, I was at Tony DeVille's place. Where's Tony?'

'Sorry... I don't know who that is?'

'How long have I been here?'

'About a week.'

'A WEEK! Who shot me? Was it that scum suckin' pig, Frankie Vitalli? I'll fuckin' kill him! Undo these cuffs! I need to speak to my father.'

'I'm sorry, but I don't have the keys for those.'

On hearing that, the man's face adopted a mean hangdog look. 'Well, you're not much fuckin' use, are you?' he said unforgivably.

Dino Marmarella's rage had peaked well beyond what many would consider acceptable behaviour, given the circumstances. And for the nurse, now he was awake, his attitude was far removed from what she had envisaged of the man. Whilst unconscious, he appeared to have a kind face. He was a good-looking man in his early thirties and, judging from his physique, he obviously kept himself fit. As she undertook her duties, nursing him back to health, Greta had plenty of opportunity to study his features and had tried to imagine how he would be when revived. She was disappointed. It appeared he was no different to the punks who would show up at the Trauma Center at Kings County Hospital at two o'clock on a Saturday morning—battered, bloodied and bruised after concluding their evening out by trying to kill one another; thugs and yobs that, in her previous job, she would have to piece back together, only for some of the same faces to show up the following week.

But now that Dino Marmarella's eyes were open, she watched him from the edge of the room as he tried to evaluate his situation. There was something about this man that frightened her. She was frightened now. He had the blank, cold, staring eyes of a serial killer. She knew nothing about him. Given the circumstances, perhaps *he* was a killer, too. Little did she know that if she had added kidnapping, sexual assault, fraud and embezzlement to that assumption, she would have accurately transcribed his resume.

'The keys!' he said, beckoning her over with the fingers of his free hand. 'You must have them.'

She shook her head. His left arm remained outstretched, hanging from the bed. He suddenly lunged at her, but she was nimble enough to dodge his attempt to grab her, and she stepped back. He collapsed back on the bed and winced.

'Humph... Jesus, my back!' he groaned, as again he yanked at the handcuffs. 'Fuck, that hurts! An' I've a pain in my ass too!'

Yes, thought the nurse, you certainly are a pain in the ass—such a disappointment after my hard work.

'Argh... I need to get outta here!' he groaned, as his wild eyes surveyed the small medical room with its monitors and racks of medical equipment. He turned to her and frowned—his piercing eyes boring into her, his mouth hanging open. 'What is it you said? Vitalli's got his own fuckin' hospital ward. Is that what you said... and that's where I am?'

'Yes.'

'Well, *he'll* fuckin' need it by the time I've finished with him. Has he got a morgue too?'

Marmarella's spat of anger seemed to recede for a moment, leaving in its wake a mood of menace as his cunning eyes again flashed around the room, evaluating, planning, looking for an angle—looking for a way out.

They eventually returned to the nurse.

After a moment of reflection, he tried a different, softer approach. 'Look, you're a pretty thing, ain't ya? Lovely girl like you stuck in this place. You should be out enjoying yourself with friends... perhaps even with me. Come on, let me have the keys.' Again, he extended his free hand like a paedophile offering sweets to a child, his eyes piercing and devoid of any genuine sentience.

The nurse looked disparagingly at him. What? An attempt at charm now?

'I don't have them,' she said.

Dino Marmarella's charm offensive did not last long. 'Fuckin' bitch!' he muttered. 'So, I'm in a facility, you say? What the fuck's that supposed to mean?'

Greta was unsure what she should do. But she knew she had had enough of this man. She needed help and turned to leave the room.

'HEY! Where you goin'? he growled. He leaned up from his bed as she disappeared. 'What is the place?' he snarled, and then he raised the volume. 'I bet Frankie's fucked you, ain't he? And why ain't there any fuckin' windows in here? BITCH!'

The room took the sound of his voice out through the open door and batted the word 'Bitch!' down and along the bunker's corridor from wall to wall. '*Bitch... Bitch... Bitch...*' Until its brutal echo decayed to silence, its venom absorbed by the cold concrete walls of the subterranean structure.

The insult rang in Greta's ears behind her as she quickly made her way along the dimly lit underground passageway back to the main house to look for someone to help.

She was annoyed with herself. She had forgotten that she had been told not to discuss anything with her patient should he come round, and she had. But none of this would have happened, she decided, had she not run out of Dexmedetomidine—a drug used for prolonged sedation. As instructed by the doctor, she had kept a supply of it in the wardroom. But earlier that morning, when she finished using the last batch went to the medical storeroom to replenish supplies, she found there was none there—although she was sure there was plenty on the shelf the last time she needed to resupply the wardroom a few days before.

Unbeknownst to her, Doctor Roberts had removed boxes of medication to conceal the packages of stolen cash in the back of his SUV on the night of the theft. But had he purposefully removed all supplies of the sedative— knowing full well the ramifications and chaos that would ensue when Dino Marmarella fully regained consciousness? Chaos that might require additional human resource and perhaps buy him a few more hours whilst making his escape.

The nurse climbed the steps from the cellar into the house. Fingers was sitting in the kitchen, keeping his best friend, Jack Daniels, company. He had been told to be ready to bring Dino up from the bunker if a meeting Salvatore Vitalli was soon to have went well. 'Everything OK,' he asked upon seeing the nurse.

'No, sir, definitely not,' she said as she began to mumble incoherently, her panicked words coming out as gibberish.

Thankfully, Fingers understood gibberish. It was his language of choice, and he could speak it fluently, but on this occasion, even *he* had to insist she slow down. 'Right,' he said. 'Eh... start again from the beginning, but slowly. What's happened?'

As Greta explained the situation, back in the wardroom, Dino Marmarella found yanking at the handcuffs was hopeless. But he *had* discovered something. The split side rail to which he was tethered, and which was designed to prevent patients from falling out of the medical bed, could be lowered. And once lowered, it might even be detachable if a couple of exposed screws were removed; that is—if he could find something within reach to unscrew them.

# # #

Meanwhile, upstairs in the main house, Salvatore Vitalli sat at his desk in his ground floor study. He had just finished a burger meal and was about to have a discussion—a discussion he had hoped to avoid, but one which he now considered vital.

Sitting opposite him wearing a pinstripe navy blue suit, was his young twenty-one-year-old nephew, Joey Vitalli, the man who had mistakenly shot Dino who, unbeknownst to them, was now lying fully conscious in the bunker's medical ward.

Joey was not hungry so had declined a takeaway meal that his uncle had requested. 'Do I have to be here, sir?' he said, as he sat anxiously wringing his hands in one of two armchairs opposite his uncle, as if waiting to be interviewed for a job.

The family leader's hooded eyes rose and met those of his favourite, but flawed nephew, as he wiped a blob of red ketchup from his white shirt. 'Godamn it!' said the big man, a sheen of perspiration glistening over his near bald head. 'Ah... look at this, I know it's no good for my cholesterol, but every time I have a Johnny Rocket burger meal, which ain't that often, this shit happens. I put a napkin there, and the spilled ketchup misses it by half an inch. Jesus! Now look at my shirt!'

He dabbed at the ketchup stain with a paper towel, which seemed to make it worse. He cursed, and then said, 'Anyway, how are you feeling now, Joey? Still in pain from that nonsense this morning?'

'I'm OK,' said Joey. 'There's just a bruise on my shoulder blade where the paintball hit.'

As he settled back into his plush leather chair, the big man, still dabbing at the red ketchup stain on his white shirt, casually said, 'You know, things could have turned out a lot worse. You might have been killed today.' He abandoned his efforts and tossed the napkin into the trash can. 'Marmarella's shooter could have used a real bullet, and you'd now be dead. Just like his asshole son, Dino, would be dead if your aim had been accurate a week ago. So, yes, you do need to be here. And yes, you need to hear this.' Salvatore Vitalli was determined to toughen his nephew.

Joey tried to object. 'But sir.'

'Joey, be quiet and listen. When you make a mistake, and you seem to make plenty, the ramifications ripple through, not just our family, but others, too. Because of your fuck up a week ago, not only do we still have that asshole in the medical bay downstairs, but now Frankie's wife is also missing. See what I mean about a ripple effect? And to cap it all, we've now got a potential war on our hands that could have, and should have, been avoided.'

'But sir...'

'Shut up and listen!' The big man leaned forward on his desk. 'When I issue a directive, Joey, it must be executed exactly per my instructions. As I said a week ago, attention to detail is paramount, otherwise shit happens. Innocent lives are lost, and the balance of order is jeopardised. There is an unwritten code that exists within our families, and certainly within *my* family. You've heard of the term Cosa Nostra, right?'

'Yes, sir.'

'Well, clearly, you do not understand its full meaning. It's a term associated with our place of origin; it goes back to the old country. It refers to 'our thing', and in particular, our way of doing things. It's an old traditional term that spans decades and relates to our code of business, our organisational prowess, if you will... how we manage our affairs.'

The discussion between Salvatore Vitalli and Joey continued, but was only a prelude to the real discussion, which was to come later.

On the other side of the house, the nurse and Fingers quickly made their way down the steps to the cellar and along the passageway back to Dino Marmarella in the bunker complex.

'That's strange,' said Greta as they approached the medical wardroom.

'What's strange?' asked Fingers.

'The door's closed. When I left, I'm sure I left it open.'

'Did you?'

'Yes.'

'And *he* was still handcuffed to the bed?'

'Yes.' The nurse anxiously bit her lip. 'Although he was very angry and was trying to free himself. He kept asking for the keys.'

'Where are the keys?'

'They're out or reach locked in the cupboard.'

'That cupboard?' Fingers pointed to an overhead locker that had been forced open. Greta winced. 'Sorry.'

'It's not your fault.'

Fingers immediately pulled his old-fashioned .22 calibre revolver from his hip holster. In his broad hand, the nickel-plated weapon looked like a kid's toy and, although not as powerful as a .38 handgun, it would still pack a punch if the bullets were put in the right place. Initially, when he acquired it many years ago, he thought the trigger had a heavy pull weight, but a spring conversion fixed that. And now he preferred it as it had an eight-shot capacity, was lightweight and ideal for concealed carry, and as such, it was always with him. 'Get behind me,' he said sharply, as they emerged from the passageway into the adjoining corridor.

He scanned the corridor and gently pushed open the wardroom door with his foot. The bed and the room were empty, and the dismantled side rail to which Dino Marmarella had been tethered lay on the floor.

'Oh, no!' gasped the nurse. 'Where is he?' she whispered.

'Shhh... I think it's better you stay in the wardroom,' said Fingers.

'No. I'm coming with you.'

'OK... stay close behind me then.'

Fingers backed out of the room into the dimly lit corridor. He closed the door to the passageway leading to the main house and headed towards where the large, open-plan living quarters were situated. Greta mimicked his every stride as he quietly made his way along the shadowy darkness. The door to the room was open, and the lights were lit.

'The lights were off in that room,' whispered the nurse behind him. 'I was in there earlier; I remember switching them off.'

Leading the way, Fingers stepped into the room. 'If you're in here, Dino!' he called, 'I have a weapon! If you show yourself, I will not shoot you.'

They waited and scanned the room, which had chairs, sofas, a dining table and an extensive kitchen area, as well as bookcases, a Large TV and other bits of furniture. There was no sign of him, although plenty of places for him to hide. With the gun leading the way, they crept around the room, Greta clinging to the back of Fingers' jacket, following closely in his footsteps.

'He's not in here,' whispered Fingers.

'Are there any weapons down here?' asked Greta.

'Yeah, but they're locked away in a gun safe.'

Suddenly, a dull explosion reverberated from the distant wing of the bunker complex. It came from the sleeping quarters along the connecting hallway, the sound travelling down the corridor toward them, bouncing off the concrete walls. Fingers pivoted and sprinted the length of the passage toward the blast. Despite his imposing build, he moved with surprising agility and speed. Upon entering the largest of the three bedrooms, he was met with a billowing cloud of suffocating dust that filled the room. In the corner was situated the bunker's emergency exit, which had been activated, small charges blowing out the vehicle inspection pit in the garage high above, as it was designed to do.

'Godamn it!' yelled Fingers, as he left the nurse behind and weaved his way between the bunk beds towards the escape shaft, where a twenty-foot vertical ladder led to the garage complex above. He looked up the narrow shaft, peering through the cloud of debris that was floating down like confetti, the gun poised in his hand.

'I can't see him. He's not up there,' he said. 'And I don't think he'd have had time to climb up there that quick.' He looked back towards the nurse. 'Let's go back and check...'

'DROP THE GUN!' came the short, sharp order.

Dino Marmarella, still wearing his open-backed pale blue hospital gown, was standing in the doorway behind. He was holding the nurse in a chokehold and had a scalpel against her neck.

As straight as you could point, Fingers had his gun trained on him.

'I said, drop the fucking gun, didn't I?' Dino pressed the blade into the woman's flesh. There was a muffled scream from her as a stream of blood seeped over his right hand—his left, covering the struggling girl's mouth.

'You fuckin' BASTARD!' said Fingers.

'DO IT THEN! Drop the gun, you pudgy fuck! Or I'll slit her jugular.'

'OK... OK!' said Fingers. He dropped the weapon.

'Kick it towards me.'

Fingers did as he was told. The nurse had passed out and was now dead weight. The brute released her to the floor. He quickly stepped over her body and grabbed the weapon. He cocked the hammer and pointed it at Fingers.

'Right! I want some fuckin' answers,' said the desperate thug, who still appeared to be drowsy from his medication. 'Was it you who shot me?'

'No,' said Fingers. 'But I wish I had.'

'Well, one of you did. Who was it? Was it Frankie fuckin' faggot Vitalli?'

'No.'

'Johnny Vitalli?'

'No.'

'Oh, I know… it was the fuckin' Easter bunny, right?'

'No, I don't think so. It's the wrong time of year.'

'Who was it then?'

'Huh… might have been the Tooth Fairy.'

'Oh, that's funny.'

Fingers fully expected to be shot, but knew that with such a small calibre weapon, the bullets would have to be accurate to be fatal.

He did not have to wait long.

'I ain't got time for this shit!' snarled Marmarella. 'Here… have some payback, you fat fuck!' He fired from the hip twice… *BANG! BANG!* And Tony 'Fingers' Vitalli collapsed to the floor.

Without waiting, Marmarella stepped over the nurse and stumbled back along the corridor towards the wardroom, but became disorientated. He again found himself in the living room. He cursed, and then span round and backtracked, and after trying a few doors, eventually, he found the door to the long connecting passageway leading to the cellar in the main house.

Chapter 22: Tomorrow Never Comes

As twilight faded, an unsettling stillness enveloped Salvatore Vitalli's house as the last traces of amber sunlight retreated from the gnarled oak trees in the grounds of the property, their branches and twigs scratching against one another like bony, arthritic fingers casting their black shadows across the walls of the house as if the hands of a spectre were trying to climb the building. The blustery winds that had raged all afternoon had abated for now, replaced by a graveyard quietness that so often precedes the arrival of a storm.

A car entered through the gates of the property and sedately followed the sweeping curve of the drive and parked beneath the steps leading to the main entrance. A man got out, climbed the steps to the house and approached the door, which opened as if anticipating his arrival. There was a brief exchange as the man entered the house, and he was asked to take a seat and wait in the foyer.

Unaware of the activities taking place in the bunker complex, Johnny Vitalli limped from the foyer along to the west wing of the large house towards Salvatore Vitalli's ground floor study, his leg still sore from where he had been stabbed the day before. He knocked on the door, opened it, and leaned in. 'He's arrived,' he said, screwing up his face as if he had a bad smell under his nose.

Salvatore Vitalli looked up. He got up from his chair and slipped on his jacket to conceal the red stain on his white shirt, and said, 'OK. Is he packing?'

'I don't know. He wouldn't let me frisk him. Do you wanna chance it?'

'I don't think we got much choice. Send him in.'

Johnny hesitated and then asked, 'Do you wanna have me in here, Boss?'

'Eh, no. The agreement was just him, me and Joey.' Salvatore Vitalli was well aware of how short Johnny's fuse could be, and that his mouth had a tendency to utter anything before his brain was fully engaged.

'OK, but if you need me, Boss… I'll be just outside.'

'Right… take these with you, will you? The big man pointed to a tray containing his empty plate and utensils.'

'What… you're not offering our guest any dinner, then?' asked Johnny. The family Don fired him a threatening look. 'OK, I'll take that as a no.'

The leader turned his attention to Joey as Johnny left the room. 'Joey, I've arranged a sit-down this evening,' he said. 'A meeting, to see if order can be restored between our two families.'

Joey looked puzzled and apprehensive as to why only he was involved. A few seconds later the door again opened and the imposing figure of Louie Marmarella, wearing an expensive looking plain black suit, white shirt with a red silk tie, and his usual patent leather shoes walked slowly and confidently into the room as if he owned the place.

'Oh, shit!' mouthed Joey beneath his breath. He rose to his feet.

'Hey, relax,' said Louie Marmarella, gesturing with his hand for the young man to sit back down. 'Talking to your associate out there, Joey. I understand you had some back pain today. That's a shame. How the hell did that happen? I could probably recommend a good chiropractor, if you need one.'

Joey bit his lip and glanced at his uncle, not quite knowing how to respond to the sneering man.

Marmarella grinned. 'Huh… what's the matter? Cat got ya tongue, Joey? The kid needs to toughen up a bit, don't ya think, Sal? You're all good now though, right Joey?'

'Eh…I guess so, yes.'

'I told my sharpshooter to aim for ya head, but he said you got up just as he fired. You spoiled the moment. It could have been a JFK thing. You know, a recreation of his head exploding in a cloud of red goo from that shot on Dealey Plaza?'

Joey eyed Marmarella with scorn. It's *re-creation*, you idiot, he wanted to say, but kept his mouth shut. He felt uncomfortable being so close to the man.

Marmarella was referring to that fateful day in Dallas, Texas, on November 22nd, 1963—when President John F. Kennedy was assassinated. Such was the enormity of that historic event everyone alive on that day remembers not only where they were when they heard the devastating news, but what they were doing.

It was a Friday.

Following the shooting, confusion reigned for almost an hour over the President's condition, despite the fact his head had clearly been blown apart by the gunman on the grassy knoll in Dealey Plaza. And yes, that *is* also what Salvatore Vitalli believed, for he too had never subscribed to the generally accepted narrative that a lone gunman had fired those three shots from the book depository building.

Contrary to the findings of the official Warren Commission inquiry, Salvatore Vitalli believed—like many others—that Lee Harvey Oswald never fired a single shot on that day. The chances of anyone firing three shots with precision using a bolt-action Carcano infantry rifle from a height of six stories in 8.3 seconds, and at a target moving away, were improbable at best. Factor in fear, stress; the enormity of the moment; heightened adrenaline rush, and improbable turns to impossible.

In Salvatore Vitalli's view, Oswald was just a spectator on that day. He believed *four* shooters were involved; one on the grassy knoll, two positioned at the rear of the motorcade, and one in front on top of the railroad overpass, who fired a bullet through the limousine's wind-shield, thought by some to be the bullet which struck the Presidents throat and ended being lodged beneath the skin near his shoulder—the same bullet that would miraculously end up completely undamaged on the president's gurney in Parkland Hospital.

Some believed the Secret Service later replaced the limousine's windshield as the hole created by the bullet was forensically conducive, with a bullet fired from the front. And in order to frame Oswald, they needed to show that all three bullets came from the rear of the car, and from the direction of the book depository building.

Salvatore Vitalli's opinion was that after the first two bullets hit the President, the final devastating head-shot was delivered, not by the snipers, but by a young 21-year-old mafia hitman, using a bolt-action scoped Remington Fireball pistol, which he fired from the other side of the grassy knoll's white picket fence.

The weapon, which was experimental at the time, was easy to conceal and extremely accurate, especially in the hands of an experienced ex-army marksman, a man who had honed his skills whilst serving in Vietnam. He was positioned on the grassy knoll with the specific instruction to shoot only if the riflemen failed to deliver a head-shot. In that cataclysmic moment, he counted the sound of the rounds being fired whilst tracking the President through his telescopic sight, but counting each shot, not as a number, but as a head-shot 'miss'... 'miss'... 'miss'.

Then, upon seeing that none had struck the President's head, he fired the fatal shot. The famous Zapruder film captures perfectly when his 'special round', a mercury-tipped explosive bullet, struck the President's head. The debris pattern, which included blood spatter to a police outrider at the right rear of the motorcade, and the manner in which Kennedy's head recoiled backwards, further substantiates a bullet impacting from the direction of the grassy knoll.

Furthermore, the petulant young shooter left a calling card on that day. Years later, he would claim that after taking the deadly shot, he bit the spent cartridge case with his teeth and left it on the picket fence—a symbolic gesture typical of a mafia style contract killing, and one which would have got him in trouble with his 'Controller' had the shell casing been found at the time.

But was this the claim of a hoaxer? For there are a multitude of conspiracy theories. Maybe. But decades later, unbeknown to the alleged shooter, it is said a garden serviceman found the shell casing buried beneath five inches of soil a few feet from the fence. Apparently, a professor in orthodontology, unaware that it was being linked to Kennedy's assassination, was asked to inspect it, and later determined that the indentations on the casing *were* indeed made by human teeth. Evidence, like the discovered shell casing—buried, for fear it would substantiate government and CIA involvement in JFK's killing and, heaven forbid, confirm an affiliation with members of the mob.

Louie Marmarella turned his attention to the Vitalli family leader. 'So how are things with you, Sal,' he said calmly, his sour expression devoid of any genuine feeling of interest, despite the pasty smile he had brought with him? 'I figured I might be hearing from you today.'

Salvatore Vitalli rose from his desk. He leaned over, and to Joey's dismay, offered his hand.

'Things could be better,' he said, as they awkwardly reached to shake hands. On this occasion, there was no respectful kiss on the cheek, or an exchange of intimate hugs, as is so often the case when mafia bosses meet. These two men had long since forgone those pleasantries. Such was the vitriol that existed between them, a simple pressing of the hand seemed to be all they could stomach.

Salvatore Vitalli glanced at the palm of his now sticky hand and frowned. It wasn't the first time he felt as though he'd molested a piece of haddock after shaking hands with his counterpart. 'Take a seat, Louie,' he said, as he pulled out a handkerchief, mopped his brow and wiped his hands.

They both sat, Marmarella occupying the armchair alongside Joey, who was feeling intensely vulnerable given he was now in the same room as the man who ordered to have him shot earlier that day, albeit only with a projectile loaded with paint.

'Nice place you got here, Sal,' said Marmarella, looking around and noting the cluster of security monitors set neatly within Vitalli's mahogany bookcase—monitors that only catered for the outside of the premises. 'Business must be good.'

'I can't complain,' said Vitalli, himself noticing from one of the cameras

Marmarella's silver Mercedes parked outside. 'I see, as we agreed, you haven't brought the Capelli brothers with you,' he said.

'No, they're busy doin' something,' said Marmarella, secure in the knowledge that as a 'Made Man' talking with a 'Made Man', he was untouchable and didn't need them today. 'And likewise, with you,' he added. 'No Frankie or Layzee Dawson here to screw up our discussion?'

'That's right. They're busy too,' said Vitalli.

'Good.' Marmarella eyed Vitalli inquisitively. 'Looks like you've lost a few pounds since we last met, Sal.'

Salvatore Vitalli noted that Louie Marmarella always seemed to comment on his weight when they met.

Marmarella's continued, 'But word on the street seems to suggest it ain't pounds you've lost, Sal, it's dollars—a lot of dollars.'

Vitalli smarted at the comment but ignored Marmarella's sly inference regarding the doctor's theft from his safe. He said, 'Word gets around quick, don't it, Louie?'

'Yes, it does. You just don't know who you can trust nowadays, do ya, Sal?' Marmarella paused for effect and then added. 'Are you aware your doctor friend, or should I say former friend, owes me one hundred G's?'

Vitalli frowned.

'Thought not,' mused Marmarella as he glanced at Joey sitting to his right. 'And as he has defaulted on his payment, he also now owes me his life. Which, when he eventually surfaces, and he will, I intend to take. Another job for my friend Tony DeVille... that is, when the police finally release him.'

Joey, upon hearing that and who always liked the doctor, shifted uncomfortably in his chair.

The Vitalli family leader leaned forward on his desk. 'Sounds like you're trying your best to wipe us all out, Louie?' he said. 'First, there was my brother Sam, then Layzee Dawson, now the doctor. Not to mention the disappearance of Debbie Vitalli. And after that stunt you played today on young Joey here, it makes me wonder just what your intentions are. I thought we were meeting today to build bridges, Louie.'

'Well, you can think what you like, Sal. But sometimes you have to cull to be kind. Debts have to be honoured… you know that.'

A frown of ridges appeared across Salvatore Vitalli's brow. 'Cull to be kind? Where the fuck are you coming from, Louie?'

Once again, Joey felt the creeping sensation of anxiety building, or was it something else stirring within him, as he listened to Marmarella speak.

There was an uncomfortable silence as Salvatore Vitalli thought for a moment, and then said, 'OK, let's cut to the chase, shall we, Louie?'

'Yeah, let's,' said Marmarella. 'So, where is he?'

'Your son? He's safe,' said Vitalli. 'He's recovering.'

'Recovering? Recovering from what, exactly? Sounds like he's here in the house. Have you been lying to me, Sal? What have you done to him, you fuckin' COCKSUCK…'

'Calm the fuck down, Louie!' interrupted Vitalli. 'He's not *in* the house, but he's nearby. Take it easy. He's OK. And I'll get back to the subject of your son in a minute. But first… where's Frankie's wife?' Salvatore Vitalli had no intention of releasing Louie Marmarella's son without first agreeing an exchange for Debbie Vitalli.

Marmarella, who was clearly disgruntled, said, 'She's recovering too.'

Salvatore Vitalli's frown deepened. 'Recovering from what?'

'Well, she wouldn't answer a few questions when asked.' Marmarella's face formed a cynical smile as he glanced over at Joey.

'What questions, Louie?'

'I asked her the whereabouts of my son. Perfectly reasonable question, I thought. And she refused to answer.'

'That's because she wouldn't know the whereabouts of your son, Louie. Frankie never discusses business with her.'

'Yeah, that's what she said. But we found that difficult to swallow.'

'Who's we?'

'Me and the brothers.'

'You let the Capelli brothers near her? Those fuckin' psychopaths!'

'I prefer to call them friends. We're all friends, aren't we, Sal? They certainly made friends with her, if you know what I mean. I'll send you the tape.'

'What?'

Marmarella's smirk widened. He was feeling content that he had the upper hand. After all, he was about to get his son back. And he had the added assurance that not only did he have Frankie Vitalli's wife still seconded, or so he thought, he also had Salvatore Vitalli's brother—a brother who the Vitalli's all thought was dead.

Salvatore Vitalli swallowed hard. 'So, what else did those hyenas do to her? Did they beat her?'

'She had a slap.'

'A slap?' said Joey.

Marmarella glanced at Joey. 'Oh, he speaks. Ha...ha! Yeah, she had a slap, Joey. Quite a few slaps, actually.'

'Define what you mean by *slap*, Louie,' said the head of the Vitalli family.

Joey looked from one man to the other as if he was watching a fast-paced rally at a tennis match.

Salvatore Vitalli leaned across his desk. He had a dour look on his face. 'Is she alive?' he asked.

There was a sharp intake of breath from Joey at the inference that Mrs Vitalli might be dead. He sat trembling in his chair, but not through fear. Anger had appeared on the scene and had seemingly banished fear. And there was no sign at all of the panic that usually triggered Joey's childhood phobia.

Marmarella stiffened in his chair. 'Look,' he said. 'We both know how these things work, Sal. You take a bite outta me. I take a bite outta you. But, when you take a bite out of a Made Man... a Made Man who just happens to be my son, Sal, things get serious... and FAST!'

An evil sneer formed across Louie Marmarella's face. Only that morning, he had issued an instruction demonstrating just how serious his intentions were. He had sent an order to the Siberian Star moored in New York Harbour to have both Debbie and Samuel Vitalli executed and their bodies disposed of at sea. He smiled to himself.

Salvatore Vitalli glared at him. 'So, where's Frankie's wife, Louie? And what condition is she in?'

'Look, I admit there's been some collateral damage to her, but at least I didn't rip her guts open and mail her spleen to you, did I? Not yet, anyway. You should be thankful for that.'

Joey looked on disbelievingly. He couldn't believe what he was hearing. Mrs. Vitalli beaten? And Marmarella's blasé threat to have her carved up. And then a plan to kill not just Layzee Dawson, but also Joey's friend Doctor Roberts. Not to mention what Frankie had told him about the fate of his parents. And this, from the man everyone suspected of killing Spaghetti Sam.

Joey felt something barely recognisable; rage burning within. This was all so one-sided.

'So, here we go again, Louie,' said Salvatore Vitalli. 'Round and round in circles. Reminds me of that old riddle. How does it go... what's always coming but never arrives?'

Joey had a glazed look about him as he tried to process what was being discussed. Almost blindly, he found himself answering the question. 'Tomorrow,' he said, a dazed expression pasted on his face.

'Yeah, that's right... tomorrow,' said Marmarella. 'Tomorrow is always coming, but never arrives.' He looked at Joey with that smug look. 'The kid's sharp. I'm surprised. I always thought he was a fuckin' retard, like his father back in the day.'

'Don't you dare talk of my father,' said Joey.

'Oh, have I hit a nerve...ha, ha!'

Joey was struggling to maintain his cool. But then, as Marmarella leaned forward, the gape of his jacket revealed he was carrying a gun. It was a flash of a moment, gone in a split second, but enough for Joey to see that he was wearing a quick draw horizontal shoulder holster, the weapon concealed neatly beneath his left armpit. If he was to nonchalantly cross his arms, thought Joey, he could so easily pull the weapon and have it on target in less than a second.

Joey recognised the holster because, unbeknown to Salvatore Vitalli, he was wearing one just like it.

'So, where's my son, Dino, Sal?' said Marmarella, a no-nonsense sneer across his taut face.

'OK,' said Salvatore Vitalli. 'There's no easy way to put this. So, I'll just come straight out with it. Your son was mistakenly shot a week ago, Louie. It was an accident, and he's since been receiving the best medical care.'

'YOU MOTHAFUC...!'

'SHUT UP, LOUIE! He's recovering, and he's gonna be fine. I had him treated here because I knew how badly you would take that news, and I wanted to ensure he would survive and get the best treatment, and he has. He's received 24-hour nursing, and he's on the mend.'

As Vitalli spoke, the sun-tanned colour in Marmarella's face drained to a pale grey, and even though he had heard everything Vitalli had said, there was only one word that registered with him.

'SHOT?' What are you talking about, shot? What d'ya mean, shot? Shot by who? Who shot him?'

Joey stood up from his chair. 'I did,' he said.

There was a moment of incredulity as both men turned their heads to face the younger man.

'I shot him with this.' Joey was holding a gun and was pointing it directly at Louie Marmarella. His arm was extended, his hand steady and sure, his voice now articulate and devoid of any sign of anxiety or fear.

Both leaders looked astonished—but astonished for two very different reasons. Marmarella, because if it were true, how could such a young, ineffectual kid like Joey Vitalli ever get the better of his perfect, athletic son? And Salvatore Vitalli, astonished not for that reason, but that his timid nephew had somehow found the courage to not just admit his indiscretion to Louie Marmarella, but he had a gun levelled at his head.

What the hell?

But Joey had not yet finished.

'Now come on, son,' said Marmarella, rising to his feet from the chair, his usual plastic smile slipping from his wet, fat lips as he looked down the barrel of Joey's gun. 'You holding that don't look right, does it? Don't be ridiculous. You know who I am. I'm a Made Man. Do you even know how to use that thing?'

'Yes,' said Joey. 'Like I said, I shot your son with it.'

Marmarella looked at him sourly, and then across the desk to Salvatore Vitalli. 'Sal, sort this out, will you?'

'I ain't finished,' grimaced Joey. 'You absolute utter asshole of a human being! You remind me of something I sometimes step in on the sidewalk.'

Marmarella's mouth hung open, saliva pooling between his bottom gum and lip. 'Oh, have your balls suddenly dropped, Joey?' he said, his hateful eyes fixed and staring. 'Have you finally grown a pair?'

Shocked by what was playing out before him, Salvatore Vitalli implored his nephew. 'Come on, Joey, put the gun down.'

But Joey remained magnificently poised, his arm rigid, his gun hand steady and unwavering.

Just then, the study door crashed open as if kicked, and Johnny Vitalli entered the room, followed by Dino Marmarella, who was still garbed in his hospital gown. Dino had a firm grip on the back of Johnny's shirt collar and was holding a gun against his head.

Upon seeing his father under threat, Dino shoved Johnny to the floor and retrained his aim at Joey.

'Ah, nice of you to show up,' snarled his father. 'Just in time. Where you been?'

'Shut up!' said Dino. 'What the hell's going on here?'

Marmarella turned to his son. 'Don't you speak to me like that!'

With the gun still raised, Joey said, 'Well, let me speak to you then.'

Marmarella, who appeared amused, turned to face him. 'OK, shoot. That is... I don't literally mean shoot. I mean speak.'

Joey's face was morose. 'On behalf of Debbie and Sam Vitalli, and Layzee Dawson, Doc Roberts, and my parents... and the other lives you've destroyed and are planning to destroy... you deserve much worse than this, Mr. Marmarella.'

'Huh, nice speech,' said Dino Marmarella, who also appeared amused. 'Has he finished?'

'No...I haven't! And you... SHUT UP! I know you were involved in the death of my parents!'

There was no attempt by Louie Marmarella's son to refute the allegation, just a widening of the sneer on his face.

Lying on the floor alongside Dino, Johnny Vitalli slowly extended his hand down his leg towards his foot. Although Dino had relieved him of his gun, Johnny was wearing the Russian's boot knife—retrieved from when he was stabbed in Franko's hair salon the day before.

Still feeling completely secure in the iron clad armour of his Made Man status, Louie Marmarella's face wore a mask of invincibility. 'Look,' he said. 'Just put the guns down, everyone. Let's talk.'

'You're not listening to me,' snapped Joey, the pressure of his finger on the weapon's trigger visibly increasing. 'Nobody ever seems to listen to me.' The pressure intensified. 'Well, perhaps now they will.'

Louie Marmarella watched with morbid fascination as he saw the trigger slowly being squeezed, his eyes widening as he knew at some point it would reach its threshold and the gun would fire. He slowly crossed his arms, his right hand slipping between his shirt and jacket, his fingers snaking in and taking hold of something. 'Shoot him!' he said to his son. 'What are you waiting for you? SHOOT HIM! HE SHOT YOU!'

Dino frowned. 'Did he?'

'YES... YOU DUMB FUCK!'

Suddenly, bodies moved and there was an explosive flash of fire as a single bullet blasted across the room. But the flash did not come from Dino's gun, neither did it come from Louie Marmarella's fast draw. The flash came from Joey's gun.

Less than a second later, the room erupted in chaos as Johnny withdrew the boot knife and plunged it into Dino Marmarella's bare foot, who cried out and began firing indiscriminately in all directions, his finger ratcheting the trigger of Fingers' revolver until all six remaining bullets had been discharged. As lead flew across the room and splintered wood and glass shattered all around, Joey's reflexes were God given. He stooped to one side and fired twice...!!

Dino Marmarella took one slug to the chest and another just below his right eye, both whipping him sideways against a bookcase as if thrown by a herculean cage fighter. He crashed face down to the floor in a crumpled heap, the split on the back of his hospital gown exposing his near naked body and the scars left by Joey's original two bullets fired a week ago.

Everyone remained stationary, like pieces on a chessboard, waiting for the next move.

Louie Marmarella remained standing. He had been struck by Joey's first bullet. His hand was clutching a pistol, which he had pulled from within his jacket. It slid from his fingers and dropped to the floor. He began to shudder, his legs buckling, no longer capable of supporting the weight of his short, stout frame. He collapsed into the chair in a sitting position, a perfectly formed hollow black hole appearing in his forehead, seconds before blood began to ooze from it, a river of crimson cascading down between his wide, surprised eyes and onto his crisp, white shirt—perfectly matching the red of his silk tie. Then, his heavy head fell forward, and his chin slumped into the bloody pool of mess on his chest.

He was dead—unquestionably dead.

'You're done!' said Joey. 'Both of you!'

The aftermath of piercing gunfire had numbed everyone's senses, a high-pitched, muffled hum ringing in their ears as if their heads had been plunged beneath water. From the first bullet to the last, time and motion had slowed to a crawl—each second seemingly taking four times that to play out.

Gun smoke filled the air as the sound abated, its shadowy echo fading as the passage of time reset to normal speed.

'Fuck me!' said Johnny Vitalli, raising his head from the floor, dumbfounded by the sheer seismic intensity of what had just happened. 'That's not something you see every day, is it? Did you see that? When he was standing there, Marmarella was already dead... he just didn't know it.'

Johnny clambered to his feet and looked around. 'Is everyone OK?'

Joey quietly placed his weapon on the desk. 'Yes,' he said.

Salvatore Vitalli raised his hand. 'Eh... perhaps not too good over here, boys,' he said. 'I took one.'

'Jesus Christ!' said Joey, as he and Johnny quickly stepped around his desk to assist. 'Where?'

'Up here,' the big man pointed to his right bicep, blood seeping through the hole in his jacket as they carefully removed it. 'And one here too,' said Joey. Another bullet had hit his right shoulder.

'And another one here?' said Johnny, inspecting his chest. 'Christ, that's a big fuckin' wound!'

'No. That's ketchup... you idiot!' snarled the big man.

Johnny frowned. 'Oh, right! Can you walk?' he asked.

'Probably. But do I wanna? No! Why the fuck would I wanna walk? I've just been shot, you mother-head!'

'We need to get you to a hospital, sir,' said Joey.

'No, no! I'm OK. It hurts like hell, but there're no vitals involved. Medics will only call the cops. We don't want no badges involved with this. We keep this strictly in-house, understand? I'll be alright. Greta will fix me up. I need to keep pressure on it, though. There's napkins in that drawer.'

'Where is Greta?' asked Joey. 'And Fingers, where's he?'

'Oh, shit!' said Johnny, pointing to the nickel-plated revolver on the floor. 'That gun there, ain't that Fingers' gun?'

'Yes, it is,' said the big man. 'Mother of God! Where are they?'

'We're here!' called two voices in unison. The nurse, her neck wrapped with gauze, was helping support Fingers as they both hobbled into the room.

'Christ, you got shot up too, Fingers?' queried the big man.

'Yeah. Mothafucker shot me with my own gun. Can you believe that? Thankfully, he's got a worse aim than Joey. He got me in both legs. Almost hit the crown jewels. And poor Greta here. He stuck her with a scalpel!'

'WHAT?' said Johnny. He leaned across Dino Marmarella's lifeless body and lifted his head. 'You stabbed the nurse that saved your ass? You cowardly fuck! If I could, I'd resuscitate you and kill you all over again... you piece of shit!'

'You OK, Greta?' asked Joey.

'Yes. I'll be fine,' said the nurse, holding the gauze dressing against her neck. 'Two or three stitches, maybe.'

Fingers looked around, perplexed. 'Jesus Christ! Who shot them two?' he asked. 'You Johnny?'

Johnny grinned. 'Uh-uh,' he said, shaking his head. 'Not me.'

'Who then?'

Salvatore Vitalli provided the answer as he placed his good arm around the shoulder of his young prodigy, a rare smile emerging on his face.

'He's come of age, boys,' he said, with a growing sense of pride. 'What d'ya know? My little nephew, Joey, has finally come of age.'

Fingers turned his head and looked at Joey. 'What? You clipped both of them, Joey?'

'Yeah, he did,' said Johnny. 'You should have seen him move. He's a regular gunslinger.'

The leader eventually got to his feet, and they all gathered, transfixed by the dead man sitting slumped in the chair and his wretch of a son lying on the floor alongside.

The cloud of gun smoke and the firework smell of cordite had hardly dispersed before Salvatore Vitalli felt the need to confront the rather large elephant in the room—the two bodies.

'Listen up,' he said. 'Gentlemen... and lady, there's been some scores settled today. But do you remember that conversation we had in the restaurant a week ago?'

Johnny, Fingers and Joey looked at one another.

'You mean the one when we discussed burying stiffs in the woods?' asked Johnny.

'Yeah, that one. Well, the plan's the same, only now there's *two* bodies. So, let's get ourselves patched up. We got some spring cleaning to do, and a woman to find. Let's get to work. And by the way, I had a call earlier today. Our doctor friend managed to escape.'

'Really?' said Joey. There was a glimmer of relief in his eyes.

'Yeah. Frankie and Layzee are flying back home. Although apparently, they're on separate planes. But the missing money? That's still here in New York somewhere.'

It was as he said that, that a car's headlamps appeared. The car pulled up in a hurry and screeched to a halt at the rear of the house, triggering the external flood lamps which illuminated it. Three people got out. Debbie

Vitalli, Sash and Salvatore Vitalli's brother, Spaghetti Sam.

'Well, I'll be damned,' said Fingers, looking out through the French doors. 'You're not gonna believe this. Guess who's just turned up?'

'Hey!' said the big man, as Salvatore Vitalli remembered back to Alberto's restaurant a week ago. 'I've heard that before. That's how this shit started!'

He looked out through the doors—and beamed the largest smile.

Epilogue

On the other side of town, an old beaten up rusty green Chevy pickup truck continued to gather dust in a residential garage. It had sat there forgotten, unused and unloved, for over twenty years. The truck had been ready for the scrap yard years ago, but in the back of it, beneath a crusty, frayed green tarpaulin sheet, was a long side-mounted metal toolbox welded to the truck's flatbed. There was not one single tool in it, although it was not empty. What it contained—was seven million reasons for the truck to remain exactly where it was.

About the Author

Michael Paul is an English author who lives in Shropshire, England. His debut novel 'Blood Money Betrayal - A New York Mafia Tale,' was inspired by his many visits to the USA over the years.

Many years ago, Mike presented a weekly one-hour radio show which was recorded in his home multi-track recording studio. At the time, his show was unique, and featured various characters, all played by Mike. The colourful characters would interact with him as the show's presenter and was very popular with listeners. Mike would write and perform comedy sketches and jingles, using various sound effect material (courtesy mostly thanks to the BBC sound effects library) and would integrate the mastered segways seamlessly within the running order of the music. The segways were recorded on his Teac four track open reel tape deck and then mixed and mastered, much the same as multi channel music is produced. His diverse range of characters included a pair of troublesome cowboys, a charming caretaker with a dodgy penchant for dark dealings, a sexy seductress, and many more. Owing to the show's dynamic complexity, it took a week of preparation to produce a one hour show and had to be pre-recorded prior to being broadcast. Mike was justifiably proud of his unique show, but his greatest compliment was when other radio presenters would turn up at the studio at 10am on a Sunday morning to listen to his latest production.

Mike also recorded voice over commercials which aired on his local radio station.

Throughout his career, Mike spent countless hours travelling the UK, using his driving time to immerse himself in audiobooks borrowed from his local library. These journeys further sparked his creativity, leading him to craft his own short stories which he later recorded as audiobooks for his family. His writing spans a diverse range of genres, from short story crime thrillers and suspense tales to romantic narratives often infused with dark humour and irreverent anecdotes. Each story is a tapestry woven from the author's imagination, rich life experiences and accumulated wisdom.

Bolstered by the encouragement of his family and friends, Mike decided to finish and publish a novel he had long been developing. Now in retirement, he has seized the opportunity to share his work with readers worldwide. 'Blood Money Betrayal' is touted as a raw, unfiltered, and uncompromising narrative centred on two New York crime families.

"For the audiobook, I have endeavoured to incorporate my experience as a voice actor within the narration," says Mike, wherein he narrates the story and seamlessly voice acts each of the characters featured in his novel. A sprinkling of dramatic sound effects at key moments ignite the story and brings the book to life.

The printed book and the immersive audiobook, which incorporates many of the techniques Mike utilised as a radio presenter, took two years to complete and is also available as an e-book, and in print format as a paperback and hardback.

"Whichever format you choose," says Mike, "I really hope you enjoy my first novel. It has been challenging but great fun to produce. Thank you very much for your interest."

Hints of a potential sequel are already circulating, suggesting more to come from this emerging author.

With his background in storytelling, audio recording expertise, and passion for crafting compelling narratives, Michael Paul is set to leave his mark on the literary world with 'Blood Money Betrayal — A New York Mafia Tale.'

Also by Michael Paul

Why not bring this novel to life? Available now on Audible is the exciting audiobook version of Blood Money Betrayal, narrated by the author.

To hear an audio sample of the book, visit www.audible.com or Amazon—search for 'Blood Money Betrayal' and click 'Preview'.

Thank you and enjoy.

Blood Money Betrayal – Audiobook Version
Written and narrated by author and voice actor, Michael Paul